W9-BRF-542

NIGHTMARES

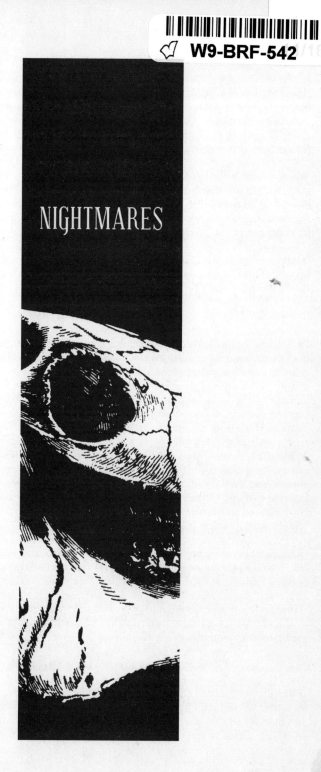

— PRAISE FOR **NIGHTMARES** —

"Ellen Datlow is a tremendously influential figure in horror circles, and this collection is one more significant milestone to be set among the score or so other titles and collections listed in its front matter…[*Nightmares*] delivers on its intention of showcasing the best in a decade of fantastically ambitious and creative dark and frightful fiction, as well as following up on a past classic." —*Metaphysical Circus*

"An excellent collection over all, featuring some of the best voices in horror. It has something to suit a wide variety of tastes, blending stories about real life trauma and bloodshed, to stories that pass into the realms of cosmic terror, horror in the old west and even those with a grim fairytale-like feel. In these pages you will find a nightmare for every horror fan." —*This Is Horror*

"Datlow offers another impressive, diverse and hugely enjoyable collection of short fiction…This is a great collection of horror fiction. I'd highly recommend it." —*The Book Lover's Boudoir*

— PRAISE FOR **THE MONSTROUS** —

"★ Datlow, horror anthologist extraordinaire, brings together all things monstrous in this excellent reprint anthology of 20 horror stories that explore the ever-widening definition of what makes a monster, with nary a misstep. The varied sources of monstrosity include a very troubled kindergarten teacher, a catering company that puts humans on the menu, and spirit-devouring creatures out of Japanese mythology, all creating distinctive microcosms where monsters reign in many forms. In Gemma Files's 'A Wish from a Bone,' an archeological reality show filming in Sudan uncovers evidence of the Terrible Seven, ancient beings who are bent on destruction and domination. Adam-Troy Castro's 'The Totals' skewers bureaucracy and the daily grind by populating a drinking hole with monsters, who create mayhem, commit murder, and kvetch with their deadly coworkers with the same sense of ennui felt by any office drone. Other standouts by Sofia Samatar, Dale Bailey, and Christopher Fowler round out this atmospheric and frequently terrifying collection." —*Publishers Weekly*, starred review

"The list of contributors, including Gemma Files, Caitlín R. Kiernan, Adam L. G. Nevill, and Kim Newman, will be enough to get horror fans excited. The assortment of styles means that there is a monster here for everyone's taste." —*Library Journal*

"Honestly, every story in this anthology is excellent. It's really a testament to Datlow's wealth of experience in the genre, and her masterful touch in editing and compiling the best stories around." —*The Warbler*

— PRAISE FOR **LOVECRAFT'S MONSTERS** —

"Ellen Datlow's second editorial outing into the realm of Lovecraft proves even more fruitful than the first. Focusing on Lovecraftian monsters, Datlow offers readers sixteen stories and two poems of a variety that should please any fans of the genre." —*Arkham Digest*

"[An] amazing and diverse treasure trove of stories. As an avid fan of Lovecraft's monstrous creations, THIS is the anthology I've been waiting for." —*Shattered Ravings*

"Datlow brings together some of the top SF/F and horror writers working today and has them play in Lovecraft's bizarre world. And that's a delight." —*January Magazine*

— PRAISE FOR **DARKNESS: TWO DECADES OF MODERN HORROR** —

"★ This diverse 25-story anthology is a superb sampling of some of the most significant short horror works published between 1985 and 2005. Editor extraordinaire Datlow (*Poe*) includes classic stories from horror icons Clive Barker, Peter Straub, and Stephen King as well as SF and fantasy luminaries Gene Wolfe, Dan Simmons, Neil Gaiman, and Lucius Shepard....This is an anthology to be cherished and an invaluable reference for horror aficionados." —*Publishers Weekly*, starred review

"Make sure you are in a safe place before you open it up." —*New York Journal of Books*

"*Darkness* promises to please both longtime fans and readers who have no clue what 'splatterpunk' was supposed to mean." —*San Francisco Chronicle*

"I can't recommend this book highly enough, and no, that's not just the rabid fanboy inside me talking. This is my serious critic's voice. I know it doesn't translate well in the written word, but trust me. I give my highest recommendation for this book." —*Hellnotes*

— PRAISE FOR **HAUNTINGS** —

"This anthology of 24 previously published dark fantasy and horror stories, edited by the ever-adept Datlow (*Blood and Other Cravings*), explores a variety of situations in which people encounter literal or figurative specters from beyond....Solid entries by Neil Gaiman, Caitlín R. Kiernan, and Joyce Carol Oates capture the mood perfectly and will thrill fans of the eerie." —*Publishers Weekly*

"Datlow once again proves herself as a master editor. Her mission to broaden readers' concepts of what a haunting can be is nothing short of a success, and the twenty-four stories on display run the gamut from explicitly terrifying to eerily familiar. Readers who wish to be haunted themselves should not miss this one. Highly recommended." —*Arkham Digest*

"Ms. Datlow has assembled a formidable community of eminent genre artists working at the very heights of their literary powers to create this outstanding dark fantasy anthology. This is the best of the best—don't miss it!" —*The Tomb of Dark Delights*

"I have a short list of editors that I will buy an anthology of, regardless of whether or not I have even heard of the writers it contains, and Ellen Datlow is at the top of that list. She has this crazy knack of consistently putting together stellar anthologies and *Hauntings* is no different." —*Horror Talk*

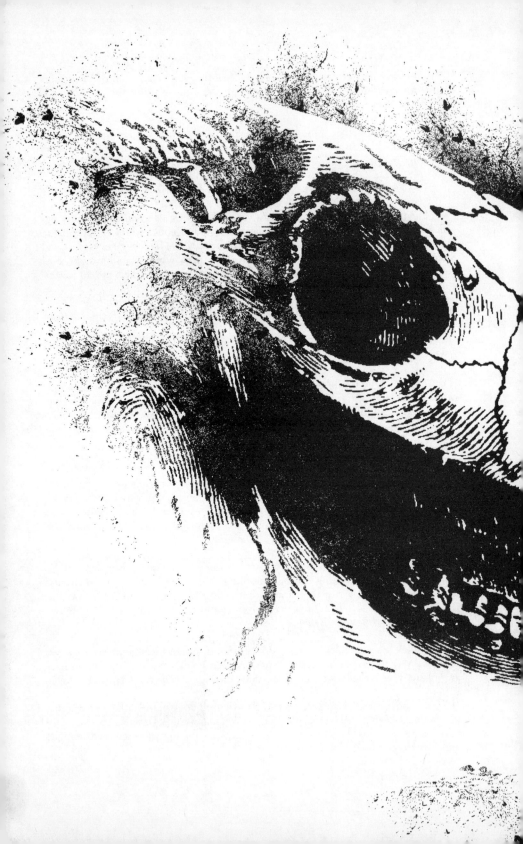

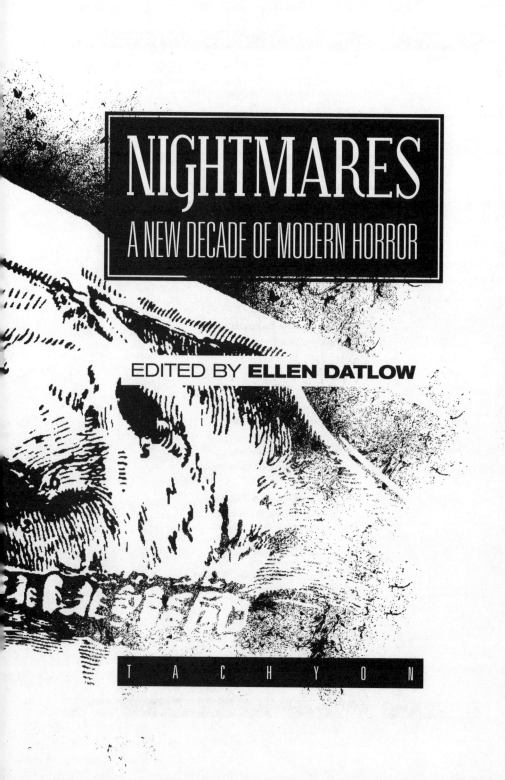

NIGHTMARES

A NEW DECADE OF MODERN HORROR

EDITED BY **ELLEN DATLOW**

TACHYON

Nightmares: A New Decade of Modern Horror

Copyright © 2016 by Ellen Datlow

This is a work of collected fiction. All events portrayed in this book are fictitious and any resemblance to real people or events is purely coincidental. All rights reserved, including the right to reproduce this book or portions thereof in any form without the express permission of the editor and the publisher.

Introduction copyright © 2016 by Ellen Datlow
Page 425 represents an extension of this copyright page.

Cover art "Silence" copyright © 2012 by Nihil
Cover design by Elizabeth Story
Interior illustrations and design
copyright © 2016 by John Coulthart

Tachyon Publications LLC
1459 18th Street #139
San Francisco, CA 94107
(415) 285-5615
WWW.TACHYONPUBLICATIONS.COM
TACHYON@TACHYONPUBLICATIONS.COM

Series Editor: Jacob Weisman
Project Editor: Jill Roberts

ISBN 13: 978-1-61696-232-6

Printed in the United States of America
by Worzalla

First Edition: 2016

9 8 7 6 5 4 3 2 1

C   O   N   T

E   N   T   S

Ellen Datlow has been editing science fiction, fantasy, and horror short fiction for over thirty-five years. She currently acquires short fiction for *Tor.com*. In addition, she has edited more than ninety science fiction, fantasy, and horror anthologies, including *Lovecraft's Monsters*, *Fearful Symmetries*, *The Monstrous*, *The Doll Collection*, and *Children of Lovecraft*.

She's won multiple World Fantasy Awards, Locus Awards, Hugo Awards, Stoker Awards, International Horror Guild Awards, Shirley Jackson Awards, and the 2012 Il Posto Nero Black Spot Award for Excellence as Best Foreign Editor. Datlow was named recipient of the 2007 Karl Edward Wagner Award, given at the British Fantasy Convention for "outstanding contribution to the genre," and was honored with the Life Achievement Award given by the Horror Writers Association, in acknowledgment of superior achievement over an entire career, and the Life Achievement Award given by the World Fantasy Convention.

She lives in New York and cohosts the monthly Fantastic Fiction Reading Series at KGB Bar. More information can be found at www.datlow.com, on Facebook, and on Twitter as @EllenDatlow.

Introduction
Ellen Datlow

Nightmares: A New Decade of Modern Horror could be considered a sequel to *Darkness: Two Decades of Modern Horror*, an anthology that covers the years 1985 to 2005. 2005–2015 has been a great period for short horror fiction, as new writers have entered the field, established writers have either dipped their feet into horror or jumped in wholeheartedly, and those who have been writing in the field for decades have continued to create great new stories. As I said in the last volume, I'm not a horror critic or *expert*. I'm an enthusiast who has dipped into horror fiction my whole life and who became totally immersed in the short-story form of it during the mid-1980s.

My intention for this anthology was to choose stories that I love. Stories that have had a lasting impact on me (that might or might not be well known within or outside the field). I've selected some of these stories for annual and themed anthologies, and commissioned several stories as original publications, including Garth Nix's Shirley Jackson Award nominee, "Shay Corsham Worsted." I've mostly included writers who were not in *Darkness*. Although several important new writers have emerged during the past decade, their foci are quite varied. Some write what might be referred to as "psychological" horror or "terror tales," some have embraced cosmic horror, creating a boomlet of Lovecraftian fiction. And there are still monsters: vampires, zombies, ghosts and other haunts, madmen.

As with *Darkness*, the stories herein are organized by year of publication. It seems the most natural way. Because the period is half that covered in *Darkness*, there is often more than one story chosen per year. So in those years, I've ordered the stories with intent.

By necessity, I've not been able to include every writer or every story that continues to make an impression on me. Juggling any anthology's contents is challenging, but in one like this, it's even more difficult than usual. Space is always a consideration. There were some excellent horror novellas (stories between 17,500 and 39,999 words) published during the period I've covered, but there's not enough space for them. I've also tried to avoid publishing stories that are readily available, but if a story seems to be *the* one by a writer that has made the most impression on me, it's difficult to not include it.

I'm often asked to name my favorite horror story. I always respond that I have no one favorite, but you can ascertain *some* of my favorites by checking out my *Best of the Year* anthologies. And you can narrow that down even further by reading *Darkness: Two Decades of Modern Horror* and *Nightmares: A New Decade of Modern Horror*. These two volumes will point you to some of my favorites published since 1985. Consider them a guide to some of the best short-story writers currently working in the field of horror fiction. And in this volume specifically, a good representation of the excellent horror that was published between 2005 and 2015.

Dedicated to the writers of short horror fiction.
Without you, I'd have no career. Without you,
we'd have no field. Thank you all.

Mark Samuels is the author of five short-story collections—*The White Hands and Other Weird Tales, Black Altars, Glyphotech & Other Macabre Processes, The Man Who Collected Machen & Other Weird Tales,* and *Written in Darkness*— as well as the short novel *The Face of Twilight.*

His tales have appeared in many prestigious anthologies on both sides of the Atlantic, including *The Mammoth Book of Best New Horror, The Year's Best Fantasy and Horror, The Weird, Inferno,* and *A Mountain Walks.*

Shallaballah
Mark Samuels

A WIG COVERED his bald scalp. His face was a patchwork of skin joined together by ugly black stitches. Mr. Punch told him that, given time, the resulting scars would be scarcely noticeable. Eventually they would almost fade away and leave only thin lines that could not be seen except under an extremely bright light. But as Sogol examined his own features in the mirror, tracing his fingers over the threads that held the flesh together, he found it difficult to believe that what he saw would ever again resemble his old familiar face. His reflection was like a mask, dead and expressionless. Sogol tried to remember that Mr. Punch had told him this was to be expected and that nerve-to-muscle control would take a few days to return, yet he had not really been prepared for the reality of just how ghastly he would appear in the interim. He poked a fingernail into the skin but felt nothing. It was like touching another person.

A gigantic industrial estate with narrow walkways, corridors and alleys. The squat, square buildings are made of concrete. They are run-down and dismal. Many of the windows are broken. On the flat roofs there are crooked TV aerials and grimy satellite dishes. They look like bizarre scarecrows and are framed against an orange-coloured sky. Subsidence and age have made the structures lean together. Flights of twisted stairs link one level to another.

Sogol sat on the edge of the camp-bed. Its mattress was soiled and hollowed in the centre, a reminder of all those who had been here before him. Mr. Punch's "clinic" offered the most meagre hospitality, despite the exorbitant cost of his special type of treatment. Those who went under his knife did so in the knowledge that the gentleman was a criminal, possibly even insane. But still his patients came. There was nowhere else for them to go. This horrible little building with its dusty windows and peeling paintwork, hidden away in a run-down ghetto estate, was a recondite Lourdes where one offered up hard cash in exchange for miracles.

He'd heard rumours about the celebrities that had passed through here. Film actresses who, beyond the help of lighting and make-up, even of face-lifts or plastic surgery, had extended their shelf-life by more than a decade by utilising the services of Mr. Punch. One did not approach him. There was no way to contact him. Mr. Punch would call on the telephone offering his services to those he knew were most in need. Celebrities of course. Only ever celebrities who could afford the fees he charged. And then his black ambulance would call in secret at an appointed time.

In Sogol's case it was after the car accident. The TV company had paid a lot of money to hush the thing up. This was, after all, right in the middle of filming the episode that was going to be next year's ratings triumph. Only Mr. Punch could repair the damage that Sogol had suffered in the crash; only Mr. Punch could reconstruct his monstrously burnt face in time.

Sogol coked up to the eyeballs, driving a sports car, a bottle of scotch with just a dribble left in it laying beside him on the passenger seat, and a hairpin bend on the hillside road…leaving behind some woman…who meant nothing to him…

Three days ago. Strange to think it had only been less than a week.

The interiors of the dismal buildings are not homes. They contain no dwellings. Inside one would find a series of strange rooms cluttered with all manner of what appears to be junk: pot plants, framed pictures, coat stands, mounds of clothes and painted backdrops.

"You cannot leave," Mr. Punch had told him in a letter passed to Sogol, "until your treatment is complete. You must follow my instructions in each and every detail. If you fail to do so I cannot be held responsible for what might happen to your face."

Sogol had groaned at this statement and crumpled the letter in his hands. He was desperate to leave this anonymous ghetto in a town whose name he could not even recall. God knows in the past he had spent time in enough sleazy hotels in pursuit of fame, playing bit parts where he might be called to the set at any moment in order to wander in front of the cameras and utter a line or two of dialogue. But that was before he had struck it big, before his face was known to everyone he met, before he'd graced the cover of gossip magazines, before interviews with him were sought by all the TV chat-show hosts.

But if he left now people would turn their heads in horror, not in awed recognition, as he passed them by. A man with a cracked face. A freak. A refugee from a sideshow who happened to bear a passing resemblance to a famous TV soap opera star.

Sogol, winner of three prestigious awards for best leading male role, one of the most highly paid actors on television, a man whom the public adored, a man who was witty, charming and handsome. Handsome above all, but now reduced to this intolerable, pitiful state of existence.

There are dusty corridors within the structures of immense industrial estate. Faded TV schedules are pinned to the walls. The same programmes are broadcast at the same time day after day, night after night. The same films, the same episodes of soap operas, the same documentaries, the same panel games and quiz shows. In the photos accompanying the text all the celebrities wear fixed smiles. Their eyes are open too wide as if they regard the camera with fear.

Sogol made his way along the passageway outside his room. At the end was the payphone that he was permitted to use. Mr. Punch had banned mobile phones from his clinic. He confiscated them from patients as soon as they were admitted.

"No distractions," Mr. Punch had explained, "no stress-inducing conversations. Complete rest. If you must make an urgent call, then there is a telephone available. Calls are monitored, however, for your own benefit. Unnecessary exploitation of this service will result in the connection being terminated and the privilege withdrawn."

Up in the corner of the middle of the passageway, in the angle between the far wall and the ceiling, was a surveillance camera. It moved through an arc on its wall-mount base in order to keep Sogol in its line of sight as he passed by. He cradled the receiver between his ear and shoulder, and dialled the number with his right hand as he scanned the little black phone book in his left. Just then he felt the beginnings of a dull pain well up around his forehead and along his jawline. A sure sign that the nurse would soon be making her rounds with the drug trolley; strange that he was now marking time by the effects of painkillers wearing off.

"Ketch Entertainments." The sound of a bored, unfamiliar female voice came down the line.

Ketch *what*? Had Sogol heard her right?

"Put me through to Joey," he said through stiffened lips, "tell him it's Sogol."

There was a pause and some tinny muzak played as his call was transferred. After a few seconds Joey spoke.

"Hi Joey, it's me."

"Sogol? Where the bloody hell are you?"

What was his problem?

"Where do you think I am, you idiot? Still in the clinic of course."

"What clinic? Why haven't you phoned in? I've gone half-crazy sorting out the seaside shows that have had to be cancelled. You've lost us a lot of money. If you think you're still represented by this agency think again."

Had Joey lost his mind? What was this? His idea of a joke?

"I'm having my face reconstructed here and you're acting like an arsehole..." Sogol hissed through his teeth, but in mid-sentence the line went dead. There was a loud click and then a droning, recorded voice said:

"This call is terminated. Please return to your room at once."

Sogol replaced the receiver and then tried to dial again. However before he'd even completed entering the whole telephone number, he heard the same recorded instruction.

"This call is terminated. Please return to your room at once."

Sogol looked back over his shoulder. The surveillance camera was trained on him. Right now someone was doubtless watching him on one of the pictures from a bank of CCTV screens. Watching and waiting to see whether he would comply. I'm not being treated like some nobody, Sogol thought, I'm not standing for this anymore. I'm Sogol! I'm not in prison!

Just then a set of double doors at the end of the corridor opened and two huge men clad in three-quarter-length black coats and bowler hats strode purposefully towards him. They looked like undertakers rather than orderlies. Nevertheless, rather than displaying any sign of his being intimidated, Sogol advanced to meet the pair. But within moments, despite his screams of protest, his arms were pinned behind his back and he was frog-marched back along the corridor and thrown into his room. They locked the door behind them once they left. Neither of them had uttered a word to him but had been cold and silent, going about their business of restraint and coercion in a mechanical, indifferent fashion. Had the situation required it, Sogol was sure that they would not have balked at actually beating him into submission.

Within the structures with the twisted TV aerials on the roofs one can hear sounds. They echo along the corridors coated with peeling paintwork. There is laughter without any humour in it; shrill, cold laughter. And it is accompanied by a series of groans. The groans seem to come from weakened lungs and throats. When the groans falter there is a horrible tittering, like that of a demented child, and then they begin all over again. This goes on for hours and hours. Finally, the sounds are suddenly replaced by the dim hiss of static. This lasts for a few seconds and then the whole process repeats itself without cessation.

Sogol was perched on the edge of the camp-bed waiting for someone to come and attend to him. He'd pushed the summons button over and over again but the nurse had not responded. Was he being punished for his actions? He knew that it was long past the time he was due his medication. The flesh beneath the skin of his face itched unbearably, as if it were infested with spectral bugs, and despite the consequences Sogol could not stop scratching. He felt nothing; the outer layers of his facial skin were as numb as before, but at least it brought some temporary relief farther down. Perhaps the bugs stopped crawling when they were sure that he was still alive.

He'd taken off the wig and sat there staring at the shoddy thing as he turned it over repeatedly in his hands. It was made of rough, artificial fibres and the brown fake hair was held together by a mesh that rested next to the scalp when worn. Mr. Punch had advised him that Sogol's own hair would begin to grow back within days but there was no sign of bristle on his skull, simply the same bald mottled patchwork he'd discovered when he'd awoken after the operation.

Up in the corner of the room was a fixture that he couldn't remember having seen previously. It was a dusty old light fitting with a bulb screwed into the socket. Underneath was a small rectangular panel that was covered in a thick layer of dust. Sogol got up to examine it more closely. He scraped away the debris to reveal the words "On Air" etched into its glass front. The bulb above the lettering was coloured a deep red.

Perhaps Mr. Punch had it put there as a tribute to his patients, in recognition of their celebrity status. It was a weird thing to do since in every other detail he had made no similar gestures. How could he possibly consider this seedy flea-pit as suitable for the glitterati? What matter that such an absurd concession had been made when compared to the grubby cells and corridors, the lack of proper heating and basic facilities?

Outside, in the corridor, he could hear the sound of the nurse finally making her rounds with the drugs trolley. It rattled like a jar of nails as she slowly wheeled the thing along the uneven linoleum. Sogol banged ferociously on the door, in an attempt to attract her attention. He began shouting at the top of his voice that he demanded she see to him first and that he was suffering terrible pain.

"I'm next, you old bitch! I'm next! I'm dying in here!"

A grille in the door opened and through the latticework her thin, doll-like head hoved into view. The nurse wore an old-fashioned mobcap. She looked at him with small black eyes, devoid of emotion.

"Stage fright, eh? Stage fright?" The words came from a toothless hole ringed by a gaudy mess of smeared lipstick. Saliva oozed down out of it onto a flabby chin dotted with hairs. "Open wide, ugly. Open wide for Nurse Judy."

She thrust two green-coated pills through the interstices and dropped them. Sogol scrambled to the floor and then swallowed them eagerly. When he looked up, the grille was closed again and he heard her continuing her rounds, whistling a discordant melody.

After fifteen minutes had passed the two grim-faced orderlies entered his room, picked Sogol up from the floor and slung him onto the bed, strapping him down to it. They left the door open, on purpose it seemed, and he stared at the aperture with dry, unblinking eyes. There were moments when the uninterrupted light affecting his retina turned everything into a hazy fog of white blindness.

There is an old television set dating from the 1930s or '40s. It is housed in a four-foot-tall wooden cabinet with a ten-inch-high flickering blue screen on the front. In a darkened, derelict room a shadowy figure with a patchwork face silently watches the display. The signal that the device is receiving is an image of a long out-of-date test card. In the centre of the image is a circle with vertical lines that thicken from right to left. Outside the circle is a black space that fills the rest of the screen. Written in white lettering on the space are the following words:

Above the circle are a logo and a slogan: "Shallaballah," "Television is the New Afterlife." Right: "Delayed images (ghosts) may appear on the black or white strips." Left: "Reception reports may be sent to Mr. Punch. College of Professors. Eng. Div., London N.19." Underneath: "Test Transmission."

Accompanying the visual broadcast is a monaural sound; a four-frequency tone that ranges from a very low droning whine to a very high shrill pitch. It is played on a continuous loop. The individual watching and listening to the broadcast is humming to himself, and he eerily mimics the noise coming from the television set's speaker, as if hypnotised.

Sogol heard footsteps and murmuring voices from outside in the corridor. It sounded like someone was conversing with the nurse and he was certain that he heard his name mentioned, though exactly what they were discussing was too indistinguishable to make out. When she came into the room she was carrying an old suitcase which she set down on the end of his bed. The nurse opened it, and took out items of stage make-up, foundation, powder and natural skin colourings, as well as a small set of scissors and tweezers. She began to cut and unpick his stitches from his skin. Once she'd finished she applied some of the make-up to his face, doing her best to mask his blemishes and wounds.

A TV studio with a set designed to look like an operating theatre from the 1930s or 1940s. The cameras that the operators are using are as out-of-date as the mock surroundings. Each device requires not only someone to point the lens but also someone else to wheel it around at the base as it closes in on a shot. At the operating table are life-size Punch and Judy puppets in white smocks, masks and gloves. Their movements are stiff and awkward although Punch tries occasionally to caper. Judy passes surgical implements over to him as he tinkers with the exposed brain of a man whose skull has been sawn open. Punch makes incisions in the man's frontal lobe with a scalpel and inserts a series of wires into the holes. The wires are connected to an obsolete television set next to the operating table. The TV is switched on. During the operation a camera draws closer and on the screen next to the table the heavily made-up face of the man being operated on can be seen quite clearly, though the image is grainy and slightly distorted. His eyes are open. They move from side to side. Not once does he blink.

During the operation Punch and Judy quarrel with each other. Punch throws Judy to the floor and changes the channel on the TV set, moving a frequency dial until it's tuned into a station showing a programme in which the patient on the table is the star.

Sogol wandered along the corridors beyond his own room. The effects of the drug had worn off some hours before although he still suffered from stiffness in his legs and back, making him walk with a shuffling gait, like that of an elderly man. It seemed that his treatment was over, for a note left in his room had advised him that he was to be released after a final interview and examination by Mr. Punch.

He ran his fingers over the flesh of his face. It was almost totally smooth except for some very thin scar-lines, and all the lost sensation and movement had now returned. As the CCTV cameras tracked Sogol's movement through

the passageways, he could not resist turning his gaze upon them so that whoever was observing him could not help but see him more clearly. Once, he
even flashed one of his best trademark smiles at the indifferent lens. The only
thing that continued to trouble him was the damned wig. But he had to wear
it in order to cover the fresh stitches that had been sewn all the way around
his head. Anyway, as soon as he was on the outside it would be easy enough
to find a more sophisticated and comfortable hairpiece.

He passed through a set of double doors. Above the entrance Sogol saw a
green sign that read "Studio 7." He gazed around him with bemused astonish-
ment at what he saw in the room. It was dusty and almost bare. At the far end
stood a portable canvas booth, like those used for puppet theatre. However,
where the stage opening should be there was instead a television screen. The
device inside was switched on but the picture showed only a card with the
words "An Announcement Is Being Made in Sound" on a black background.
The sound it emitted was a four-frequency tone, its pitch rising and falling. In
the centre of the room a hangman's noose dangled from the ceiling. Directly
beneath it was a trapdoor, operated by a lever mechanism fixed onto the bare
floorboards.

Then Punch and Judy appeared from behind him. They seized Sogol, and
although he struggled wildly, the two of them quickly had his hands bound
behind his back with a length of cord. Mr. Punch placed a noose over his
neck and tightened the knot until the rope chafed his throat. Judy dragged his
body by its legs into a standing position above the trapdoor. Neither of them
spoke a word, maintaining a grim, terrifying silence. Mr. Punch beat Sogol
about his head viciously with a stick, until he stopped resisting.

When Sogol was in the right position, the test-card on the screen faded
out although the four-frequency tone continued to be broadcast. The inky
blackness slowly gave way to black and white static. Inside the chaos of the
electronic snow features began to coalesce and take shape; a deformed maw
that might have been a mouth and twin holes that might have been empty
eye sockets.

Mr. Punch covered Sogol's head with a cloth bag. For some reason it had
mouth- and eye-holes cut into the rough material. Then the lever was pulled
and Sogol's flailing body dropped into the opening that appeared beneath
him. He fell for fifteen feet before the rope reached its full length and the knot
at the base of his skull snapped his neck.

Up in Studio 7 the face on the television screen in the booth continued to take shape. Its features became more distinct and more like those of Sogol with each moment that passed.

Gene Wolfe is best known for his Book of the New Sun series and his tetralogy *The Book of the Long Sun*. He also wrote the trilogy *The Book of the Short Sun* and many stand-alone novels, including most recently *A Borrowed Man*. He's at work on a sequel titled *Interlibrary Loan*.

He has won the World Fantasy Award three times (most recently for his novel *Soldier of Sidon*) and the World Fantasy Life Achievement Award.

He has also written many shorter works, including the interconnected trio of novellas called *The Fifth Head of Cerberus* and the stories in his several collections, the most recent being *The Best of Gene Wolfe: A Definitive Retrospective of His Finest Short Fiction*.

Sob in the Silence
Gene Wolfe

"This," the horror writer told the family visiting him, "is beyond any question the least haunted house in the Midwest. No ghost, none at all, will come within miles of the place. So I am assured."

Robbie straightened his little glasses and mumbled, "Well, it looks haunted."

"It does, young man." After teetering between seven and eight, the horror writer decided that Robbie was about seven. "It's the filthy yellow stucco. No doubt it was a cheerful yellow once, but God only knows how long it's been up. I'm going to have it torn off, every scrap of it, and put up fresh, which I will paint white."

"Can't you just paint over?" Kiara asked. (Kiara of the all-conquering pout, of the golden hair and the tiny silver earrings.)

Looking very serious, the horror writer nodded. And licked his lips only mentally. "I've tried, believe me. That hideous color is the result of air pollution—of smoke, soot, and dirt, if you will—that has clung to the stucco. Paint over it, and it bleeds out through the new paint. Washing—"

"Water jets under high pressure." Dan was Robbie's father, and Kiara's. "You can rent the units, or buy one for a thousand or so."

"I own one," the horror writer told him. "With a strong cleaning agent added to the water, it will do the job." He paused to smile. "Unfortunately, the stucco's old and fragile. Here and there, a good jet breaks it."

"Ghosts," Charity said. Charity was Mrs. Dan, a pudgy woman with a soft, not unattractive face and a remarkable talent for dowdy hats. "Please go back to your ghosts. I find ghosts far more interesting."

"As do I." The horror writer favored her with his most dazzling smile. "I've tried repeatedly to interest psychic researchers in the old place, which has a—may I call it fascinating—history. I've been persuasive and persistent, and no less than three teams have checked this old place out as a result. All three have reported that they found nothing. No evidence whatsoever. No spoor of spooks. No cooperative specters a struggling author might use for research purposes."

"And publicity," Kiara said. "Don't forget publicity. I plan to get into public relations when I graduate."

"And publicity, you're right. By the time you're well settled in public relations, I hope to be wealthy enough to engage you. If I am, I will. That's a promise."

Charity leveled a plump forefinger. "You, on the other hand, have clearly seen or heard or felt something. You had to have something more than this big dark living-room to get the psychics in, and you had it. Tell us."

The horror writer produced a sharply bent briar that showed signs of years of use. "Will this trouble anyone? I rarely smoke in here, but if we're going to have a good long chat—well, a pipe may make things go more smoothly. Would anyone care for a drink?"

Charity was quickly equipped with white wine, Dan with Johnnie Walker and water, and Robbie with cola. "A lot of the kids drink beer at IVY Tech," Kiara announced in a tone that indicated she was one of them. "I don't, though."

"Not until you're twenty-one," Dan said firmly.

"You see?" She pouted.

The horror writer nodded. "I do indeed. One of the things I see is that you have good parents, parents who care about you and are zealous for your welfare." He slipped Kiara a scarcely perceptible wink. "What about a plain soda? I always find soda water over ice refreshing, myself."

Charity said, "That would be fine, if she wants it."

Kiara said she did, and he became busy behind the bar.

Robbie had been watching the dark upper corners of the old, high-ceilinged room. "I thought I saw one."

"A ghost?" The horror writer looked up, his blue eyes twinkling.

"A bat. Maybe we can catch it."

Dan said, "There's probably a belfry, too."

"I'm afraid not. Perhaps I'll add one once I get the new stucco on."

"You need one. As I've told my wife a dozen times, anybody who believes in ghosts has bats in his belfry."

"It's better, perhaps," Charity murmured, "if living things breathe and move up there. Better than just bells, rotting ropes, and dust. Tell us more about this place, please."

"It was a country house originally." With the air of one who performed a sacrament, the horror writer poured club soda into a tall frosted glass that already contained five ice cubes and (wholly concealed by his fingers) a generous two inches of vodka. "A quiet place in which a wealthy family could get away from the heat and stench of city summers. The family was ruined somehow—I don't recall the details. I know it's usually the man who kills in murder-suicides, but in this house it was the woman. She shot her husband and her stepdaughters, and killed herself."

Charity said, "I could never bring myself to do that. I could never kill Dan. Or his children. I suppose I might kill myself. That's conceivable. But not the rest."

Straight-faced, the horror writer handed his frosted glass to Kiara. "I couldn't kill myself," he told her. "I like myself too much. Other people? Who can say?"

Robbie banged down his cola. "You're trying to scare us!"

"Of course I am. It's my trade."

Dan asked, "They all died? That's good shooting."

The horror writer resumed his chair and picked up his briar. "No. As a matter of fact they didn't. One of the three stepdaughters survived. She had been shot in the head at close range, yet she lived."

Dan said, "Happens sometime."

"It does. It did in this case. Her name was Maude Parkhurst. Maude was a popular name back around nineteen hundred, which is when her parents and sisters died. Ever hear of her?"

Dan shook his head.

"She was left penniless and scarred for life. It seems to have disordered her thinking. Or perhaps the bullet did it. In any event, she founded her own church and was its pope and prophetess. It was called—maybe it's still called, since it may still be around for all I know—the Unionists of Heaven and Earth."

Charity said, "I've heard of it. It sounded innocent enough."

The horror writer shrugged. "Today? Perhaps it is. Back then, I would say no. Decidedly no. It was, in its own fantastic fashion, about as repellent as a cult can be. May I call it a cult?"

Kiara grinned prettily over her glass. "Go right ahead. I won't object."

"A friend of mine, another Dan, once defined a cult for me. He said that if the leader gets all the women, it's a cult."

Dan nodded. "Good man. There's a lot to that."

"There is, but in the case of the UHE, as it was called, it didn't apply. Maude Parkhurst didn't want the women, or the men either. The way to get to Heaven, she told her followers, was to live like angels here on Earth."

Dan snorted.

"Exactly. Any sensible person would have told them that they were not angels. That it was natural and right for angels to live like angels, but that men and women should live like human beings."

"We really know almost nothing about angels." Charity looked pensive. "Just that they carry the Lord's messages. It's Saint Paul, I think, who says that each of us has an angel who acts as our advocate in Heaven. So we know that, too. But it's really very little."

"This is about sex," Kiara said. "I smell it coming."

The horror writer nodded. "You're exactly right, and I'm beginning to wonder if you're not the most intelligent person here. It is indeed. Members of the UHE were to refrain from all forms of sexual activity. If unmarried, they were not to marry. If married, they were to separate and remain separated."

"The University of Heaven at Elysium. On a T-shirt. I can see it now."

Charity coughed, the sound of it scarcely audible in the large, dark room. "Well, Kiara, I don't see anything wrong with that if it was voluntary."

"Neither do I," the horror writer said, "but there's more. Those wishing to join underwent an initiation period of a year. At the end of that time, there was a midnight ceremony. If they had children, those children had to attend, all of them. There they watched their parents commit suicide—or that's how it looked. I don't know the details, but I know that at the end of the service they were carried out of the church, apparently lifeless and covered with blood."

Charity whispered, "Good God...."

"When the congregation had gone home," the horror writer continued, "the children were brought here. They were told that it was an orphanage, and it was operated like one. Before long it actually was one. Apparently there was some sort of tax advantage, so it was registered with the state as a church-run foundation, and from time to time the authorities sent actual orphans here. It was the age of orphanages, as you may know. Few children, if any, were put in foster homes. Normally, it was the orphanage for any child without parents or close relatives."

Dan said, "There used to be a comic strip about it, 'Little Orphan Annie.'"

The horror writer nodded. "Based upon a popular poem of the nineteenth century.

"'Little Orphant Annie's come to our house to stay,
An' wash the cups an' saucers up,
an' brush the crumbs away,
An' shoo the chickens off the porch,
an' dust the hearth an' sweep,
An' make the fire, an' bake the bread,
an' earn her board an' keep.
An' all us other children,
when the supper things is done,
We set around the kitchen fire an' has the mostest fun
A-list'nin' to the witch tales 'at Annie tells about,
An' the Gobble-uns 'at gets you
Ef you
Don't
Watch
Out!'

"You see," the horror writer finished, smiling, "in those days you could get an orphan girl from such an orphanage as this to be your maid of all work and baby-sitter. You fed and clothed her, gave her a place to sleep, and paid her nothing at all. Despite being showered with that sort of kindness, those girls picked up enough of the monstrosity and lonely emptiness of the universe to become the first practitioners of my art, the oral recounters of horrific tales whose efforts preceded all horror writing."

"Was it really so bad for them?" Kiara asked.

"Here? Worse. I haven't told you the worst yet, you see. Indeed, I haven't even touched upon it." The horror writer turned to Dan. "Perhaps you'd like to send Robbie out. That might be advisable."

Dan shrugged. "He watches TV. I doubt that anything you'll say will frighten him."

Charity pursed her lips but said nothing.

The horror writer had taken advantage of the pause to light his pipe. "You don't have to stay, Robbie." He puffed fragrant white smoke, and watched it begin its slow climb to the ceiling. "You know where your room is, and you may go anywhere in the house unless you meet with a locked door."

Kiara smiled. "Secrets! We're in Bluebeard's cashel—castle. I knew it!"

"No secrets," the horror writer told her, "just a very dangerous cellar stair—steep, shaky, and innocent of any sort of railing."

Robbie whispered, "I'm not going."

"So I see. From time to time, Robbie, one of the children would learn or guess that his parents were not in fact dead. When that happened, he or she might try to get away and return home. I've made every effort to learn just how often that happened, but the sources are contradictory on the point. Some say three and some five, and one says more than twenty. I should add that we who perform this type of research soon learn to be wary of the number three. It's the favorite of those who don't know the real number. There are several places on the grounds that may once have been graves—unmarked graves long since emptied by the authorities. But—"

Charity leaned toward him, her face tense. "Do you mean to say that those children were killed?"

The horror writer nodded. "I do. Those who were returned here by their parents were. That is the most horrible fact attached to this really quite awful old house. Or at least, it is the worst we know of—perhaps the worst that occurred."

He drew on his pipe, letting smoke trickle from his nostrils. "A special midnight service was held here, in this room in which we sit. At that service the church members are said to have flown. To have fluttered about this room like so many strange birds. No doubt they ran and waved their arms, as children sometimes do. Very possibly they thought they flew. The members of medieval witch cults seem really to have believed that they flew to the gatherings of their covens, although no sane person supposes they actually did."

Charity asked, "But you say they killed the children?"

The horror writer nodded. "Yes, at the end of the ceremony. Call it the children's hour, a term that some authorities say they used themselves. They shot them as Maude Parkhurst's father and sisters had been shot. The executioner was chosen by lot. Maude is said to have hoped aloud that it would fall to her, as it seems to have done more than once. Twice at least."

Dan said, "It's hard to believe anybody would really do that."

"Perhaps it is, although news broadcasts have told me of things every bit as bad. Or worse."

The horror writer drew on his pipe again, and the room had grown dark enough that the red glow from its bowl lit his face from below. "The children were asleep by that time, as Maude, her father, and her sisters had been. The lucky winner crept into the child's bedroom, accompanied by at least one other member who carried a candle. The moment the shot was fired, the candle was blown out. The noise would've awakened any other children who had been sleeping in that room, of course; but they awakened only to darkness and the smell of gun smoke."

Dan said, "Angels!" There was a world of contempt in the word.

"There are angels in Hell," the horror writer told him, "not just in Heaven. Indeed, the angels of Hell may be the more numerous."

Charity pretended to yawn while nodding her reluctant agreement. "I think it's time we all went up bed. Don't you?"

Dan said, "I certainly do. I drove one hell of a long way today."

Kiara lingered when the others had gone. "Ish really nice meeting you." She swayed as she spoke, though only slightly. "Don' forget I get to be your public relations agent. You promised."

"You have my word." The horror writer smiled, knowing how much his word was worth.

For a lingering moment they clasped hands. "Ish hard to believe," she said, "that you were Dad's roommate. You sheem—seem—so much younger."

He thanked her and watched her climb the wide curved staircase that had been the pride of the Parkhursts long ago, wondering all the while whether she knew that he was watching. Whether she knew or not, watching Kiara climb stairs was too great a pleasure to surrender.

On the floor above, Charity was getting Robbie ready for bed. "You're a brave boy, I know. Aren't you a brave boy, darling? Say it, please. It always helps to say it."

"I'm a brave boy," Robbie told her dutifully.

"You are. I know you are. You won't let that silly man downstairs fool you. You'll stay in your own bed, in your own room, and get a good night's sleep.

We'll do some sight-seeing tomorrow, forests and lakes and rugged hills where the worked-out mines hide."

Charity hesitated, gnawing with small white teeth at her full lower lip. "There's no night-light in here, I'm afraid, but I've got a little flashlight in my purse. I could lend you that. Would you like it?"

Robbie nodded, and clasped Charity's little plastic flashlight tightly as he watched her leave. Her hand—the one without rings—reached up to the light switch. Her fingers found it.

There was darkness.

He located the switch again with the watery beam of the disposable flashlight, knowing that he would be scolded (perhaps even spanked) if he switched the solitary overhead light back on but wanting to know exactly where that switch was, just in case.

At last he turned Charity's flashlight off and lay down. It was hot in the too-large, too-empty room. Hot and silent.

He sat up again, and aimed the flashlight toward the window. It was indeed open, but open only the width of his hand. He got out of bed, dropped the flashlight into the shirt pocket of his pajamas, and tried to raise the window farther. No effort he could put forth would budge it.

At last he lay down again, and the room felt hotter than ever.

When he had looked out through the window, it had seemed terribly high. How many flights of stairs had they climbed to get up here? He could remember only one, wide carpeted stairs that had curved as they climbed; but that one had been a long, long stair. From the window he had seen the tops of trees.

Treetops and stars. The moon had been out, lighting the lawn below and showing him the dark leaves of the treetops, although the moon itself had not been in sight from the window.

"It walks across the sky," he told himself. Dan, his father, had said that once.

"You could walk...." The voice seemed near, but faint and thin.

Robbie switched the flashlight back on. There was no one there.

Under the bed, he thought. They're under the bed.

But he dared not leave the bed to look, and lay down once more. An older person would have tried to persuade himself that he had imagined the voice, or would have left the bed to investigate. Robbie did neither. His line between palpable and imagined things was blurred and faint, and he had not the slightest desire to see the speaker, whether that speaker was real or make-believe.

There were no other windows that might be opened. He thought of going out. The hall would be dark, but Dan and Charity were sleeping in a room not very far away. The door of their room might be locked, though. They did that sometimes.

He would be scolded in any event. Scolded and perhaps spanked, too. It was not the pain he feared, but the humiliation. "I'll have to go back here," he whispered to himself. "Even if they don't spank me, I'll have to go back."

"You could walk away...." A girl's voice, very faint. From the ceiling? No, Robbie decided, from the side toward the door.

"No," he said. "They'd be mad."

"You'll die...."

"Like us...."

Robbie sat up, shaking.

Outside, the horror writer was hiking toward the old, rented truck he had parked more than a mile away. The ground was soft after yesterday's storm, and it was essential—absolutely essential—that there be tracks left by a strange vehicle.

A turn onto a side road, a walk of a hundred yards, and the beam of his big electric lantern picked out the truck among the trees. When he could set the lantern on its hood, he put on latex gloves. Soon, very soon, the clock would strike the children's hour and Edith with the golden hair would be his. Beautiful Kiara would be his. As for laughing Allegra, he neither knew nor cared whose she might be.

"Wa' ish?" Kiara's voice was thick with vodka and sleep.

"It's only me," Robbie told her, and slipped under the covers. "I'm scared." She put a protective arm around him.

"There are other kids in here. There are! They're gone when you turn on the light, but they come back. They do!"

"Uh huh." She hugged him tighter and went back to sleep.

In Scales Mound, the horror writer parked the truck and walked three blocks to his car. He had paid two weeks' rent on the truck, he reminded himself.

Had paid that rent only three days ago. It would be eleven days at least before the rental agency began to worry about it, and he could return it or send another check before then.

His gun, the only gun he owned, had been concealed in a piece of nondescript luggage and locked in the car. He took it out and made sure the safety was on before starting the engine. It was only a long-barreled twenty-two; but it looked sinister, and should be sufficient to make Kiara obey if the threat of force was needed.

Once she was down there...Once she was down there, she might scream all she liked. It would not matter. As he drove back to the house, he tried to decide whether he should hold it or put it into one of the big side pockets of his barn coat.

Robbie, having escaped Kiara's warm embrace, decided that her room was cooler than his. For one thing, she had two windows. For another, both were open wider than his one window had been. Besides, it was just cooler. He pulled the sheet up, hoping she would not mind.

"Run...." whispered the faint, thin voices.

"Run.... Run...."

"Get away while you can...."

"Go...."

Robbie shook his head and shut his eyes.

Outside Kiara's bedroom, the horror writer patted the long-barreled pistol he had pushed into his belt. His coat pockets held rags, two short lengths of quarter-inch rope, a small roll of duct tape, and a large folding knife. He hoped to need none of them.

There was no provision for locking Kiara's door. He had been careful to see to that. No key for the quaint old lock, no interior bolt; and yet she might have blocked it with a chair. He opened it slowly, finding no obstruction.

The old oak doors were thick and solid, the old walls thicker and solider still. If Dan and his wife were sleeping soundly, it would take a great deal of commotion in here to wake them.

Behind him, the door swung shut on well-oiled hinges. The click of the latch was the only sound.

Moonlight coming through the windows rendered the penlight in his shirt pocket unnecessary. She was there, lying on her side and sound asleep, her lovely face turned toward him.

As the horror writer moved toward her, Robbie sat up, his mouth a dark circle, his pale face a mask of terror. The horror writer pushed him down again.

The muzzle of his pistol was tight against Robbie's head; this though the horror writer could not have said how it came to be there. His index finger squeezed even as he realized it was on the trigger.

There was a muffled bang, like the sound of a large book dropped. Something jerked under the horror writer's hand, and he whispered, "Die like my father. Like Alice and June. Die like me." He whispered it, but did not understand what he intended by it.

Kiara's eyes were open. He struck her with the barrel, reversed the pistol, and struck her again and again with the butt, stopping only when he realized he did not know how many times he had hit her already or where his blows had landed.

After pushing up the safety, he put the pistol back into his belt and stood listening. The room next to that in which he stood had been Robbie's. Presumably, there was no one there to hear.

The room beyond that one—the room nearest the front stair—was Dan's and Charity's. He would stand behind the door if they came in, shoot them both, run. Mexico. South America.

They did not.

The house was silent save for his own rapid breathing and Kiara's slow, labored breaths; beyond the open windows, the night-wind sobbed in the trees. Any other sound would have come, almost, as a relief.

There was none.

He had broken the cellar window, left tracks with the worn old shoes he had gotten from a recycle store, left tire tracks with the old truck. He smiled faintly when he recalled its mismatched tires. Let them work on that one.

He picked up Kiara and slung her over his shoulder, finding her soft, warm, and heavier than he had expected.

The back stairs were narrow and in poor repair; they creaked beneath his feet, but they were farther—much farther—from the room in which Dan and Charity slept. He descended them slowly, holding Kiara with his right arm while his left hand grasped the rail.

She stirred and moaned. He wondered whether he would have to hit her again, and decided he would not unless she screamed. If she screamed, he would drop her and do what had to be done.

She did not.

The grounds were extensive, and included a wood from which (long ago) firewood had been cut. It had grown back now, a tangle of larches and alders, firs and red cedars. Toward the back, not far from the property line, he had by merest chance stumbled upon the old well. There had been a cabin there once. No doubt it had burned. A cow or a child might have fallen into the abandoned well, and so some prudent person had covered it with a slab of limestone. Leaves and twigs on that stone had turned, in time, to soil. He had moved the stone away, leaving the soil on it largely undisturbed.

When he reached the abandoned well at last, panting and sweating, he laid Kiara down. His penlight showed that her eyes were open. Her blood-stained face seemed to him a mask of fear; seeing it, he felt himself stand straighter and grow stronger.

"You may listen to me or not," he told her. "What you do really doesn't matter, but I thought I ought to do you the kindness of explaining just what has happened and what will happen. What I plan, and your place in my plans."

She made an inarticulate sound that might have been a word or a moan.

"You're listening. Good. There's an old well here. Only I know that it exists. At the bottom—shall we say twelve feet down? At the bottom there's mud and a little water. You'll get dirty, in other words, but you won't die of thirst. There you will wait for me for as long as the police actively investigate. From time to time I may, or may not, come here and toss down a sandwich."

He smiled. "It won't hurt you in the least, my dear, to lose a little weight. When things have quieted down, I'll come and pull you out. You'll be grateful—oh, very grateful—for your rescue. Soiled and starved, but very grateful. Together we'll walk back to my home. You may need help, and if you do I'll provide it."

He bent and picked her up. "I'll bathe you, feed you, and nurse you."

Three strides brought him to the dark mouth of the well. "After that, you'll obey me in everything. Or you had better. And in time, perhaps, you'll come to like it."

He let her fall, smiled, and turned away.

There remained only the problem of the gun. Bullets could be matched to barrels, and there was an ejected shell somewhere. The gun would have to be destroyed; it was blued steel; running water should do the job, and do it swiftly.

Still smiling, he set off for the creek.

It was after four o'clock the following afternoon when Captain Barlowe of the Sheriff's Department explained the crime. Captain Barlowe was middle-aged and heavy-limbed. He had a thick mustache. "What happened in this house last night is becoming pretty clear." His tone was weighty. "Why it happened..." He shook his head.

The horror writer said, "I know my house was broken into. One of your men showed me that. I know poor little Robbie's dead, and I know Kiara's missing. But that's all I know."

"Exactly." Captain Barlowe clasped his big hands and unclasped them. "It's pretty much all I know, too, sir. Other than that, all I can do is supply details. The gun that killed the boy was a twenty-two semi-automatic. It could have been a pistol or a rifle. It could even have been a sawed-off rifle. There's no more common caliber in the world."

The horror writer nodded.

"He was killed with one shot, a contact shot to the head, and he was probably killed for being in a room in which he had no business being. He'd left his own bed and crawled into his big sister's. Not for sex, sir. I could see what you were thinking. He was too young for that. He was just a little kid alone in a strange house. He got lonely and was murdered for it."

Captain Barlowe paused to clear his throat. "You told my men that there had been no cars in your driveway since the rain except your own and the boy's parents'. Is that right?"

The horror writer nodded. "I've wracked my brain trying to think of somebody else, and come up empty. Dan and I are old friends. You ought to know that."

Captain Barlowe nodded. "I do, sir. He told me."

"We get together when we can, usually that's once or twice a year. This year he and Charity decided to vacation in this area. He's a golfer and a fisherman."

Captain Barlowe nodded again. "He should love our part of the state."

"That's what I thought, Captain. I don't play golf, but I checked out some of the courses here. I fish a bit, and I told him about that. He said he was coming, and I told him I had plenty of room. They were only going to stay for two nights."

"You kept your cellar door locked?"

"Usually? No. I locked it when I heard they were coming. The cellar's dirty and the steps are dangerous. You know how small boys are."

"Yes, sir. I used to be one. The killer jimmied it open."

The horror writer nodded. "I saw that."

"You sleep on the ground floor. You didn't hear anything?"

"No. I'm a sound sleeper."

"I understand. Here's my problem, sir, and I hope you can help me with it. Crime requires three things. They're motive, means, and opportunity. Know those, and you know a lot. I've got a murder case here. It's the murder of a kid. I hate the bastards who kill kids, and I've never had a case I wanted to solve more."

"I understand," the horror writer said.

"Means is no problem. He had a gun, a car, and tools. Maybe gloves, because we haven't found any fresh prints we can't identify. His motive may have been robbery, but it was probably of a sexual nature. Here's a young girl, a blonde. Very good-looking, to judge by the only picture we've seen so far."

"She is." The horror writer nodded his agreement.

"He must have seen her somewhere. And not just that. He must have known that she was going to be in this house last night. Where did he see her? How did he know where she was going to be? If I can find the answers to those questions we'll get him."

"I wish I could help you." The horror writer's smile was inward only.

"You've had no visitors since your guests arrived?"

He shook his head. "None."

"Delivery men? A guy to fix the furnace? Something like that?"

"No, nobody. They got here late yesterday afternoon, Captain."

"I understand. Now think about this, please. I want to know every-body—and I mean everybody, no matter who it was—you told that they were coming."

"I've thought about it. I've thought about it a great deal, Captain. And I didn't tell anyone. When I went around to the golf courses, I told people I was expecting guests and they'd want to play golf. But I never said who those guests were. There was no reason to."

"That settles it." Captain Barlowe rose, looking grim. "It's somebody they told. The father's given us the names of three people and he's trying to come up with more. There may be more. He admits that. His wife…"

"Hadn't she told anyone?"

"That's just it, sir. She did. She seems to have told quite a few people and says she can't remember them all. She's lying because she doesn't want her friends bothered. Well by God they're going to be bothered. My problem— one of my problems—is that all these people are out of state. I can't go after them myself, and I'd like to. I want to have a good look at them. I want to see their faces change when they're asked certain questions."

He breathed deep, expanding a chest notably capacious, and let it out. "On the plus side, we're after a stranger. Some of the local people may have seen him and noticed him. He may—I said *may*—be driving a car with out-of-state plates."

"Couldn't he have rented a car at the airport?" the horror writer asked.

"Yes, sir. He could, and I hope to God he did. If he did, we'll get him sure. But his car had worn tires, and that's not characteristic of rentals."

"I see."

"If he did rent his car, it'll have bloodstains in it, and the rental people will notice. She was bleeding when she was carried out of her bedroom."

"I didn't know that."

"Not much, but some. We found blood in the hall and more on the back stairs. The bad thing is that if he flew in and plans to fly back out, he can't take her with him. He'll kill her. He may have killed her already."

Captain Barlowe left, Dan and Charity moved into a motel, and the day ended in quiet triumph. The experts who had visited the crime scene earlier reappeared and took more photographs and blood samples. The horror writer asked them no questions, and they volunteered nothing.

He drove to town the next morning and shopped at several stores. So far as he could judge, he was not followed. That afternoon he got out the binoculars he had acquired years before for bird-watching and scanned the surrounding woods and fields, seeing no one.

At sunrise the next morning he rescanned them, paying particular attention to areas he thought he might have slighted before. Selecting an apple from the previous day's purchases, he made his way through grass still wet with dew to the well and tossed it in.

He had hoped that she would thank him and plead for release; if she did either her voice was too faint for him to catch her words, this though it seemed to him there was a sound of some sort from the well, a faint, high humming. As he tramped back to the house, he decided that it had probably been an echo of the wind.

The rest of that day he spent preparing her cellar room.

He slept well that night and woke refreshed twenty minutes before his clock radio would have roused him. The three-eighths-inch rope he had bought two days earlier awaited him in the kitchen; he knotted it as soon as he had finished breakfast, spacing the knots about a foot apart.

When he had wound it around his waist and tied it securely, he discovered bloodstains—small but noticeable—on the back of his barn coat. Eventually it would have to be burned, but a fire at this season would be suspicious in itself; a long soak in a strong bleach solution would have to do the job—for the present, if not permanently. Pulled out, his shirt hid the rope, although not well.

When he reached the well, he tied one end of the rope to a convenient branch and called softly.

There was no reply.

A louder "Kiara!" brought no reply either. She was still asleep, the horror writer decided. Asleep or, just possibly, unconscious. He dropped the free end of the rope into the well, swung over the edge, and began the climb down.

He had expected the length of his rope to exceed the depth of the well by three feet at least; but there came a time when his feet could find no more rope below him—or find the muddy bottom either.

His pen light revealed it, eight inches, perhaps, below the soles of his shoes. Another knot down—this knot almost the last—brought his feet into contact with the mud.

He released the rope.

He had expected to sink into the mud, but had thought to sink to a depth of no more than three or four inches; he found himself floundering, instead, in mud up to his knees. It was difficult to retain his footing; bracing one hand against the stone side of the well, he managed to do it.

At the first step he attempted, the mud sucked his shoe from his foot. Groping the mud for it got his hands thoroughly filthy, but failed to locate it. Attempting a second step cost him his other shoe as well.

This time, however, his groping fingers found a large, soft thing in the mud. His pen light winked on—but in the space of twenty seconds or a little less its always-faint beam faded to darkness. His fingers told him of hair matted with mud, of an ear, and then of a small earring. When he took his hand from it, he stood among corpses, shadowy child-sized bodies his fingers could not locate. Shuddering, he looked up.

Above him, far above him, a small circle of blue was bisected by the dark limb to which he had tied his rope. The rope itself swayed gently in the air, its lower end not quite out of reach.

He caught it and tried to pull himself up; his hands were slippery with mud, and it escaped them.

Desperately, almost frantically, he strove to catch it again, but his struggles caused him to sink deeper into the mud.

He tried to climb the wall of the well; at his depth its rough stones were thick with slime.

At last he recalled Kiara's body, and by a struggle that seemed to him long he managed to get both feet on it. With its support, his fingertips once more brushed the dangling end of the rope. Bracing his right foot on what felt like the head, he made a final all-out effort.

And caught the rope, grasping it a finger's breadth from its frayed end. The slight tension he exerted on it straightened it, and perhaps stretched it a trifle. Bent the limb above by a fraction of an inch. With his right arm straining almost out of its socket and his feet pressing hard against Kiara's corpse, the fingers of his left hand could just touch the final knot.

Something took hold of his right foot, pinning toes and transverse arch in jaws that might have been those of a trap.

The horror writer struggled then, and screamed again and again as he was drawn under—screamed and shrieked and begged until the stinking almost liquid mud stopped his mouth.

Brian Hodge is one of those people who always has to be making something. So far, he's made ten novels, with number eleven due out in late 2016. He's also authored more than 120 shorter works and four full-length collections. His first collection, *The Convulsion Factory*, was ranked by critic Stanley Wiater among the 113 best books of modern horror.

Other upcoming works for 2016 include "The Weight of the Dead," slated for June from *Tor.com*, and "The Burning Times v2.0," in *2113: Stories Inspired by the Music of Rush*.

He lives in Colorado, where he also likes to make music and photographs; loves everything about organic gardening except the thieving squirrels; and trains in Krav Maga and kickboxing, which are of no use at all against the squirrels.

Connect with him at WWW.BRIANHODGE.NET or Facebook (WWW.FACE-BOOK.COM/BRIANHODGEWRITER).

Our Turn Too Will One Day Come
Brian Hodge

THEY'RE THE PHONE calls we hate most. That unnerving 2 a.m. jangle that drills your gut the way a dentist drills a tooth. If you've been out of college for much longer than a year, nobody has anything to tell you after midnight that you want to hear.

And could you bring a shovel? I can't find ours.

Things like that least of all.

Yes, I went to college. Took a year or two longer than it should have. I had a habit of arguing with professors. Except for the extended trip back to the auld ancestral homeland—a given, in our family, a rite of passage that somewhere along the way seems to have lost most of its original significance—college was the farthest away from home I'd ever gotten for any length of time.

Otherwise, thirty-eight miles—that's it. I rolled down the mountains, bounced across the foothills of the Rockies, and had just enough momentum to make it as far as Boulder. Not a bad place to land, really. It put a little distance between me and where I grew up, but not so much that I didn't have a ready sanctuary close by in case I ever needed it. In case I had another of those phases in which I couldn't quite trust my eyes and ears.

The drive back up, I've never minded it in the day. At night, that's something else. Get past a town called Lyons and the spine of the North American continent starts to wrap around you. The road winds. A lot. Cliffs tower on one side while gorges yawn on the other. Narrow, as gorges go, and not terribly deep, but enough to swallow your car and leave you broken on a rocky streambed below.

When the settlers of the New World left their homes in the Old, it was only natural that they look for things that would be a reminder of what they would never see again. The Dutch who founded New Amsterdam, later to become New York, were drawn to Manhattan because the encircling river there reminded them of the lowland waters back home. Germans who made it past the Mississippi found, another hundred or so miles west, a region around the Missouri River that seemed very much like the Rhineland.

And the Scots from whom my sister and I descended? They had to go farther before they were satisfied. Occasionally I've wondered whether it was blind chance or ordained fate that drew them up into the Rocky Mountains until, at the site of what would one day become Estes Park, they looked around at the peaks and crags, and knew that here was as passable a substitute for the Highlands as they were ever likely to find.

While staking their claims in a world that could be as hostile as it was unfamiliar, these immigrants couldn't have helped but take comfort in whatever semblances of home they could find. I've always understood that.

What I never really thought about was what they might have brought with them.

She was waiting for me outside the front door, Noelle sitting on the ground with a candle. I didn't know if the candle was for her benefit, to keep her occupied, or for mine, so I wouldn't trip over her in the dark. This house sits on the edge of town, up against the old scar where pines were cleared to make room for cattle, so you can't see much here at night. There are no streetlights here. There never have been. There probably never will be.

Not much of a street, either. More like a neglected road and a pervading sense that what happens around these old pines and aspens stays within them.

Noelle's candle was a big, fat pillar brimming over with melted wax. My sister took hold of it and tipped it, poured the molten wax over her hand, over the crust already there. Turning her hand as it ran, cooled, hardened. She must have done that when we were kids, although now wasn't the moment to ask. There were times when we were growing up that I wondered how her hand got so chapped looking, but only ever the left one, and just as often in the middle of summer as the dead of winter.

"Brandt," she said. The name of her ex-husband came out of her as if it had been lodged deep, had to be yanked out skewered on the barbs of a fishhook. "He killed her. He's killed my baby."

It cut the legs right out from under me. Down on the ground, hugging my sister, feeling that if I didn't have her to hold onto, I'd just keep falling, up to my clawing fingertips in clotted earth.

Should I lie, to pound home the sense of tragedy? Prattle on about what a little beauty queen my niece was, radiant and full of poise and charm beyond her years? That's what sells the grief: the image of a potential that people can recognize at once, without having to look deeper or think; someone they want to wrap their arms around and protect from every bad thing until she's old enough to fuck.

Except she wasn't a cute child. Not on the outside. It was like she'd taken the least appealing attributes from both parents, then made the worst of them. Maybe she would have grown out of it, duckling into swan, but probably not. So this is what she would've grown into: a homely young woman ignored by the world, except for the parts that she touched directly because she loved the world anyway. Six years old and already, on some level, she knew what lay ahead, so she'd begun to prepare. Bugs and plants and mammals, Joy just couldn't get enough of them…especially the herds of elk that ambled through Estes Park every autumn rutting season. I adored her all the more for it—that hopeful, melancholy spark of awareness.

So did her father. That's what I want to think: that he loved her more than he simply hated losing. Loved her enough to break into his one-time home and try to take her away into his new world. Except he didn't love her enough to do it competently. In the middle of the night, the haste with which he was trying to get the job done…maybe she didn't realize who it was, just that she was draped over some man's shoulder and that was how you made the news, as long as you were cute enough. No wonder she fought. Six years old and groggy and still she sent a grown man down a flight of 125-year-old stairs.

In a just world, Joy would've landed on her father, not the other way around. He would have broken her fall instead of her neck.

Noelle's hand was starting to look truly deformed. I should've blown out the candle, except that would've left us in the dark, and just hearing her cry would've been worse somehow than seeing her.

"A shovel—did you bring one? I looked and looked for ours, but…."

No one could blame her for not thinking straight. What jury would fault her for finishing the job on her ex-husband that the stairs had started? What cop wouldn't have coached her, however subtly, to spin her story to eliminate her culpability? Okay, she took the big iron fireplace tongs to the back of his skull—so?

"You didn't do anything wrong," I told her. "There's nothing to bury here."

I'm more familiar than I would like to be with how, even in the most crushing moments of her life, a woman can look at you as though you're the biggest fool she's ever seen.

Noelle peeled the wax from her hand and snuffed the candle, then stood, and like a wraith, turned and walked toward the front door.

This house. We've always lived in this house.

It was built by ancestors who died when my grandparents were young, by that first generation of immigrants who came and saw and set down roots, sinking them deep in the cool, mist-dampened earth.

This house. Sprawling and dark, its timbers hug the land as if it had come to a respectful truce with the hills and trees rather than trying to defy them. When it was new, could anyone have looked at this house and not seen that it was built by people who were determined to dig in, hunker down, and stay? Could anyone have failed to recognize that these were people who would love the land and bring down a terrible wrath on neighbors who might oppose or try to cheat them?

It's their blood that flows through my veins, even if these people couldn't be much more remote if they were characters from myth. Their names were spoken with reverence even in my own lifetime, during my first few years, with my grandparents living in their own wing of the house.

We've always lived in this house. But there was never the remotest chance that it could one day be mine. It's always been passed down to the daughters.

Tradition like that, you change it at your peril.

As for the boys, I suppose we learned to never ask why.

Inside the house, Brandt lay where he'd died. He had managed to get up and stagger away from where he'd landed at the foot of the stairs, but appeared not to have made it far before Noelle brained him.

"I hit him once to keep him still right after it happened. So he wouldn't get in the way while I was taking care of Joy," Noelle told me. "Then...when I knew...I must have come back and hit him some more."

The back of his head was buckled and broken, mostly intact but smashed in like the shell of a hard-boiled egg. His face seemed to have shifted, displaced from the inside, his eyes protruding and his jaw jutting crooked. Everything a head could leak had oozed out of one orifice or crack or other.

The fireplace tongs lay nearby, a huge iron scissors-like utensil ending in curved pincers big enough to grapple onto burning logs. This contraption had fascinated me as a boy, one of those things that you instinctively know has a history, has been gripped by generations of hands, as much a part of the fireplace as the flat blackened stones of its hearth. I would imagine our great-great-grandfather pausing in negotiations with someone who had come to buy cattle, or sell him horses, stooping before a blazing fire and using the tongs to wrestle the biggest log into place. I imagined him standing up straight again without setting the tongs aside, instead flexing their heavy, hinged handles and clanging the pincers together to knock loose the ash—once, twice, three times—but eyeing his guest in such a way as to tell him that this display was really to demonstrate that my family had a long reach.

I can only think that this forefather would've been fiercely proud of Noelle.

What about Joy, though—would he have thought much of her? Her ungainly little body, her inquisitive scrunched-up monkey face? He probably would have, for her love of animals, but even if not, one thing mattered much more: She was one of ours, and she'd been taken from us by a thief in the night.

I'd always sensed that, both here and in Scotland, our family was no stranger to feuds and blood.

Joy lay on the sofa where Noelle had put her, still wearing her pajamas, pale blue and full of Dalmatians. My sister had straightened her head so she would look like she was only sleeping, but then, there was that awful bruise down the side of her neck.

I knelt to hold her, and remembered so much, and never until this moment knew which of my feelings for her had outweighed the other: love, or pity.

Noelle leaned against my back, her freshest tears on my shoulder.

"You should start digging," she said, finally. "One for each of them. Near the treeline. Anywhere along there should be good. And not too deep."

"Wouldn't *in* the trees be better?" I still wasn't sure why we were going through with this. Maybe I would strain and sweat awhile before she came to her senses and realized, no, that's not the way we handle things in this day and age. "Not so...in the open?"

"It needs to be away from too many roots," she said. "So you really never knew? You never actually saw anything before, or figured anything out on your own?"

Whatever that implied, I had to tell her no, I must not have.

"I want to stay in here with Joy as long as I can. But not with *him* around." She pointed at Brandt. "Can you get him out back on your own?"

I found an old blanket that would do for dragging him. Didn't much want to touch him to get him onto it, though.

But the fireplace tongs fit his neck just fine.

It wasn't until I was old enough to not much care that I realized our family was different in some ways. Like my grandparents, and the flashes of memory that I swear I have of my great-grandmother, although everyone says I was too little when she died to have remembered anything.

In virtually all the families I've known, or heard friends reminisce about, it's the grandfathers who like to scare you—all in fun—while the grandmothers sit back and shake their heads and tut-tut and warn the grinning old men that they're going to give the children nightmares.

In our family it was the other way around. Which isn't to say that our grandfather couldn't play the game, it's just that our grandmother was the one to send us off to sleep burrowing under our blankets and watching for shadows.

Bedtime stories—if Noelle and I heard this one once, we must've heard some variation of it two dozen times:

My grandparents—your great-greats—they wasn't poor when they come over. Not like so many of 'em back then, especially them filthy Irish. No, they had a nice tidy sum that had come down through the family. Always been wealth in cattle. And there always will be.

But back then, there wasn't no planes to fly in, the way there is today. Back then, if you had a long trip you needed to take, you had to do it slow, no matter how fast you wanted to put some distance between you and wherever you was coming from. So to cross that wide old ocean, they had to get on a big ship. That was the only way in them days. It was one of them big pretty ships like the Titanic, *except older and not as fancy, plus this was one of the ones that didn't sink.*

So it was big and pretty enough, all right, but it was slow. Some of 'em took over a week to cross the ocean, but that's if you got a captain on board that knew his business. Not all of them captains did, you know. Some of them captains were just as dumb as rocks and didn't even have the good sense to realize it, so they'd get lost and the trip might take a little longer. And some of 'em took a lot longer. They might be out there a month or two. And some of 'em never did find their way into port, so they must still be out there today, sailing 'round and 'round and not even knowing it, maybe not even knowing they've been dead most of this time, too. Terrible, just terrible.

But the voyage our family come over on was one of the regular length ones, or near to it. Except it was long enough for what usually couldn't be avoided on trips like that. People died during the middle of it. Nothing sinister about that, just tragic, from natural causes. It's bound to happen. You get that many people together on one boat, especially when they're packed together the way them Irish traveled, and some of 'em are bound to turn toes up. They show up sick and near to dead already, and the strain of the trip finishes 'em off. Or they show up not too bad off and might've survived the crossing, except for breathing somebody else's sick air, and the combination takes its toll.

Now, they couldn't just give them poor folks a burial at sea. It wasn't like the Navy. Their families was right there, and if the sailors had've dumped them bodies over the sides and let the waves take 'em, the families would've raised holy hell. Maybe there would've even been a mutiny, and throats would've got cut, and that wouldn't've been good for anybody. So what they done was wrap them bodies up decent and respectful, and box 'em up in crates, and put 'em way down in the hold, in the bottom of the ship, where it was nice and cool and they might keep a little fresher.

Except what do you think they found after they got to port and it was time to give them families back their dead?

It was only a surprise the first time. All the other times I knew what was coming. I kept hoping that somehow the story would turn out differently for a change, and this part never did.

That's right—there wasn't any bodies left. Just the biggest of the bones and some old dried stains, and the tore-up shrouds, and the holes in the crates where they'd been pried into.

But our family was lucky. They was healthy and strong when they stepped on the ship, and they stepped off the same way. And down that gangplank they walked, your two great-great-grandparents, and my own momma, just a girl then, and my two uncles, and the two babes in arms that my grandma and momma held close and wouldn't ever let another soul see, and nobody kept asking once it was explained how sickly the pair was.

And that's how we come from Scotland to America, so you could grow up in this big house and lay there in that nice bed.

Then she would kiss us goodnight and turn out the light.

There were many other stories that she told my sister and wouldn't tell me, and worse, had instructed Noelle that she was to *never* share them with me, under penalty of…well, I never knew what that would've been, either.

At first I believed Noelle, that for some reason I'd been excluded. Then I refused to believe her at all, figured she was just being malicious, only trying to make me *think* I'd been excluded—looking for that wounding edge the way siblings do. Because she never once cracked and uttered a word of what those other stories were about. That isn't natural. If she'd had anything, wouldn't she have let it slip? Teased me with a few hints?

I'm not sure when I reverted and started believing her all over again.

Maybe soon after our grandmother was dead, and our mother had indisputably assumed the mantle of matriarch, with Noelle grown old enough to feel weighed down by secrets and obligations, and her hand looking chapped sometimes, but only ever the left one, and just as often in the middle of summer as the dead of winter.

Like the opposite of a grave robber working by moonlight, I put shovel to earth and broke the soil.

A few yards in front of me, the pines and aspens rose in a dense, murmuring thicket, poured full of night. Their tops were black cones against the sky, sometimes swaying as if to swat down the stars, blind the only witnesses. Behind me was the house where we've always lived, vast and dark, lights showing in only a couple of windows. Such a big house for so few people these days, with both our parents gone.

And in between, closer to the house than to the treeline, stood the stout wooden post that supported the iron bell. Just as we've always lived in the house, the post has always stood there—replaced each time it grew weathered and weak—and the bell has always hung from it, as much a part of each generation as the fireplace tongs.

I'd never dug a grave before, let alone two. Noelle had stressed that she wanted plenty of space between them. To dig them side by side would have been an insult to Joy and the way she'd died. It would have given Brandt more consideration than he was due, either on the earth or under it.

No doubt there are men for whom gravedigging feels like honest work, or the last kindness they can show the dead. There was none of that for me and my shovel. We were accomplices, guilty of something I couldn't specify, although it mattered less here than it might have elsewhere. It may have been wrong, but down deep I knew that the greater right was to stand with family.

One adult, one child....

The thing about graves, I learned, is knowing when to stop. Six feet under is the rule of thumb, and even though I wouldn't be digging that far—not too deep, Noelle had said—I knew even that wouldn't feel far down enough. Things like this, they feel as though they should be buried deeper.

Behind me, nearer to the house than to the graves, the bell seemed to watch, to make sure it was all done properly.

At just past three feet, the shovel blade scraped something hard and unyielding, although it didn't feel big. Easy to pry out of the hole, caked with earth like a flattened dirt clod, and wash off with the bottled water I'd brought from the kitchen.

Even in the moonlight I could tell what it was. It was corroded by perhaps decades underground, but so thick and sturdy it was still mostly intact: a gigantic belt buckle of brass or iron. Just the kind of thing a man might wear if he had a lot of cattle and not much taste.

It should've been a bigger surprise to think, finally, that I hadn't really known my family at all. But it wasn't.

During the years I spent growing up, I couldn't think of a single occasion, with absolute certainty, that I'd heard the bell ring. A time or two, maybe, or three or four, late at night, the sort of event you can't be sure whether it really happened or whether you'd dreamed it. The sort of thing you might ask about over breakfast, like any boy trying to satisfy his curiosity without going too far, making someone angry. And of course they never got angry, my parents. They would just look at each other, blank and quizzical, as if to silently inquire of each other how I could ever have gotten such an idea. Then they would tell me no, no, the bell hadn't rung. How could it? The bell was just for show, remember. The bell wasn't for ringing.

And it wasn't, so far as I knew. It was the only bell I'd ever seen that spent its life with a sleeve secured over its clapper. A thick old leather sheath with an intricate weave of ancient rawhide that laced up one side, and whose tip, like some kind of strange condom, was stuffed with fresh-shorn wool.

I would've only been a toddler the afternoon my great-grandmother caught me staring up at the bell with helpless longing. The time they later told me I would've been too young to remember, so I must've been making it up.

"Don't you ever ring that bell there just to be ringing it," she warned me, as if I were tall enough to even try. "Do that, and you just might look down to find your toes gone."

The holes were dug, the bodies placed inside—Joy's lowered with tender care, Brandt's rolled in the way you'd kick a can to the gutter. All that was left was to replace the upturned earth. Because Noelle never had come to her senses. She was adamant: *This had to be done.*

So I did it, and night was kind, keeping me from seeing the soil in much detail. I imagined that mingled within the two mounds, in each shovelful, there must have been other trinkets: buttons and rings and boot nails and scraps of rotted leather. But as long as I didn't notice bones or teeth, I could tell myself that those pale glints were bits of milk glass, chips of ceramic.

"Thank you. So much," Noelle told me after it was done. "You should go now."

"That's it? Just *go*—like that?"

"It would be better if you did."

"I'm not some hired hand," I said, and thought of my niece in the ground. "Family, *that's* who comes out in the middle of the night, no questions asked." Thought of the little girl to whom, last Christmas, I had given a telescope, and how much she'd loved it, even though she quickly grew bored with looking at the sky and instead wanted to turn it on the earth, the woods. Looking for her cherished elk and whatever else that roamed. "Is there something that makes you more family than I am?"

"So what if there is? That doesn't have to mean it's a *good* thing." She wiped dirt from my cheek. "So please…just leave now and be glad you grew up sheltered."

"I didn't grow up sheltered, Noelle. I grew up being lied to. Sheltered is when you're blissfully ignorant. Lied to, that's when you know there's something not right but everyone you trust tells you you're imagining things. Tells you that so often that one day you're just not sure when you can believe your eyes and ears, and when you can't. Was that somebody's idea of doing me a favor? Because there were some years there that I was pretty well unemployable."

"There was always money. You never had to worry about that."

"Aren't you even listening? Isn't that kind of beside the point?"

That was the remark that made me decide to shut up, no matter what. For a woman who's just buried her only child, the point is whatever she says it is.

Noelle draped both hands onto my shoulders, on the verge of...something. Tears, yes, always those, but now more, as if she wanted to tell me something but didn't yet dare to. She had looked this way so many times while we were growing up that I was used to it. Or just decided that I was imagining it.

Gran's not here anymore to punish you if you tell me anything, I almost said, and any other night, would have. It wasn't that I knew for sure Gran used to do anything. It's just that I started to wonder where Noelle had picked up the bit with the hot wax.

"Okay. Stay," she said. "You can't say you weren't warned."

She went for the bell, hanging from the post with its clapper sheathed, and in the near-dark Noelle untied the complex knotwork of the rawhide lacing as though her fingers had always known how.

She struck the bell then, a short but consistent pattern rung three times, and left to hang in the pre-dawn chill like so many recollections from dreams that they'd never entirely managed to convince me weren't real.

Here's another one that never happened:

There was this boy, see, who grew up in a mountain valley on the edge of a one-time resort town whose main streets had gradually become clogged with touristy kitsch. But the past was never entirely out of reach there. On a prominent hill, presiding over Estes Park like a dignified old mayor, stood the rambling Stanley Hotel and the ghosts that called it home. Below, sometimes all but forgotten, were even older pockets of time, bygone traces of the trappers and hunters and prospectors and ranchers who settled the valley first, fighting—sometimes to the death—for their rights to take and make, as settlers always do.

The boy's roots went deep here, even if he was too young to know it at the time.

He must have been four, maybe closer to five, because his sister was still in the crib that summer. Even today he remembers that part quite clearly, and how attentively their grandmother used to watch over her as she slept. There were times the old woman seemed to see everything, but not while she was tending the baby. This, and their father and grandfather's habit of retreating to the den after dinner, was what finally gave him the courage to slip outside one evening. Because lately he'd been wondering where their mother disappeared to this time of evening.

At first he looked for her up and down the empty road, trying to push back the gnawing sense of dread he got whenever he wondered what would happen if one evening she never came back.

He tried behind the house next, past the muffled bell hanging like a poison fruit he was already too intimidated to touch, and followed his instincts into the pines and aspens. They were as good a place to walk alone as any. There seemed to be no end to them, their depth unknowable, and you might walk and walk for days, yet never come close to emerging on the other side.

Her back was to him when he first spotted her in a cluster of trees going dark with pooled shadows, as she sat upon a sun-bleached fallen log. Before her, obscured by the log, he could see the upper curve of a dark bulky stone. Her hair was long then, halfway down her spine. For a moment he stood and watched. Her elbows were thrust out behind her, as if she were holding something close to her body. Whatever it was, it seemed to be squirming.

Pretty soon, he started forward again, to close the gap between them.

It was inevitable that she would hear him eventually. Even a woodland filled mostly with evergreens can be a noisy place to walk. She whirled, her hair like a lashing whip, her eyes fixing on him first with fright and then with fury and, if his memory could be trusted, something he later identified as guilt.

His gaze lowered to the bundle in her arms—the wrinkled pink-gray skin that seemed to bristle with coarse dark hairs, and the conical face whose spade-like snout was clamped over her exposed breast. Surely he hadn't imagined the little peg teeth; why else would he have wondered if they hurt? Surely he hadn't imagined the way it seemed to sense his mother's abrupt distress, and pulled away to open its mouth—inside, the roof was ridged and spotted—with a squall like that of a bear cub.

When the stone sitting before his mother rose with a shudder and a thick wet snort, he turned and ran.

She was all smiles the next morning. Made him his favorite breakfast—waffles and bacon. Told him what an imagination he had, that she'd only been out there with Noelle, in a small threadbare blanket, the same blanket she used to carry him out as a baby too, to nurse him within the trees so that he would learn to love nature and its bounty. Like everyone in the family.

The boy ate his waffles. He let her stroke his hair. He decided to try harder to believe.

"I guess if you take most any family that has old money coming down through the generations," Noelle said, "the farther back you go, the more likely you are to find that so much of what they have is built on the bodies of people who got in their way."

We were sitting on the wide, open porch along the back of the house, where we used to play as children and dream of the adventures the world held for us. It had been a long night, and the sky was beginning to lighten with pink and blue and orange, just enough dawn to make out the pair of dark rounded mounds near the treeline.

"We were never the Hearsts or the Rockefellers, not even close," she said. "But there still were bodies."

The last echoes of the bell had faded minutes ago, but I thought I could still hear them, pealing across the open ground and ricocheting among tree trunks.

"It started in Scotland, but not even Gran was sure how far back it actually went, or who was the first. I mean, Gran used to tell me stories about those parts, too. But not long before she died she told me that she'd made up parts of them herself, because she had to tell me something. It was easier than admitting she didn't know. You can't tell little kids stories without personalities in them."

If the look on Noelle's face some mornings had been anything to go by, there were stories you shouldn't tell kids at all.

"So let's call her Jenny, okay? Our great-great-great-whatever grandmother. And even though she was a good woman, she always turned a blind eye to what her father and grandfather and brothers and uncles and husband did: stealing cattle—those big shaggy Scottish cattle that look like walking carpets—and sometimes killing the rightful owners and *their* men when they came to get them back. Or killing other thieves who tried to take what they'd stolen first."

Stolen fair and square, I imagined our grandmother saying. I could hear none of her voice in Noelle's hollow recitation, my sister murmuring her way through this as if she'd waited so long it finally seemed to involve some other family. Except I still couldn't help but think of the words that Gran might use instead, the old woman forcing herself between us even though she'd been dead for years.

"So Jenny had seen enough men in her life get hanged for murder by sheriffs, and wanted to do something about it before it reached her own sons. Only she was enough of a pragmatist to realize that she couldn't stop them from following the same path if that's what they meant to do. So instead of trying prevention, Jenny turned to the cleanup."

By now, long minutes after the bell had rung its last, I could hear something heavy crashing through the still-darkened woods.

"God knows how she did it. How she managed to find them. And then how she managed to communicate with them. It's not like they speak, you know. But when you're looking in their eyes...you see something there that gives you the impression that some part of them is listening." Noelle kept watch, her eyes as dead now as the daughter we'd buried. "I don't know, maybe I'm giving them too much credit. Gran never said so, but more than once I've wondered if we weren't only descended from cattle thieves and killers, but a witch, too."

From out of the trees, where the dawn had not yet reached, they came: six dark shapes, thick and low to the ground, like boars, their round muscled shoulders and backs bouncing along with eager purpose.

"They're called yird swine," Noelle said. "They like to dig into graves for food. And these are ours. They've always been ours."

They attacked the fresh shallow graves with snorts and squeals, sounding not quite like any hogs I'd ever heard—like if you listened closely enough to the grunting, you could make out the rudiments of voices. And they were ravenous, burrowing into the mounds and churning through earth with forelimbs that I was too far away to see, with too little light yet, but their snouts, their claws...the soil flew as though they'd been made for this and nothing else.

You can watch things that hold you rapt with fascination even as they sicken you. And so it was, here and now. Because I began to understand. They weren't merely ours; we were theirs, too. Just as the murderous blood of our fathers ran through our veins, the milk of our mothers ran through theirs. They would demand it as part of their bargain.

"So Jenny, whatever her name really was, she went out in secret to these *things*, that her neighbors felt nothing but dread for. However she managed it—and I don't think I ever want to know—she turned them into allies. Then she came home and demanded of the men left in her family that if they took another's life, she had to know about it immediately…and that she would take care of it. At least that's the way Gran told it. More or less."

Over at the mounds, they were shoulders deep and going strong.

"Why wasn't I supposed to know any of this?" I asked her.

"That's just how it all came about. Having a way to get rid of the bodies… quickly, completely…it only made things worse, in a way."

Yes. I imagined that it did. It gave our forefathers a license to kill. Made them arrogant, maybe even prolific. I could imagine sons, brothers, uncles, cousins, drunk on ale and their own impunity, battering on Jenny's door in the middle of the night, their saddles draped with the corpses of those they'd killed on the road after some trivial insult in the taverns.

"So you—all the men in the family, I mean—weren't supposed to know until there wasn't any way to avoid it," Noelle said. "Gran loved men, I know. But she didn't have a very high opinion of your self-control."

Over at the graves, they'd reached the bodies. Noelle snapped out of her muted trance and buried her face in her hands.

"I can't watch it. Not this time," she said, and the slammed door off the end of the porch was the last I would hear of her for hours.

So I stayed to do my family duty, because while Noelle hadn't said so, I suspected that this was a vital part of the process; that *they* expected one of us to remain and bear witness, remembering the covenant between our species, our clans.

So I stayed, and watched as they ferociously tugged the bodies halfway from their graves, to feed on what lay helpless and exposed, then tug a little more to expose that too. I listened as their tusks ripped through skin and muscle, to the bursting of tender organs, to the grinding of their teeth on bones.

It was clear to me now, finally, Gran's old story about our family coming over on that ship: what was really swaddled in the blankets and what they'd grown into, what they'd bred. I'd always thought we'd come because this was the land of opportunity, and maybe that's really how my ancestors saw it… but only after they'd done things so terrible they could no longer remain on the far side of the ocean.

So because of their sins, I watched, listened, as their youngest descendant was ground into gristle.

We, too, were a part of the old bargain. Noelle hadn't said this either, but didn't have to. She'd been raised to believe, obviously, that there was no other way. Why else would she turn her daughter over to *this*? I could imagine the things our grandmother must have told her, things that Gran maybe even believed herself: *You've seen them things dig, so don't think you could ever get away. They got the smell of you in their noses, you know, and they was fed on the same milk that you suckled from your momma, so there's no place you could go that they couldn't sniff you out and dig their way to, some day.*

And still, I loved her.

It all explained some things—why I had never once visited the graves of my grandparents—but called so many others into question: If my mother, after the cancer took her, had really donated her remains to science. If my father, the day he left, had truly left for the reasons he'd said, and why he hadn't tried harder to take me with him.

And because I knew so much more now about where and what I came from, I thought about families, and the roles everyone seems to fall into: givers and takers, the feeders and the fed upon.

Turns out we were a lot more normal than I ever gave us credit for.

Bram Stoker Award nominee, two-time World Fantasy Award nominee, and Shirley Jackson Award winner Kaaron Warren has lived in Melbourne, Sydney, Canberra, and Fiji. She's sold more than two hundred short stories, three novels (the multi-award-winning *Slights*, *Walking the Tree*, and *Mistification*), and six short-story collections, including the multi-award-winning *Through Splintered Walls*. Her latest novel is *The Solace of Saint Theresa* (IFWG Publishing, Australia) and her latest short-story collection is *Cemetery Dance Select: Kaaron Warren*.

You can find her at KAARONWARREN.WORDPRESS.COM and she Tweets @KAARONWARREN.

Dead Sea Fruit
Kaaron Warren

I HAVE A collection of baby teeth, sent to me by recovered anorexics from the ward. Their children's teeth, proof that their bodies are working.

One sent me a letter. "Dear Tooth Fairy, you saved me and my womb. My son is now six, here are his baby teeth."

They call the ward Pretty Girl Street. I don't know if the cruelty is intentional; these girls are far from pretty. Skeletal, balding, their breath reeking of hard cheese, they languish on their beds and terrify each other, when they have the strength, with tales of the Ash Mouth Man.

I did not believe the Pretty Girls. The Ash Mouth Man was just a myth to scare each other into being thin. A moral tale against promiscuity. It wouldn't surprise me to hear that the story originated with a group of protective parents, wanting to shelter their children from the disease of kissing.

"He only likes fat girls," Abby said. Her teeth were yellow when she smiled, though she rarely smiled. Abby lay in the bed next to Lori; they compared wrist thickness by stretching their fingers to measure.

"And he watches you for a long time to make sure you're the one," Lori said.

"And only girls who could be beautiful are picked," Melanie said. Her blonde hair fell out in clumps and she kept it in a little bird's nest beside her bed. "He watches you to see if you could be beautiful enough if you were thinner then he saunters over to you."

The girls laughed. "He saunters. Yes," they agreed. They trusted me; I listened to them and fixed their teeth for free.

"He didn't saunter," Jane said. I sat on her bed and leaned close to hear. "He beckoned. He did this," and she tilted back her head, miming a glass being poured into her mouth. "I nodded. I love vodka," she said. "Vodka's made of potatoes, so it's like eating."

The girls all laughed. I hate it when they laugh. I have to maintain my smile. I can't flinch in disgust at those bony girls, mouths open, shoulders shaking. All of them exhausted with the effort.

"I've got a friend in New Zealand and she's seen him," Jane said. "He kissed a friend of hers and the weight just dropped off her."

"I know someone in England who kissed him," Lori said.

"He certainly gets around," I said. They looked at each other.

"I was frightened at the thought of him at first," Abby said. "Cos he's like a drug. One kiss and you're hooked. Once he's stuck in the tongue, you're done. You can't turn back."

They'd all heard of him before they kissed him. In their circles, even the dangerous methods of weight loss are worth considering.

I heard the rattle of the dinner trolley riding the corridor to Pretty Girl Street. They fell silent.

Lori whispered, "Kissing him fills your mouth with ash. Like you pick up a beautiful piece of fruit and bite into it. You expect the juice to drip down your chin but you bite into ashes. That's what it's like to kiss him."

Lori closed her eyes. Her dry little tongue snaked out to the corners of her mouth, looking, I guessed, for that imagined juice. I leaned over and dripped a little water on her tongue.

She screwed up her mouth.

"It's only water," I said. "It tastes of nothing."

"It tastes of ashes," she said.

"They were hoping you'd try a bite to eat today, Lori," I said. She shook her head.

"You don't understand," she said. "I can't eat. Everything tastes like ashes. Everything."

The nurse came in with the dinner trolley and fixed all the Pretty Girls' IV feeds. The girls liked to twist the tube, bend it, press an elbow or a bony buttock into it to stop the flow.

"You don't understand," Abby said. "It's like having ashes pumped directly into your blood."

They all started to moan and scream with what energy they could muster. Doctors came in, and other nurses. I didn't like this part, the physicality of the feedings, so I walked away.

I meet many Pretty Girls. Pretty Girls are the ones who will never recover, who still see themselves as ugly and fat even when they don't have the strength to defecate. These ones the doctors try to fatten up so they don't scare people when laid in their coffins.

The recovering ones never spoke of the Ash Mouth Man. And I did not believe, until Dan entered my surgery, complaining he was unable to kiss women because of the taste of his mouth. I bent close to him and smelt nothing. I found no decay, no gum disease. He turned his face away.

"What is it women say you taste like?" I said.

"They say I taste of ashes."

I blinked at him, thinking of Pretty Girl Street.

"Not cigarette smoke," the girls had all told me. "Ashes."

"I can see no decay or internal reason for any odour," I told Dan.

After work that day I found him waiting for me in his car outside the surgery.

"I'm sorry," he said. "This is ridiculous. But I wondered if you'd like to eat with me." He gestured, lifting food to his mouth. The movement shocked me. It reminded me of what Jane had said, the Ash Mouth Man gesturing a drink to her. It was nonsense and I knew it. Fairy tales, any sort of fiction, annoy me. It's all so very convenient, loose ends tucked in and no mystery left unsolved. Life isn't like that. People die unable to lift an arm to wave and there is no reason for it.

I was too tired to say yes. I said, "Could we meet for dinner tomorrow?"

He nodded. "You like food?"

It was a strange question. Who didn't like food? Then the answer came to me. Someone for whom every mouthful tasted of ash.

"Yes, I like food," I said.

"Then I'll cook for you," he said.

He cooked an almost perfect meal, without fuss or mess. He arrived at the table smooth and brown. I wanted to sweep the food off and make love to him right there. "You actually like cooking," I said. "It's nothing but a chore for me. I had to feed myself from early on and I hate it."

"You don't want the responsibility," he said. "Don't worry. I'll look after you."

The vegetables were overcooked, I thought. The softness of them felt like rot.

He took a bite and rolled the food around in his mouth.

"You have a very dexterous tongue," I said. He smiled, cheeks full of food, then closed his eyes and went on chewing.

When he swallowed, over a minute later, he took a sip of water then said, "Taste has many layers. You need to work your way through each to get to the base line. Sensational."

I tried keeping food in my mouth but it turned to sludge and slipped down my throat. It was fascinating to watch him eat. Mesmerizing. We talked at the table for two hours, then I started to shake.

"I'm tired," I said. "I tend to shake when I'm tired."

"Then you should go home to sleep." He packed a container of food for me to take. His domesticity surprised me; I laughed on entering his home at the sheer seductiveness of it. The masculinity masquerading as femininity. Self-help books on the shelf, their spines unbent. Vases full of plastic flowers with a fake perfume.

He walked me to my car and shook my hand, his mouth pinched shut to clearly indicate there would be no kiss.

Weeks passed. We saw each other twice more, chaste, public events that always ended abruptly. Then one Wednesday, I opened the door to my next client and there was Dan.

"It's only me," he said.

My assistant giggled. "I'll go and check the books, shall I?" she said. I nodded. Dan locked the door after her.

"I can't stop thinking about you," he said. "It's all I think about. I can't get any work done."

He stepped towards me and grabbed my shoulders. I tilted my head back to be kissed. He bent to my neck and snuffled. I pulled away.

"What are you doing?" I said. He put his finger on my mouth to shush me. I tried to kiss him but he turned away. I tried again and he twisted his body from me.

"I'm scared of what you'll taste," he said.

"Nothing. I'll taste nothing."

"I don't want to kiss you," he said softly.

Then he pushed me gently onto my dentist's chair. And he stripped me naked and touched every piece of skin, caressed, squeezed, stroked until I called out.

He climbed onto the chair astride me, and keeping his mouth well away, he unzipped his pants. He felt very good. We made too much noise. I hoped my assistant wasn't listening.

Afterwards, he said, "It'll be like that every time. I just know it." And it was. Even massaging my shoulders, he could make me turn to jelly.

I had never cared so much about kissing outside of my job before but now I needed it. It would prove Dan loved me, that I loved him. It would prove he was not the Ash Mouth Man because his mouth would taste of plums or toothpaste, or of my perfume if he had been kissing my neck.

"You know we get pleasure from kissing because our bodies think we are eating," I said, kissing his fingers.

"Trickery. It's all about trickery," he said.

"Maybe if I smoke a cigarette first. Then my breath will be ashy anyway and I won't be able to taste you."

"Just leave it." He went out, came back the next morning with his lips all bruised and swollen. I did not ask him where he'd been. I watched him outside on the balcony, his mouth open like a dog's tasting the air, and I didn't want to know. I had a busy day ahead, clients all through and no time to think. My schizophrenic client tasted yeasty; they always did if they were medicated.

Then I kissed a murderer; he tasted like vegetable waste. Like the crisper in my fridge smells when I've been too busy to empty it. They used to say people who suffered from tuberculosis smelled like wet leaves; his breath was like that but rotten. He had a tooth he wanted me to fix; he'd cracked it on a walnut shell.

"My wife never shelled things properly. Lazy. She didn't care what she ate. Egg shells, olive pits, seafood when she knew I'm allergic. She'd eat anything."

He smiled at me. His teeth were white. Perfect. "And I mean anything." He paused, wanting a reaction from me. I wasn't interested in his sexual activities. I would never discuss what Dan and I did. It was private, and while it remained that way I could be wanton, abandoned.

"She used to get up at night and raid the fridge," the murderer said after he rinsed. I filled his mouth with instruments again. He didn't close his eyes. Most people do. They like to take themselves elsewhere, away from me. No matter how gentle a dentist is, the experience is not pleasant.

My assistant and I glanced at each other.

"Rinse," I said. He did, three times, then sat back. A line of saliva stretched from the bowl to his mouth.

"She was fat. Really fat. But she was always on a diet. I accused her of secretly bingeing and then I caught her at it."

I turned to place the instruments in my autoclave.

"Sleepwalking. She did it in her sleep. She'd eat anything. Raw bacon. Raw mince. Whole slabs of cheese."

People come to me because I remove the nasty taste from their mouths. I'm good at identifying the source. I can tell by the taste of them and what I see in their eyes.

He glanced at my assistant, wanting to talk but under privilege. I said to her, "Could you check our next appointment, please?" and she nodded, understanding.

I picked up a scalpel and held it close to his eye. "You see how sharp it is? So sharp you won't feel it as the blade gently separates the molecules. Sometimes a small slit in the gums releases toxins or tension. You didn't like your wife getting fat?"

"She was disgusting. You should have seen some of the crap she ate."

I looked at him, squinting a little.

"You watched her. You didn't stop her."

"I could've taken a football team in to watch her and she wouldn't have woken up."

I felt I needed a witness to his words, and knowing Dan was in the office above, I pushed the speaker phone extension to connect me to him.

"She ate cat shit. I swear. She picked it off the plate and ate it," the murderer said. I bent over to check the back of his tongue. The smell of vegetable waste turned my stomach.

"What was cat shit doing on a plate?" I asked.

He reddened a little. When I took my fingers out of his mouth he said, "I just wanted to see if she'd eat it. And she did."

"Is she seeking help?" I asked. I wondered what the breath of someone with a sleep disorder would smell like.

"She's being helped by Jesus now," he said. He lowered his eyes. "She ate a bowlful of dishwashing powder with milk. She was still holding the spoon when I found her in the morning."

There was a noise behind me as Dan came into the room. I turned to see he was wearing a white coat. His hands were thrust into the pockets.

"You didn't think to put poisons out of reach?" Dan said. The murderer looked up.

"Sometimes the taste of the mouth, the smell of it, comes from deep within," I said to the murderer. I flicked his solar plexus with my forefinger and he flinched. His smile faltered. I felt courageous.

As he left, I kissed him. I kiss all of my clients, to learn their nature from the taste of their mouths. Virgins are salty, alcoholics sweet. Addicts taste like fake orange juice, the stuff you spoon into a glass then add water.

Dan would not let me kiss him to find out if he tasted of ash.

"Now me," Dan said. He stretched over and kissed the man on the mouth, holding him by the shoulders so he couldn't get away.

The murderer recoiled. I smiled. He wiped his mouth. Scraped his teeth over his tongue.

"See you in six months' time," I said.

I had appointments with the Pretty Girls, and Dan wanted to come with me. He stopped at the ward doorway, staring in. He seemed to fill the space, a door himself.

"It's okay," I said. "You wait there."

Inside, I thought at first Jane was smiling. Her cheeks lifted and her eyes squinted closed. But there was no smile; she scraped her tongue with her teeth. It was an action I knew quite well. Clients trying to scrape the bad taste out of their mouths. They didn't spit or rinse, though, so the action made me feel queasy. I imagined all that buildup behind their teeth. All the scrapings off their tongue.

The girls were in a frenzy. Jane said, "We saw the Ash Mouth Man." But they see so few men in the ward I thought, "Any man could be the Ash Mouth Man to these girls." I tended their mouths, tried to clear away the bad taste. They didn't want me to go. They were jealous of me, thinking I was going to kiss the Ash Mouth Man. Jane kept talking to make me stay longer, though it took her strength away. "My grandmother was kissed by him. She always said to watch out for handsome men, cos their kiss could be a danger. Then she kissed him and wasted away in about five days."

The girls murmured to each other. *Five days! That's a record! No one ever goes down in five days.*

In the next ward there are Pretty Boys, but not so many of them. They are much quieter than the girls. They sit in their beds and close their eyes most of the day. The ward is thick, hushed. They don't get many visitors and they don't want me as their dentist. They didn't like me to attend them. They bit at me as if I were trying to thrust my fingers down their throats to choke them.

Outside, Dan waited, staring in.

"Do you find those girls attractive?" I said.

"Of course not. They're too skinny. They're sick. I like healthy women. Strong women. That's why I like you so much. You have the self-esteem to let me care for you. Not many women have that."

"Is that true?"

"No. I really like helpless women," he said. But he smiled.

He smelt good to me, clean, with a light flowery aftershave that could seem feminine on another man. He was tall and broad; strong. I watched him lift a car to retrieve a paper I'd rolled onto while parking.

"I could have moved the car," I said, laughing at him.

"No fun in that," he said. He picked me up and carried me indoors.

I quite enjoyed the sense of subjugation. I'd been strong all my life, sorting myself to school when my parents were too busy to care. I could not remember being carried by anyone, and the sensation was a comfort.

Dan introduced me to life outside. Before I met him, I rarely saw daylight; too busy for a frivolous thing like the sun. Home, transport, work, transport, home, all before dawn and after dusk. Dan forced me to go out into the open. He said, "Your skin glows outdoors. Your hair moves in the breeze. You couldn't be more beautiful." So we walked. I really didn't like being out. It seemed like time wasting.

He picked me up from the surgery one sunny Friday and took my hand. "Come for a picnic," he said. "It's a beautiful day."

In my doorway, a stick man was slumped.

"It's the man who killed his wife," I whispered.

The man raised his arm weakly. "Dentist," he rattled. "Dentist, wait!"

"What happened to you? Are you sleepwalking now?" I asked.

"I can't eat. Everything I bite into tastes of ash. I can't eat. I'm starving." He lisped, and I could see that many of his white teeth had fallen out.

"What did you do to me?" he whispered. He fell to his knees. Dan and I stepped around him and walked on. Dan took my hand, carrying a basket full of food between us. It banged against my legs, bruising my shins. We walked to a park and everywhere we went girls jumped at him. He kissed back, shrugging at me as if to say, "Who cares?" I watched them.

"Why do it? Just tell them to go away," I said. They annoyed me, those silly little girls.

"I can't help it. I try not to kiss them but the temptation is too strong. They're always coming after me."

I had seen this.

"Why? I know you're a beautiful-looking man, but why do they forget any manners or pride to kiss you?"

I knew this was one of his secrets. One of the things he'd rather I didn't know.

"I don't know, my love. The way I smell? They like my smell."

I looked at him sidelong. "Why did you kiss him? That murderer. Why?"

Dan said nothing. I thought about how well he understood me. The meals he cooked, the massages he gave. The way he didn't flinch from the job I did.

So I didn't confront him. I let his silence sit. But I knew his face at the Pretty Girls ward. I could still feel him fucking me in the car, pulling over into a car park and taking me, after we left the Pretty Girls.

"God, I want to kiss you," he said.

I could smell him, the ash-fire warmth of him, and I could feel my stomach shrinking. I thought of my favourite cake, its colour leached out and its flavour making my eyes water.

"Kissing isn't everything. We can live without kissing," I said.

"Maybe you can," he said, and he leant forward, his eyes wide, the white parts smudgy, grey. He grabbed my shoulders. I usually loved his strength, the size of him, but I pulled away.

"I don't want to kiss you," I said. I tucked my head under his arm and buried my face into his side. The warm fluffy wool of his jumper tickled my nose and I smothered a sneeze.

"Bless you," he said. He held my chin and lifted my face up. He leant towards me.

He was insistent.

It was a shock, even though I'd expected it. His tongue was fat and seemed to fill my cheeks, the roof of my mouth. My stomach roiled and I tried to pull away but his strong hands held my shoulders till he was done with his kiss.

Then he let me go.

I fell backward, one step, my heels wobbling but keeping me standing. I wiped my mouth. He winked at me and leant forward. His breath smelt sweet, like pineapple juice. His eyes were blue, clear and honest. You'd trust him if you didn't know.

The taste of ash filled my mouth.

Nothing else happened, though. I took a sip of water and it tasted fresh, clean. A look of disappointment flickered on his face before he concealed it. I thought, "You like it. You like turning women that way."

I said, "Have you heard of the myth the Pretty Girls have? About the Ash Mouth Man?"

I could see him visibly lifting, growing. Feeling legendary. His cheeks reddened. His face was so expressive I knew what he meant without hearing a word. I couldn't bear to lose him but I could not allow him to make any more Pretty Girls.

I waited till he was fast asleep that night, lying back, mouth open. I sat him forward so he wouldn't choke, took up my scalpel, and with one perfect move I lifted his tongue and cut it out of his mouth.

Lisa Tuttle has been writing strange, weird stories nearly all her life, making her first professional sale in 1971. She has won the John W. Campbell Award, the British Science Fiction Award, and the International Horror Guild Award.

Her short stories have been widely published and reprinted, and gathered into five published collections to date. Her first novel, written in collaboration with George R. R. Martin, *Windhaven*, originally published in 1981, is still in print, and has been translated into many other languages. Her other novels include *Lost Futures*, *The Mysteries*, *The Silver Bough*, and, forthcoming in 2016, *The Curious Affair of the Somnambulist and the Psychic Thief*.

Born and raised in Texas, she now lives with her family in the Highlands of Scotland.

Closet Dreams
Lisa Tuttle

SOMETHING TERRIBLE HAPPENED to me when I was a little girl.

I don't want to go into details. I had to do that far too often in the year after it happened, first telling the police everything I could remember in the (vain) hope it would help them catch the monster, then talking for hours and hours to all sorts of therapists, doctors, shrinks and specialists brought in to help me. Talking about it was supposed to help me understand what had happened, achieve closure, and move on.

I just wanted to forget—I thought that's what "putting it behind me" meant—but they said to do that, first I had to *remember*. I thought I did remember—in fact, I was sure I did—but they wouldn't believe what I told them. They said it was a fantasy, created to cover something I couldn't bear to admit. For my own good (and also, to help the police catch that monster) I had to remember the truth.

So I racked my brain and forced myself to relive my darkest memories, giving them more and more specifics, suffering through every horrible moment a second, third and fourth time before belatedly realizing it wasn't the stuff the monster had done to me that they could not believe. There was nothing at all impossible about a single detail of my abduction, imprisonment and abuse, not even the sick particulars of what he called "playing." I had been an innocent; it was all new to me, but they were adults, professionals who had dealt with too many victims. It came as no surprise to them that there were monsters living among us, looking just like ordinary men, but really the worst kind of sexual predator.

The only thing they did not believe in was my escape. It could not have happened the way I said. Surely I must see that?

But it had. When I understood what they were questioning, it made me first tearful and then mad. I was not a liar. Impossible or not, it had happened, and my presence there, telling them about it, ought to be proof enough.

One of them—her name escapes me, but she was an older lady who always wore turtle-neck sweaters or big scarves, and who reminded me a little of my granny with her high cheekbones, narrow blue eyes and gentle voice—told me that she knew I wasn't lying. What I had described was my own experience of the escape, and true on those terms—but all the same, I was a big girl now and I could surely understand that it could not have happened that way in actuality. She said I could think of it like a dream. The dream was my experience, what happened inside my brain while I was asleep, but something else was happening at the same time. Maybe, if we worked with the details of my dream, we might get some clues as to what that was.

She asked me to tell her something about my dreams. I told her there was only one. Ever since I'd escaped I'd had a recurring nightmare, night after night, unlike any dream I'd ever had before, twice as real and ten times more horrible.

It went like this: I'd come awake, in darkness too intense for seeing, my body aching, wooden floor hard beneath my naked body, the smell of dust and ancient varnish in my nose, and my legs would jerk, a spasm of shock, before I returned to lying motionless again, eyes tightly shut, trying desperately, against all hope, to fall back into the safe oblivion of sleep. Sometimes it was only a matter of seconds before I woke again in my own bedroom, where the light was always left on for just such moments, but sometimes I would seemingly remain in that prison for hours before I could wake. Nothing ever happened; I never saw him; there was just the closet, and that was bad enough. The true horror of the dream was that it didn't seem like a dream, and so turned reality inside-out, stripping my illusory freedom from me.

When I was much younger I'd made the discovery that I guess most kids make, that if you can only manage to scream out loud when you're dreaming—especially when you've started to realize that it *is* just a dream—you'll wake yourself up.

But I never tried that in the closet dream; I didn't dare. The monster had taught me not to scream. If I made any noise in the closet, any noise loud enough for him to hear from another room, he would tape my mouth shut, and tie my hands together behind my back.

I knew I was his prisoner. Before he did that, it wouldn't have occurred to me that I still had *some* freedom.

So I didn't scream.

I guess the closet dream didn't offer much scope for analysis. She tried to get me to recall other dreams, but when I insisted I didn't have any, she didn't press. Instead, she told me that it wouldn't always be that way, and taught me some relaxation techniques that would make it easier to slip into an undisturbed sleep.

It wasn't only for my peace of mind that I kept having these sessions with psychiatrists. Anything I remembered might help the police.

Nobody but me knew what my abductor looked like. I'd done my best to describe him, but my descriptions, while detailed, were probably too personal, intimate and distorted by fear. I had no idea how an outsider would see him; I rarely even saw him dressed. I didn't know what he did for a living or where he lived.

I was his prisoner for nearly four months, but I'd been unconscious when he took me into his house, and all I knew of it, all I was ever allowed to see, was one bedroom, bathroom and closet. Under careful questioning from the police, with help from an architect, a very vague and general picture emerged: it was a single-story house on a quiet residential street, in a neighborhood that probably dated back to the 1940s or even earlier. (Nobody had used bathroom tiles like that since the 1950s; the small size of the closet dated it, and so did the thickness of the internal doors.) There were no houses like that in my parents' neighborhood, and all the newer subdivisions in the city could be ruled out, but that still left a lot of ground. It was even possible, since I had no idea how long I'd been unconscious in the back of his van after he grabbed me, that the monster lived and worked in another town entirely.

I wanted to help them catch him, of course. So although I hated thinking about it, and wanted only to absorb myself back into my own life with my parents, friends and school, I made myself return, in memory, to my prison and concentrated on details, but what was most vivid to me—the smell of dusty varnish or the pictures I thought I could make out in the grain of the wood floor; a crack in the ceiling, or the low roaring surf sound made by the central air conditioning at night—did not supply any useful clues to the police.

Five mornings a week the monster left the house and stayed away all day. He would let me out to use the bathroom before he left, and then lock me into the closet. He'd fixed a sliding bolt on the outside of the big, heavy closet door, and once the door was shut and he slid the bolt home, I was trapped. But that was not enough for him: he added a padlock, to which he carried the only key. As he told me, if he didn't come home to let me out, I would *die* inside that closet, of hunger and thirst, so I had better pray nothing happened to him, because if it did, no one would ever find me.

That padlock wasn't his last word in security, either. He also locked the bedroom door, and before he left the house I always heard an electronic bleeping sound I recognized as being part of a security system. He had a burglar alarm, as well as locks on everything that could be secured shut.

All he left me with in the closet was a plastic bottle full of water, a blanket and a child's plastic potty that I couldn't bear to use. There was a light-fixture in the ceiling, but he'd removed the light-bulb, and the switch was on the other side of the locked door. At first I thought his decision to deprive me of light was just more of his meaningless cruelty, but later it occurred to me that it was just another example—like the padlock and the burglar alarm—of his overly-cautious nature. He'd even removed the wooden hanging rod from the closet, presumably afraid that I might have been able to wrench it loose and use it as a weapon against him. I might have scratched him with a broken light-bulb; big deal. It wouldn't have incapacitated him, but it might have hurt, and he wouldn't risk even the tiniest of hurts. He wanted total control.

So, all those daylight hours when I was locked into the closet, I was in the dark except for the light which seeped in around the edges of the door; mainly from the approximately three-quarters of an inch that was left between the bottom of the door and the floor. That was my window on the world. I thought it was larger than the gap beneath our doors at home; the police architect said it might have been because the carpet it had been cut to accommodate had been removed; alternatively, my captor might have replaced the original door because he didn't find it sturdy enough for the prison he had planned.

Whatever the reason, I was grateful that the gap was wide enough for me to look through. I would spend hours sometimes lying with my cheek flat against the floor, peering sideways into the bedroom, not because it was interesting, but simply for the light and space that it offered in comparison to the tiny closet.

When I was in the closet, I could use my fingernails to scrape the dirt and varnish from the floorboards, or make pictures out of the shadows all around me; there was nothing else to look at except the dirty cream walls, and the most interesting thing there—the only thing that caught my eye and made me think—was a square outlined in silvery duct tape.

I knew what it was, because there was something very similar on one wall of my closet at home, and my parents had explained to me that it was only an access-hatch, so a plumber could get at the bathroom plumbing, in case it ever needed to be fixed.

Once that had been explained, and I knew it wasn't the entrance to a secret passage or a hidden room, it became uninteresting to me. In the monster's closet, though, a plumbing access-hatch took on a whole new glamour.

I thought it might be my way out. Even though I knew there was no window in the bathroom, and the only door connected it to the bedroom—it was at least an escape from the closet. I wasn't sure an adult could crawl through what looked like a square-foot opening, but I knew I could manage; I didn't care if I left a little skin behind.

I peeled off the strips of tape, got my fingers into the gap and, with a little bit of effort, managed to pry out the square of painted Sheetrock. But I didn't uncover a way out. There were pipes revealed in a space between the walls, but that was all. There was no opening into the bathroom, no space for a creature larger than a mouse to squeeze into. And I probably don't need to say that I didn't find anything useful left behind by a forgetful plumber; no tools or playthings or stale snacks.

I wept with disappointment, and then I sealed it up again—carefully enough, I hoped, that the monster would never notice what I'd done. After that, for the next thirteen weeks or so, I never touched it.

But I looked at it often, that small square that so resembled a secret hatchway, a closed-off window, a hidden opening to somewhere else. There was so little else to look at in the closet, and my longing, my need, for escape was so strong, that of course I was drawn back to it. For the first few days I kept my back to it, and flinched away even from the thought of it, because it had been such a let-down, but after a week or so I chose to forget what I knew about it, and pretended that it really *was* a way out of the closet, a secret that the monster didn't know.

My favorite thing to think about, and the only thing that could comfort me enough to let me fall asleep, was home. Going home again. Being safely back at home with my parents and my little brother and Puzzle the cat, surrounded by all my own familiar things in my bedroom. It wasn't like the relaxation techniques the psychiatrist suggested, thinking myself into a place I loved. That didn't work. Just thinking about my home could make me cry, and bring me more rigidly awake on the hard floor in the dark narrow closet, too aware of all that I had lost, and how impossibly far away it was now. I had to do something else, I had to create a little routine, almost like a magic spell, a mental exercise that let me relax enough to sleep.

What I did was, I pretended I had never before stripped away the tape and lifted out that square of Sheetrock in the wall. I was doing it for the first time. And this time, instead of pipes in a shallow cavity between two walls, I saw only darkness, a much deeper darkness than that which surrounded me in the closet, and which I knew was the opening to a tunnel.

It was kind of scary. I felt excited by the possibility of escape, but that dark entry into the unknown also frightened me. I didn't know where it went. Maybe it didn't go anywhere at all; maybe it would take me into even greater danger. But there was no real question about it; it looked like a way out, so of course I was going to take it.

I squeezed through the opening and crawled through darkness along a tunnel which ended abruptly in a blank wall. Only the wall was not entirely blank; when I ran my hands over it I could feel the faint outline of a square that had been cut away—just like in the closet I'd escaped from, only at this end the tape was on the other side.

I gave it a good, hard punch and knocked out the piece of Sheetrock, and then I crawled through, and found myself in another closet. Only this one was ordinary, familiar and friendly, with carpet comfy underfoot, clothes hanging down overhead, and when I grasped the smooth metal of the doorknob it turned easily in my hand and let me out into my own beloved bedroom.

After that, the fantasy could take different courses. Sometimes I rushed to find my parents. I might find them downstairs, awake and drinking coffee in the kitchen, or they might be asleep in their bed, and I'd crawl in beside them to be cuddled and comforted as they assured me there was nothing to fear, it was only a bad dream. At other times I just wandered around the house, rediscovering the ordinary domestic landscape, reclaiming it for my own, until finally I fell asleep.

My captivity continued, with little to distinguish one day from another until the time that I got sick. Then, the monster was so disgusted by me, or so fearful of contagion, that he hardly touched me for a couple of days; his abstinence was no sign of compassion. It didn't matter to him if I was vomiting, or shaking with feverish chills, I was locked into the closet and left to suffer alone as usual.

I tried to lose myself in my comfort-dream, but the fever made it difficult to concentrate on anything. Even in the well-rehearsed routine, I kept mentally losing my place, having to go back and start over again, continuously peeling the tape off the wall and prying out that square of Sheetrock, again and again, until, finding it unexpectedly awkward to hold, I lost my grip and the thing came crashing down painfully on my foot.

It was only then, as I blinked away the reflexive tears and rubbed the soreness out of my foot, that I realized it had really happened: I wasn't just imagining it; in my feverish stupor I'd actually stood up, pulled off the tape and opened a hole in the wall.

And it really *was* a hole this time.

I stared, dumbfounded, not at pipes in a shallow cavity, but into blackness.

My heart began to pound. Fearful that I was just seeing things, I bent over and stuck my head into it, flinching a little, expecting to meet resistance. But my head went in, and my chest and arms…I stretched forward and wriggled into the tunnel.

It was much lower than in my fantasy, not big enough to allow me to crawl. If I'd been a couple of years older or five pounds heavier I don't think I would have made it. Only because I was such a flat-chested, narrow-hipped, skinny little kid did I fit, and I had to wriggle and worm my way along like some legless creature.

I didn't care. I didn't think about getting stuck, and I didn't worry about the absolute, suffocating blackness stretching ahead. This was freedom. I kept my eyes shut and hauled myself forward on hands and elbows, pushing myself ahead with my toes. Somehow, I kept going, although the energy it took was immense, almost more than I possessed. I was drenched in sweat and gasping—the sound of my own breathing was like that of a monster in pursuit—but I didn't give up. I could not.

And then I came to the end, a blank wall. But that didn't worry me, because I'd already dreamed of this moment, and I knew what to do. I just had to knock out the bit of plasterboard. Nothing but tape held it in. One good punch would do it.

Only I was so weak from illness, from captivity, from the long, slow journey through the dark, that I doubted I had a good punch in me. But I couldn't give up now. I braced my legs on either side of the tunnel and pushed with all my might, pushed so hard I thought my lungs would burst. I battered it with my fists, and heard the feeble sound of my useless blows like hollow laughter. Finally, trembling with exhaustion, sweating rivers, I hauled back, gathered all the power I had left, and launched myself forward, using my head as a battering ram.

And that did it. On the other side of the wall the tape tore away, and as the square of Sheetrock fell out and into my bedroom closet, so did I.

I was home. I was really and truly home at last.

I wanted to go running and calling for my mother, but first I stopped to repair the wall, carefully fitting the square of Sheetrock back into place, and restoring the pieces of tape that had held it in, smoothing over the torn bits as best I could. It seemed important to do this, as if I might be drawn back along through the tunnel, back to that prison-house, if I didn't seal up the exit.

By the time I finished that, I was exhausted. I walked out of the closet, tottered across the room to my bed, pulled back the sheet and lay down, naked as I was.

It was there, like that, my little brother found me a few hours later.

Even I knew my escape was impossible. At least, it could not have happened in the way I remembered. Just to be sure, my parents opened the plumbing access hatch in my closet, to prove that's all it was. There was no tunnel; no way in or out.

Yet I had come home.

My parents—and I guess the police, too—thought the monster had been frightened by my illness into believing I might die, and had brought me home. Maybe he'd picked the locks (we didn't have a burglar alarm), or maybe— because a small window in one of the upstairs bathrooms turned out to have been left unfastened—he'd carried me up a ladder and pushed me through. My "memory" was only a fevered, feverish dream.

Did it matter that I couldn't remember what really happened? My parents decided it did not, and that the excruciating regime of having to talk about my ordeal was only delaying my recovery, and they brought it to an end.

The years passed. I went to a new junior high, and then on to high school.

I learned to drive. I started thinking about college. I didn't have a boyfriend, but it began to seem like a possibility. I'm not saying I forgot what had happened to me, but it was no longer fresh, it wasn't present, it belonged to the past, which became more and more blurred and distant as I struck out for adulthood and independence. The only thing that really bothered me, the real, continuing legacy of those few months when I'd been the monster's prisoner and plaything, were the dreams. Or, I should say, dream, because there was just the one, the closet dream.

Even after so many years, I did not have ordinary dreams. Night after night—and it was a rare night it did not happen—I fell asleep only to wake, suddenly, and find myself in that closet again. It was awful, but I kind of got used to it. You can get used to almost anything. So when it happened, I didn't panic, but tried practicing the relaxation techniques I'd been taught when I was younger, and eventually—sometimes it took just a few minutes, while other nights it seemed to take hours—I escaped back into sleep.

One Saturday, a few weeks before my seventeenth birthday, I happened to be in a part of town that was strange to me. I was looking for a summer job, and was on my way to a shopping mall I knew only by name, and somehow or other, because I wanted to avoid the freeways, I got a little lost. I saw a sign for a U-Tote-Em and pulled into the parking lot to figure it out. Although I had an indexed map book, I must have been looking on the wrong page; after a few hot, sweaty minutes of frustration I threw it down and got out of the car, deciding to go into the store to ask directions, and buy myself a drink to cool me down.

I had just taken a Dr Pepper out of the refrigerator cabinet when something made me look around. It was him. The monster was standing in the very next aisle, a loaf of white bread in one hand as he browsed a display of chips and dips.

My hands were colder than the bottle. My feet felt very far away from my head. I couldn't move, and I couldn't stop looking at him.

My attention made him look up. For a moment he just looked blank and kind of stupid, his lower lip thrust out and shining with saliva. Then his mouth snapped shut as he tensed up, and his eyes kind of bulged, and I knew that he'd recognized me, too.

I dropped the plastic bottle and ran. Somebody said something—I think it was the guy behind the counter—but I didn't stop. I didn't even pause, just hurled myself at the door and got out. I couldn't think about anything but escape; it never occurred to me that *he* might have had more to fear than I did, that I could have asked the guy behind the counter to call the police, or just dialed 911 myself on my cell. All that was too rational, and I was way too frightened to reason. The old animal brain, instinct, had taken over, and all I could think of was running away and hiding.

I was so out of my mind with fear that instead of going back to my car I turned in the other direction, ran around to the back of the store, then past the dry cleaner's next door, and hid myself, gasping for breath in the torrid afternoon heat, behind a dumpster.

Still panting with terror, shaking so much I could barely control my movements, I fumbled inside my purse, searching for my phone. My hands were so cold I couldn't feel a thing; impatient, I sank into a squat and dumped the contents on the gritty cement surface, found the little silver gadget and snatched it up.

Then I hesitated. Maybe I shouldn't call 911; that was supposed to be for emergencies only, wasn't it? Years ago the police had given me a phone number to call if I ever remembered something more or learned something that might give them a handle on the monster's identity. That number was pinned to the bulletin board in the kitchen, where I saw it every single day. It was engraved on my memory still; although I'd never used it, I knew exactly what numbers to press. But when I tried, my fingers were still so stiff and clumsy with fear that I kept messing up.

I stopped and concentrated on calming myself. Looking around the side of the dumpster I could see a quiet, tree-lined residential street. It was an old neighborhood—you could tell that by the age of the trees, and the fact that it had sidewalks. I was gazing at this peaceful view, feeling my breath and pulse-rate going back to normal, when I caught another glimpse of the monster.

Immediately, I shrank back and held my breath, but he never looked up as he walked, hunched a little forward as he clutched a brown paper bag to his chest, eyes on the sidewalk in front of him. He never suspected my eyes were on him, and as I watched his jerky, shuffling progress—as if he wanted to run but didn't dare—I realized how much our encounter had rattled him. All at once I was calmer. He must know I would call the police, and he was trying to get away, to hide. That he was on foot told me he must live nearby;

probably the clerk in the convenience store would recognize him as a local, and the police would not have far to look for him.

But that was only if he stayed put. What if he was planning to leave? He might hurry home, grab a few things, jump in the car and lose himself in another city where he'd never be found.

I was filled with a righteous fury. I was not going to let him escape. He'd just passed out of sight when I decided to follow him.

I kept well back and off the sidewalk, darting in and out of the trees, keeping to the shade, not because I was afraid, but because I didn't want to alert him. I was determined to find out where he lived, to get his address and the license number of his car, and then I'd hand him over to the police.

After two blocks, he turned onto another street. I hung back, looking for the name of it, but the street sign was on the opposite corner where the lacy fronds of a mimosa tree hung down, obscuring it.

That didn't really matter. All I had to do was tell the police his house was two blocks off Montrose—was that the name? All at once I was uncertain of where I'd just been, the name of the thoroughfare the U-Tote-Em was on, where I'd left my car. But I could find my way back and meet the police there, just as soon as I saw which house the monster went into.

So I hurried after, suddenly fearful that he might give me the slip, and I was just in time to see him going up the front walk of a single-story, pink-brick house, digging into his pocket for the key to the shiny black front door.

I made no effort to hide now, stopping directly across the street in the open, beneath the burning sun. I looked across at the raised curb-stone where the house number had been painted. But the paint had been laid down a long time ago and not renewed; black and white had together faded into the grey of the concrete, and I couldn't be sure after the first number—definitely a 2—if the next three were sixes, or eights, or some combination.

As he slipped the key into the lock the monster suddenly turned his head and stared across the street. He was facing me, looking right at me, and yet I had the impression he didn't see me watching him, because he didn't look scared or worried any more. In fact, he was smiling; a horrible, familiar smile that I knew all too well.

I raised the phone to summon the police, but my hand was empty. I grabbed for my purse, but it had gone, too. There was no canvas strap slung across my shoulder. As I groped for it, my fingers felt only skin: my own, naked flesh. Where were my clothes? How could I have come out without getting dressed?

The smells of dust and ancient varnish and my own sour sweat filled my nose and I began to tremble as I heard the sound of his key in the lock and woke from the dream that was my only freedom, and remembered.

Something terrible happened to me when I was a little girl.

It's still happening.

Award-winning horror author Gemma Files has also been a film critic, teacher, and screenwriter. She is probably best known for her Weird Western Hexslinger series: *A Book of Tongues*, *A Rope of Thorns*, and *A Tree of Bones*, and has published two collections of short fiction, *Kissing Carrion* and *The Worm in Every Heart*, as well as two chapbooks of poetry. Her book *We Will All Go Down Together: Stories About the Five-Family Coven* was published in 2014. Her most recent novel is *Experimental Film*.

Spectral Evidence[1]

Gemma Files

> "The dust still rains and reigns."
> —Stephen Jay Gould, *Illuminations: A Bestiary*

PRELIMINARY NOTES

The following set of photographs was found during a routine reorganization of the Freihoeven Institute's ParaPsych Department files, a little over half a year after the official coroner's inquest which ruled medium Emma Yee Slaughter's death either an outright accident or unprovable misadventure. Taken with what appears to have been a disposable drug-store camera, the photographs had been stuffed into a sealed, blank envelope and then tucked inside the supplemental material file attached to Case #FI4400879, Experiment #58B (attempts at partial ectoplasmic facial reconstruction, conducted under laboratory conditions).

Scribbles on the back of each separate photo, transcribed here, appear to be jotted notes done in black ink—type of pen not readily identifiable—cross-bred with samples of automatic writing done by a blue felt-tipped pen with a fine nib; graphological analysis reveals two distinct sets of handwriting. The original messages run diagonally across the underside of the paper from left to right, while the additional commentary sometimes doubles back across itself so that sentences overlap. Where indicated, supplementary lines have often been written backwards. Footnotes provide additional exegesis.[2]

PHOTOGRAPH #1:[3]

Indistinct interior[4] of a dimly lit suburban house (foliage inconsistent with

---

1 Metaphorical license, naturally: Nothing here constitutes proper legal "evidence" of anything, by any stretch of the imagination.
2 All footnotes were compiled throughout March of 2006 by Sylvester Horse-Kicker, Freihoeven Placement Programme intern, at the request of Dr. Guilden Abbott.
3 Photographs, as indicated, are not themselves numbered; numbers assigned are solely the result of random shuffling. The fact that—when viewed in the order they achieved through this process—the eventual array appears to "tell a story" (Dr. Abbott's notes, March 3/06) must be viewed entirely as coincidence.
4 Most photos in the sequence are best described as "indistinct."

downtown Toronto is observable through one smallish window to left-hand side); the location seems to be a living room, decorated in classic polyester print, plastic-wrapped couch 1970s style. A stuffed, moulting sloth (*Bradypus pallidus*), mounted on a small wooden stand, sits off-centre on the glass-topped coffee-table.

Notes: "House A, April. Apported object was later traced back to Lurhninger Naturalichmuseum in Bonn, Germany. Occupants denied all knowledge of how it got there, paid us $800 to burn it where they could observe. Daughter of family said it followed her from room to room. She woke up in bed with it lying next to her."[5]

Commentary (Forwards): "Edentata or toothless ones: Sloths, anteaters, armadillos. Living fossils. A natural incidence of time travel; time travel on a personal scale, living in two places at once, bilocation. Phenomena as observed. I love you baby you said, I can't do it without you, I cut the key, you turn it. But who opens the door, and to what? Who knows for sure what comes through?"[6]

---

5 Research prompted by details in commentary has since indicated that "House A" may be 1276 Brightening Lane, Mimico, owned by William MacVain and family. On April 15, 2004, at the request of MacVain himself, Slaughter and her Freihoeven control partner, Imre Madach, were sent to investigate on-site poltergeist activity. Activity had apparently ceased by April 20, when they filed their report; the report contains no mention of monetary reimbursement for services, which the Freihoeven's internal code of conduct (of course) strongly discourages.

    N.B.: "There remains the question of exactly how MacVain knew *who* to contact initially, not to mention the further question of who inside the programme might have authorized Madach and Slaughter's travelling expenses—though grantedly, travel to Mimico [a suburb of the Greater Toronto Area, easily reached by following the Queen Street streetcar line to its conclusion] wouldn't have cost them much, unless they did it by taxi. Inquiries into why any letters, e-mails or phone calls exchanged between MacVain and Madach/Slaughter seem not to have been properly logged are also currently ongoing." (Dr. Abbott, ibid.)

6 Samples sent to Graphology for comparison suggest the initial notes on each photo were made by Madach, while the backwards commentary comes closest to a hurried, clumsy imitation of Slaughter's normal penmanship. Forward commentary, on the other hand, can probably be attributed to former Freihoeven intern Eden Marozzi, who was found dead in her apartment on Christmas 2005; going by records left behind, Marozzi had apparently been assisting Madach with his work on Slaughter's unfinished channelling experiments. As we all know, it was Madach's proven presence in her apartment at the time of Marozzi's death—as revealed by evidence gathered during the Metro Toronto Police Department's initial crime scene investigation—which, along with a lack of plausible alibi, would eventually lead to his subsequent arrest on charges of murder in the second degree.

Commentary (Backwards): "Apports are often difficult without help, so try using lucifuges for guidance. Circle is paramount; Tetragrammaton must be invoked. They have no names."[7]

PHOTOGRAPH #2:

Equally dim, angled upwards to trace what may be marks of fire damage—scorching of wallpaper, slight bubbling of plaster—moving from ceiling of kitchen down *towards* sink. The highest concentration of soot seems to be at the uppermost point. Wallpaper has a juniper-berry and leaf motif.[8]

Notes: "House D, May. We were becoming popular in certain circles. Family had two children, both sons, both under three years old; nanny reported the younger one was playing in his high-chair during breakfast when his 'Teddy-thing' suddenly caught fire.[9] Subsequent damage was estimated at $4,000; we received an additional $2,000 for making sure it wouldn't happen again."

Commentary (Forwards): "We need something more spectacular, baby, a display, like Hollywood. Fire eats without being eaten, consumes unconsumed, as energy attracts. Come at once from whatever part of the world and answer my questions. Come at once, visibly and pleasantly, to do whatever I desire. Come, fulfil my desires and persist unto the end in accordance to my will. I conjure thee by Him to whom all creatures are obedient, and by the name of Him who rules over thee.[10] So this one goes out to the one I love, the one who

---

7 "Mention of 'lucifuges' would seem to indicate Slaughter—and Madach?—were using hierarchical magic to accelerate or control—generate?—poltergeist activity at MacVain house. Worth further inquiry, after cataloguing rest of photos." (Dr. Abbott, ibid.)

8 Attempts to identify this location have, thus far, proved inconclusive. Dr. Abbott is undecided, but tentatively calls it either 542 McCaul or 71B Spinster, both of which were visited by Slaughter and Madach in connection with repeated pyrokinetic poltergeist incidents. Since one family has moved out leaving no forwarding address, however, while the other proved spectacularly uncooperative, no more detailed analysis seems forthcoming.

9 If we assume the photo *was* taken at 71B Spinster, it may be relevant to record that the child in question sustained burns severe enough to require partial amputation of three fingers from his left hand.

10 This "anthology incantation" seems to have been compiled from several different ones, all of which appear in the legendary grimoire *Lemegeton*. Dr. Abbott confirms that the Freihoeven's library copy of this text was misplaced for several days in November of 2004, half a year prior to when the first photo was taken; this theft coincides with Madach's brief tenure as volunteer assistant librarian, before forming an experimental field-team with Slaughter.

left me behind, a simple prop to occupy his time. And why Teddy-'thing,' anyway? God knows I couldn't tell what it was before, afterwards."

Commentary (Backwards): "By this time, I can only think they were already watching me closely."[11]

Photograph #3:

Murky yet identifiable three-quarter study of Slaughter, who appears to be in light mediumistic control-trance. Orbs[12] hover over her right eye, pineal gland and heart chakra, roughly the same areas in which she would later develop simultaneous (and fatal) aneurysms. She sits in a rust-red La-Z-Boy recliner, feet elevated, with a dust-covered television screen barely visible to her extreme right, in the background of the frame.

Notes: "House H, July. Inclement weather with continual smog-warning. Séance performed at the request of surviving family-members, with express aim of contacting their deceased father; a control spirit was used to produce and animate an ectoplasmic husk patterned after his totem photograph, freely donated for use as a guided meditational aid. Mother cashed out RRSPs and eldest daughter's college fund in order to assemble the $15,000 required to remove 'curse'[13] afflicting their bloodline."

Commentary (Forwards): "But he died of natural causes so it's not so bad, right, not like we did anything really, and if you keep having those migraines then maybe you should take something, maybe you should just relax, baby, let me help you, let me. Don't be like that, let me, why you gotta be that way? Palpitations, you say that like it's a bad thing, that's what I love about you, baby, you have such a big heart: A big fat heart full of love and warmth and plaque and knots and pain. So just breathe, just breathe, just breathe, go do some yoga, take a pill, calm the hell down. You know we can't stop yet."

---

11 By "they," this commentator may mean the aforementioned lucifuges or fly-the-lights, elemental spirits identified with fire, who Eliphas Levi calls notoriously difficult to control and naturally "hateful towards mortals."
12 Sphere-shaped visual deformities of the emulsion or pixels, often observed at sites where teams are trying to record various psychic phenomena.
13 "This just gets better and better." (Dr. Abbott, ibid.)

Commentary (Backwards): "Them either."

PHOTOGRAPH #4:
Close-angled shot of greasy black writing sprawled across what looks like the tiled wall of a bathroom shower-stall; letters vary radically in size, are imperfectly formed, seem (according to Graphology) inconsistent with "tool-bearing hands."[14] Letters read: "aLWaYs TheRe."[15]

Notes: "Automatic writing observed at Apartment C, renewed five separate times over a period of eight days. When advised that a cleansing exorcism was the best option, owner refused to cooperate."[16]

Commentary (Forwards): "We have to stop we can't. We have to stop we can't. We have to stop stop stop we can't can't can't, oh Christ I want to STOP this, what are you, stupid? There's too much at stake, we're in too deep, no going back. WE CAN'T STOP NOW."

Commentary (Backwards): "Behold, I shall show you a great mystery, for we shall not all sleep, but we shall all be changed. And you can consider this my formal letter of resignation."

PHOTOGRAPHS #5 TO #9:
After close examination by various Freihoeven staff-members, Photographs #5 through #8 have been conclusively proven to show one of the Institute's own experimental labs. The blurry image in the extreme foreground of each seems most consistent with an adjustable Remote Viewing diorama[17] which

---

14 "'Tool-bearing'? Most messages of this type are produced telekinetically." (Dr. Abbott, ibid.)
15 Naturally enough, opinions vary as to who (or what) might be responsible for these markings.
16 The single shortest annotation. This photo has since been tentatively identified—within a fairly narrow margin of error—as having been taken inside Slaughter's former condo, the site of her death. Even more significant, in hindsight, may be Dr. Abbott's recollection (confirmed through studying her coroner's inquest file) that Slaughter's body was found in her bathtub on August 23/05, partially immersed in shallow water.
17 Invented by Dr. Abbott as part of his 1978 dissertational work at the University of Toronto, these are often used as a meditational aid during guided remote viewing sessions: The "navigator" or non-psychic team-member will set the diorama up to roughly approximate the area he/she wants the viewer to access, then talk them through it on a detail-by-detail level until their trance becomes deep enough that they can guide themselves on the rest of their mental journey.

was set up in Lab Four from approximately September 15 to December 15, 2005. Much of the background area of each photo, on the other hand, has apparently been obscured by new visuals somehow imposed over an original image, by unidentifiable means; portions of the emulsion have been either destroyed or significantly altered, creating a visual illusion not unlike the "chiaroscuro" effect observed in certain Renaissance paintings which, while being restored, turn out to have been painted over a primary image that the artist may have wanted to either alter or conceal.[18]

As usual, even these partially subliminal secondary images are best described as indistinct and difficult to identify and/or categorize. Nevertheless, extensive analysis has revealed certain constants, e.g.:

• That background areas correspond with rough approximations of Photos #1 through #4, with the exception/addition of:
• A figure, face always angled away from "the camera," whose physical proportions seem to match those observed in photos taken of Slaughter, pre-mortem.[19]

Photo #9 was taken elsewhere; the diorama shown in Photos #5 through #8 is notably absent. A grey-painted stretch of wall, the hinge of a partially open door and the angle of lens during exposure all suggest that the camera may have been mounted on a tripod inside one of the Freihoeven's many industrial-sized storage closets, but not enough distinguishing marks are

---

18 "This is a prime example of what is commonly called 'spirit photography'—in this case, a Directed Imagery experiment involving Marozzi that may have been infiltrated by outside influences, producing the photo. These influences may have been, as Slaughter's commentary suggests, lucifuges originally suborned into helping her and Madach perpetrate their various psychic frauds; since Slaughter, the person with genuine paranatural power in their equation, was probably the one who did the actual invocation, the lucifuges would have seen her as their primary oppressor, and directed their revenge against her in specific. Even were we to take all of the above as being empirically 'true,' however, once the lucifuges' malefic influence had already brought about Slaughter's death (if that is, indeed, what actually happened), one would tend to assume that they would have no further interest in the case...or that, if they did, their campaign would shift focus onto Madach, the sole surviving author of the original invocation. And in that case, why harass Marozzi at all?" (Dr. Abbott, ibid.)

19 Note to self: Why am I here? Wasn't there some other, slightly less insane, place I could have gotten a summer job in? I *knew* Eden; a sweet girl, if easily influenced, overly fascinated by/ with psychic phenomena and those Freihoeven members who claimed to work with/produce them. Emma Slaughter looked at me in the halls once as I passed by, and I dreamed about it for a week—still felt her watching me, wherever I went. Is this relevant? Is recording stuff like this *science*? (S. Horse-Kicker, March 2/06)*

*"A valid question, Sylvester. Thanks for your input." (Dr. Abbott, ibid.)

visible to establish exactly which one (there are six on Floor Three alone, for example, near the location of Lab Four).

Notes [collated into list-form for easy reading]:
(#5) "Subject was asked to visualize inside of House X. One hour fifty-three minutes allowed for session; results varyingly successful."
(#6) "Subject was asked to visualize interior of Facility H, no specific target. Agreed to deepen trance through application of Batch 33. Three hours ten minutes allowed for session; results varyingly successful."
(#7) "Subject was asked to visualize office area within Facility H, with specific reference to files stored on Public Servant G's computer. Five hours seventeen minutes allowed for session; results inconclusive overall."
(#8) "Subject was asked to visualize home office area inside House Z, with specific reference to correspondence stored in file-cabinet with plaster gargoyle on top of it.[20] Given sample of handwriting to meditate on, with double dose of Batch 33. Session interrupted at eight hours two minutes, after subject began to spasm; results inconclusive."
(#9) "Subject entered trance on own time, without instruction, after having self-injected a triple dose of Batch 33; session interrupted after approximately one hour, when subject was accidentally discovered by navigator. Limited amnesia observed after recuperation. Having no idea what image is meant to represent, impossible to say if session was successful or not."

Commentary (Forwards) [as above]:
(#5) Unintelligible scrawls.
(#6) Same.
(#7) Same, interrupted only by a shaky but repetitive attempt to form the letters E, Y, S.
(#8) In very different handwriting, far more like that usually used for backwards commentary: "See here, see there, trying so hard, how could I help but answer? Because he likes girls who see things, yes he does; little pig, little pig, let me come in. This world's a big wide open place, up and down and all in between. Not so fun to see around corners when you know what's waiting, is it?"

---

20 "That sounds like *my* office. Investigate? I have vague recollection of anonymous notes sent to me last year, shortly before Emma's death..." (Dr. Abbott, ibid.)

(#9) Back to unintelligible scrawls.

Commentary (Backwards) [as above]:

(#5) "can"

(#6) "you"

(#7) "hear"

(#8) "me"

(#9) "now"

PHOTOGRAPH #10:

At first misidentified as one of the actual MTPD crime-scene photos taken at the Marozzi apartment on Christmas Day, 2005, this image also demonstrates "spirit photography" alterations of a subtly different (yet far more disturbing) sort. Analysis has revealed that the apparent main image, that of Eden Marozzi's bedroom and corpse, is actually incongruent with other elements in the photo—specifically, the time visible on Marozzi's bedside clock, which places this as having been taken a good three hours prior to what forensic experts established as her physical T.O.D.

Further examinations, including X-rays administered at the Institute's expense, have since concluded that this first image has been recorded not on the photograph's own emulsion but on a thin, rock-hard layer of biological substance[21] overlaid carefully on the original photo. Beneath this substance is a simple holiday-style snap, probably taken with the camera on a timer, that shows Marozzi and Madach embracing at Marozzi's kitchen table, both wearing party-hats and smiling. The remains of a Christmas dinner surround them; if one looks closely at the bottom centre of the photo, an opened jewel-box explains the ring visible on Marozzi's finger.

In the mirror behind them, however, a third figure—familiar from the previous array of "guided" photos—can be glimpsed sitting next to them, its hand half-raised, as though just about to touch Marozzi on the shoulder.

Notes: "Merry Christmas, Eve, from your Adam. A new Paradise begins."

Commentary (Forwards): "Fruit of knowledge, fruit of sin, snake's gift. This

---

21 Possibly ectoplasm, a substance occasionally exuded during séances, made up of various dead material from the medium's body.

is what you want? This is what you get: The bitter pill. Fly the lights, lights out; out, out, brief candle! Goodbye, my lover. Goodbye, my friend. Goodbye, little girl who didn't know enough not to get in between. You can tell her I picked the wallpaper out myself. Ask her: How you like me now? Pretty good oh God God God God God"

Commentary (Backwards): "And on that note—did it really never occur to you that allowing someone used to working outside her body to be *dis*embodied might not be the world's best idea, after all?"[22]

CONCLUSION:
With Imre Madach in jail, Emma Yee Slaughter and Eden Marozzi dead, and the official files closed on all three, the discovery of the preceding photographic array would seem—though, naturally, interesting in its own right—fairly extraneous to any new interpretation of the extant facts of the case.

RECOMMENDATIONS
- From now on, access to/possession of library books on the Freihoeven collection's "hazardous" list must obviously be tracked far more effectively.
- In the initial screening process for evaluating prospective Freihoeven employees, whether contracted freelancers or in-house, far more emphasis needs to be placed on psychological mapping. Issues thus revealed need to be recorded and rechecked, rigorously, on a regular monthly basis.

---

22 To this last bit of commentary, Dr. Abbott asks that a partial transcript of his most recent interview with Freihoeven psychic control-group member Carraclough Devize—held March 4/06, during which he showed her what are now tentatively called the Slaughter/Madach/Marozzi photos—be appended to this report:
Devize: (After 120-second pause) Oh, no. Christ, that's sad.
Abbott: What is, Carra?
Devize: That. Don't you...no, of course you don't. There, in that corner, warping the uppermost stains. See? You'll have to strain a bit.
Abbott: Is that...an orb?
Devize: That's *Emma*, Doc. Face-on, finally. God, so *sad*.
Abbott: (After 72-second pause) I'm afraid I'm still not—
Devize: (Cuts him off) I know. But there she is, right there. Just about to take shape.
Abbott: Not fly-the-lights?
Devize: *Emma* had fly-the-lights, like mice or roaches, except mice and roaches don't usually...anyway. But Madach, and that poor little spoon-bender wannabe Barbie of his? By the end, what *they* had—was Emma.

- Similarly, field-work teams should be routinely broken up after three complete assignments together, and the partners rotated into other departments. This will hopefully prevent either side of the equation developing an unhealthy dependence on the other.
- Finally, the Institute itself needs to undergo a thorough psychic cleansing, as soon as possible; lingering influences must be dispelled through expulsion or exorcism, and the wards must be redrawn over the entire building. Outside experts, rather than Freihoeven employees/experts, should be used for this task (Dr. Abbott suggests consulting Maccabee Roke, Nan van Hool, Father Akinwale Oja S.J. or—as a last resort—Jude Hark Chiuwai as to promising/economical local prospects).
- Photographs #1 through #10 will be properly refiled under #FI5556701 (cross-referentials: Madach, Marozzi, Slaughter).

Filed and signed: Sylvester Horse-Kicker, March 5/06
Witnessed: Dr. Guilden Abbott, March 5/06

Born in Wolverhampton and bred in Manchester, Simon Bestwick now lives on the Wirral with a long-suffering wife, the author Cate Gardner. He is the author of the novels *Tide of Souls*, *The Faceless*, and *Hell's Ditch*, along with four collections of short stories and a chapbook, *Angels of the Silences*. He's been a fast-food operative, an insurance salesman, and a call-center worker, all of which were horrible.

When not writing, he goes for walks, watches movies, listens to music, and does all he can to avoid having to get a proper job again. Two new novels, *Devil's Highway* and *The Feast of All Souls*, will be out later this year.

Hushabye
Simon Bestwick

MARCH STARTED LATE that year, as if waiting for a cue it had missed. The conversion back to BST was scheduled for late in the month; the days stayed short, the nights dark, long, and cold. When snow fell it lay for days in a brittle crust, and every other morning all stone was patterned with frost.

I was looking unsuccessfully for paying work that didn't drive me crazy after a fortnight, and still living out of cardboard boxes in my friend Alan's spare room. Although he'd said I could stay as long as I needed when I moved in, it'd been six months now and his patience had started to fray, all our little habits scraping at one another's nerves.

So I took to going for long walks around the area. I like walking, even in the cold night on treacherous pavements.

I went down Bolton Road to the roundabout where it met Langworthy Road, then walked down Langworthy 'til I was opposite the abandoned shell of the Mecca bingo hall; I was on the corner of Brindleheath Road, which ran under a bridge, past the edge of the industrial estate and a couple of vacant lots and up onto the A6 next to Pendleton Church and near a Chinese takeaway. I decided to get some chow mein before heading back home.

As I came out from under the bridge, I heard a child call out, "No."

That was followed by a noise somewhere between a gasp and a cry, then silence. My skin prickled; I ran up the road.

I saw them vanishing into the bushes at the edge of one of the vacant lots; a small girl, tiny in a red coat, and a figure that looked like a shadow walking at first, 'til I realised it was dressed in black, only the white of its face visible. Then they were gone into the dark. They hadn't seen me.

I pelted up the road and crashed through the bushes, shouting. They were white in the gloom, or at least the girl's body and the man's face were. Something silver, brighter than breath, glimmering like motes of powdered glass, was pouring from the girl's opened mouth and into his. The man looked up. His face was long, pale; a thin blade of nose, one thick eyebrow a line across the top. The eyes looked black too.

I kicked out at him, but he was already rolling away. He scrambled up and ran, vanishing into the shadows. I stood there, gasping for air; I couldn't see him and on the uneven ground all I'd do was break an ankle. And there was the girl to think about.

He'd worked fast; she lay with her clothes scattered about her, staring up at the night stars. For a moment I thought she was dead, but then I saw her breath. I took off my jacket and covered her; she flinched from my touch as if stung, whimpering like a hurt animal and curling up on her side. I couldn't tell if it was the cold or the hate that made my fingers so clumsy as I dug out my mobile and dialled 112.

The first assault on a local child had happened in Higher Broughton just before Christmas, in Albert Park. A six-year-old boy almost dead with hypothermia, his torn clothes scattered around him. There'd been more over the following months, the same pattern: police offering nothing but pleas for vigilance and information, the victims unwilling or unable to provide any leads.

They took the girl to Hope Hospital and me down to the police station on the Crescent. I was interviewed for two hours by a pair of detectives. Poole, the Detective Sergeant, was the hardest to handle, spending the first hour treating me as a suspect. In the end, the Detective Constable, Hardiman, put a hand on his arm and led him outside. They left me with a paused tape and a stony-faced policewoman; I heard raised voices through the breezeblock wall.

Hardiman took it from there. He was young, earnest and sympathetic. Poole stayed silent, looking at the scarred desktop, light gleaming on his bald crown. He had a drinker's lined, ruddy face. Hardiman's was smooth and pale as fibreglass. I told him everything I'd seen, except whatever it was I'd seen passing from the girl's mouth to her attacker's. I didn't want dismissing as a nutter.

"You'll have to excuse DS Poole," Hardiman said later, as we watched the Identi-Kit picture take shape. "He's got a kid of his own that age. Takes it personally."

"It's OK," I told him, meaning it. Normally I'm pretty scathing about heavy-handed policing, but having seen what had been done to the girl I'd've quite happily held Poole's coat for him while he threw the offender down the stairs several times. As long as it was the right man.

"It's not," said Hardiman. "My missus wants us to have kids, but…" He gestured at the picture to indicate all it represented. "You shouldn't have to think of this when you're thinking of starting a family."

"I know."

"You're sure this is him?"

I looked at the finished picture and nodded slowly. Hardiman rubbed his eyes and pushed his fingers through his sandy hair. "OK," he said. "Come on. I'll drive you home. And I want to thank you. This is the first clue we've had of any kind." He must've been tired, to let that one slip out.

They had my details, of course, but I didn't hear any more from them for over a fortnight. In the interim, I received bad news of a different kind: a friend of mine called Terry Browning died.

He'd choked on his own puke, sat in his armchair by the window with an empty bottle of Lone Piper beside him on the floor. It happened in his flat on Langworthy Road, a scant hundred yards from where I'd heard the little girl cry out. The funeral was at St. John's Church, in the Height, about a week later.

He'd been a priest, but had left the church with a deep loss of faith the previous year; maybe they thought it was catching, as the only dog-collar in sight was the one who read the service, which didn't mean anything to me or Terry's brother, the only other mourner, and probably wouldn't've to Terry any longer. I wasn't even sure if it meant much to the priest, but it was hard to tell. The bitter wind tore his graveside oration to shreds, like grey confetti.

Rob Browning and I went for a pint down at the Crescent afterwards, more to chase out the chill than anything else. We hardly said a dozen words to each other. He was smart and suited and had a southern accent; I knew he and Terry hadn't been close. He stayed for one drink and then left; I ordered a double Jameson's and raised the glass to the memory of a friend whose death I still felt a certain guilt for.

"Mind if I join you?"

I looked up to see DC Hardiman standing over me with a Britvic orange in his hand.

"How'd you know I was here?"

"Didn't make CID on my good looks."

I laughed. "Didn't think so."

He flipped me the bird and sat. "Sorry about your mate."

"Thanks. Looks like we're the only ones who are."

We sat in silence; I waited for him to probe about Terry but he didn't. In the end it was me who started fishing. "How's the investigation going?"

He shook his head.

"Nothing?"

"Oh no. Something. But...there's complications."

"How d'you mean?"

He didn't answer at first. "I looked you up on HOLMES. Quite the colourful character."

"Is that a compliment?"

"You say what you think and kick up a stink when you reckon you have to."

"Fair assessment," I had to admit.

"And you don't believe in keeping your trap shut or leaving things alone when not doing so would piss off certain people."

"People in high places, sort of thing?"

He nodded.

"Guilty, I suppose." I took a swallow of whisky. "Are you trying to tell me something?"

He studied his glass, turning it this way and that like a faceted gem. "The evidence I've got...it's taking me somewhere where shutting my trap and leaving things alone is pretty much what the doctor ordered."

Everything seemed to go very still. "I'm feeling on my own on this one in a big way," he said, almost to himself, then looked up. "Even Poole's not sure, and I thought he wanted that bastard more than anyone."

"Close to his pension."

"Yeah. I just thought...you'd understand where I'm at right now."

"I do." I studied my own drink for a minute, then looked up. "What are you going to do?"

Hardiman put his glass down on the table. "The little girl you found. Ellie Chatham, her name is. I visited her yesterday. To see if she remembered anything, or...I don't know. She's like an old woman. Five years old and she's like an old woman. Shuffles from place to place and just sits there. Breathing, staring. Waiting. I don't know what for. Death, maybe. Like something's just gone out of her."

I thought of the silver glittering I'd seen passing from her mouth to the attacker's. "Yeah."

"And the psychiatrist reports on the others…Christ, I don't think one of those kids'll ever be the same again. It's different for all of them, but…night terrors, rages…there's one, the boy they found in Albert Park, he flies into a rage every time he sees anybody black or Asian. Don't know why, there's no indication anyone non-white was involved. The opposite is how it looks, thanks to you. It's like he's full of hate and rage, but it's not going where it should, it's going at someone else, a scapegoat. Fuck knows why."

"I'll lend you one of my books on capitalism sometime," I said. "Might give you a few pointers."

He snorted a laugh. "That'll raise a few eyebrows in the canteen. All these kids, and he's taken something from them they'll never get back, that'll fuck them up forever. And my wife, she still wants us to try for a kid. I just…just want to know any child of mine is gonna be as safe as I can make it, from something like this. But I'm supposed to keep my trap shut and look the other way. Well, fuck that." He lifted his glass. "Here's to colourful characters."

I clinked my glass against it. "Amen."

Twenty-four hours after he spoke to me, Detective Constable Alec Hardiman's Ford Mondeo went off the motorway between Manchester and Bradford, on Saddleworth Moor. It was two in the morning, and no one ever knew what he'd been doing out there. His neck was broken in the crash. He left behind a wife, Sheila, but no children, actual or in the womb.

I would've gone to the funeral, but had a strong sense I wouldn't be welcome if I did. I watched it from a distance, saw a thin pale woman in black that I assumed to be Sheila Hardiman, leaning on two other women—mother and sister, at a guess. Other mourners included a grey-faced DS Poole and a lone man in his sixties, bald on top with a salt-and-pepper goatee.

It was this last mourner who turned up on my doorstep the following evening, with a brown paper parcel under his arm. My first thought on seeing him was: *Jesus, people still wear tweed?*

"Mr. Paul Hearn?" he asked.

"Yes."

"Don Hardiman." He offered his hand. "Alec's father."

"Please come in."

The parcel sat on the table, between us and our coffee cups. Don Hardiman's voice was quiet and modulated, very clear; he was a university lecturer. There was a black armband round one sleeve of his jacket.

"Alec came to me the day before he died, and put the package into my keeping, along with your name and address and a request to bring it here. We weren't particularly close, and I wasn't the first person anyone would think of coming to for any little…legacies of this kind. Which is why I expect Alec chose me."

My hand kept twitching towards the package, but I kept stopping it.

"My son wasn't a paranoid man, Mr. Hearn—"

"Paul."

He inclined his head. "But he was definitely afraid of something and believed he could no longer trust his colleagues. I believe I have some idea of what's in there, and I'd presume you do as well."

I nodded. "I think so."

"I suspect as well that I wasn't intended to know anything about this. Alec did love me, in his way, and would want to protect me. But I loved him in my way too. He was my son, and now he's dead. I'd like to help."

"Don—"

"Please."

"Alright." I nodded. "Let's see what we've got."

Timothy was the son of Arthur Wadham, a highly successful businessman known for his generous donations to New Labour's party funds. He'd inherited his father's charm and ruthlessness, by all accounts, but neither his looks nor his business acumen. Nearly thirty, he'd launched about half-a-dozen business ventures since returning from the all-expenses-paid-by-Daddy backpacking tour following his graduation from Cambridge.

All expenses paid by Daddy, in fact, seemed to be pretty much a—even *the*—recurrent theme in Timothy Wadham's life. All half-a-dozen business ventures had ended in financial disaster, but Wadham senior was always on hand with a blank cheque for the next one. Hard-nosed and void of sentiment he might be, but he clearly—like most parents—had a blind spot where his offspring was concerned. Under any other circumstances, a man who could cock up running a lap-dancing club in Romford would have been filed in the do-not-touch-this-fuckwit-with-a-bargepole category and left there.

Just another rich kid bombing happily through life secure in the knowledge that pater would always be there to bail him out. What money didn't solve directly, the connections it bought most assuredly would.

I picked up the photograph of Timothy Wadham; the long face and thin sharp nose, the black eyes and the unbroken line of the eyebrow. I showed it to Don Hardiman. Wadham's address was written on the back.

"Still want to help?" I asked after he'd finished reading. He looked up with a wintry smile.

"I'm not my son's father for nothing," he said. "What do you need?"

"What in the bloody hell do you think you're doing, Paul?"

When my reflection didn't reply I opened the sock drawer and rummaged around in the back. I found what I was looking for and unwrapped the old T-shirt it was folded in.

I'd taken the Browning automatic off the body of a man called Frankie Hagen in Ordsall the month before. I hadn't killed him, any more than I'd had any idea what I thought I wanted a gun for. I began to wonder if I now knew.

I unloaded the pistol—there were eight rounds left in the magazine—and looked at myself in the bedroom mirror. I was wearing black, including a wool skully and Thinsulate gloves. I dry-fired the pistol with the gloves on. They didn't get in the way of the trigger pull; that was all I needed to know.

I took a few more deep breaths, looking at myself in the mirror, and asked myself a new question. Not *what are you doing?*, but *why are you doing it?*

For Ellie Chatham, old woman of five, and all the others naked and shivering in the cold, all leeched of parts of themselves whose absence they would never overcome. For Terry Browning, who had seen reality and refused to turn away, even knowing it would destroy him, and for Alec Hardiman, who had done the same. In some way perhaps it would atone for Terry, who could and should have received more from me, even if it had only been sitting up with him for a few nights. Could that have helped? It was too late to ask now.

And perhaps most of all it was for me, in my thirty-something dread of failure and the dark, so that at the withered arse-end of my life I could look back and say, *This at least. Even if no one knows but me, I achieved this. Even if I started nothing, at least I ended something that needed ending; this, at least.*

Whether they were good enough or not, they were the only reasons I had, and so they'd have to do.

I pulled the curtains back and looked out of the window. Don Hardiman's Vauxhall Astra was parked outside. Fifteen minutes later he pulled up in a Volkswagen Polo. That one was for me. I reloaded the Browning and went out to meet him.

"Do you think Wadham did it?" he asked.

"Did what?"

"Alec."

I shrugged. "I suppose he could've. But more than likely it was someone looking out for him. Working for his dad, or one of his dad's connections. Don't suppose we'll ever know, will we?"

"No." He shook his head. "And it doesn't really matter, does it? The effect's the same."

"Yeah."

"Good luck, Paul." We shook hands.

"You too."

Don picked Wadham up first, coming out of his gravel drive in Sale in a BMW. We stayed in touch with mobiles, and I followed at a distance, picking up when I had to. We alternated pursuit like that for nearly an hour, until he reached Lower Broughton.

"He's pulled in," said Don. "Shit, Paul, he's getting out of the car. Heading up Broughton Road, on foot. What now?"

"Leave it with me," I said. I was surprised how calm I felt.

Wadham was heading up from the Irwell Valley campus. Broughton Road led ultimately to the Broad Street roundabout, a stone's throw from the vacant lots off Brindleheath Road. The arrogance of the bastard; so close to where he'd attacked Ellie Chatham. Of course, there were a lot of roads branching off along the way. I pulled in near the roundabout where Broughton crossed Seaford Road. He walked past, head down; I ducked so he wouldn't see me, in case he remembered too.

When he was gone, I got out of the Polo and followed at a distance, hands thrust into my pockets. He kept going up, over Lower Broughton Road, 'til he reached the low-rise blocks and estate terraces on the left-hand side of the road. Then he vanished down one of the walkways and was lost in the shadows.

I hung back, waiting by a small birch sapling someone had optimistically planted on the green apron outside the terrace. It occurred to me that, dressed in black and loitering in the shadows as I was, I might easily be mistaken for my prey, and I had to smile bitterly at the thought. Should I follow him? In the dark, the walkways were a maze, and what if Wadham knew I was trailing him? Before I could make a move, he came back out again, leading a small boy by the hand.

The boy was maybe eight, wearing tracksuit bottoms, a T-shirt and a base-ball cap, his hair almost shaved clean it was cut so close to the skull. The estate kids in Broughton are tough, they have to be, but the boy followed Wadham meekly as a lamb. Why he was out that late, or how Wadham charmed him so easily, I never knew.

Wadham and the boy crossed the road; they were heading for Broughton Park, a small zone of green surrounded by a multicoloured fence. Wadham climbed the gate; the boy waited patiently to be lifted over.

I ran across the road, scaled the gate, landed in a crouch. I couldn't see them. Then there was a whimpered cry from the child, and a sound of ripping cloth. I pulled the Browning from my belt, pulled back the slide, and ran.

I floundered through the bushes; the boy lay on the open grass. He was naked except for his underpants; they came away in Wadham's hand with a final rip as I ran up. Wadham's lips were skinned back from his teeth; I couldn't tell if it was a smile or the snarl of a predator about to strike. His head turned as I reached him; our eyes met for the second time. Then I swung up the Browning and shot him in the face.

The bang was sudden and deafening; there was a flash and a brass cartridge spat out of the gun. Something warm and wet splashed my cheek. Wadham's face was black with it as he fell backwards, arms flailing, then jerked once and was still.

I turned to the boy; he was sat up, hugging his knees. "Are you alright?" I asked. He nodded. Wadham hadn't had time to do whatever it was he'd done to Ellie Chatham and the rest.

I turned and Wadham's snarling face lunged up into mine, teeth bared.

One eye was gone, the socket streaming blackness down a bone-white cheek. He grabbed my throat; his hand was bitter cold. I shoved the Browning into his chest and fired twice, blowing darkness out of his back; he reeled away and fell to one knee, arms windmilling, then launched himself up and came at me again.

I aimed two-handed and shot him in the forehead, then again in the temple as he fell to his knees. He rolled onto his back and I stood over him; blood-covered, his glistening face was a blackness like the rest of him. There was a noise in his throat that was either a rattle or a laugh as he began to sit up.

I shot him in the face again and again, shell cases bucking clear of the gun, the sulphur smell of cordite in the crisp night air, and felt sprays of blood and bone hitting me. He reached out a hand to me as the gun emptied, the trigger clicking helplessly as I pulled it, then toppled back and lay still. But I could still hear him breathing, and after a while he began moving feebly. Then the breathing stopped and his limbs went slack.

I turned back to the boy. He began fumbling in the grass for his clothes. "Come on," I said, "let's get you home."

I still have nightmares about Timothy Wadham's one-eyed corpse slithering into my bedroom by night, smashed face grinning.

About a week into April, spring was finally underway. Crocuses and daffodils were in bloom. The sky was clean and blue and the air was getting warm. I opened the windows and cleaned the house; a late spring was better than none. Then the doorbell rang. When I answered it, it was DS Poole. "I think you know why I'm here," he said.

Instead of the station, he took me down the pub; Mulligan's in town, to be precise. I've always been a sucker for Irish whiskey. Over a shot each of Black Bush, we talked.

"Worst part is," he said, "that Alec went to you, not me. He didn't trust me."

"He didn't know who he could trust," I said quietly. "It wasn't just you."

He glowered at me. "You think that helps? I was his partner. I wouldn't have let him down."

I wasn't sure which of us he was trying to convince, but I didn't press the point.

"I didn't see anything about Wadham in the papers," I said at last.

Poole grunted. "That's how it'll stay. The boy's mum called us in. No chance that one could just go away. His old man's not chasing up revenge—not through us anyway. The boy gave us a description of his rescuer. Or rather, me. No one else knows and no one else will. From that I put two and two together."

"And Wadham?"

"Up in smoke, Paul. Saw to it myself." He toyed with his drink, then looked up at me. "You know, when I saw how many times you'd shot him, I thought you must've hated him even more than I did. But when we burned the fucker, I understood why."

I waited, but I knew what was coming next.

"He was banging on his coffin lid," said Poole. "And then he was banging on the oven door. All the way through, 'til all he was was ash. And the ashes went in the river. Saw to that myself, an' all. With all the shit that's gone in the Irwell over the years, who'll notice a bit more?"

"They've just had it cleaned," I pointed out.

"Well, they'll just have to clean it all over again." We finished our whiskies; Poole looked towards the bar. "What's that bottle?"

I looked. "More whiskey. Midleton."

"Any good?"

"Supposed to be, but at a tenner a shot I wouldn't know."

Poole came back with two doubles. "To Alec," he said.

"Alec," I nodded, and touched my glass to his.

Nicholas Royle is the author of *First Novel* as well as six earlier novels, including *The Director's Cut* and *Antwerp*, and a short-story collection, *Mortality*. In addition he has published more than a hundred short stories. He has edited nineteen anthologies and is series editor of *Best British Short Stories* (Salt). A senior lecturer in creative writing at Manchester Metropolitan University, he also runs Nightjar Press, which publishes new short stories as signed, limited-edition chapbooks, and is an editor at Salt Publishing.

Very Low-Flying Aircraft
Nicholas Royle

FROM A DISTANCE of thirty yards, Ray saw immediately what was happening. There was Flynn, in his new full uniform, which the two older men, in engineer's overalls, would have insisted he wear. Ray stepped back behind the trunk of a palm tree, observing.

Several ginger-cream chickens pecked in the sand, looking for seed that the two engineers, whom Ray recognised as Henshaw and Royal, would have scattered there. Ray could see Henshaw talking to Flynn, explaining what he needed to do, Flynn looking unsure in spite of the new recruit's desire to please. Henshaw was a big man with red hair cut severely short at the back and sides of his skull. Royal—the shorter of the two engineers, with a greased quiff—who had been bending down watching the chickens, stood up and took something from the pocket of his overalls, which he handed to Flynn.

Ray caught the flash of sunlight on the blade.

Henshaw mimed the action Flynn would need to copy.

Ray considered stepping in, stopping the ritual, for it *was* a ritual. He hadn't had to suffer it on his arrival on the island, but only because he had been a little older than Flynn on joining up. Henshaw and Royal were younger than Ray, which would have been enough to dissuade them.

But for the time being, he remained where he was.

Flynn, his golden hair falling in front of his face, took the knife in his left hand. With his right, he loosened his collar. He would have been very warm in his blue airman's uniform, and he clearly wasn't looking forward to using the knife. His shoulders drooping, he made a last, half-hearted appeal to the two engineers. Henshaw made a dismissive gesture with his hands as if to say it wasn't such a big deal. It was just something that had to be done. The squadron had to eat.

Flynn tried to catch one of the wary chickens, but found it difficult to do so and hang on to the knife at the same time. Henshaw swooped down, surprisingly quickly for such a big man, and grabbed a chicken. Flynn bent over beside him and switched the knife to his right hand, looking set to do the job while the bird was held still, but Henshaw indicated that Flynn needed to hold the chicken himself. He passed it over and swiftly withdrew. Royal took several steps back as well.

Flynn secured the chicken between his legs and encircled its neck with his left hand, then glanced over his shoulder for encouragement. Royal gave a vigorous nod, and as Flynn turned back to the chicken the two older men exchanged broad smiles.

Ray knew this was the moment at which he ought to step in, but still he made no move from behind the tree.

To his credit, Flynn got through the neck of the struggling chicken with a single slice and leapt back as a jet of red spurted. Liberated, the chicken's body spun, spraying the airman with arterial blood until his uniform was soaked. The recruit dropped the severed head as if it were an obscene object, which of course suddenly it was.

The butchered bird ran round in ever decreasing circles still pumping out blood. At a safe distance the two engineers laughed. Ray glared at them as he approached. He put a protective arm around the shoulders of Flynn and muttered comforting words, but the young airman, not yet out of his teens, seemed traumatised.

"Come on," said Ray. "They were just having a bit of fun." Though he didn't know why he should excuse their behaviour.

Flynn wouldn't move. The chicken's body had given up and had slumped to the sand. But it was the bird's head that transfixed Flynn. It twitched. The eye moved in its socket. A translucent film closed over the eyeball and then retracted again.

"It can still see," Flynn whispered.

"It's just a nervous spasm," Ray said.

"No, it's still conscious," said the teenager. "Look."

As they watched, the bird blinked one more time, then the eye glazed over and it finally took on the appearance of death.

Ray looked over his shoulder and saw that Henshaw and Royal were now a long way down the beach, their dark overalls shimmering in the heat haze, which caused their bodies to elongate and become thinner, while their heads became distended, like rugby balls hovering above their shoulders.

Insulated from the pain that had cut him off from England for ever, Raymond Cross prospered in the Royal Air Force, which had a small presence on Zanzibar. Prospered insofar as he seemed to find satisfying the narrow range of tasks assigned to him. He ticked boxes on checklists, got his hands dirty in the engines of the few planes that were maintained daily. They were taken up only once or twice a week, to overfly the island and to hop across to Mombasa to pick up supplies. Ray was allowed to accompany the tiny flight crew if he wasn't busy: he could be made useful loading and unloading.

In his spare time in the barracks, Ray listened to jazz records on an old gramophone the base commander had picked up on a trip to the mainland. Milt Jackson and Thelonious Monk riffed until the needle was practically worn away. No one could say where the records had come from. Some nights he got out of his head on Kulmbacher lager they had flown over from Germany. It was dropped at night, illegally, in wooden crates that burst open on the beach, scattering the ghost crabs that rattled about on the foreshore. He drank steadily—sometimes with the other men, usually on his own—and spoke to none of his comrades about his reasons for joining the RAF.

When the conditions were right—and they usually were between June and March, outside the rainy season—and Squadron Leader William Dunstan was piloting the mission, they would take a small detour before heading for the airstrip. On returning from Mombasa or a tour of the island, Billy Dunstan would take the Hercules north to Uroa, where he would swoop down over the beach and buzz the aircraftmen and flight lieutenants stationed there. Ray was soon organising his time around Dunstan's schedule, so that when the flamboyant squadron leader was in charge, Ray was invariably waiting at the airstrip to go up with the crew. Dunstan ran a pretty relaxed ship.

The men at Uroa station would hear the Hercules's grumbling approach rise above the constant susurration of the wind in the palms and run out onto the beach waving their arms. Dunstan would take the plane down as low as possible; on occasion he even lowered the landing gear and brushed the surface of the beach a few hundred yards before or after the line of men, raising huge ballooning clouds of fine white sand.

After his pass, the line of men on the beach applauding as they turned to watch, Dunstan would tilt to starboard over the ocean and climb to a few hundred feet before doubling back and flying down the coast to the base at Bwejuu. Every time, Ray would be standing hunched up in the cockpit behind Dunstan for the best view. The squadron leader enjoyed showing off; Ray's enjoyment lay in watching Dunstan's reaction as he risked going lower and lower each time, but there was more to it than that. There was another element to it for which Ray had yet to find expression.

The next day, during a break from duties, Ray saw a lone figure standing by the shoreline. He wandered over, clearing his throat once he was within earshot, and came to a halt only when he had drawn alongside. The two men looked out at the horizon. Some three hundred yards out, the reef attracted a flurry of seabirds. They hung in the air as if on elastic, a short distance above the water.

"I'm sorry I didn't get there sooner," Ray said. "In time to stop them, I mean."

Flynn shrugged. "They'd have got me another time," he said.

"Probably. No harm done, eh?"

"I was scrubbing away at my uniform for at least an hour this morning," the younger man said.

Ray felt the breeze loosen his clothes and dry the sweat on his body.

"I've heard stories," Flynn continued, "about beheadings in the Mau Mau Uprising. They used machetes. They'd cut someone's head off and the eyes would still be blinking, still watching them. What must that be like? Still being able to see."

They watched the horizon without speaking for a few moments. Ray broke the silence.

"I'm not sure you should be left alone with your thoughts."

They watched the rise and fall of the seabirds, at this distance like a cloud of midges.

"Do you leave the base much?" Ray asked.

"I go to Stone Town..."

Ray turned to look at the young airman. He was wearing fatigues and a white vest. His eyes, which didn't deviate from the view in front of him, were a startling blue. He didn't seem to want to elaborate on what he got up to in

Stone Town. Ray bent down and picked up a shell. He turned it over and ran his thumb over the ridges and grooves.

"There you go," he said, handing it to Flynn. "Don't say I never give you anything."

Ray had joined the RAF as a way of getting out of Britain in the early 1960s. His wife had died giving birth to their only child and it would have broken him if he hadn't got out. Some say it did break him anyway. Others that it just changed him. The pinched-faced moralisers among his family said it had no effect on him: he'd always only ever been in it for himself. These are the people you might have expected to have got their heads together to decide who was best placed to offer the infant a home, until such time as his father tired of the tropics. But they didn't exactly fight among themselves for that right.

Ray himself had been born into a community so tightly knit it cut off the circulation. His own domineering mother and subjugated father, all his uncles and aunts, were regular church-goers. Some gritty, northern, unforgiving denomination, it would have been, where prayer cushions would have been considered a luxury.

It wouldn't have mattered who Ray brought back to the house in Hyde as his intended, they weren't going to like her. They'd have looked down on her whatever she was, princess or pauper. Not that they had any money of their own to speak of, they didn't. But pride they had.

Perhaps Ray bore all of this in mind when he took the Levenshulme bingo caller to the Kardomah in St. Anne's Square. *Victoria.* Vic, Ray called her— his queen. She may have been only a bingo caller to the family, but Ray worshipped her. She turned up in the Cross household one blustery night in a new mini-skirt. "Legs eleven," he blurted out, ill-advisedly. "Your father and I will be in here," his mother said, frowning in disapproval and pointing to the front room; Ray's father shuffled obediently. "You can sit in t' morning room," she said to Ray.

The morning room, an antechamber to the kitchen, was dim and soulless in the morning and didn't get any lighter or warmer as the day wore on. Somehow it failed to benefit from its proximity to the kitchen. No one used it, not even his mother, despite her being temperamentally suited to its ambience.

Ray and Victoria's options were few, if they had any at all, and sticking around wasn't one of them. Ray got a job with the Post Office in Glossop, so they packed what little they had and moved out along the A57. He worked hard and earned more than enough for two, so that when the first signs of pregnancy appeared, they didn't think twice. It didn't matter that the baby hadn't been planned; it was welcome.

After the birth, Ray held the tiny baby once, for no more than a few seconds. Victoria lost so much blood, the hospital ran out of supplies. She suffered terribly for the next twelve hours, during which time Ray stayed by her side. Twice the nurses asked him if they'd thought of a name for the baby. Each time he waved them away.

When the RAF asked Ray his reasons for wanting to join up, he said he liked the uniform and had no objection to travelling, the latter being an understatement. They sent him to the island of Zanzibar, thirty miles or so off the coast of Tanganyika in East Africa. A greater contrast with east Manchester must have been hard to imagine. The family declared him heartless and cruel, swanning off to a tropical island when he should have been mourning his wife and looking after his kid. Their hypocrisy galvanised him, and he brought his departure date forward. He needed to put some distance between himself and his family in order to mourn. Five thousand miles wasn't bad going.

Ray wasn't surprised when Billy Dunstan invited the two girls to join them on a flight around the island. Joan and Frankie were English nurses working in a clinic in Zanzibar Town. Dunstan and one of his fellow officers, Flight Lieutenant Campbell, had met the pair one evening on the terrace of the Africa House Hotel where all the island's expats went to enjoy a drink and to watch the sun go down in the Indian Ocean.

On the agreed afternoon, the nurses were brought to the base at Bwejuu by an RAF auxiliary. Ray looked up from polishing his boots and saw all the men stop what they were doing as the women entered the compound. Henshaw stepped forward with a confident smirk, wiping his hands on an oily rag. The other men watched, with the exception of Flynn, whose uniform still bore one or two of the more obstinate traces of the engineers' ritual humiliation of him on the beach. The airman coloured up and looked away.

Dunstan appeared and made a swift assessment of the situation.

"Henshaw," he said, "shouldn't you be driving the supply truck up to Uroa? You'll have it dark, lad. Take Flynn with you."

Flight Lieutenant Campbell had been called away to deal with a discipline problem on Pemba Island, Dunstan explained to the two women. Because of the nurses' schedule, there wouldn't be another opportunity for a fortnight and Dunstan didn't want them to go away disappointed. Ray watched him stride out across the landing strip to the Hercules, his white silk scarf, an affectation only he had the dashing glamour to carry off, and then possibly only in Ray's opinion, flapping in the constant onshore breeze. Joan trotted behind him. Frankie stopped to fiddle with her heel and while doing so looked back at the men watching from the paved area outside the low huts. Ray, who was among those men, was struck for the first time by her resemblance to Victoria. When she smiled, it seemed directed straight at him. A nudge in the ribs from Henshaw confirmed this.

"Didn't you receive an order?" muttered Ray.

"Yes, Corporal," Henshaw replied sarcastically.

Ray looked away from Henshaw towards Flynn, who had also been watching the exchange of looks between Ray and Frankie with, it seemed to Ray, a look of hurt in his blue eyes.

"Corporal Cross," came a cry from the airstrip. "Get your flying jacket."

"Now it's your turn to be ordered about," said Henshaw. "Lucky bastard."

As Ray left to join Dunstan and the two girls, he passed close to Flynn.

"You'll get your chance, son," he said quietly.

As they taxied to the beginning of the landing strip, Ray looked out of the cockpit to see the fair head of Flynn bobbing into the supply truck alongside Henshaw.

"Hold tight, ladies," shouted Dunstan over the noise of the four engines as the plane started to rumble down the runway.

They flew across the island to Zanzibar Town. Dunstan pointed out the Arab Fort and the Anglican cathedral. Frankie spotted the clinic where she and Joan worked on the edge of Stone Town. Dunstan turned the plane gently over the harbour and flew back over the so-called New City in a south-easterly direction so that he was soon flying parallel with the irregular south-west coastline.

"Uzi Island," shouted Dunstan as he pointed to the right. The two girls leaned over the back of his seat to get the best view. Ray watched the way their hips and bellies pressed into Dunstan's shoulders. The squadron leader seemed to sit up straighter, flexing the muscles at the top of his back, as if maximising the contact between them, his hands maintaining a firm grip on the controls.

"Where's that?" asked Joan, pointing to a tiny settlement in the distance.

"Kizimkazi. Not much there. Hang on." So saying, he banked sharply to the left, unbalancing both girls, who toppled over then picked themselves up, giggling. Ray watched a twitch of pleasure in Dunstan's cheek. Frankie smiled hopefully in Ray's direction. He smiled back instinctively, but looked away somewhat awkwardly at the same time.

They crossed the southern end of the island, then kept going out to sea before turning left again and gradually describing an arc that would eventually bring the plane back over land north of Chwaka Bay. The horizon—an indistinct line between two blocks of blue—had become a tensile bow, twisted this way and that in the hands of a skilled archer: the plane itself was Dunstan's arrow. Ray watched the squadron leader's hands on the controls, a shaft of sunlight edging through the left-side window and setting the furze of reddish hairs on his forearm ablaze.

The RAF station at Uroa came into view: a couple of low-lying buildings in a small compound, a handful of motorbikes, a jeep and one truck that Ray surmised would be the supply vehicle driven there by Henshaw and Flynn. As they overflew the station, several men appeared from inside one of the huts, running out onto the beach waving their arms. Ray looked back as Dunstan took the Hercules into a steep left-hander and headed away from the island once more.

"They're moving the truck," Ray said. "They're driving it onto the beach."

"They must want to play," said Dunstan with a grin as he maintained the angle of turn.

The nurses grabbed onto the back of the pilot's seat.

"This is like going round that roundabout," said Frankie to Joan, "on the back of your Arthur's motorbike."

Dunstan looked around.

"My ex," Joan elucidated.

"What we're about to do," Dunstan yelled, "you can't do on a motorbike, no matter who's driving it. Hold on tight and don't look away."

Dunstan took the plane lower and lower. The beach was a mile away, the altitude dropping rapidly.

"Five hundred feet," Dunstan shouted. "At five hundred feet you can make out cows' legs."

"There aren't any cows," Frankie shouted back.

"That's why I'm using this," said Dunstan, tapping the altimeter with his fingernail.

Ray watched the needle drop to four hundred, three hundred and fifty, three hundred.

"Two hundred and fifty!" Dunstan roared. "Sheep's legs at two hundred and fifty. Not that there's any sheep either. We are now officially low flying, and below two hundred and fifty," he shouted as he took the rattling hull down even lower, "is classified as *very* low flying."

The ground looked a lot closer than two hundred and fifty feet to Ray, who knew that the palm trees on this side of the island grew to a height of more than thirty feet. He watched their fronds shudder in the plane's wake, then turned to face forward as the station appeared beneath them once more. The truck had been parked in the middle of the beach, the men standing in a ragged line on either side of it, raising their hands, waving at the plane. From this distance—by now, free of the palm trees, no more than fifty feet—it was easy to recognise Henshaw, and Flynn, who was jumping up and down in boyish enthusiasm. The girls whooped as the Hercules buzzed the truck, leaving clearance of no more than thirty feet. Ray turned to watch the men raise their hands to cover their faces in the resulting sandstorm.

"Fifty feet, ladies," Dunstan boasted, enjoying showing off. "We're allowed to fly this low to make free drops."

"What are free drops when they're at home?" asked Joan.

"When we want to drop stuff without parachutes. Boxes of supplies. Equipment. Whatever."

Frankie had fallen silent and was looking back at the line of men.

"What is it?" Joan asked her.

"That young one, the blond one, I'm sure I've seen him before."

"He's been in the clinic, Frankie. I saw him in the waiting room. He must have been your patient, because he wasn't mine. I'd have remembered him, if you know what I mean."

Frankie put her hand up to her mouth as she did remember.

"Oh God, yes," she said. "Such a nice boy. He was so embarrassed. I felt terribly sorry for him."

Dunstan had already started to go around again. The blue out of the left-hand side of the plane was now exclusively that of the ocean, the sky having disappeared. Ray waited to see if Frankie would say more about Flynn. She saw him watching her and fell silent.

She was similar to Victoria, but when Ray looked at her he felt nothing. Victoria was gone and the feelings he had had for her were gone also. It didn't mean they hadn't existed. But they could not be reawakened. Something in Ray had changed, even if he didn't understand the full nature of the change. He didn't doubt that he was still grieving for Victoria, but living on the island, in the company of Dunstan and the other men, was changing him. He couldn't have said what he did feel, only what he didn't.

"Can you take it any lower this time?" Joan was asking Dunstan as she leaned over the back of his seat and the line of men grew bigger in the pilot's windshield.

"What's that boy doing?" Ray muttered, as Flynn clambered on top of the cab of the supply truck that was still parked on the beach.

"Sometimes we fly as low as fifteen feet," Dunstan shouted, sweat standing out on his forehead as he clung to the controls and fought to keep the plane steady. He knew that one mistake would be fatal. If the right-hand wing tip caught the trunk of a palm tree, if the wake of the aircraft created an updraught that interfered with the rudder, control would be wrested from him in an instant, setting in motion a chain of events that would be as swift as it would be inevitable. Ray knew this and he knew that Dunstan knew it. He could sense that the two girls were beginning to realise it, as they watched, wide-eyed and white-knuckled.

The line of men was no more than a hundred yards away, the plane travelling at 140 knots.

"Be careful, sir," Ray murmured. "Watch Flynn."

The youngster was standing on the roof of the cab, stretching his arms in the air, his face ecstatic, hair swept back.

As the plane passed over him, they felt a bump. It would have felt harmless to the nurses, but Ray knew nothing is harmless in a plane of that size flying at that kind of altitude. He twisted around and looked back through the side window. He saw a figure in a blue uniform falling from the roof of the truck and something the size of a football rolling down the beach towards the sea.

"Christ!" said Ray.
One of the girls started screaming.

The golden sand, the turquoise sea. Rolling and rolling. A line of palm trees, the outermost buildings of the station. Henshaw, eyes wide, mouth hanging open. Another engineer bent double. Over and over. The golden sand, darker now, black, the sea, fringe of white foam, the vast blue sky. The black cross of the Hercules climbing steeply, banking sharply, heading out to sea. The golden sand. A body, damaged, somehow not right, lying on the sand by the supply truck. A quickly spreading pool of blood. The golden sand, line of trees, the vast empty sky, the distant plane, a line of men, men running, a body on the sand. The golden sand. Ghost crabs. A shell. Shells. The vast blue sky, line of trees. The supply truck. The golden sand. Palm trees swaying, blown by the wind. Henshaw. The golden sand again, darker, wetter. White foam, tinged pink. The blue of the sky. The body by the truck. Line of men, line of trees. The golden sand.

Margo Lanagan writes novels and short stories. Her work has won many awards, including four World Fantasy Awards (for novel, novella, short story, and collection), and been translated into many languages.

Her most recent novel is *Sea Hearts*, and her most recent collection of short stories is *Cracklescape*. She is currently collaborating with Scott Westerfeld and Deborah Biancotti on the Zeroes trilogy, Book 2 of which was published in September 2016.

Lanagan lives in Sydney.

The Goosle
Margo Lanagan

"THERE," SAID GRINNAN as we cleared the trees. "Now, you keep your counsel, Hanny-boy."

Why, that is the mudwife's house, I thought. Dread thudded in me. Since two days ago among the older trees when I knew we were in my father's forest, I'd feared this.

The house looked just as it did in my memory: the crumbling, glittery yellow walls, the dreadful roof sealed with drippy white mud. My tongue rubbed the roof of my mouth just looking. It is crisp as wafer-biscuit on the outside, that mud. You bite through to a sweetish sand inside. You are frightened it will choke you, but you cannot stop eating.

The mudwife might be dead, I thought hopefully. So many are dead, after all, of the black.

But then came a convulsion in the house. A face passed the window-hole, and there she was at the door. Same squat body with a big face snarling above. Same clothing, even, after all these years, the dress trying for bluishness and the pinafore for brown through all the dirt. She looked just as strong. However much bigger I'd grown, it took all my strength to hold my bowels together.

"Don't come a step nearer." She held a red fire-banger in her hand, but it was so dusty—if I'd not known her I'd have laughed.

"Madam, I pray you," said Grinnan. "We are clean as clean—there's not a speck on us, not a blister. Humble travellers in need only of a pig-hut or a chicken-shed to shelter the night."

"Touch my stock and I'll have you," she says to all his smoothness. "I'll roast your head in a pot."

I tugged Grinnan's sleeve. It was all too sudden—one moment walking wondering, the next on the doorstep with the witch right there, talking heads in pots.

"We have pretties to trade," said Grinnan.

"You can put your pretties up your poink-hole where they belong."

"We have all the news of long travel. Are you not at all curious about the world and its woes?"

"Why would I live here, tuffet-head?" And she went inside and slammed her door and banged the shutter across her window.

"She is softening," said Grinnan. "She is curious. She can't help herself."

"I don't think so."

"You watch me. Get us a fire going, boy. There on that bit of bare ground."

"She will come and throw her bunger in it. She'll blind us, and then—"

"Just make and shut. I tell you, this one is as good as married to me. I have her heart in my hand like a rabbit-kitten."

I was sure he was mistaken, but I went to, because fire meant food and just the sight of the house had made me hungry. While I fed the fire its kindling I dug up a little stone from the flattened ground and sucked the dirt off it.

Grinnan had me make a smelly soup. Salt-fish, it had in it, and sea-celery and the yellow spice.

When the smell was strong, the door whumped open and there she was again. Ooh, she was so like in my dreams, with her suddenness and her ugly intentions that you can't guess. But it was me and Grinnan this time, not me and Kirtle. Grinnan was big and smart, and he had his own purposes. And I knew there was no magic in the world, just trickery on the innocent. Grinnan would never let anyone else trick me; he wanted that privilege all for himself.

"Take your smelly smells from my garden this instant!" the mudwife shouted.

Grinnan bowed as if she'd greeted him most civilly. "Madam, if you'd join us? There is plenty of this lovely bull-a-bess for you as well."

"I'd not touch my lips to such mess. What kind of foreign muck—"

Even I could hear the longing in her voice, that she was trying to shout down.

There before her he ladled out a bowlful—yellow, splashy, full of delicious lumps. Very humbly—he does humbleness well when he needs to, for such a big man—he took it to her. When she recoiled he placed it on the little table by the door, the one that I ran against in my clumsiness when escaping, so hard I still sometimes feel the bruise in my rib. I remember, I knocked it skittering out the door, and I flung it back meaning to trip up the mudwife.

But instead I tripped up Kirtle, and the wife came out and plucked her up and bellowed after me and kicked the table onto the path, and ran out herself with Kirtle like a tortoise swimming from her fist and kicked the table aside again—

Bang! went the cottage door.

Grinnan came laughing quietly back to me.

"She is ours. Once they've et your food, Hanny, you're free to eat theirs. Fish and onion pie tonight, I'd say."

"Eugh."

"Jealous, are we? Don't like old Grinnan supping at other pots, hnh?"

"It's *not* that!" I glared at his laughing face. "She's so ugly, that's all. So old. I don't know how you can even think of—"

"Well, I am no primrose myself, golden boy," he says. "And I'm grateful for any flower that lets me pluck her."

I was not old and desperate enough to laugh at that joke. I pushed his soup-bowl at him.

"Ah, bull-a-bess," he said into the steam. "Food of gods and seducers."

When the mudwife let us in, I looked straight to the corner, and the cage *was still there*! It had been repaired in places with fresh plaited withes, but it was still of the same pattern. Now there was an animal in it, but the cottage was so dim…a very thin cat, maybe, or a ferret. It rippled slowly around its borders, and flashed little eyes at us, and smelled as if its own piss were combed through its fur for pomade. I never smelled that bad when I lived in that cage. I ate well, I remember; I fattened. She took away my leavings in a little cup, on a little dish, but there was still plenty of me left.

So that when Kirtle freed me I *lumbered* away. As soon as I was out of sight of the mud-house I stopped in the forest and just stood there blowing from the effort of propelling myself, after all those weeks of sloth.

So that Grinnan when he first saw me said, *Here's a jubbly one. Here's a cheese cake. Wherever did you get the makings of those round cheeks?* And he fell on me like a starving man on a roasted mutton-leg. Before too long he had used me thin again, and thin I stayed thereafter.

He was busy at work on the mudwife now.

"Oh my, what an array of herbs! You must be a very knowledgeable woman. And hasn't she a lot of pots, Hansel! A pot for every occasion, I think."

Oh yes, I nearly said, *including head-boiling, remember?*

"Well, you are very comfortably set up here, indeed, madam." He looked about him as if he's found himself inside some kind of enchanted palace, instead of in a stinking hovel with a witch in the middle of it. "Now, I'm sure you told me your name—"

"I did not. My name's not for such as you to know." Her mouth was all pruny and she strutted around and banged things and shot him sharp looks, but I'd seen it. We were in here, weren't we? We'd made it this far.

"Ah, a guessing game!" says Grinnan delightedly. "Now, you'd have a good strong name, I'm sure. Bridda, maybe, or Gert. Or else something fiery and passionate, such as Rossavita, eh?"

He can afford to play her awhile. If the worst comes to the worst, he has the liquor, after all. The liquor has worked on me when nothing else would, when I've been ready to run, to some town's wilds where I could hide—to such as that farm-wife with the worried face who beat off Grinnan with a broom. The liquor had softened me and made me sleepy, made me give in to the old bugger's blandishments; next day it had stopped me thinking with its head-pain, further than to obey Grinnan's grunts and gestures.

How does yours like it? said Gadfly's red-haired boy viciously. *I've heard him call you "honey," like a girl-wife; does he do you like a girl, face to face and lots of kissing? Like your boy-bits, which they is so small, ain't even there, so squashed and ground in?*

He calls me Hanny, because Hanny is my name. Hansel.

Honey is your name, eh? said the black boy—a boy of black skin from naturalness, not illness. *After your honey hair?*

Which they commenced patting and pulling and then held me down and chopped all away with Gadfly's good knife. When Grinnan saw me he went pale, but I'm pretty sure he was trying to cut some kind of deal with Gadfly to swap me for the red-hair (with the *skin like milk, like freckled milk,* he said), so the only thing it changed, he did not come after me for several nights until the hair had settled and I did not give off such an air of humiliation.

Then he whispered, *You were quite handsome under that thatch, weren't you? All along.* And things were bad as ever, and the next day he tidied off the stragglier strands, as I sat on a stump with my poink-hole thumping and the other boys idled this way and that, watching, warping their faces at each other and snorting.

The first time Grinnan did me, I could imagine that it didn't happen. I thought, I had that big dump full of so much nervous earth and stones and some of them must have had sharp corners and cut me as I passed them, and the throbbing of the cuts gave me the dream, that the old man had done that to me. Because I was so fearful, you know, frightened of everything coming straight from the mudwife, and I put fear and pain together and made it up in my sleep. The first time I could trick myself, because it was so terrible and mortifying a thing, it could not be real. It could not.

I have watched Grinnan a long time now, in success and failure, in private and on show. At first I thought he was too smart for me, that I was trapped by his cleverness. And this is true. But I have seen others laugh at him, or walk away from his efforts easily, shaking their heads. Others are cleverer.

What he does to me, he waits till I am weak. Half-asleep, he waits till. I never have much fight in me, but dozing off I have even less.

Then what he does—it's so simple I'm ashamed. He bares the flesh of my back. He strokes my back as if that is all he is going to do. He goes straight to the very oldest memory I have—which, me never having told him, how does he know it?—of being sickly, of my first mother bringing me through the night, singing and stroking my back, the oldest and safest piece of my mind, and he puts me there, so that I am sodden with sweetness and longing and nearly-being-back-to-a-baby.

And then he proceeds. It often hurts—it *mostly* hurts. I often weep. But there is a kind of bargain goes on between us, you see. I pay for the first part with the second. The price of the journey to that safe, sweet-sodden place is being spiked in the arse and dragged kicking and biting my blanket back to the real and dangerous one.

Show me your boy-thing, the mudwife would say. *Put it through the bars.*

I won't.

Why not?

You will bite it off. You will cut it off with one of your knives. You will chop it with your axe.

Put it out. I will do no such thing. I only want to wash it.

Wash it when Kirtle is awake, if you so want me clean.

It will be nice, I promise you. I will give you a nice feeling, so warm, so wet. You'll feel good.

But when I put it out, she exclaimed, *What am I supposed to do with that?*

Wash it, like you said.

There's not enough of it even to wash! How would one get that little peepette dirty?

I put it away, little shred, little scrap I was ashamed of.

And she flung around the room awhile, and then she sat, her face all red crags in the last little light of the banked-up fire. *I am going to have to keep you forever!* she said. *For* years *before you are any use to me. And you are expensive! You eat like a pig! I should just cook you up now and enjoy you while you are tender.*

I was all wounded pride and stupid. I didn't know what she was talking about. *I can do anything my sister can do, if you just let me out of this cage. And I'm a better wood-chopper.*

Wood-chopper! she said disgustedly. *As if I needed a wood-chopper!* And she went to the door and took the axe off the wall there, and tested the edge with one of her horny fingertips, and looked at me in a very *thoughtful* way that I did not much like.

Sometimes he speaks as he strokes. *My Hanny,* he says, very gentle and loving like my mother, *my goosle, my gosling, sweet as apple, salt as sea.* And it feels as if we are united in yearning for my mother and her touch and voice.

She cannot have gone forever, can she, if I can remember this feeling so clearly? But, ah, to get back to her, so much would have to be undone! So much would have to un-happen: all of Grinnan's and my wanderings, all the witch-time, all the time of our second mother. That last night of our first mother, our real mother, and her awful writhing and the noises and our father begging, and Kirtle weeping and needing to be taken away—that would have to become a nightmare, from which my father would shake me awake with the news that the baby came out just as Kirtle and I did, just as easily. And our mother would rise from her bed with the baby; we would all rise into the baby's first morning, and begin.

It is very deep in the night. I have done my best to be invisible, to make no noise, but now the mudwife pants, *He's not asleep.*

Of course he's asleep. Listen to his breathing.

I do the asleep-breathing.

Come, says Grinnan. *I've done with these, bounteous as they are. I want to go below.* He has his ardent voice on now. He makes you think he is barely in control of himself, and somehow that makes you, somehow that flatters you enough to let him do what he wants.

After some uffing and puffing, *No,* she says, very firm, and there's a slap. *I want that boy out of here.*

What, wake him so he can go and listen at the window?

Get him out, she says. *Send him beyond the pigs and tell him to stay.*

You're a nuisance, he says. *You're a sexy nuisance. Look at this! I'm all misshapen and you want me herding children.*

You do it, she says, rearranging her clothing, *or you'll stay that shape.*

So he comes to me and I affect to be woken up and to resist being hauled out the door, but really it's a relief of course. I don't want to hear or see or know. None of that stuff I understand, why people want to sweat and pant and poke bits of themselves into each other, why anyone would want to do more than hold each other for comfort and stroke each other's back.

Moonlight. Pigs like slabs of moon, like long, fat fruit fallen off a moonvine. The trees tall and brainy all around and above—*they* never sweat and pork; the most they do is sway in a breeze, or crash to the ground to make useful wood. The damp smell of night forest. My friends in the firmament, telling me where I am: two and a half days north of the ford with the knotty rope; four and a half days north and a bit west of "Devilstown," which Grinnan called it because someone made off in the night with all the spoils *we'd* made off with the night before.

I'd thought we were the only ones not black in their beds! he'd stormed on the road.

They must have come very quiet, I said. *They must have been accomplished thieves.*

They must have been sprites or devils, he spat, *that I didn't hear them, with my ears.*

We were seven and a half days north and very very west of Gadfly's camp, where we had, as Grinnan put it, *tried the cooperative life for a while.* But those boys, *they were a gang of no-goods,* Grinnan says now. Whatever deal he had tried to make for Freckled-Milk, they laughed him off, and Grinnan could not stand it there having been laughed at. He took me away before dawn one morning, and when we stopped by a stream in the first light he showed me the brass candlesticks that Gadfly had kept in a sack and been so proud of.

And what'll you use those for? I said foolishly, for we had managed up until then with moon and stars and our own wee fire.

I did not take them to use them, Hanny-pot, he said with glee. *I took them because he loved and polished them so.* And he flung them into the stream, and I gasped—and Grinnan laughed to hear me gasp—at the sight of them cutting through the foam and then gone into the dark cold irretrievable.

Anyway, it was new for me still, there beyond the mudwife's pigs, this knowing where we were—though I had lost count of the days since Ardblarthen when it had come to me how Grinnan looked *up* to find his way, not down among a million tree-roots that all looked the same, among twenty million grass-stalks, among twenty million million stones or sand-grains. It was even newer how the star-pattern and the moon movements had steadied out of their meaningless whirling and begun to tell me whereabouts I was in the wide world. All my life I had been stupid, trying to mark the things around me on the ground, leaving myself trails to get home by because every tree looked the same to me, every knoll and declivity, when all the time the directions were hammered hard into their system up there, pointing and changing-but-never-completely-changing.

So if we came at the cottage from this angle, whereas Kirtle and I came from the front, that means...but Kirtle and I wandered so many days, didn't we? I filled my stomach with earths, but Kirtle was piteous weeping all the way, so hungry. She would not touch the earth; she watched me eating it and wept. I remember, I told her, *No wonder you are thirsty! Look how much water you're wasting on those tears!* She had brown hair, I remember. I remember her pushing it out of her eyes so that she could see to sweep in the dark cottage—the cottage where the mudwife's voice is rising, like a saw through wood.

The house stands glittering and the sound comes out of it. My mouth waters; they wouldn't hear me over that noise, would they?

I creep in past the pigs to where the blobby roof-edge comes low. I break off a blob bigger than my hand; the wooden shingle it was holding slides off, and my other hand catches it soundlessly and leans it against the house.

The mudwife howls; something is knocked over in there; she howls again and Grinnan is grunting with the effort of something. I run away from all those noises, the white mud in my hand like a hunk of cake. I run back to the trees where Grinnan told me to stay, where the woman's howls are like mouse-squeaks and I can't hear Grinnan, and I sit between two high roots and I bite in.

Once I've eaten the mud I'm ready to sleep. I try dozing, but it's not comfortable among the roots there, and there is still noise from the cottage—now it is Grinnan working himself up, calling her all the things he calls me, all the insults. *You love it,* he says, with such deep disgust. *You filth, you filthy cunt.* And she *oh*'s below, not at all like me, but as if she really does love it. I lie quiet, thinking, Is it true, that she loves it? That I do? And if it's true, how is it that Grinnan knows, but I don't? She makes noise, she agrees with whatever he says. *Harder, harder,* she says. *Bang me till I burst. Harder!* On and on they go, until I give up waiting—they will never finish!

I get up and go around the pigsty and behind the chicken house. There is a poor field there, pumpkins gone wild in it, blackberry bushes foaming dark around the edges. At least the earth might be softer here. If I pile up enough of this floppy vine, if I gather enough pumpkins around me—

And then I am holding, not a pale baby pumpkin in my hand but a pale baby skull.

Grinnan and the mudwife bellow together in the house, and something else crashes broken.

The skull is the colour of white-mud, but hard, inedible—although when I turn it in the moonlight I find tooth-marks where someone has tried.

The shouts go up high—the witch's loud, Grinnan's whimpering.

I grab up a handful of earth to eat, but a bone comes with it, long, white, dry. I let the earth fall away from it.

I crouch there looking at the skull and the bone, as those two finish themselves off in the cottage.

They will sleep now—but I'm not sleepy any more. The stars in their map are nailed to the inside of my skull; my head is filled with dark clarity. When I am sure they are asleep, I scoop up a mouthful of earth, and start digging.

Let me go and get the mudwife, our father murmured. *Just for this once.*

I've done it twice and I'll do it again. Don't you bring that woman here! Our mother's voice was all constricted, as if the baby were trying to come up her throat, not out her nethers.

But this is not like the others! he said, desperate after the following pain. *They say she knows all about children. Delivers them all the time.*

Delivers them? She eats them! said our mother. *It's not just this one. I've two others might catch her eye, while I feed and doze. I'd rather die than have her near my house, that filthy hag.*

So die she did, and our new brother or sister died as well, still inside her. We didn't know whichever it was. *Will it be another little Kirtle-child?* our father had asked us, bright-eyed by the fire at night. *Or another baby woodcutter, like our Hans?* It had seemed so important to know. Even when the baby was dead, I wanted to know.

But the whole reason! our father sobbed. *Is that it could not come out, for us to see!* Which had shamed me quiet.

And then later, going into blackened towns where the only way you could tell man from woman was by the style of a cap, or a hair-ribbon draggling into the dirt beneath them, or a rotted pinafore, or worst by the amount of shrunken scrag between an unclothed person's legs—why, then I could see how small a thing it was not to know the little one's sex. I could see that it was not important at all.

When I wake up, they are at it again with their sexing. My teeth are stuck to the inside of my cheeks and lips by two ridges of earth. I have to break the dirt away with my finger.

What was I thinking, last night? I sit up. The bones are in a pile beside me; the skulls are in a separate pile—for counting, I remember. What I thought was: Where did she *find* all these children? Kirtle and I walked for days, I'm sure. There was nothing in the world but trees and owls and foxes and that one deer. Kirtle was afraid of bats at night, but I never saw even one. And we never saw people—which was what we were looking for, which was why we were so unwise when we came upon the mudwife's house.

But what am I going to do? What was I planning, piling these up? I thought I was only looking for all Kirtle's bits. But then another skull turned up and I thought, Well, maybe this one is more Kirtle's size, and then skull after skull—I dug on, crunching earth and drooling and breathing through my nose, and the bones seemed to rise out of the earth at me, seeking out the moon the way a tree reaches for the light, pushing up thinly among the other trees until it finds light enough to spread into, seeking out *me*, as if they were thinking, Here, finally, is someone who can do something for us.

I pick up the nearest skull. Which of these is my sister's? Even if there were just a way to tell girls' skulls from boys'! Is hers even here? Maybe she's still buried, under the blackberries where I couldn't go for thorns.

Now I have a skull in either hand, like someone at a market weighing one cabbage against another. And the thought comes to me: Something is different. Listen.

The pigs. The mudwife, her noises very like the pigs'. There is no rhythm to them; they are random grunting and gasping. And I—

Silently I replace the skulls on the pile.

I haven't heard Grinnan this morning. Not a word, not a groan. Just the woman. The woman and the pigs.

The sunshine shows the cottage as the hovel it is, its saggy sides propped, its sloppy roofing patched with mud-splats simply thrown from the ground. The back door stands wide, and I creep up and stand right next to it, my back to the wall.

Wet slaps and stirrings sound inside. The mudwife grunts—she sounds muffled, desperate. Has he tied her up? Is he strangling her? There's not a gasp or word from him. That *thing* in the cage gives off a noise, though, a kind of low baying. It never stops to breathe. There is a strong smell of shit. Dawn is warming everything up; flies zoom in and out the doorway.

I press myself to the wall. There is a dip in the doorstep. Were I brave enough to walk in, that's where I would put my foot. And right at that place appears a drop of blood, running from inside. It slides into the dip, pauses modestly at being seen, then shyly hurries across the step and dives into hiding in the weeds below.

How long do I stand there, looking out over the pigsty and the chicken house to the forest, wishing I were there among the trees instead of here clamped to the house wall like one of those gargoyles on the monks' house in Devilstown, with each sound opening a new pocket of fear in my bowels? A fly flies into my gaping mouth and out again. A pebble in the wall digs a little chink in the back of my head, I'm pressed so hard there.

Finally, I have to know. I have to take one look before I run, otherwise I'll dream all the possibilities for nights to come. She's not a witch; she can't spell me back; I'm thin now and nimble; I can easily get away from her.

So I loosen my head, and the rest of me, from the wall. I bend one knee and straighten the other, pushing my big head, my popping eyes, around the doorpost.

I only meant to glimpse and run. So ready am I for the running, I tip outward even when I see there's no need. I put out my foot to catch myself, and I stare.

She has her back to me, her bare, dirty white back, her baggy arse and thighs. If she weren't doing what she's doing, that would be horror enough, how everything is wet and withered and hung with hair, how everything shakes.

Grinnan is dead on the table. She has opened his legs wide and eaten a hole in him, in through his soft parts. She has pulled all his innards out onto the floor, and her bare bloody feet are trampling the shit out of them, her bare shaking legs are trying to brace themselves on the slippery carpet of them. I can smell the salt-fish in the shit; I can smell the yellow spice.

That devilish moan, up and down it wavers, somewhere between purr and battle-yowl. I thought it was me, but it's that shadow in the cage, curling over and over itself like a ruffle of black water, its eyes fixed on the mess, hungry, hungry.

The witch pulls her head out of Grinnan for air. Her head and shoulders are shiny red; her soaked hair drips; her purple-brown nipples point down into two hanging rubies. She snatches some air between her red teeth and plunges in again, her head inside Grinnan like the bulge of a dead baby, but higher, forcing higher, pummelling up inside him, *fighting* to be un-born.

In my travels I have seen many wrongnesses done, and heard many others told of with laughter or with awe around a fire. I have come upon horrors of all kinds, for these are horrible times. But never has a thing been laid out so obvious and ongoing in its evil before my eyes and under my nose and with the flies feasting even as it happens. And never has the means to end it hung as clearly in front of me as it hangs now, on the wall, in the smile of the mud-wife's axe-edge, fine as the finest nail-paring, bright as the dawn sky, the only clean thing in this foul cottage.

I reach my father's house late in the afternoon. How I knew the way, when years ago you could put me twenty paces into the trees and I'd wander lost all day, I don't know; it just came to me. All the loops I took, all the mistakes I made, all laid themselves down in their places on the world, and I took the right way past them and came here straight, one sack on my back, the other in my arms.

When I dreamed of this house it was big and full of comforts; it hummed with safety; the spirit of my mother lit it from inside like a sacred candle. Kirtle was always here, running out to greet me all delight.

Now I can see the poor place for what it is, a plague-ruin like so many that Grinnan and I have found and plundered. And tiny—not even as big as the witch's cottage. It sits in its weedy quiet and the forest chirps around it. The only thing remarkable about it is that I am the first here; no one has touched the place. I note it on my star map—there *is* safety here, the safety of a distance greater than most robbers will venture.

A blackened boy-child sits on the step, his head against the doorpost as if only very tired. Inside, a second child lies in a cradle. My father and second-mother are in their bed, side by side just like that lord and lady on the stone tomb in Ardblarthen, only not so neatly carved or richly dressed. Everything else is exactly the same as Kirtle and I left it. So sparse and spare! There is nothing of value here. Grinnan would be angry. *Burn these bodies and beds, boy!* he'd say. *We'll take their rotten roof if that's all they have.*

"But Grinnan is not here, is he?" I say to the boy on the step, carrying the mattock out past him. "Grinnan is in the ground with his lady-love, under the pumpkins. And with a great big pumpkin inside him, too. And Mrs. Pumpkin-Head in his arms, so that they can sex there underground forever."

I take a stick and mark out the graves: Father, Second-Mother, Brother, Sister—and a last big one for the two sacks of Kirtle-bones. There's plenty of time before sundown, and the moon is bright these nights, don't I know it. I can work all night if I have to; I am strong enough, and full enough still of disgust. I will dig and dig until this is done.

I tear off my shirt.

I spit in my hands and rub them together.

The mattock bites into the earth.

Steve Duffy's work has appeared in numerous magazines and anthologies in Europe and North America, and has been collected in four books of short stories. His most recent collection of weird fiction, *The Moment of Panic*, was published in 2013 and includes the International Horror Guild Award–winning short story "The Rag-and-Bone Men."

Duffy lives in North Wales.

The Clay Party
Steve Duffy

FROM THE *Sacramento Citizen-Journal*, NOVEMBER 27, 1846
Disquieting news reaches the offices of the *Citizen-Journal* from our corre-
spondent at Sutter's Fort, where the arrival of a party of settlers embarked on
an untried and hazardous new crossing has been anxiously expected since the
beginning of the month. November having very nearly elapsed with no word
of these prospective Californians as yet received, it is feared by all that their
party is become stranded in the high passes with the onset of winter. There is
a general agreement among mountain men and seasoned wagoneers alike that
the route believed travelled by these unfortunate pilgrims is both unorthodox
and perilous in the extreme, it being the handiwork of a Mr. Jefferson Clay
of New Hampshire, a stranger to these parts with no reputation as a pioneer
or a capable navigator. We hear anxious talk of a rescue party being recruited,
once the worst of the snow has passed…

►─≫•❖•≪─◄

FROM *The Diary of John Buell*, 1846
May 17th, Independence, Missouri: Embarkation day. At last! Set out at nine
sharp with our fellow Californians—for so we shall be entitled to call ourselves, in but a little while. A great clamour of oxen and horses along Main
Street, and the most uproarious cheering from all the townsfolk as they bid us
farewell. It is sad to reflect that among these friendly multitudes there should
be faces—dear faces, friends and relatives among them—that we shall never
see again; and yet the prospect of that providential land in the West recalls us
to our higher purpose, and strengthens us in our resolve. We carry the torch
of Progress, as our mentor Mr. Clay has written, and it is most fitting that he
should be at the head of our party as we depart. We are forty-eight in number:

seven families, a dozen single men, our great wagons pulled by sturdy oxen. Surely nothing can stop us.

Elizabeth concerned at the possible effects of the crossing on little Mary-Kate; also, that the general health of her mother is not all it might be. Again I remind her that the balmy air of California can only strengthen the old lady's general constitution, and that no other place on God's earth affords such opportunities for our daughter and ourselves. This she accepts, and we are fairly bound on our way. So it's "three cheers for Jeff Clay, boys," as the wagoneers sang out at our departure—and onwards into the West. Lord, guide us in this great undertaking!

May 26th: The plains. An infinite expanse of grassy prairie, profoundly still and empty. Surely God created no more unfrequented space among all His mighty works. Thunder in the nights, and storms away off on the horizon. Mud along the trail, thick and treacherous, so that we must double-team the oxen on the inclines. The rate of our advance is measured, yet perfectly steady. If only there were some sign by which we could mark our progress! I long for mountains, such as we knew back home in Vermont. Elizabeth's mother no better; she eats but little, and is silent as these endless brooding plains. Mary-Kate in excellent health, thank God.

May 31st: The Big Blue, and our first real reverse. River swollen with much rain: unfordable. We are obliged to construct a temporary ferry. It will take time.

June 3rd: On our way again. It was the Lord's own struggle crossing the Big Blue, and we were fortunate not to lose more than a couple of our oxen, but now at least we have an opportunity to make up for lost time. Mrs. Stocklasa now very weak, though generally quiet and uncomplaining. Elizabeth says little, except to cheer me up with her words of tender encouragement, but I know her every waking hour is filled with anxiety for her ailing mama. Perhaps at Fort Laramie we shall find a doctor.

June 16th: Laborious progress up the Platte; mud still obliging us to double-team on the slightest incline. Found Elizabeth outside the wagon this evening after settling Mary-Kate for the night, weeping freely and most bitterly. She fears her mother's mortal crisis is approaching. God grant it may not be so. Throughout the night she watches over her, soothing her when she wakes, speaking to her in that strange language of her homeland. It gives the old lady much comfort—which may be all that we have left to give her.

June 18th: With a heavy heart I must record the most sorrowful of all tidings: Elizabeth's mother died around sunset yesterday. The entire party much distressed and brought low by this melancholy event. We dug her grave at a pretty spot on a little knoll overlooking the valley, with up ahead the still-distant prospect of mountains. Would that she had been destined to stand on their peaks with us, and gain a Pisgah view of the promised land! The Lord giveth and the Lord taketh away. One of the wagoneers has inscribed with hot-iron a simple wooden marker for her grave: *JULIA STOCKLASA—Born 1774, Wallachia, Died 1846, Missouri Territory, bound for California—Tarrying here awhile.* It is a curious thing to come across in such a lonely place, the humble marker atop its little cairn of rocks; and a sad enough sight for we who mourn, to be sure. But may it not be the case that for those Westerners yet to pass along this trail, it will speak, however haltingly, of home and God and goodness, and may even serve as a first, albeit melancholy sign of civilisation in this great American wilderness? It is hard to envisage this now, as the wolves cry out in the night-time, and Elizabeth starts into wakefulness once more, her features drawn and thin, her eyes reddened with much sorrow. But it may be so.

June 30th: Fort Laramie, at the foothills of the mountains. Revictualling and recuperating after our grim passage across the plains, for which we paid with much hardship and great sorrow.

July 4th: Celebrations in the evening, sky-rockets and dancing to fiddle music; all marred somewhat by an altercation between our leader Jefferson Clay and certain of the mountain men. These rough-hewn, barbarous individuals are much in evidence at the fort, paying homage to the independence of our fair Republic by drinking strong whiskey till they can barely stand. Some of these fine fellows engaged Mr. Clay in conversation, in the course of which he showed them the maps laid out in his booklet *California, Fair Garden of the West.* Herein lay the roots of the discord. The mountain men would not concede that his route—a bold and imaginative navigation of the Great Salt Desert and the mountain passes beyond—represents the future of our nation's westward migration. Harsh words were exchanged, till Mr. Clay suffered himself to be led away from the scene of the quarrel. I was among those who helped remove him, and I recall in particular his strong patrician countenance flushed with rage, as he shouted at the top of his voice—"It's the nigher way, I tell you! The nigher way!"

July 5th: On our way again. We were happy enough to arrive at Fort Laramie, but I guess we shall not miss it overmuch.

July 12th: Another black day for our party: Mrs. Hiderick dead of a fit in the night. Hiderick, a silent black-browed German-Pennsylvanian, buried her himself before sunup.

July 20th: Hard going. Storms bedevil us still, and we are pretty well accustomed now to our night-time serenades of rolling thunder and the howling of far-off coyotes and wolves. Even Mary-Kate does not stir from her childish slumbers. On nights when the storms are at their worst, the oxen stampede, half-mad from the thunder and the lightning. Regrouped only with much labour. And then the endless sage, and the all-enveloping solitude of the plains. The passage through to California must indeed be a great prize, to be gained at such a cost.

July 25th: The Continental Divide, or so we reckon. From here on in, Oregon country. A thousand miles out, a thousand still to go, says Mr. Clay. It is comforting to know that the greater part of our endeavours are now over. I say this to Elizabeth, who I know is grieving still for her beloved mama, and she agrees with me.

July 27th: A curious conversation with Elizabeth, late last night. She asked me if there was anything I would not do to protect our family. Of course I said there was nothing—that her safety, and the safety of our beloved daughter, must always be foremost in my mind, and if any action of mine could guarantee such an outcome, then I would not hold back from it for an instant. She said she knew it, and rallied a little from her gloom; or tried to. What can all this mean? She pines for her mother, of course; and fears what lies ahead. I must seek to reassure her.

July 28th: The Little Sandy River. Here we arrive at the great parting of the ways; while the other wagon trains follow the deep ruts of the regular Oregon trail to our right, heading north, we shall strike out south along Mr. Clay's cut-off. A general air of excitement throughout the company. Even Elizabeth rallies somewhat from her melancholy reveries.

July 31st: Fort Jim Bridger. Supplies and rest. Elizabeth and Mary-Kate the subject of some wonderment among the bachelor gentlemen of the fort, when taking the air outside the wagon this morning. It is quite comical to see such grizzled individuals turn as silent and bashful as a stripling lad at his first dance. Such is the effect of my schoolteacher lady, and our little angel!

August 2nd: Bad feeling again in the fort. Cagie Bowden came to our wagon this morning, with news that Mr. Clay was once more in dispute with the mountain men last night. Bowden says that together with Mr. Doerr & Mr. Shorstein he was obliged to remove Mr. Clay from the proceedings; also, that in their opinion he was every bit as drunk as the mountain men. Let us not tarry overlong in this place.

August 3rd: On our way once more, along the cut-off. Thus we reckon to save upwards of three-hundred and fifty miles, and should reach Sutter's Fort within six or seven weeks.

August 9th: Ten, fifteen miles a day, when we had reckoned on twenty. Reasonable progress, still we must not fall behind our schedule. Difficult terrain ahead.

August 17th: A wilderness of canyons. Impassable except by much labour. Entire days wasted in backing out of dead-ends and searching for another route. We are falling behind, and the seasons will not wait. Mr. Clay delivered the harshest of rebukes to Cagie Bowden for suggesting we turn back to Fort Jim Bridger and the northern trail. (And yet it is only what some of the others are saying.) Too late now in any case.

August 23rd: Lost for the last six days. Only this morning, when Mr. Doerr climbed a tall peak and scouted out a surer way, were we freed at last from the hell of the canyons. Much time lost here. Mr. Clay is now generally unapproachable except by a very few. He will not suffer the Bowdens to come nigh him. It is regrettable.

August 27th: Into the trackless wastes along the Wasatch. Two and three miles' progress in a day. Aspen and cottonwoods choking up the canyons; cleared only with superhuman effort. Weary to my very bones. Elizabeth tells me not to over-exert myself, but there is no choice. I brought my wife & baby daughter into this place, and now they must always be at the forefront of my thoughts. We *must not* be caught here in the wilderness when winter comes.

August 29th: Some of the other families have proposed that we abandon the larger wagons, which they believe cannot be driven through this mountainous territory. They called a meeting tonight, at which Mr. Clay overruled them, assuring the party that we have passed through the worst of the broken land, and speaking passionately of the ease and speed with which our passage shall be completed once we leave behind the canyon country. Cagie Bowden pressed him on the details, upon which he became much agitated, and attempted to expel the Bowden wagon from the party. On this he was overruled, by a clear majority of the settlers. He retired with much bitterness to his wagon, as did we all. A general air of foreboding over all the party.

August 30th: Seven of the single men missing this morning; gone with their horses. The party is fractured clean down the middle. No one looks up from his labours save with a grave and troubled face. Double-teaming all day. Elizabeth urges me to rest tonight, and cease from writing. God grant we shall one day read these words, settled safe in California, and wonder at the tribulations of the passage across.

September 1st: Out of the canyons at last! and on to the low hilly land above the salt flats. Six hundred miles from our destination. A chance to recoup lost time, and fresh springs in abundance. Charley and Josephus, the Indian guides we engaged at Fort Bridger, went from wagon to wagon warning us to take on board all the water we might carry, and to hoard it well—no good springs, they said, for many days' march ahead. On hearing of this Mr. Clay had the men brought to him, and cursed them for a pair of craven panic-mongers and Godless savages. Hiderick was for lashing them to a wagon-wheel and whipping them—restrained with some difficulty by the rest of us men. Heaven help us all.

September 2nd: A note found stuck to the prickerbushes by the side of the trail, by the Indian Charley scouting ahead. He brought it to me at the head of the wagon train, and with some difficulty Bowden and I pieced it together. We believe it to be the work of several of the single men who cleared out last week—it tells of hard going up ahead, and warns us to turn back and make for Fort Bridger while we have the chance. I was for keeping it from Jefferson Clay till we had spoken to the other families, but nothing would do for Bowden but to force the issue. Once more Clay and Bowden wound up at each other's throats, and were separated only by the combined exertions of all present. An ill omen hangs over this party. Ahead lies the desert. Into His hands we commend our spirits, who brought His chosen ones through forty years of wandering to the promised land.

September 3rd: Slow passage across the face of the great salt desert. Hard-baked crust over limitless salty mud, bubbling up to the surface through the ruts left by our wagon wheels. The wagons sink through to above the wheel-hubs, and the going is most laborious. Again we fall behind, and the season grows late.

September 4th: Endless desolation—no safe land—no fresh water. This is a hellish place.

September 5th: Disaster in the night. The oxen, mad with thirst, stampeded in the night; all but a handful lost out on the salt pans. Four of the wagons have been abandoned, and the families must carry what they can. All have taken on board as much as they can carry, and the overloaded wagons sink axle-deep into the mud. Surely God has not set his face against us?

September 7th: Passage still devilish slow; no sign of an end to the desert. Bitter cold in the night-time—we huddle with the dogs for warmth, like beasts in the wilderness. Little Mary-Kate screams in disgust at the bitter salt taste that fills her pretty rosebud mouth. Vainly she tries to spit it out, as her mother comforts her. Would that I could rid my own mouth of the bitter taste of defeat. ~~I have led them into this hell~~ [*remainder of sentence erased—Ed.*]

September 9th: Off the salt pans at last. Oxen lost, wagons abandoned, and no prospect of a safe retreat to Fort Bridger. To go back now would surely finish us off. In any case, the provisions would not last—Bowden says they will barely serve for the passage through the mountains. He is for confronting Clay, once and for all, and holding a popular vote to determine who should lead the party from here on into California. I counsel him to wait till our strength is somewhat recouped. None of us have the belly for such a confrontation at present.

September 13th: Ahead in the distance, the foothills of the Sierras. White snow on the hilltops. Dear God, that it should come to this.

September 20th: No slackening in our progress, no rest for any man; but we are slow, we are devilish slow. Without the oxen and the wagons we lost out on the salt pans, our progress is impeded mightily, and much effort is expended in the securing of provisions. Clay now wholly removed from the rest of the party; like a general he rides alone at the head of the column, seeing nothing but the far horizon while all around him his troops suffer, close to mutiny. Around our wagons each night, the howling of wolves.

September 23rd: Desperation in the camp, which can no longer be hidden. The remaining single men have volunteered to ride on ahead, that they might alert the Californian authorities to our plight; they set out this morning. All our chances of success in this forlorn undertaking ride with them.

October 2nd: The Humboldt River. According to Charley the Indian guide, we are now rejoined with the main trail, and done at last with Clay's damned cut-off. No sign of any other parties along the banks of the river. It is late in the season—they will be safe across the mountains and in California now. A note from the men riding on ahead was discovered on the side of the trail, and brought straight to Clay. He will not disclose its contents. I am persuaded at last that the time has come to follow Bowden's counsel, and force a reckoning.

October 3rd: A catastrophe. The thing I most feared has come to pass. Last night Cagie Bowden led a deputation of the men to Clay's wagon and demanded he produce the note. Clay refused, and upon Bowden's pressing him, drew a pistol and shot him through the chest. Instantly Clay was seized by the men, while aid was summoned for the stricken Bowden; alas, too late. Within a very little time he expired.

I was for burying him, then abandoning Clay in the wilderness and pressing on. Hiderick would have none of it, calling instead for frontier justice and a summary settling of accounts. His hotter temper won the day. Hiderick caused Clay's wagon to be tipped over on its side, and then hanged him from the shafts. It was a barbarous thing to watch as he strangled to death at the end of a short rope. Are we no better than beasts now? Have our hardships brought us to such an extremity of animal passion? Back in the wagon, I threw myself to the floor in a perfect storm of emotion; Elizabeth tried to comfort me, but I could take no solace even from her sweet voice. I have failed her—we have all failed, all of us men who stood by and let vanity and stupidity lead us into this hell on earth. Now on top of it all we are murderers. The mark of Cain lies upon us.

October 4th: In all my anguish of last night I forgot to set down that the note was found on Clay's body after all, tucked inside his pocketbook. It read— "Make haste. Indians in the foothills. Snow already on the peaks. Waste no time."

October 11th: Forging on down the valley of the Humboldt. Such oxen as remain alive are much weakened through great exertion and lack of fodder, and to save their strength we walk where we can. No man talks to his neighbour; our gazes are bent to the trail ahead, and our heads hang low. Why should we look up? Snowcaps clearly visible atop the mountains in the west.

October 23rd: In the night, a great alarm: Indians, howling down from the hills, attacking our wagons. Four wagons lost before we knew it—nine men dead in the onslaught. They have slaughtered half of the oxen too, the brutes. As they vanished back into the hills, we heard them laughing—a terrible and callous sound. I hear it now as I write, and it may be that it shall follow me to my grave: the mocking of savages in this savage land. Savages, I say? At least they do not kill their own as we have done.

October 31st: Our progress is so slow as to be hardly worth recording. Oxen dying between the wagon-shafts; if we are to make the crossing into California, I believe we shall have to rely on the mules and upon our own feet. Thunder atop the peaks, and the laughter of the Paiutes, echoing through these lonely canyons. They do not bother us much now, though; even the wolves leave us alone. We are not worth the bothering.

November 4th: Very nigh to the mountains now—can it be that the Lord will grant us safe passage before the winter comes? Dark clouds over all the white-capped peaks. One more week, Lord; one more week. At night on our knees by the bunks we pray, Elizabeth & I—God grant us another week.

November 8th: In the high passes. So close! Lord, can it be?

November 9th: Snow in the night, great flakes whirling out of a black sky. We pressed on without stopping, but in the morning it commenced again, and mounted to a wild flurry by midday. The oxen are slipping, and the wagons wholly ungovernable. We made camp by the side of a lake nigh to the tree-line, where some party long since departed fashioned four or five rough cabins out of logs. For tonight we must bide here by the lakeside, and pray for no more snow.

November 10th: Snow all through the night. Trail impassable—neither man nor beast can battle through the drifts. Exhausted, hope gone. Wind mounting to a howling frenzy, mercury falling, sky as black as lead. We have failed. The winter is upon us and we are lost in the high passes. God help us.

►≫❄≪◄

FROM THE *Sacramento Citizen-Journal,* **FEBRUARY 2, 1847**
Our readers, anxious for fresh news of the wagon-train of settlers trapped in the mountains, will doubtless remember our interview with Mr. Henry Garroway, one of the outriders sent on ahead of the party who arrived in California last November, with the first of winter's storms at his heels. Mr. Garroway, it will be recalled, announced it as his intention to lead a rescue company at the earliest opportunity, made up of brave souls from the

vicinity of Sutter's Fort, kitted out and victualled by the magnanimous Mr. John Augustus Sutter himself. Alas, grave news reaches us from the fort: the ferocity of the January storms has rendered even the lowest of the western passes wholly impenetrable. Drifts higher than a man on horseback have been reported as the norm, and even the most sanguine estimate cannot anticipate the departure of any rescue party until March at the earliest…

►─⫸•❋•⫷─◄

ADDENDUM TO *The Diary of John Buell* (UNDATED, MADE BY HIS WIFE, ELIZABETH)

I had not thought to take up my dear husband's pen and bring the story of our family's tribulations to its conclusion; however, should this diary be all that remains of us, then it may serve as a testament—to much bravery, and also to wickedness beyond measure.

We have been snowed in at the lakeside for nigh on three months now. Things have gone hard with us since the beginning: our provisions were scanty on arrival, and dwindled soon enough to nothing. I have seen people trying to eat shoe-leather and the binding of books; bark and grass and dirt they have eaten, twigs and handfuls of leaves. We were thirty-five on our arrival, thirty-two adults and three nursing children including my angel Mary-Kate. Now we are reduced to three.

The hunger swallows all things. Whole days will pass, and we think of nothing save food, how it would be to fill our bellies to repletion. There is a narcotic in it; it lulls one into a dangerous inactivity, a dull vacant torpor. I have seen this look settle upon a score of people; in each case the end came very nigh after. Daily I look for it in myself. I must be strong, for my angel's sake.

The provisions ran out before the end of November: the last of the oxen were slaughtered and eaten by then, and the mules too. One of the children was the first to die, Sarah Doerr's little Emily; soon after her, Missy Shorstein, and her father the next day. Our sorrow was great—we had no way of knowing that all too soon death would become a familiar thing with us. It is hard to mourn, when horror is piled upon horror and the bodies are beyond counting or remembrance; but it is necessary. It is the most human of emotions, and we must remain human, even in this uttermost remove of hell.

From the start it was clear that some would not last the year out. A great depression settled over our camp like a funeral pall, and many succumbed to its all-embracing pressure. It was most prevalent among the men—not least in my dear husband John. From the first he reproached himself, and for many days after our arrival, half-crazy with remorse, he would not stir from his bed of leaves and moss in our cabin. Many times I spoke with him, and sought to assure him he was not to blame for our predicament; but he would not be consoled, and turned his head away to the wall. Greatly I feared for his life; that he would give up the will to live, and fade away like so many of the others.

But my husband John Buell was a strong man, and a brave one, and soon enough he arose from his bed and was about the general business. He managed to trap some small animals for the pot; hares and crows and the like. He helped weather-proof our cabin, and the cabins of our neighbours. And around the middle of December, when folks were dying and all hope seemed forlorn, he set forth a plan.

Together with three of the other man—Bill Doerr, Martin Farrow and young Kent Shorstein—he purposed to cross the mountains on foot and fetch help. The Indians, Charley and Josephus, would accompany them, guiding them safe through to California. It was a desperate plan, fraught with much peril and offering but little chance of success, but it was voted the last best hope of our pitiful assembly, for all were in agreement when the plan was presented for approval. Here I must be honest, and record that in private I counselled against the expedition—I wept and pleaded with John, that he should stay with us and not throw his life away on such a rash and impetuous undertaking. He would not listen, though: it was as if he saw in this reckless plan a last chance, not just for our beleaguered party, but for himself—as if he might thus redeem himself in my eyes, when all along he was my hero and my one true love.

They set out in the second week of December; and soon afterwards Hiderick presented his awful proposition to the remainder of the party.

Now I must be brave, and record the facts of the matter without flinching. Hiderick said that the rescue party were doomed to failure, and would undoubtedly die in the mountain passes; we should not rely on them for assistance. I could have struck him—that he could thus impugn my husband, and his brave allies, when he had not the courage to do aught save cower in his cabin! But I must tell it aright, and not let myself be sidetracked.

Hiderick said that we were doomed, and should not make it through to the spring, save for one chance. He said that we were surrounded by fresh meat, if we had only the brains to see it, and the nerve to do something about it; he said he was a butcher by trade, and would show us what he meant. If I live another fifty years I shall not forget what he did next.

He went to the door of the big cabin and flung it wide open. The snow rose up in drifts all around, parted only where a path had been cleared between the cabins. All around were the graves of those who had already succumbed to the hunger and the cold; maybe nine or ten by that time. We could not dig them in the ground, for that lay ten feet beneath the snowdrifts, and was frozen hard as iron. Instead we lay them wrapped in blankets in the snow, where the cold would preserve them till the spring.

Hiderick pointed to the nearest of the graves—little Missy Shorstein's. "There's your meat," he said, in his thick guttural voice. "Like it or not, it's the only vittles you'll get this side of the thaw."

There was an uproar. Old Man Shorstein struck Hiderick full in the face, and swore he would take a pistol and spill Hiderick's brains on the snow before he ever disturbed the grave of his daughter. Hiderick wiped the blood from his cheek, licking his hand clean in a way that made me sick to watch, and merely said, "You'll see. None need eat his own kin, if we handle it right."

But Mr. Shorstein himself was in his grave before Christmas Day, and two others with him. Two more the next day, and three the next—and soon after that the first of the families took to eating the dead.

Hiderick dressed the bodies, and distributed the parcels of meat. Like a terrible black-bearded devil he passed from cabin to cabin; always he would knock upon our door, and always I would refuse to answer. Sometimes the ghoul would show his grinning face at the window; I would hold little Mary-Kate close to my bosom, and pray for our deliverance. Five of the seven families partook; let the record show that the Buells and the Shorsteins never ate human flesh. It is not my place to judge them—Mama told me more than once that survival runs close to the bone, closer than anything save the blood. But the flesh of our friends and fellow Christians! Dear Lord, no.

I trapped what I could, enough for Mary-Kate at least: back in Vermont when I was but a little child, Mama had showed me many ways to catch the small creatures of hills and woodland. Still the hunger was always with us, and Mary-Kate grew awful thin and pale; yet no unholy flesh passed our lips.

As for the rest of them: they ate or fasted according to their consciences, and yet even for those who chose to partake there was scarce enough meat to grow fat on, so little was there left on the bones of the dead. They cheated death for but a little while, but at what cost, Lord? At what cost?

Even this grisly feasting was all but through by the January, and folk were dying again almost daily, when out of the mountains staggered Kent Shorstein and the Indian Josephus, carrying between them the body of my dear brave husband John Buell.

We buried John in the snowdrifts out back of the cabin. Kent Shorstein told me of the great hardships endured by the five of them up in the mountains; he said that they lost their way searching for a pass that was not entirely blocked, and so within a week they were starving and nigh to death themselves. Doerr and Farrow were for killing the Indians, and eating their flesh; on this Charley rose up and ran Martin Farrow through with a knife, and Bill Doerr shot Charley dead on the spot. Josephus would have killed him for it, but John and young Kent restrained him. Best if they had not, maybe, for next morning when they awoke they found Doerr eating Charley's liver by the campfire. Kent and my dear John refused to join him in the gruesome repast, and instead they entreated Josephus to lead them away, back to our camp by the lake. The last they saw of Bill Doerr was him raving and singing to himself among the pine trees, waving a gobbet of meat on a stick.

Poor Kent Shorstein told me all this from his sickbed; he shivered like a man with the ague, and I was not surprised when two days later, his body was taken for burial by his grieving sisters. Soon they too had joined him at rest; and then began the grimmest passage of my travails.

With John dead and the last of the Shorsteins gone also, there now remained of the party only Mary-Kate and I who refused to eat the flesh of the deceased. Hiderick was now pre-eminent among us; he roamed from cabin to cabin like a robber baron, adorned—I can scare bring myself to speak of it!—adorned with a gruesome sort of necklace, fashioned from small knucklebones and vertebrae strung on a leather strip. He said they were from the mules and the oxen, though everybody knew this to be a lie. Who though could reproach him? He fed them, and they depended on him. On his shoulders he wore a cape of wolfskin—the wolves surrounded the camp but would not come close, for I had set up snares all around as Mama showed me how to do, and we still had ammunition enough to shoot them.

It was the practice of the families to place over the bodies of their loved ones a marker made of wood, together with a small tag hung round the neck, lest anyone should eat his own kin. In the cases of the Shorsteins and us Buells, this marker served to warn away the ghoul Hiderick entirely. Imagine then the distress and the horror with which I found, when going to pray awhile at John's graveside, that the bodies of Adolph and Bella Shorstein had been dragged from their sacred resting-place around to Hiderick's cabin, whither I dared not go. What to do?

In the presence of all those remaining in the party—few enough, Lord, few enough! and yet sufficient to deal with Hiderick, had they but dared—I confronted him with the foul deed. He merely laughed and said, "Hain't I got to put meat on the table? They ain't so particular about their food now, I reckon." No one would take my part in it; they slunk away like so many starving jackals, licking the bloody hand that feeds them. I took Mary-Kate back to our cabin, and wept throughout the night. I vowed to myself: she is my angel, and I will do what I must to protect her. Let the others throw in their lots with the ghoul, I said, and see what comes of it.

Death came of it, I believe as much of shame as hunger in the end. People could scarce bear to look at one another, and took to their beds, and come morning they were dead; only Hiderick seemed to thrive on his grisly diet. He ruled over all, and grew fat on the bodies of his erstwhile subjects.

Josephus would have taken my part, for he too—let his name be recorded among the virtuous!—never ate of the cursed meat; but he was gone. After bringing John back to the camp he spent a night resting, then another day crouching out in the snow beneath the mightiest of the trees around the camp, muttering to himself some words of heathen prayer. The wolves came right up to him, but did not touch him; for his part, he hardly seemed to heed their presence. At dusk he came down from the treeline to knock on my cabin door and tell me he was departing. Would I come with him, he asked? I said I could not, and showed him Mary-Kate asleep in her rough cot. He nodded, and said a curious thing: "You are best fitted of all of them to look after her, maybe. I will see you again." Then he looked at me for the longest time, so long that I felt uncomfortable and averted my eyes from his keen and curious gaze—upon which he turned on his heel and departed. That night—I am sure it was him—he left the dressed-out carcass of a deer at our door. We never saw him again.

Now we are through February and into March, and still no sign of a thaw, nor any hope of rescue. Instead the snow redoubles, and my traps are empty come the morning. There were upward of a dozen souls remaining in our party when John's companions dragged him back into camp. Today, there are but three remaining, Mary-Kate and me—and Hiderick.

Oh, unutterable horror! That such things could exist under the sun! The deserted camp is like some awful frozen abattoir. Long streaks of blood disfigure the white snowdrifts. Here and there lie the horrible remains of some devil's feast—a long bone picked clean, a shattered skull—and barricaded inside our cabin we hear, Mary-Kate and I, the ravings of the maniac outside.

This afternoon—I can scarce bear to set the words down. I must be strong. This afternoon, he came to the cabin door and hammered it till I opened. He was stripped to the waist, I thought at first; then I realised I could not see his mop of greasy black hair and bristling beard, and thought he wore some sort of leathern cap over all. What it was—

What he wore was the skin of my dear husband John Buell, stretched over his head and shoulders like an awful mask. He was laughing like a madman, and bawling at the top of his cracked and shrieking voice: "You like me? You like me now, huh? I fitten enough for you now, maybe?"

I raised John's pistol level with my eyes, and said, I know not how I managed it but I said: "Get out." He scarcely heard me, so filled with the spirit of devilishness and insanity was he. I did not hesitate. I fired the pistol. The load flew so close by his head—closer than I had intended it to, I think—that it served to rouse him from his madness. He stared at me, but all I could see were the features, blackened and distorted, of my dear sweet John. The horror of it—the horror—

"Get out now," I said.

"I'll come fer you," he said, and I swear there was nothing in his voice that was halfway human any more. "I'm your husband, now, don't you see, and I'll come fer you. You'll want me by and by, I reckon. I got meat—got good meat—" and he raised his hand to show me some hideous gobbet of flesh—please God let it not have been *his*, oh merciful Lord please! He brandished it before him like a dreadful prize.

I fired again, and this time the bullet took the greater part of his ear off. He dropped the stinking piece of carrion and screamed; with the incredible clarity of great stress and panic, I saw his traitor's blood spilling out on the white and blameless snow. Like the basest coward in creation he scuttled back to his shack, shrieking and cursing all the while. For the time being he is quiet; but I doubt not that he will come for us, maybe tonight when the moon is up. My bullet only wounded him, he will survive. But shall we, Mary-Kate and I?

Alone; abandoned; forsaken. How shall I protect my darling babe from this madman, from this wolf at the door? All that drives me on is the remembrance of Mama, those nights she lay nigh death in the wagon, how she clasped my hand in hers and gripped it and told me that I would survive, though she might not. I said Mama, Mama, no, it shan't be, you're strong, you're so strong, and I am weak, but she said I would change. When the time came I would change. I do not know whether she was right, but I feel at the end of myself.

The moon is up. Its broad full face smiles down on this stained defiled earth. The howling of the wolves echoes out across the frozen lake and through the deserted cabins, up into the snow-choked trees. Four bullets left. Not near enough, I fear, but one each for me and Mary-Kate at need. Grant me the strength to do what I must, to survive this night!

►≫·❈·≪◄

FROM THE *Sacramento Citizen-Journal*, APRIL 27, 1847

THE MIRACLE OF THE MOUNTAINS
A CHILD FOUND IN THE WILDERNESS
Guarded by Wolves—Horrors Strewn All About
Full particulars

The most shocking and incredible news from Mr. Henry Garroway's rescue party, who rode to the assistance of the wagon train forced to winter in the high mountains, is setting all California ablaze. Wild rumors have been bruited on all sides, and it is incumbent upon the *Citizen-Journal* to set down the facts as we have learned them, *directly from Mr. Garroway himself.*

The party set out from Sutter's Fort in the last week of March, and battled through mighty snow-drifts to the far side of the peaks, where lay the encampment of the unfortunate settlers stranded by the winter storms. The first of the outriders drew up short on reaching the outskirts of the camp, so appalling was the scene which lay before their eyes. Together the would-be rescuers prayed for strength and marshalled their forces, before entering into a scene of horror no pen can describe, fit only for some grim courageous Dante of the New World.

Five cabins of rough construction lay before them, their roofs alone visible above the snow. No sign of chimney-smoke, or indeed of any human activity, could be seen; instead, between the cabins, there were bloodied trails, as of the aftermath of a great slaughter. One veteran member of the party, Mr. Frederick Marchmont of Sacramento, swears that the carnage wreaked upon that place surpassed in horror anything seen by the most hardened of frontier campaigners; not even the savage Apache, he avers, could have left in his wake so much bloodshed and butchery.

Great was the dismay with which the rescuing party gazed upon this devastation; heavy were the hearts of all as the search from cabin to cabin began. Horrible to relate, all about the cabins were portions of human flesh and bone, torn as if by wild animals; so atrocious was the general aspect of the place that several of the rescuers were all but unmanned, falling to their knees and praying to the Lord that this bitter cup should pass them by.

Imagine, then, the wonderment with which the assembled men of the rescue party heard, in all that great stillness of desolation, the crying of a little child!

►─❈─◄

FROM A PRIVATE LETTER OF ELIZABETH BUELL TO HER DAUGHTER MARY-KATE, HELD WITHIN THE GARROWAY FAMILY

My darling, I believe they are coming soon. Last night I heard them, ever so far off, up in the peaks—I smell them now, their scent travels on the thin spring wind. Tomorrow they will arrive, and they will find you.

It will be the cruellest and most bitter thing to leave you, crueller even than the burying of my own dear husband, your loving father John Buell. I saw his body once Hiderick had done with it: oh, my child, pray you never have to look on such a sight! Hard it was to look upon; till now, the hardest thing in that long season of sadness and hardship that began with the death of your grandmother, Julia Stocklasa, at the commencement of all our wanderings.

Your father, as he lay raving in his cabin by the lakeside, called this a god-less place; and then cursed himself for a blasphemer. God has abandoned us, he screamed into the night; better say that God was never here, my darling. Better say that we rode beyond His grace into some strange and ancient land, where the old gods still hold sway, where blood and death and the animal passions yet contend for mastery of the earth. Your grandmother knew it, Mary-Kate; as she lay on her deathbed she whispered it in my ear. Remember, she said, you will change at need. You will change, she said, and I did not know what she meant at first. Then she told me of the shapeshifter women of her homeland, those that go out into the woods on nights when the moon is full, and the change comes upon them. She told me what to do if I wished to survive the peril she foresaw, and to protect you. I did not believe her at first, but perhaps only in the uttermost desperation can such things ring true. I did what she told me, and everything changed, my darling—everything, save my love for you.

I thought I could come back, after it was done. For it was only to protect you, my darling, that I did what I did that night of the full moon when Hiderick came for us; little did I care for my own life, only for yours, since to stay alive would be to keep you safe from harm, and that was all that mattered to me. How could I know that what is done, is done, once and for all; that *there can be no changing back*? How could I live among men again, after such a fearful alteration? Now I have other family, and must leave you to your own kind.

They wait for me among the trees, my new kin, tongues lolling from their strong jaws as they grin and pant, coats wet from the melting snow. How it feels to run with them, to fling myself into snowbanks and roll and play and lie together—this you can never know, my darling. Josephus, who helped save you, knew: straight away I recognised him, after the deed was done and the rest of the wolves came down to the camp to look upon the slaughter. I looked into his eyes as I lay there full changed, streaked and clotted still with Hiderick's reeking blood, and he looked back into mine. This time I did not turn away.

Did I do wrong? I did what I had to do. Did I betray my dear husband? At least I did not fail our beautiful and most perfect daughter, first in both our affections and ever dearest to us. So how bitter, my darling, to leave you for these men to find. They will take you across the mountains, whither your father and I cannot follow: we shall remain here as you ride away. At least you shall find your home in the new Eden: east of Eden is fit enough for such as we, who have the stain of blood on us.

Perhaps this land, that has so much escaped God's grace, may still be subject to His justice; perhaps I will be punished for what I have done. As if there could be a worse punishment than knowing you to be alive and well in that promised land beyond the mountains, and I not able to see you, or hold you in my arms and hear your pretty laugh.

Hark! They are coming down from the mountain. I must go, and leave you now. All my love goes with you. Be good, my darling; be kind, be honest, be faithful, and know that your Mama will love you always. Listen for me, nights when you lie abed and the moon is up. The pack are waiting for me. I must go—

Laird Barron is the author of several books, including *The Croning, Occultation,* and *The Beautiful Thing That Awaits Us All.* His work has also appeared in many magazines and anthologies. An expatriate Alaskan, Barron currently resides in upstate New York.

Strappado
Laird Barron

KENSHI SUZUKI AND Swayne Harris had a chance reunion at a bathhouse in an Indian tourist town. It had been five or six years since their previous Malta liaison, a cocktail party at the British consulate that segued into a branding iron-hot affair. They'd spent a long weekend of day cruises to the cyclopean ruins on Gozo, nightclubbing at the elite hotels and casinos, and booze-drenched marathon sex before the dissolution of their respective junkets swept them back to New York and London in a storm of tears and bitter farewells. For Kenshi, the emotional hangover lasted through desolate summer and into a melancholy autumn. And even now, when elegant, thunderously handsome Swayne materialized from the crowd on the balcony like the Ghost of Christmas Past—!

Kenshi wore a black suit; sleek and polished as a seal or a banker. He swept his single lock of gelled black hair to the left, like a gothic teardrop. His skin was sallow and dewlapped at his neck, and soft at his belly and beneath his Italian leather belt. He'd been a swimmer once, earnestly meant to return to his collegiate form, but hadn't yet braced for the exhaustion of such an endeavor. He preferred to float in hotel pools while dreaming of his supple youth, once so exotic in the suburbs of white-bread Connecticut. Everyone but his grandparents (who never fully acclimated to their transplantation to the West) called him Ken. A naturalized U.S. citizen, he spoke meager Japanese, knew next to zero about the history or the culture and had visited Tokyo a grand total of three times. In short, he privately acknowledged his unworthiness to lay claim to his blood heritage and thus lived a life of minor, yet persistent regret.

Swayne wore a cream-colored suit of a cut most popular with the royalty of South American plantations. *It's in style anywhere I go,* he explained later as they undressed one another in Kenshi's suite at the Golden Scale. Swayne's complexion was dark, like fired clay. His slightly sinister brows and waxed imperial lent him the appearance of a Christian devil.

In the seam between the electric shock of their reunion and the resultant delirium fugue of violent coupling, Kenshi had an instant to doubt the old magic before the question was utterly obliterated. And if he'd forgotten Swayne's sly, wry demeanor, his faith was restored when the dark man rolled to face the ceiling, dragged on their shared cigarette and said, "Of all the bathhouses in all the cities of the world…"

Kenshi cheerfully declared him a bastard and snatched back the cigarette. The room was strewn with their clothes. A vase of lilies lay capsized and water funneled from severed stems over the edge of the table. He caught droplets in his free hand and rubbed them and the semen into the slick flesh of his chest and belly. He breathed heavily.

"How'd you swing this place all to yourself?" Swayne said. "Big promotion?"

"A couple of my colleagues got pulled off the project and didn't make the trip. You?"

"Business, with unexpected pleasure, thank you. The museum sent me to look at a collection—estate sale. Paintings and whatnot. I fly back on Friday, unless I find something extraordinary, which is doubtful. Mostly rubbish, I'm afraid." Swayne rose and stretched. Rich, gold-red light dappled the curtains, banded and bronzed him with tiger stripes.

The suite's western exposure gave them a last look at the sun as it faded to black. Below their lofty vantage, slums and crooked dirt streets and the labyrinthine wharfs in the shallow, blood-warm harbor were mercifully obscured by thickening tropical darkness. Farther along the main avenue and atop the ancient terraced hillsides was a huge, baroque seventeenth-century monastery, much photographed for feature films, and farther still, the scattered manors and villas of the lime nabobs, their walled estates demarcated by kliegs and floodlights. Tourism pumped the lifeblood of the settlement. They came for the monastery, of course, and only a few kilometers off was a wildlife preserve. Tour buses ran daily and guides entertained foreigners with local folklore and promises of tigers, a number of which roamed the high grass plains. Kenshi had gone on his first day, hated the ripe, florid smell of the jungle, the heat, and the sullen men with rifles who patrolled the electrified perimeter fence in halftracks. The locals wore knives in their belts, even the urbane guide with the Oxford accent, and it left Kenshi feeling shriveled and helpless, at the mercy of the hatefully smiling multitudes.

Here, in the dusty, grimy heart of town, some eighty kilometers down the coast from grand old Mumbai, when the oil lamps and electric lamps fizzed alight, link by link in a vast, convoluted chain, it was only bright enough to help the muggers and cutthroats see what they were doing.

"City of romance," Swayne said with eminent sarcasm. He opened the door to the terrace and stood naked at the rail. There were a few tourists on their verandas and at their windows. Laughter and pop music and the stench of the sea carried on the lethargic breeze as it snaked through the room. The hotel occupied the exact center of a semicircle of relatively modernized blocks—the chamber of commerce's concession to appeasing Westerners' paranoia of marauding gangs and vicious muggers. Still, three streets over was the Third World, as Kenshi's colleagues referred to it while they swilled whiskey and goggled at turbans and sarongs and at the Buddhists in their orange robes. It was enough to make him ashamed of his continent, to pine for his father's homeland, until he realized the Japanese were scarcely more civilized as guests.

"The only hotel with air conditioning and you go out there. You'll be arrested if you don't put something on!" Kenshi finally dragged himself upright and collected his pants. "Let's go to the discothèque."

"The American place? I'd rather not. Asshole tourists swarm there like bees to honey. I was in the cantina a bit earlier and got stuck near a bunch of Hollywood types whooping it up at the bar. Probably come to scout the area or shoot the monastery. All they could talk about is picking up on 'European broads.'"

Kenshi laughed. "Those are the guys I'm traveling with. Yeah, they're scouting locations. And they're all married, too."

"Wankers. Hell with the disco."

"No, there's another spot—a hole in the wall I heard about from a friend. A local."

"Eh, probably a seedy little bucket of blood. I'm in, then!"

Kenshi rang his contact, one Rashid Obi, an assistant to an executive producer at a local firm that cranked out several dozen Bollywood films every year. Rashid gave directions and promised to meet them at the club in forty-five minutes. Or, if they were nervous to travel the streets alone, he could escort them.... Kenshi laughed, somewhat halfheartedly, and assured his acquaintance there was no need for such coddling. He would've preferred Rashid's company, but knew Swayne was belligerently fearless regarding forays into foreign environments. His lover was an adventurer and hard-bitten in his own charming fashion. Certainly Swayne would mock him for his timidity and charge ahead regardless. So, Kenshi stifled his misgivings and led the way.

The discothèque was a quarter mile from the hotel and buried in a mis-shapen block of stone houses and empty shops. They found it mostly by accident after stumbling around several narrow alleys that reeked of urine and the powerful miasma of curry that seeped from open apartment windows. The entry arch was low and narrow and blackened from soot and antiquity. The name of the club had been painted into the worn plaster, illegible now from erosion and neglect. Kerosene lamps guttered in inset sconces and shadows gathered in droves. A speaker dangled from a cornice and projected scratchy sitar music. Two Indian men sat on a stone bench. They wore baggy, lemon shirts and disco slacks likely purchased from the black market outlets in a local bazaar. They shared the stem of the hookah at their sandaled feet. Neither appeared interested in the arrival of the Westerners.

"Oh my God! It's an opium den!" Swayne said and squeezed Kenshi's buttock. "Going native, are we, dear?"

Kenshi blushed and knocked his hand aside. He'd smoked half a joint with a dorm mate in college and that was the extent of his experimentation with recreational drugs. He favored a nice, dry white wine and the occasional import beer, preferably Sapporo.

The darkness of the alley followed them inside. The interior lay in shadow, except for the bar, which glowed from a strip along its edge like the bioluminescent tentacle of a deep sea creature, and motes of gold and red and purple passing across the bottles from a rotating glitter ball above the tiny square of dance floor wedged in the corner. The sitar music issued from a beat box and was much louder than it had been outside. Patrons were jammed into the little rickety tables and along the bar. The air was sharp with sweat and exhaled liquor fumes.

Rashid emerged from the shadows and caught Kenshi's arm above the elbow in the overly familiar manner of his countrymen. He was shorter than Kenshi and slender to the point of well-heeled emaciation. He stood so close Kenshi breathed deeply of his cologne, the styling gel in his short, tightly coiled hair. He introduced the small man from Delhi to a mildly bemused Swayne. Soon Rashid vigorously shepherded them into an alcove where a group of Europeans crowded together around three circular tables laden with beer bottles and shot glasses and fuming ashtrays heaped with the butts of cigarettes.

Rashid presented Swayne and Kenshi to the evening's co-host, one Luis Guzman, an elderly Argentinean who'd lived abroad for nearly three decades in quasi political exile. Guzman was the public relations guru for a profoundly large international advertising conglomerate, which in turn influenced, or owned outright, the companies represented by the various guests he'd assembled at the discothèque.

Kenshi's feet ached, so he wedged in next to a reedy blonde Netherlander, a weather reporter for some big market, he gathered as sporadic introductions were made. Her hands bled ink from a mosaic of nightclub stamps, the kind that didn't easily wash off, so like rings in a tree, it was possible to estimate she'd been partying hard for several nights. This impression was confirmed when she confided that she'd gone a bit wild during her group's whirlwind tour of Bangkok, Mumbai, and this "village" in the space of days. She laughed at him from the side of her mouth, gaped fishily with her left eye, a Picasso girl, and pressed her bony thigh against him. She'd been drinking boleros, and lots of them, he noted. *What goes down must come up,* he thought and was sorry for whomever she eventually leeched onto tonight.

The Viking gentleman looming across from them certainly vied for her attention, what with his lascivious grimaces and bellowing jocularity, but she appeared content to ignore him while trading glances with the small, hirsute Slav to the Viking's left and occasionally brushing Kenshi's forearm as they shared an ashtray. He soon discovered Hendrika the weathergirl worked for the Viking, Andersen, chief comptroller and inveterate buffoon. The Slav was actually a native of Minsk named Fedor; Fedor managed distribution for a major vodka label and possessed some mysterious bit of history with Hendrika. Kenshi idly wondered if he'd been her pimp while she toiled through college. A job was a job was a job (until she found the job of her dreams) to a certain subset of European women, and men too, as he'd been pleased to discover during his many travels. In turn, Hendrika briefly introduced Kenshi to the French contingent of software designers—Françoise, Jean Michelle, and Claude—the German photographer Victor and his assistant Nina, and Raul, a Spanish advertising consultant. They extended lukewarm handshakes and one of them bought him a glass of bourbon, which he didn't want but politely accepted. Then, everyone resumed roaring, disjointed conversations and ignored him completely.

Good old Swayne got along swimmingly, of course. He'd discarded his white suit for an orange blazer, black shirt, and slacks and Kenshi noted with equal measures of satisfaction and jealousy that all heads swiveled to follow the boisterous Englishman. Within moments he'd shaken hands with all and sundry and been inducted by the club of international debauchers as a member in good standing. That the man didn't even speak a second language was no impediment—he vaulted such barriers by shamelessly enlisting necessary translations from whomever happened to be within earshot. Kenshi glumly thought his friend would've made one hell of an American.

Presently Swayne returned from his confab with Rashid and Guzman and exclaimed, "We've been invited to the exhibition. A *Van Iblis!*" Swayne seemed genuinely enthused, his meticulously cultivated cynicism blasted to smithereens in an instant. Kenshi barely made him out over the crossfire between Andersen and Hendrika and the other American, Walther. Walther was fat and bellicose, a colonial barbarian dressed for civilized company. His shirt was untucked, his tie an open noose. Kenshi hadn't caught what the fellow did for a living, however Walther put whiskey after whiskey away with the vigor of a man accustomed to lavish expense accounts. He sneered at Kenshi on the occasions their eyes met.

Kenshi told Swayne he'd never heard of Van Iblis.

"It's a pseudonym," Swayne said. "Like Kilroy, Or Alan Smithee. He, or she, is a guerilla. Not welcome in the U.K.; persona non grata in the free world you might say." When Kenshi asked why Van Iblis wasn't welcome in Britain, Swayne grinned. "Because the shit he pulls off violates a few laws here and there. Unauthorized installations, libelous materials, health code violations. Explosions!" Industry insiders suspected Van Iblis was actually comprised of a significant number of member artists and exceedingly wealthy patrons. Such an infrastructure seemed the only logical explanation for the success of these brazen exhibitions and their participants' elusiveness.

It developed that Guzman had brought his eclectic coterie to this part of the country after sniffing a rumor of an impending Van Iblis show and, as luck would have it, tonight was the night. Guzman's contacts had provided him with a hand-scrawled map to the rendezvous, and a password. A password! It was all extraordinarily titillating.

Swayne dialed up a slideshow on his cell and handed it over. Kenshi remembered the news stories once he saw the image of the three homeless men who'd volunteered to be crucified on faux satellite dishes. Yes, that had caused a sensation, although the winos survived relatively intact. None of them knew enough to expose the identity of his temporary employers. Another series of slides displayed the infamous pigs' blood carpet bombing of the Viet Nam War Memorial from a blimp that then exploded in midair like a Roman candle. Then the so called "corpse art" in Mexico, Amsterdam, and elsewhere. Similar to the other guerilla installations, these exhibits popped up in random venues in any of a dozen countries after the mildest and most surreptitious of advance rumors and retreated underground within hours. Of small comfort to scandalized authorities was the fact the corpse sculptures, while utterly macabre, were allegedly comprised of volunteers with terminal illnesses who'd donated their bodies to science, or rather, art. Nonetheless, at the sight of grimly posed seniors in antiquated bathing suits, a bloated, eyeless Santa in a coonskin cap, the tri-headed ice cream vendor and his chalk-faced Siamese children, Kenshi wrinkled his lip and pushed the phone at Swayne. "No, I think I'll skip this one, whatever it is, thank you very much."

"You are such a wet blanket," Swayne said. "Come on, love. I've been dying to witness a Van Iblis show since, well forever. I'll be the envy of every art dilettante from Birmingham to Timbuktu!"

Kenshi made polite yet firm noises of denial. Swayne leaned very close; his hot breath tickled Kenshi's ear. He stroked Kenshi's cock through the tight fabric of his designer pants. Congruently, albeit obliviously, Hendrika continued to rub his thigh. Kenshi choked on his drink and finally consented to accompany Swayne on his stupid side trek, would've promised anything to spare himself this agonizing embarrassment. A lifetime in the suburbs had taught him to eschew public displays of affection, much less submit to a drunken mauling by another man in a foreign country not particularly noted for its tolerance.

He finished his drink in miserable silence and awaited the inevitable.

They crowded aboard Guzman's two Day-Glo rental vans and drove inland. There were no signs to point the way and the road was narrow and deserted.

Kenshi's head grew thick and heavy on his neck and he closed his eyes and didn't open them until the tires made new sounds as they left paved road for a dirt track and his companions gently bumped their legs and arms against his own.

It wasn't much farther.

Daylight peeled back the layers of night and deposited them near a collection of prefabricated warehouse modules and storage sheds. The modules were relatively modern, yet already cloaked in moss and threaded with coils of vine. Each was enormous and had been adjoined to its siblings via additions and corrugated tin walkways. The property sat near the water, a dreary, fog-shrouded expanse surrounded by drainage ditches and marshes and a jungle of creepers and banyan trees.

Six or seven dilapidated panel trucks were parked on the outskirts; 1970s Fords imported from distant USA, their white frames scorched and shot with rust. Battered insignia on the door panels marked them as one-time property of the ministry of the interior. Alongside the trucks, an equally antiquated, although apparently functional, bulldozer squatted in the high grass; a dull red model one would expect to see abandoned in a rural American pasture. To the left of the bulldozer was a deep, freshly ploughed trench surmounted by plastic barrels, unsealed fifty-five-gallon drums and various wooden boxes, much of this half-concealed by canvas tarps. Guzman commented that the owners of the land were in the embryonic stage of prepping for large-scale development—perhaps a hotel. Power lines and septic systems were in the offing.

Kenshi couldn't imagine who in the hell could possibly think building a hotel in a swamp represented a wise business investment.

Guzman and Rashid's groups climbed from the vans and congregated, faces slack and bruised by hangovers, jet lag, and burgeoning unease. What had seemed a lark in the cozy confines of the disco became a more ominous prospect as each took stock and realized he or she hadn't a bloody clue as to north or south, or up and down, for that matter. Gnats came at them in quick, sniping swarms, and several people cursed when they lost shoes to the soft, wet earth. Black and white chickens scratched in the weedy ruts.

A handful of Indians dressed in formal wear grimly waited under a pavilion to serve a buffet. None of them smiled or offered any greeting. They mumbled amongst themselves and loaded plates of honeydew slices and crepes and poured glasses of champagne with disconsolate expressions. A

Victrola played an eerie Hindu-flavored melody. The scene reminded Kenshi of a funeral reception. Someone, perhaps Walther, muttered nervously, and the sentiment of general misgiving palpably intensified.

"Hey, this is kinda spooky," Hendrika stage-whispered to her friend Fedor. Oddly enough, that cracked everybody up and tensions loosened.

Guzman and Rashid approached a couple of young, drably attired Indian men who were scattering corn from gunny sacks to the chickens, and started a conversation. After they'd talked for a few minutes, Guzman announced the exhibition would open in about half an hour and all present were welcome to enjoy the buffet and stretch their legs. Andersen, Swayne, and the French software team headed for the pavilion and mosquito netting.

Meanwhile, Fedor fetched sampler bottles of vodka supplied by his company and passed them around. Kenshi surprised himself by accepting one. His throat had parched during the drive and he welcomed the excuse to slip away from Hendrika, whose orbit had yet again swung her all too close to him.

He strolled off a bit from the others, swiping at the relentless bugs and wishing he'd thought to wear that rather dashing panama hat he'd "borrowed" from a lover on location in the Everglades during a sweltering July shoot. His stroll carried him behind a metal shed overgrown with banyan vines. A rotting wooden addition abutted the sloppy edge of a pond or lagoon; it was impossible to know because of the cloying mist. He lit a cigarette. The porch was cluttered with disintegrating crates and rudimentary gardening tools. Gingerly lifting the edge of a tarp slimy with moss, he discovered a quantity of new plastic barrels. Hydrochloric Acid, CORROSIVE! and a red skull and crossbones warned of hazardous contents. He quickly snatched back his hand and moved away lest his cigarette trigger a calamity worthy of a Darwin Award.

"Uh, yeah—good idea, Sulu. Splash that crap on you and your face will melt like glue." Walther had sneaked up behind him. The man drained his mini vodka bottle and tossed it into the bushes. He drew another bottle from the pocket of his sweat-stained dress shirt and had a pull. The humidity was awful here; it pressed down in a smothering blanket. His hair lay in sticky clumps and his face was shiny and red. He breathed heavily, laboring as if the brief walk from the van had led up several flights of stairs.

Kenshi stared at him considering and discarding a series of snappy retorts. "Asshole," he finally said under his breath. He flicked his cigarette butt toward the scummy water and edged around Walther and made for the vans.

Walther laughed. "Jap fag," he said. The fat man unzipped and began pissing off the end of the porch.

"I'm not even fucking Japanese, you idiot," Kenshi said over his shoulder. No good, he realized; the tremor in his voice, the quickening of his shuffle betrayed his cowardice in the face of adversity. This instinctive recoil from trouble, the resultant wave of self-loathing and bitter recriminations was as it ever had been with Kenshi. Swayne would've smashed the jerk's face.

Plucking the thought from the air, Walther called, "Don't go tell your Limey boyfriend on me!"

Guzman gathered everyone into a huddle as Kenshi approached. He stood on the running board of a van and explained the three rules regarding their impending tour of the exhibition: no touching, no souvenirs, no pictures. "Mr. Vasilov will come around and secure all cell phones, cameras and recorders. Don't worry, your personal effects will be returned as soon as the tour concludes. Thank you for your cooperation."

Fedor dumped the remaining limes and pears from a hotel gift basket and came around and confiscated the proscribed items. Beyond a few exaggerated sighs, no one really protested; the prohibition of cameras and recording devices at galleries and exclusive viewings was commonplace. Certainly, this being Van Iblis and the epitome of scofflaw art, there could be no surprise regarding such rules.

At the appointed time the warehouse doors rattled and slid aside and a blond man in a paper suit emerged and beckoned them to ascend the ramp. He was large, nearly the girth of Andersen the Viking, and wore elbow-length rubber gloves and black galoshes. A black balaclava covered the lower half of his face. The party filed up the gangway in pairs, Guzman and Fedor at the fore. Kenshi and Swayne were the next to last. Kenshi watched the others become swiftly dissolving shadows backlit as they were by a bank of humming fluorescent lamps. He thought of cattle and slaughter pens and fingered his passport in its wallet on a string around his neck. Swayne squeezed his arm.

Once the group had entered, five more men, also clothed in paper suits and balaclavas, shut the heavy doors behind them with a clang that caused Kenshi's flesh to twitch. He sickly noted these five wore machetes on their belts. Blood rushed to his head in a breaker of dizziness and nausea. The reek of alcohol sweat and body odor tickled his gorge. The flickering light washed over his companions, reflected in their black eyes, made their faces pale and strange and curiously lifeless, as if he'd been suddenly trapped with brilliantly sculpted automatons. He understood then that they too had spotted the machetes. Mouths hung open in moist exclamations of apprehension and dread and the inevitable thrill derived from the alchemy of these emotions. Yet another man, similarly garbed as his compatriots, wheeled forth a tripod-mounted Panaflex motion picture camera and began shooting the scene.

The floor creaked under their gathered weight. Insulating foam paneled the walls. Every window was covered in black plastic. There were two narrow openings at the far end of the entry area; red paint outlined the first opening, blue paint the second. The openings let into what appeared to be darkened spaces, their gloom reinforced by translucent curtains of thick plastic similar to the kind that compartmentalized meat lockers.

"You will strip," the blond man said in flat, accented English.

Kenshi's testicles retracted, although a calmness settled over his mind. He dimly acknowledged this as the animal recognition of its confinement in a trap, the inevitability of what must ultimately occur. Yet, one of this fractious group would argue, surely Walther the boor, or obstreperous Andersen, definitely and assuredly Swayne. But none protested, none resisted the command, all were docile. One of the anonymous men near the entrance took out his machete and held it casually at his waist. Wordlessly, avoiding eye contact with each other, Kenshi's fellow travelers began to remove their clothes and arrange them neatly, or not so much, as the case might've been, in piles on the floor. The blond instructed them to form columns and face the opposite wall. The entire affair possessed the quality of a lucid dream, a not-happening-in-the-real-world sequence of events. Hendrika was crying, he noted before she turned away and presented him with her thin backside, a bony ridge of spine, spare haunches. She'd drained white.

Kenshi stood between oddly subdued Swayne and one of the Frenchmen. He was acutely anxious regarding his sagging breasts, the immensity of his scarred and stretched belly, his general flaccidity, and almost chuckled at the absurdity of it all.

When the group had assembled with their backs to him, the blond man briskly explained the guests would be randomly approached and tapped on the shoulder. The designated guests would turn and proceed into the exhibit chambers by twos. Questions? None were forthcoming. After a lengthy pause it commenced. Beginning with Guzman and Fedor, each of them were gradually and steadily ushered out of sight with perhaps a minute between pairings. The plastic curtains swished and crackled with their passage. Kenshi waited his turn and stared at the curdled yellow foam on the walls.

The tap on the shoulder came and he had sunk so far into himself it was only then he registered everyone else had gone. The group comprised an uneven number, so he was odd man out. Abruptly, techno music blared and snarled from hidden speakers, and beneath the eardrum-shattering syncopation, a shrill screeching like the keening of a beast or the howl of a circular saw chewing wood.

"Well, friend," said the blond, raising his voice to overcome the music, "you may choose."

Kenshi found it difficult to walk a straight line. He staggered and pushed through the curtain of the blue door into darkness. There was a long corridor and at its end another sheet of plastic that let in pale light. He shoved aside the curtain and had a moment of sick vertigo upon realizing there were no stairs. He cried out and toppled, arms waving, and flopped the eight or so feet into a pit of gravel. His leg broke on impact, but he didn't notice until later. The sun filled his vision with white. He thrashed in the gravel, dug furrows with elbows and heels and screamed soundlessly because the air had been driven from his lungs. A shadow leaned over him and brutally gripped his hair and clamped his face with what felt like a wet cloth. The cloth went into his nose, his mouth, choked him.

The cloth tasted of death.

Thanks to a series of tips, authorities found him three weeks later in the closet of an abandoned house on the fringes of Bangalore. Recreating events, and comparing these to the experiences of those others who were discovered at different locations but in similar circumstances, it was determined he'd been pacified with drugs unto a stupor. His leg was infected and he'd lost a terrible amount of weight. The doctors predicted scars, physical and otherwise.

There'd been police interviews; FBI, CIA, NSA. Kenshi answered and answered and they eventually let him go, let him get to work blocking it, erasing it to the extent erasing it was possible. He avoided news reports, refused the sporadic interviews, made a concentrated effort to learn nothing of the aftermath, although he suspected scant evidence remained, anyway. He took a leave of absence and cocooned himself.

Kenshi remembered nothing after the blue door and he was thankful.

Months after their second and last reunion, Swayne rang him at home and asked if he wanted to meet for cocktails. Swayne was in New York for an auction, would be around over the weekend, and wondered if Kenshi was doing all right, if he was surviving. This was before Kenshi began to lie awake in the dark of each new evening, disconnected from the cold pulse of the world outside the womb of his apartment, his hotel room, the cabs of his endless stream of rental cars. He dreamed the same dream; a recurring nightmare of acid-filled barrels knocked like dominoes into a trench, the grumbling exertions of a red bulldozer pushing in the dirt.

I've seen the tape, Swayne said through a blizzard of static.

Kenshi said nothing. He breathed, in and out. Starless, the black ceiling swung above him, it rushed to and fro, in and out like the heartbeat of the black Atlantic tapping and slapping at old crumbling seawalls, not far from his own four thin walls.

I've seen it, Swayne said. After another long pause, he said, *Say something, Ken.*

What?

It does exist. Van Iblis made sure copies were circulated to the press, but naturally the story was killed. Too awful, you know? I got one by post a few weeks ago. A reporter friend smuggled it out of a precinct in Canada. The goddamned obscenity is everywhere. And I didn't have the balls to look. Yesterday, finally.

That's why you called. Kenshi trembled. He suddenly wanted to know. Dread nearly overwhelmed him. He considered hanging up, chopping off Swayne's distorted voice. He thought he might vomit there, supine in bed, and drown.

*Yeah. We were the show. The red door people were the real show, I guess. God help us, Ken. Ever heard of a Palestinian hanging? Dangled from your wrists, cinder blocks tied to your ankles? That's what the bastards started with. When they were done, while the people were still alive...*Swayne stopped there, or his next words were swallowed by the static surf.

Of course, Van Iblis made a film. No need for Swayne to illuminate him on that score, to open him up again. Kenshi thought about the empty barrels near the trench. He thought about what Walther said to him behind the shed that day.

I don't even know why I picked blue, mate, Swayne said.

He said to Swayne, *Don't ever fucking call me again.* He disconnected and dropped the phone on the floor and waited for it to ring again. When it didn't, he slipped into unconsciousness.

One day his copy arrived in a plain envelope via an anonymous sender. He put the disk on the sidewalk outside of his building and methodically crushed it under the heel of his wingtip. The doorman watched the whole episode and smiled indulgently, exactly as one does to placate the insane.

Kenshi smiled in return and went into his apartment and ran a bath. He slashed his wrists with the broken edge of a credit card. Not deep enough; he bled everywhere and was forced to hire a service to steam the carpets. He never again wore short-sleeve shirts.

Nonetheless, he'd tried. There was comfort in trying.

Kenshi returned to the Indian port town on company business a few years later. Models were being flown in from Mumbai and Kolkata for a photo shoot near the old monastery. The ladies wouldn't arrive for another day and he had time to burn. He hired a taxi and went looking for the Van Iblis site.

The field wasn't difficult to find. Developers had drained the swamp and built a hotel on the site, as advertised. They'd hacked away nearby wilderness and plopped down high-rise condos, two restaurants and a casino. The driver dropped him at the Ivory Tiger, a glitzy, towering edifice. The lobby was marble and brass and the staff a pleasant chocolate mahogany, all of whom dressed smartly, smiled perfectly white smiles and spoke flawless English.

He stayed in a tenth floor suite, kept the blinds drawn, the phone unplugged, the lights off. Lying naked across crisp, snow-cool sheets was to float disembodied through a great silent darkness. A handsome businessman, a fellow American, in fact, had bought him a white wine in the lounge; a sweet talker, that one, but Kenshi retired alone. He didn't get many erections these days and those that came ended in humiliating fashion. Drifting through insoluble night was safer.

In the morning, he ate breakfast and smoked a few cigarettes and had his first drink of the day. He was amazed how much he drank anymore and how little effect it had on him. After breakfast he walked around the hotel grounds, which were very much a garden, and stopped at the tennis courts. No one was playing; thunderclouds massed and the air smelled of rain. By his estimation, the tennis courts were near to, if not directly atop, the old field. Drainage grates were embedded at regular intervals and he went to his knees and pressed the side of his head against one until the cold metal flattened his ear. He listened to water rushing through subterranean depths. Water fell through deep, hollow spaces and echoed, ever more faintly. And, perhaps, borne through yards of pipe and clay and gravel that hold, some say, fragments and frequencies of the past, drifted whispery strains of laughter, Victrola music.

He caught himself speculating about who else went through the blue door, the exit to the world of the living, and smothered this line of conjecture with the bribe of more drinks at the bar, more sex from this day on, more whatever it might take to stifle such thoughts forever. He was happier thinking Hendrika went back to her weather job once the emotional trauma subsided, that Andersen the Viking was ever in pursuit of her dubious virtue, that the Frenchmen and the German photographer had returned to their busy, busy lives. And Rashid.... Blue door. Red door. They might be anywhere.

The sky cracked and rain poured forth.

Kenshi curled into a tight ball, chin to chest, and closed his eyes. Swayne kissed his mouth and they were crushingly intertwined. Acid sluiced over them in a wave, then the lid clanged home over the rim of the barrel and closed them in.

Stephen Graham Jones is the author of sixteen novels and six story collections. Most recent is *Mongrels*, from William Morrow. Stephen lives in Boulder, Colorado.

Lonegan's Luck
Stephen Graham Jones

LIKE EVERY MONTH, the horse was new. A mare, pushing fifteen years old. Given his druthers, Lonegan would have picked a mule, of course, one that had had its balls cut late, so there was still some fight in it, but, when it came down to it, it had either been the mare or yoking himself up to the buckboard, leaning forward until his fingertips touched the ground.

Twenty years ago, he would have tried it, just to make a girl laugh.

Now, he took what was available, made do.

And anyway, from the way the mare kept trying to swing wide, head back into the shade of town, this wasn't going to be her first trip across the Arizona Territories. Maybe she'd even know where the water was, if it came down to that. Where the Apache weren't.

Lonegan brushed the traces across her flank and she pulled ahead, the wagon creaking, all his crates shifting around behind him, the jars and bottles inside touching shoulders. The straw they were packed in was going to be the mare's forage, if all the red baked earth ahead of them was as empty as it looked.

As they picked their way through it, Lonegan explained to the mare that he never meant for it to be this way. That this was the last time. But then he trailed off. Up ahead a black column was coming into view.

Buzzards.

Lonegan nodded, smiled.

What was dead there was pungent enough to be drawing them in for miles.

"What do you think, old girl?" he said to the mare. She didn't answer. Lonegan nodded to himself again, checked the scattergun under his seat, and pulled the mare's head towards the swirling buzzards. "Professional curiosity," he told her, then laughed because it was a joke.

The town he'd left that morning wasn't going on any map.

The one ahead of him, as far as he knew, probably wasn't on any map either. But it would be there. They always were.

When the mare tried shying away from the smell of death, Lonegan got down, talked into her ear, and tied his handkerchief across her eyes. The last little bit, he led her by the bridle, then hobbled her upwind.

The buzzards were a greasy black coat, moved like old men walking barefoot on the hot ground.

Instead of watching them, Lonegan traced the ridges of rock all around.

"Well," he finally said, and leaned into the washed-out little hollow.

The buzzards lifted their wings in something like menace, but Lonegan knew better. He slung rocks at the few that wouldn't take to the sky. They just backed off, their dirty mouths open in challenge.

Lonegan held his palm out to them, explained that this wasn't going to take long.

He was right: the dead guy was the one Lonegan had figured it would be. The thin deputy with the three-pocketed vest. He still had the vest on, had been able to crawl maybe twenty paces from where his horse had died. The horse was a gelding, a long-legged bay with a white diamond on its forehead, three white socks. Lonegan distinctly remembered having appreciated that horse. But now it had been run to death, had died with white foam on its flanks, blood blowing from its nostrils, eyes wheeling around, the deputy spurring him on, deeper into the heat, to warn the next town over.

Lonegan looked from the horse to the deputy. The buzzards were going after the gelding, of course.

It made Lonegan sick.

He walked up to the deputy, facedown in the dirt, already rotting, and rolled him over.

"Not quite as fast as you thought you were, eh deputy?" he said, then shot him in the mouth. Twice.

It was a courtesy.

Nine days later, all the straw in his crates hand-fed to the mare, his jars and bottles tied to each other with twine to keep them from shattering, Lonegan looked into the distance and nodded: a town was rising up from the dirt. A perfect little town.

He snubbed the mare to a shuffling stop, turned his head to the side to make sure they weren't pulling any dust in. That would give them away.

Then he just stared at the town.

Finally the mare snorted a breath of hot air in, blew it back out.

"I know," Lonegan said. "I know."

According to the scrap of paper he'd been marking, it was only Friday.

"One more night," he told the mare, and angled her over to some scrub, a ring of blackened stones in the packed ground.

He had to get there on a Saturday.

It wasn't like one more night was going to kill him, anyway. Or the mare.

He parked the buckboard on the town side of the ring of stones, so they wouldn't see his light, find him before he was ready.

Before unhooking the mare, he hobbled her. Four nights ago, she wouldn't have tried running. But now there was the smell of other horses in the air. Hay, maybe. Water.

And then there was the missing slice of meat Lonegan had cut from her haunch three nights ago.

It had been shallow, and he'd packed it with a medley of poultices from his crates, folded the skin back over, but still, he was pretty sure she'd been more than slightly offended.

Lonegan smiled at her, shook his head no, that she didn't need to worry. He could wait one more day for solid food, for water that wasn't briny and didn't taste like rust.

Or—no: he was going to get a *cake*, this time. All for himself. A big white one, slathered in whatever kind of frosting they had.

And all the water he could drink.

Lonegan nodded to himself about this, leaned back into his bedroll, and watched the sparks from the fire swirl up past his battered coffee pot.

When it was hot enough, he offered a cup to the mare.

She flared her nostrils, stared at him.

Before turning in, Lonegan emptied the grains from his cup into her open wound and patted it down, told her it was an old medicine man trick. That he knew them all.

He fell asleep thinking of the cake.

The mare slept standing up.

By noon the next day, he was set up on the only street in town. Not in front of the saloon but the mercantile. Because the men bellied up to the bar would walk any distance for the show. The people just in town for flour or salt though, you had to step into their path some. Make them aware of you.

Lonegan had polished his boots, shaved his jaw, pulled the hair on his chin down into a waxy point.

He waited until twenty or so people had gathered before reaching up under the side of the buckboard, for the secret handle.

He pulled it, stepped away with a flourish, and the panel on the buckboard opened up like a staircase, all the bottles and jars and felt bags of medicine already tied into place.

One person in the crowd clapped twice.

Lonegan didn't look around, just started talking about how the blue oil in the clear jar—he'd pilfered it from a barber shop in Missouri—how, if rubbed into the scalp twice daily and let cook in the sun, it would make a head of hair grow back, if you happened to be missing one. Full, black, Indian hair. But you had to be careful not to use too much, especially in these parts.

Now somebody in the crowd laughed.

Inside, Lonegan smiled, then went on.

The other stuff, fox urine he called it, though assured them it wasn't, it was for the women specifically. He couldn't go into the particulars in mixed company though, of course. This was a Christian settlement, right?

He looked around when no one answered.

"Amen," a man near the front finally said.

Lonegan nodded.

"Thought so," he said. "Some towns I come across…well. Mining towns, y'know?"

Five, maybe six people nodded, kept their lips pursed.

The fox urine was going to be sold out by supper, Lonegan knew. Not to any of the women, either.

Facing the crowd now, the buckboard framed by the mercantile, like it was just an extension of the mercantile, Lonegan cycled through his other bottles, the rest of his jars, the creams and powders and rare leaves. Twice a man in the crowd raised his hand to stop the show, make a purchase, but Lonegan held his palm up. Not yet, not yet.

But then, towards mid-afternoon, the white-haired preacher finally showed up, the good book held in both hands before him like a shield.

Lonegan resisted acknowledging him. But just barely.

They were in the same profession, after all.

And the preacher was the key to all this, too.

So Lonegan went on hawking, selling, testifying, the sweat running down the back of his neck to wet his shirt. He took his hat off, wiped his forehead with the back of his sleeve, and eyed the crowd now, shrugged.

"If you'll excuse me a brief moment," he said, and stepped halfway behind the ass-end of the buckboard, swigged from a tall, clear bottle of nearly-amber liquid.

He swallowed, lifted the bottle again, and drew deep on it, nodded as he screwed the cap back on.

"What is that?" a woman asked.

Lonegan looked up as if caught, said, "Nothing, ma'am. Something of my own making."

"We—" another man started, stepping forward.

Lonegan shook his head no, cut him off: "It's not *that* kind of my own making, sir. Any man drinks whiskey in the heat like this is asking for trouble, am I right?"

The man stepped back without ever breaking eye contact.

"Then what is it?" a boy asked.

Lonegan looked down to him, smiled.

"Just something an old—a man from the Old Country taught this to me on his deathbed. It's kind of like...you know how a strip of dried meat, it's like the whole steak twisted into a couple of bites?"

The boy nodded.

Lonegan lifted the bottle up, let it catch the sunlight. Said, "This is like that. Except it's the good part of water. The cold part."

A man in the crowd muttered a curse. The dismissal cycled through, all around Lonegan. He waited for it to abate, then shrugged, tucked the bottle back into the buckboard. "It's not for sale anyway," he said, stepping back around to the bottles and jars.

"Why not?" a man in a thick leather vest asked.

By the man's bearing, Lonegan assumed he was law of some kind.

"Personal stock," Lonegan explained. "And—anyway. There's not enough. It takes about fourteen months to get even a few bottles distilled the right way."

"Then I take that to mean you'd be averse to sampling it out?" the man said.

Lonegan nodded, tried to look apologetic.

The man shook his head, scratched deep in his matted beard, and stepped forward, shouldered Lonegan out of the way.

A moment later, he'd grubbed the bottle up from the bedclothes Lonegan had stuffed it in.

With everybody watching, he unscrewed the cap, wiped his lips clean, and took a long pull off the bottle.

What it was was water with a green juniper leaf at the bottom. The inside of the bottle cap dabbed with honey. A couple drops of laudanum, for the soft headrush, and a peppermint candy ground up, to hide the laudanum.

The man lowered the bottle, swallowed what was left in his mouth, and smiled.

Grudgingly, Lonegan agreed to take two dollars for what was left in the bottle. And then everybody was calling for it.

"I don't—" he started, stepping up onto the hub of his wheel to try to reach everybody, "I don't have—" but they were surging forward.

"*Okay*," he said, for the benefit of the people up front, and stepped down, hauled a half-case of the water up over the side of the buckboard.

Which was when the preacher spoke up.

The crowd fell silent like church.

"I can't let you do this to these good people," the preacher said.

"I think—" Lonegan said, his stutter a practiced thing, "I think you have me confused with the k-kind of gentlemen who—"

"I'm not confused at all, sir," the preacher said, both his hands still clasping the Bible.

Lonegan stared at him, stared at him, then took a respectful step forward. "What could convince you then, Brother?" he said. "Take my mare there. See that wound on her haunch? Would you believe that four days ago that was done by an old blunderbuss, fired on accident?"

"By you?"

"I was cleaning it."

The preacher nodded, waiting.

Lonegan went on. "You could reach your hand into the hole, I'm saying."

"And your medicine fixed it?" the preacher anticipated, his voice rising.

Lonegan palmed a smoky jar from the shelves, said, "This poultice, yes sir. A man named Running Bear showed me how to take the caul around the heart of a dog and grind—"

The preacher blew air out his nose.

"He was Oglala Sioux," Lonegan added, and let that settle.

The preacher just stared.

Lonegan looked around at the faces in the crowd, starting to side with the preacher. More out of habit than argument. But still.

Lonegan nodded, backed off, hands raised. Was quiet long enough to let them know he was just thinking of this: "These—these snake oil men you've taken me for, Brother. People. A despicable breed. What would you say characterizes them?"

When the preacher didn't answer, a man in the crowd did: "They sell things."

"I sell things," Lonegan agreed.

"Medicine," a woman clarified.

"Remedies," Lonegan corrected, nodding to her to show he meant no insult.

She held his eyes.

"What else?" Lonegan said, to all.

It was the preacher who answered: "You'll be gone tomorrow."

"—before any of our hair can get grown in," an old man added, sweeping his hat off to show his bald head.

Lonegan smiled wide, nodded. Cupped a small bottle of the blue oil from its place on the panel, twirled it to the man.

He caught it, stared at Lonegan.

"I'm not leaving," Lonegan said.

"Yeah, well—" a man started.

"I'm *not*," Lonegan said, some insult in his voice now. "And, you know what? To prove it, today and today only, I'll be accepting checks, or notes. Just write your name and how much you owe me on any scrap of paper—here, I've got paper myself, I'll even supply that. I won't come to collect until you're satisfied."

As one, a grin spread across the crowd's face.

"How long this take to work?" the bald man asked, holding his bottle of blue up.

"I've seen it take as long as six days, to be honest."

The old man raised his eyebrows. They were bushy, white.

People were already pushing forward again.

Lonegan stepped up onto his hub, waved his arms for them to slow down, slow down. That he wanted to make a gift first.

It was a tightly-woven cloth bag the size of a man's head.

He handed it to the preacher, said, "Brother."

The preacher took it, looked from Lonegan to the string tying the bag closed.

"Traveling like I do," Lonegan said, "I make my tithe where I can. With what I can."

The preacher opened it.

"The sacrament?" he said.

"Just wafers for now," Lonegan said. "You'll have to bless them, of course."

Slowly at first, then altogether, the crowd started clapping.

The preacher tied the bag shut, extended his hand to Lonegan.

By dinner, there wasn't a drop of fox urine in his possession.

When the two women came to collect him for church the next morning, Lonegan held his finger up, told them he'd be right there. He liked to say a few prayers beforehand.

The women lowered their bonneted heads that they understood, then one of them added that his mare had run off in the night, it looked like.

"She does that," Lonegan said with a smile, and closed the door, held it there.

Just what he needed: a goddamn prophetic horse.

Instead of praying then, or going to the service, Lonegan packed his spare clothes tight in his bedroll, shoved it under the bed then made the bed so nobody would have any call to look under it. Before he ever figured this whole thing out, he'd lost two good suits just because he'd failed to stretch a sheet across a mattress.

But now, now his bedroll was still going to be there Monday, or Tuesday, or whenever he came for it.

Next, he angled the one chair in the room over to the window, waited for the congregation to shuffle back out into the streets in their Sunday best.

Today, the congregation was going to be the whole town. Because they felt guilty about the money they'd spent yesterday, and because they knew this morning there was going to be a Communion.

In a Baptist church, that happened little enough that it was an event.

With luck, nobody would even have noticed Lonegan's absence, come looking for him.

With luck, they'd all be guilty enough to palm an extra wafer, let it go soft against the roofs of their mouths.

After a lifetime of eating coarse hunks of bread, the wafer would be candy to them. So white it had to be pure.

Lonegan smiled, propped his boots up on the windowsill, and tipped back the bottle of rotgut until his eyes watered. If he'd been drinking just to feel good, it would have been sipping bourbon. For this, though, he needed to be drunk, and smell like it.

Scattered on the wood-plank floor all around him, fallen like leaves, were the promissory notes for yesterday's sales.

He wasn't going to need them to collect.

It was a funny thing.

Right about what he figured was the middle of lunch for most of the town—he didn't even know its name, he laughed to himself—he pulled the old Colt up from his lap, laid the bottom of the barrel across the back of his left wrist, and aimed in turn at each of the six panes in his window, blew them out into the street.

Ten minutes and two reloads later, he was fast in jail.

"Don't get too comfortable in there now," the bearded man Lonegan had made for the law said. He was wearing a stiff collar from church, a tin star on his chest.

Lonegan smiled, leaned back on his cot, and shook his head no, he wouldn't.

"When's dinner?" he slurred out, having to bite back a smile, the cake a definite thing in his mind again.

The Sheriff didn't respond, just walked out.

Behind him, Lonegan nodded.

Sewed into the lining of his right boot were all the tools he would need to pick the simple lock of the cell.

Sewed into his belt, as back-up, was a few thimblefuls of gunpowder wrapped in thin oilcloth, in case the lock was jammed. In Lonegan's teeth, a sulfur-head match that the burly man had never even questioned.

Lonegan balanced it in one of the cracks of the wall.

He was in the best room in town, now.

That afternoon he woke to a woman staring at him. She was sideways—*he* was sideways, on the cot.

He pushed the heel of his right hand into one eye then the other, sat up.

"Ma'am," he said, having to turn his head sideways to swallow.

She was slight but tall, her face lined by the weather it looked like. A hard woman to get a read on.

"I came to pay," she said.

Lonegan lowered his head to smile, had to grip the edge of his cot with both hands to keep from spilling down onto the floor.

"My father," the woman went on, finding her voice, "he—I don't know why. He's rubbing that blue stuff onto his head. He smells like a barbershop."

Lonegan looked up to this woman, wasn't sure if he should smile or not. *She* was, anyway.

"You don't see its efficacy," he said, "you don't got to pay. Ma'am."

She stared at him about this, finally said, "Can you even spell that?"

"What?"

"Efficacy."

Now it was Lonegan's turn to just stare.

"Got a first name?" she said.

"Lonegan," Lonegan shrugged.

"The rest of it?"

"Just Lonegan."

"That's how it is then?"

"Alone, again…" he went on, breaking his name down into words for her.

"I get it," she told him.

"Regular-like, you mean?"

She caught his meaning about this as well, set her teeth, but then shook her head no, smiled instead.

"I don't know what kind of—what kind of affair you're trying to pull off here, Mister Alone Again."

"My horse ran off," Lonegan said, standing, pulling his face close to the bars now. "Think I'm apt to make a fast getaway in these?"

For illustration, he lifted his right boot. It was down at heel. Shiny on top, bare underneath.

"You meant to get thrown in here, I mean," she said. "Shooting up Molly's best room like that."

"Who are you, you don't mind my asking?"

"I'm the daughter of the man you swindled yesterday afternoon. I'm just here to complete the transaction."

"I told you—"

"And I'm telling you. I'm not going to be indebted to a man like you. Not again."

Lonegan cocked his head over to her, narrowed his eyes. "Again?" he said.

"How much it going to cost me?"

"Say my name."

"How much?"

Lonegan tongued his lower lip out, was falling in love just a little bit, he thought. Wishing he wasn't on this side of the bars, anyway.

"You like the service this morning?" he asked.

"I don't go to church with my father anymore," the woman said. "Who do you think swindled us the first time?"

Lonegan smiled, liked it.

"Anyway," the woman went on. "My father tends to bring enough church home with him each Sunday to last us the week through. And then some."

"What's your name?" Lonegan said, watching her.

"That supposed to give you some power over me, if you know?"

"So you think I'm real then?"

Lonegan shrugged, waiting for her to try to back out of the corner she'd wedged herself into.

"You can call me Mary," she said, lifting her chin at the end.

"I like Jezebel better," he said. "Girl who didn't go to church."

"Do you even know the Bible?" she asked.

"I know I'm glad you didn't go to church this morning."

"How much, Mister *Lonegan*?"

He nodded thanks, said, "For you, Jezebel. For you—"

"I don't want a deal."

"Two dollars."

"They sold for two bits, I heard."

"Special deal for a special lady."

She held his stare for a moment longer then slammed her coin purse down on the only desk in the room, started counting out coins.

Two dollars was a full week's work, Lonegan figured.

"What do you do?" he said, watching her.

"Give money to fools, it would seem," she muttered.

Lonegan hissed a laugh, was holding the bars on each side of his face, all his weight there.

She stood with the money in her hand.

"I *bake*," she said—spit, really.

Lonegan felt everything calming inside him.

"Confectionary stuff?" he said.

"Why?" she said, stepping forward. "You come here for a matrimony?"

"…Mary Lonegan," Lonegan sung out, like trying it out some.

She held the money out, her palm down so she'd just have to open her fingers.

Lonegan worked it into a brush of skin anyway, said at the last moment, "Or you could just—you could stay and talk. In the next cell, maybe."

"It cost me two more dollars not to?" she said back, her hand to her coin purse again, then stared at Lonegan until he had to look away. To the heavy oak door that opened onto the street.

The sheriff was stepping through, fumbling for the peg on the wall, to hang his holster on.

"Annie," he said to the woman.

Her top lip rose in what Lonegan took for anger, disgust. Not directed at the lawman, but at her own name spoken aloud.

"'Annie,'" Lonegan repeated.

"You know this character?" the man said, cutting his eyes to Lonegan.

"We go back a long ways, Sheriff," Lonegan said.

Annie laughed through her nose, pushed past the lawman, stepped out into the sunlight.

Lonegan watched the door until it was closed all the way, then studied the floor.

Finally he nodded, slipped his belt off with one hand, ferreted the slender oilcloth of gunpowder out.

"For obvious reasons, she didn't bake it into a cake," he said, holding the oilcloth up for the lawman to see.

"Annie?" the lawman said, incredulous.

"If that's the name you know her by," Lonegan said, then dropped the oilcloth bag onto the stone floor.

The lawman approached, fingered the black powder up to his nose. Looked to the door as well.

By nightfall, Annie Jorgensson was in the cell next to Lonegan's.

"Was hoping you'd bring some of those pastries you've been making," he said to her, nodding down to the apron she was still wearing, the flour dusting her forearms.

"Was hoping you'd be dead by now, maybe," she said back, brushing her arms clean.

"You could have brought something, I mean."

"That why you lied about me?"

"What I said, I said to save your life. A little courtesy might be in order."

"You think talking to you's going to save me?" she said. "Rather be dead, thanks."

Lonegan leaned back on his cot, closed his eyes.

All dinner had been was some hardtack the Sheriff had had in his saddlebag for what tasted like weeks.

Lonegan had made himself eat all of it, though, every bite.

Not for strength, but out of spite. Because he knew what was coming.

"You're sure you didn't go to church this morning?" he said to Annie Jorgensson.

She didn't answer. It didn't matter much if she had though, he guessed, and was just lying to him about it, like she had with her name. Either way there was still a wall of bars between them. And he didn't know what he was going to do with her anyway, after. Lead her by the hand into the saloon, pour her a drink?

No, it was better if she was lying, really. If she was a closet Baptist.

It would keep him from having to hold her down with his knee, shoot her in the face.

Ten minutes after a light Lonegan couldn't see the source of was doused, the horses at the livery took to screaming.

Lonegan nodded, watched for Annie's reaction.

She just sat there.

"You alive?" he called over.

Her eyes flicked up to him, but that was all.

Yes.

Soon enough the horses kicked down a gate or a wall, started crashing through the town. One of them ran up onto the boardwalk it sounded like, then, afraid of the sound of its own hooves, shied away, into a window. After that, Lonegan couldn't tell. There was gunfire, for the horse maybe. Or not.

The whole time he watched Annie.

"Mary," he said to her once, in play.

"Jezebel to you," she hissed back.

He smiled.

"What's happening out there?" she asked, finally.

"I'm in here," Lonegan shrugged back to her. "You saying this doesn't happen every night?"

She stood, leaned against the bars at the front of her cell.

One time before, Lonegan had made it through with a cellmate. Or, in the next cell, like this.

He'd left that one there, though. Not turned, like the rest of the town, but starved inside of four days anyway. Five if he ate the stuffing from his mattress.

It had been interesting, though, the man's reactions—how his back stiffened with each scream. The line of saliva that descended from his lip to the ground.

"I've got to piss," Lonegan said.

Annie didn't turn around.

Lonegan aimed it at the trap under the window, was just shaking off when a face appeared, nearly level with his own.

It was one of the men from the crowd.

His eyes were wild, roving, his cheeks already shrunken, making his teeth look larger. Around his mouth, blood.

He pulled at the bars of the window like the animal he was.

"You're already dead," Lonegan said to him, then raised his finger in the shape of a pistol, shot the man between the eyes.

The man grunted, shuffled off.

"That was Sid Masterson," Annie said from behind him. "If you're wondering, I mean."

"Think he was past the point where an introduction would have done any good," Lonegan said, turning to catch her eye.

"This is supposed to impress me?" Annie said, suddenly standing at the wall of bars between them.

"You're alive," Lonegan told her.

"What are they?" she said, lifting her chin to take in the whole town.

Lonegan shrugged, rubbed the side of his nose with the side of his finger.

"Some people just get caught up when they're dying, I guess," he said. "Takes them longer."

"How long?"

Lonegan smiled, said, "A day. They don't last so long in the sun. I don't know why."

"But you can't have got everybody."

"They'll get who I didn't."

"You've done this before."

"Once or twice, I suppose. My oxen gets in the ditch like everybody else's..."

For a long time, Annie just stared at him. Finally she said, "We would have given you whatever, y'know?"

"A good Christian town," Lonegan recited.

"You didn't have to do this, I mean."

"They were asking for it," Lonegan said, shrugging it true. "They paid me, even, if I recall correctly."

"It was that poppy water."

Lonegan raised his eyebrows to her.

"I know the taste," she said. "What was it masking?"

In reply, Lonegan pursed his lips, pointed with them out to the town: that.

"My father?" Annie said, then.

Lonegan kept looking at the front door.

Her father. That was definitely going to be a complication. There was a reason he usually passed the night alone, he told himself.

But she was a *baker*.

Back in her kitchen there was probably all manner of frosting and sugar.

Lonegan opened his mouth to ask her where she lived, but then thought better of it. He'd find her place anyway. After tonight, he'd have all week to scavenge through town. Every house, every building.

Towards the end of the week, even, the horses would come back, from downwind. They'd be skittish like the mare had been—skittish that he was dead like the others had been, just not lying down yet—but then he'd have oats in a sack, and, even if they had been smart enough to run away, they were still just horses.

Or, he hoped—this time—a *mule.*

Something with personality.

They usually tasted better anyway.

He came to again sometime before dawn. He could tell by the quality of light sifting in through the bars of his window. There were no birds singing, though. And the smell. He was used to the smell by now.

Miles east of town, he knew, a tree was coated with buzzards.

Soon they would rise into an oily black mass, ride the heat into town, drift down onto the bodies that would be in the street by now.

Like with the deputy Lonegan had found, though, the buzzards would know better than to eat. Even to them, this kind of dead tasted wrong.

With luck, maybe one of the horses would have run its lungs bloody for them, collapsed in a heap of meat.

With luck, it'd be that ornery damn mare.

They'd start on her haunch, of course, finish what Lonegan had started.

He nodded, pulled a sharp hank of air up his nose, and realized what had woke him: the oak door. It was moving, creaking.

In the next cell, Annie was already at the bars, holding her breath.

"They can't get in," Lonegan told her.

She didn't look away from the door.

"What were you dreaming about there?" she said, her voice flat and low.

Lonegan narrowed his eyes at her.

Dream?

He looked at his hands as if they might have been involved, then touched his face.

It was wet.

He shook his head no, stood, and the oak door swung open.

Standing in the space it had been was the sheriff.

He'd seen better days.

Annie fell back to her cot, pulled the green blanket up to her mouth.

Lonegan didn't move, just inspected. It wasn't often he got to see one of the shufflers when they were still shuffling. This one, he surmised, he'd fallen down in some open place. While he was turning, too, another had fed on him, it looked like. His face on the right side was down to the bone, one of his arms gone, just a ragged sleeve now.

Not that he was in a state to care about any of that.

This was probably the time he usually came into work on Monday.

It was all he knew anymore.

"Hey," Lonegan called out to it, to be sure.

The thing had to look around for the source of the sound.

When he found it, Lonegan nodded.

"No…" Annie was saying through her blanket.

"He can't get through," Lonegan said again. "They can't—keys, tools, guns."

For a long time, then—it could sense the sun coming, Lonegan thought—the thing just stood there, rasping air in and out.

Annie was hysterical in a quiet way, pushing on the floor with her feet over and over, like trying to back herself out of this.

Lonegan watched like she was a new thing to him.

Maybe if he was just seeing his first one too, though. But…no. Even then—it had been a goat—even then he'd known what was happening. It was the goat he'd been trying all his mixtures out on first, because it would eat anything. And because it couldn't aim a pistol.

When it had died, Lonegan had nodded, looked at the syrup in the wooden tube, already drying into a floury paste, and been about to sling it out into the creek with all the other bad mixes when the goat had kicked, its one good eye rolling in its skull, a sound clawing from its throat that had pushed Lonegan up onto his buckboard.

Finally, when the horse he'd had then wouldn't calm down, Lonegan had had to shoot the goat.

The goat had looked up to the barrel like a child, too.

It was the same look the thing in the doorway had now. Like it didn't understand just how it had got to be where it was.

The front of its pants were wet, from the first time it had relaxed into death.

Lonegan watched it.

In its other hand—and this he'd never seen—was one of the bottles of what Annie had called poppy water.

The thing was holding it by the neck like it knew what it was.

When it lifted it to its mouth, Annie forgot how to breathe a little.

Lonegan turned to her, then to the thing, and got it: she knew what that water tasted like, still thought it *was* the water, doing all this to her town.

He smiled to himself, came back to the thing, the shuffler.

It was making its way across the floor, one of its ankles at a bad angle.

Now Annie was screaming, stuffing the blanket into her mouth. The thing noticed, came to her cell.

"You don't want to—" Lonegan started, but it was too late.

Make them take an interest in you, he was going to say.

Like anything with an appetite, jerky motions drew its attention.

Annie was practically convulsing.

Lonegan came to the wall of bars between them, reached for her hand, just to let her know she was alive, but, at the touch she cringed away, her eyes wild, breath shallow.

"You should have gone to church," Lonegan said, out loud he guessed, because she looked over, a question on her face, but by then the thing was at the bars. It wasn't strong enough to come through them of course, but it didn't understand things the way a man would either.

Slowly, as if *trying* to, it wedged its head between two of the bars—leading with its mouth—and started to push and pull through.

The first thing to go was its one good eye. It ran down its cheek.

Next was its jaw, then its skull, and still it kept coming, got halfway through before it didn't have anything left.

Annie had never been in danger. Not from the thing, anyway.

She wasn't so much conscious anymore either, though.

For a long time, Lonegan sat on the edge of his cot, his head leaned down into his hands, the thing in the bars still breathing somehow, even when the sunlight spilled through, started turning its skin to leather.

It was time.

Lonegan worked his pants leg up, slid the two picks out, had the door to his cell open almost as fast as if he'd had the key.

The first thing he did was take the shotgun off the wall, hold the barrel to the base of the thing's skull. But then Annie started to stir. Lonegan focused in on her, nodded, and turned the gun around, slammed the butt into the thing until its head lolled forward, the skin at the back of the neck tearing into a mouth of sorts, that smiled with a ripping sound.

When the thing fell, it gave Lonegan a clear line on Annie.

She was dotted with black blood now.

He might as well have just shot the thing, he figured.

"Well," he said to her.

She was crying, hiding inside herself.

"You don't catch it from the blood," he told her, "don't worry," but she wasn't listening anymore.

Lonegan pulled the keys up from the thing's belt, and unlocked her cell, let the door swing wide.

"But—but—" she said.

Lonegan shrugged, disgusted with her.

"*What?*" he said, finally. "I saved your life, Mary, Jezebel. Annie Jorgensson."

She shook her head no, more of a jerk than a gesture.

Lonegan twirled the shotgun by the trigger guard, held it down along his leg.

The easy thing to do now would be to point it at her, get this over with.

Except she was the cake lady.

For the first time in years, he wasn't sure if he'd be able to stomach the cake, later, if he did this to her now.

"What's the name of this town?" he said to her.

She looked up, the muscles in her face dancing.

"Name?"

"This place."

For a long time she didn't understand the question, then she nodded, said it: "Gultree."

Lonegan nodded, said, "I don't think I'll be staying in Gultree much longer, Miss Jorgensson. Not to be rude."

She shook her head no, no, he wasn't being rude.

"I'm sorry about your father," he said then. It even surprised him.

Annie just stared at him, her mouth working around a word: "…why?"

"The world," he said to her, "it's a—it's a hard place. I didn't make it. It just is."

"Somebody told you that," she said weakly, shaking her head no. "You don't…you don't believe it."

"Would I do this if I didn't?"

She laughed, leaned back. "You're trying to convince yourself, Mister Alone Again," she told him.

And then she didn't stop laughing.

Lonegan stared hard at her, hated Gultree. Everything about it. He was glad he'd killed it, wiped it off the map.

"Goodbye then," he said to her, lifting the fingers of his free hand to the hat he'd left…where?

He looked around for it, finally just took a sweated-through brown one off the peg by the door.

It fit. Close enough, anyway.

For a moment longer than he meant to, he stood in the doorway, waiting for Annie to come up behind him, but she didn't. Even after the door of her cell made its rusty moan.

Lonegan had to look back.

Annie was on her knees behind the thing the sheriff had become.

She'd worked his revolver up from his holster, was holding it backwards, the barrel in her mouth, so deep she was gagging.

Lonegan closed his eyes, heard her saying it again, from a few minutes ago: "But—but—"

But she'd drank the poppy water too. Thought she was already dead like the rest of them.

She only had to shoot herself once.

Lonegan narrowed his lips, made himself look at what was left of her, then turned, pulled the door shut.

Usually he took his time picking through town, filling saddlebags and feed-sacks with jewelry and guns and whatever else would sell.

This time was different, though.

This time he just walked straight down Main Street to his buckboard, folded the side panel back into itself, and looked around for a horse.

When there wasn't one, he started walking the way he'd come in. Soon enough a horse whinnied.

Lonegan slowed, filled his stolen hat with pebbles and sand, started shaking it, shaking it.

Minutes later, the mare rose from the heat.

"Not you," he said.

She was briny with salt, from running. Had already been coming back to town for the water trough.

Lonegan narrowed his eyes at the distance behind her, for another horse. There was just her, though. He dumped the hat, turned back around.

Twenty minutes later, her nose to the ground like a dog, she trotted into town.

Lonegan slipped a rope over her head and she slumped into it, kept drinking.

All around them were the dead and the nearly dead, littering the streets, coming half out of windows.

Ahead of him, in the straight line from the last town to this one, there'd be another town, he knew. And another, and another. Right now, even, there was probably a runner out there from *this* town, trying to warn everybody of the snake oil man.

Lonegan would find him like he'd found the last, though. Because anybody good enough to leave his own family to ride all night, warn people twenty miles away, anybody from that stock would have been at the service Sunday morning too, done a little partaking.

Which meant he was dead in the saddle already, his tongue swelling in his mouth, a thirst rising from deeper than any thirst he'd ever had before.

Lonegan fixed the yoke on the mare, smeared more poultice into her wound.

If things got bad enough out there this time, he could do what he'd always thought would work: crush one of the wafers up, rub it into her nostrils, make her breathe it in.

She'd die, yeah, but she'd come back too. If she was already in the harness when she did, then he could get a few more miles out of her, he figured.

But it would spoil her meat.

Lonegan looked ahead, trying to figure how far it was going to be this time. How many days. Whether there was some mixture or compound or extract he hadn't found yet, one that could make him forget Gultree altogether. And Annie. Himself.

They'd been asking for it though, he told himself, again.

If it hadn't been him, it would have been somebody else, and that other person might not have known how to administer it, then it would have been one half of the town—the *live* half—against the other.

And that just plain took too long.

No, it was better this way.

Lonegan leaned over to spit, then climbed up onto the seat of the buckboard. The mare pulled ahead, picking around the bodies on her own. The one time one of them jerked, raising its arm to her, Lonegan put it down with the scattergun.

In the silence afterwards, there wasn't a sound in Gultree.

Lonegan shook his head, blew his disgust out his nose.

At the far edge of town was what he'd been counting on: a house with a name gold-lettered onto the back of one of the windows: *Wm. Jorgensson.* It was where Annie lived, where she cooked, where she'd *been* cooking, until the sheriff came for her.

Lonegan tied the mare to a post, stepped into Annie's living room, found himself with his hat in his hands for some reason, the scattergun in the buckboard.

They were all dead, though.

"Cake," he said aloud, trying to make it real.

It worked.

In the kitchen, not even cut, was a white cake. It was smeared with lard, it looked like. Lard thick with sugar.

Lonegan ran his finger along the edge, tasted it, breathed out for what felt like the first time in days.

Yes.

He took the cake and the dish it was on too, stepped back into the living room.

The father was waiting for him, a felt bowler hat clamped down over his skull. He was dead, clutching a Bible the same way the sheriff had been carrying the bottle.

The old man was working his mouth and tongue like he was going to say something.

Lonegan waited, waited, had no idea what one of these could say if it took a mind to.

Finally he had to say it for the old man, though, answer the only question that mattered: Annie.

"I got her out before," he said. "You don't need to worry about her none, sir."

The old man just creaked, deep in his throat.

Walking across his left eyeball was a wasp.

Lonegan took a step back, angled his head for another door then came back to the old man.

If—if the buzzards knew better than to eat these things, shouldn't a wasp too?

Lonegan narrowed his eyes at the old man, walked around to see him from the side.

He was dead, a shuffler, but—but not *as* dead.

It hadn't been a bad mixture, either. Lonegan had made it like every other time. No, it was something else, something…

Lonegan shook his head no, then did it anyway: tipped the old man's bowler hat off.

What spilled out was a new head of hair. It was white, silky, dripping blue.

The old man straightened his back, like trying to stand from the hair touching his neck now, for the first time ever.

"No," Lonegan whispered, still shaking his head, and then the old man held the Bible out to him.

It pushed Lonegan backwards over a chair.

He caught himself on his hand, rolled into a standing position in the kitchen doorway. Never even spilled the cake.

"You've been using the oil," he said to the old man, touching his own hair to show.

The old man—William Jorgensson: a *he*, not an it—didn't understand, just kept leading with the Bible.

Lonegan smiled, shook his head no. Thanks, but no.

The old man breathed in sharp then, all at once, then out again, blood misting out now. Meaning it was almost over now, barbershop oil or no.

Again, he started making the creaking sound with his throat. Like he was trying to talk.

When he couldn't get it out, and Lonegan wouldn't take the Bible, the old man finally reached into his pocket, came out with a handful of broken wafers, stolen from the pan at church.

It was what Annie had said: her father bringing the church back to her, since she wouldn't go.

Lonegan held his hands away, his fingertips even, and stepped away again. Not that the wafers could get through boot leather. But still.

The Bible slapped the wooden floor.

"You old thief," Lonegan said.

The old man just stood there.

"What else you got in there, now?" Lonegan asked.

The old man narrowed his half-dead eyes, focused on his hand in his pocket, and came up with the bottle Lonegan had given him for free. It was empty.

Lonegan nodded about that, got the old man nodding too.

"That I can do something about, now," he said, and stepped long and wide around the old man, out the front door.

The heat was stifling, wonderful.

Lonegan balanced the cake just above his shoulder, unhooked the panel on the side of the buckboard. It slapped down, the mare spooking ahead a step or two, until the traces stopped her.

Lonegan glared at her, looked back to the house, then did it anyway, what he knew he didn't have to: palmed up the last two bottles of barbershop oil. They were pale blue in the sunlight, like a cat's eyes.

He stepped back into the living room, slapped the wall to let the old man know he was back.

The old man turned around slow, the soles of his boots scraping the wood floor the whole way.

"Here," Lonegan said, setting the two bottles down on the table, holding up the cake to show what they were in trade for.

The old man just stared, wasn't going to make it. His index finger twitching by his thigh, the nail bed stained blue.

"I'm sorry," Lonegan said. "For whatever that's worth."

By the time he'd pulled away, the old man had shuffled to the door, was just standing there.

"Give it six days," Lonegan said, touching his own hair to show what he meant, then laughed a nervous laugh, slapped the leather down on the mare's tender haunch.

Fucking Gultree.

He pushed out into the heat, was able to make himself wait all the way until dark for the cake. Because it was a celebration, he even sedated the mare, cut another flank steak off, packed it with poultice.

He'd forgot to collect any water, but then he'd forgot to collect all the jewelry and guns too.

There'd be more, though.

In places without women like Annie Jorgensson.

Lonegan wiped the last of the mare's grease from his mouth, pulled his chin hair down into a point, and pulled the cake plate into his lap, started fingering it in until he realized that he was just eating the sweet off the top, like his aunt had always warned him against. It needed to be balanced with the dry cake inside.

He cut a wedge out with his knife, balanced it into his mouth, and did it again and again, until something popped under his blade, deep in the cake.

It was a half a wafer.

Lonegan stared at it, stared at it some more. Tried to control his breathing, couldn't seem to.

Was it—was it from *this* Sunday's service, or from last?

Had what was in the old man's pocket been the whole take, or just part of it?

Lonegan's jaws slowed, then he gagged, threw up onto his chest, and looked all the way back to town, to the old man in the door, smiling now, lifting his Bible to show that he knew, that he'd known, that he'd been going to get religion into his daughter's life whether she wanted it or not.

Lonegan shook his head no, no, told the old man that—that, if she'd just waited to pull the trigger, he would have *told* her that it wasn't the poppy water. But then too was dead certain he could feel the wafer inside him, burrowing like a worm for his heart, his life.

He threw up again, but it was thin now, weak.

"...no," he said, the wet strings hanging from his chin. It didn't—it couldn't...it didn't happen *this* fast. Did it? Had it ever?

His fingers thick now, he sifted through the cake for another wafer, to see if he could tell which Sunday it had been from, but all the shards were too small, too broken up.

Annie. Goddamn you. *Which Sunday?*

But—but...

The oil, the barbershop oil. Hell yes. It slowed the wafers.

Lonegan stumbled up through the fire, scattering sparks, the cake plate shattering on a rock, and started falling towards the mare. To ride fast back to Gultree, back to the old man, those two blue bottles.

But the mare saw him coming, jerked her head away from the wagon wheel she was tied to.

The reins held. The spoke didn't.

She skittered back, still sluggish from what he'd dosed her with, and Lonegan nodded, made himself slow down. Held his hat out like there was going to be something in it this time, really, come on, old gal.

The mare opened her nostrils to the night, tasting it for oats, then turned her head sideways to watch Lonegan with one eye, then shied back when he stepped forward, shaking her mane in warning, flicking her tail like she was younger than her years, and when he took another step closer, leading with the hat, she ducked him, and in this way they danced for the rest of the night, her reins always just within reach, if he could just time his steps right. Or what he thought was his reach.

Reggie Oliver is an actor, director, playwright, and author of fiction. Published work includes six plays; two novels; six volumes of short stories, including *Mrs Midnight* (2012 winner of Children of the Night Award for best work of supernatural fiction); and the biography of Stella Gibbons, *Out of the Woodshed*.

His stories have appeared in more than fifty anthologies. *The Sea of Blood*, selected stories including some new, was published in 2015. To be published in 2016: *The Boke of the Divill*—novel (Dark Renaissance); *Holidays from Hell*—new collection of stories (Tartarus); and *The Hauntings at Tankerton Park and How They Got Rid of Them*—children's book with illustrations by the author (Zagava Press).

Mr. Pigsny
Reggie Oliver

I

IT WAS, I suppose, a typical gangster's funeral. There were the extravagantly insincere floral tributes: To REG, A DIAMOND GEEZER in white carnations; there was "My Way" played by the reluctant organist; there was the coffin borne by six burly, black-coated thugs into a church which Reg would never have entered in his lifetime except to marry or to bury.

And why was I, Housman Professor of Classical Epigraphy at Cambridge University, there? Well, my sister, in some unaccountable hour of rebellious madness, had once married the late Reg McCall's younger brother Den and borne him two sons, before finally divorcing him and marrying a merchant banker instead. Because my sister Gwen "simply could not face" the funeral, and it was still the vacation, I had been deputised to accompany my two teenage nephews Robert and Arthur to the obsequies. Reg had no living children. His daughter Janet had predeceased him in a dreadful drug-fueled car crash some years previously, so Robert and Arthur were possible heirs. It would have shown "disrespect," that great gangland sin, had they not been present at their uncle's interment.

To be honest, I had rather liked Reg on the few occasions I had met him. Certainly, I always preferred him to Den, a "cold fish" if ever there was one. Of course I knew that Reg had been a ruthless underworld tyrant of the old school. I knew that he had had people "slapped," the criminal's euphemism for beaten up, and even "cut" (knifed) for betraying him. I knew that he had run protection rackets and brothels, and masterminded bank raids, and that he had once personally killed a man. The victim's name apparently was Maltese Percy, and the deed had been done in the cellars of the Dog and Gibbet in Hoxton. Everyone knew it had happened, but there had been, of course, no witnesses. I had also discovered that his proud boast that he never had anything to do with drug dealing was a lie, given out for the benefit of journalists, eager to perpetuate the myth of the loveable rogue. Nevertheless, I had liked him.

Because our paths would never have crossed other than for family reasons, Reg and I could take a dispassionate interest in one another. I heard that Reg used to boast about me to his cronies—"my brother-in-law, you know, the Cambridge professor"—and I must admit that I have occasionally dined out at high tables on *him*. At family gatherings Reg was a lavish and attentive host with the kind of courtesy, when he had a mind to it, that had earned him the sentimental East End reputation of being "a real gentlemen." In my experience real gentlemen don't have people cut or slapped, and rarely kill petty criminals in pub cellars, but let that pass. He was genial and friendly towards me, unlike his brother Den, "the quiet one," the backstairs fixer of the outfit, who always gave the impression of harbouring a grudge against the world.

I had been hoping, rather unrealistically perhaps, that once we had seen the body safely interred in the little Essex churchyard, my nephews and I could slip away. But of course, it was not to be; we were "asked back to the house" and it would have been disrespectful to refuse. We were even offered a lift in Reg's widow's stretch limousine because we had arrived at the church by train and taxi.

Even before we entered the limousine, I sensed an atmosphere. Den was already there, and Reg's widow Maureen was tucked into a corner. She was a small, neat woman who had retained her figure and her striking blonde hair with a strenuousness that showed in her face. Though she was barely in her mid-fifties, it looked ten years older, withered and pinched by anxiety. She glared at us from her corner while Den explained the situation briskly to her.

"Larry here and the boys are coming up to the house with us. All right Maureen?" That last question expected no reply and got none. (My name incidentally is *not* Larry and never has been: it is Lawrence, Professor Lawrence Chibnall.)

I knew the reason for the atmosphere and could, to some extent, sympathise with her. Now that Reg was dead, from natural causes incidentally, what little importance Maureen possessed in the McCall family hierarchy would dwindle to nothing. Den had already assumed a greater measure of control over the firm after Reg's first stroke eighteen months before; now the takeover was complete. Maureen would be comfortably off, but she would be ignored. Had she had sons as Den had, the role of matriarch might still be hers.

My nephews Robert and Arthur were behaving well. They did their best to ignore Maureen's resentful, tearstained stare and talked quietly to each other about neutral subjects. They were both at good public schools. Though they had been taught by their mother to hate Den they had the sense never to show any hostility. I was amused to learn from them that the fact that their father was a notorious underworld figure was regarded as "cool" by their school fellows and they were more than happy to take advantage of the fact.

Just before we set off for the house, someone else joined us in the limousine. Though there was plenty of room Den tried to prevent it on the spurious grounds that the car was reserved for close family only, but Maureen, for once, asserted herself.

"It's all right," she said. "It's Mr. Pigsny."

"Oh, yeah?"

"He was very close to Reg when he was dying. Let him in, Den."

The man who clambered aboard was very small, almost a dwarf, with a disproportionately large head. Long strands of sparse red hair had been combed across his domed cranium and lay there lank and damp, like seaweed on a rock after the tide has retreated. He wore a neat black suit and black tie, and, somewhat incongruously, a dark red rose in his buttonhole. He sat himself beside Maureen, smiling and nodding at the rest of us.

Den had decided to ignore him altogether, so I introduced myself and the boys. Mr. Pigsny shook hands smilingly with all three of us, but, as far as I can remember, said nothing. The drive to the house took place in the purring near silence of the great black limousine, punctuated only by the occasional sniffle from Maureen.

Reg's house was a detached mock Tudor mansion in an avenue of similar leafy refuges just outside Thurrock, that part of Essex being the place where all good criminals go to die. The lawns were clean shaven, the gravel deep in the drive, the leylandii high and dense enough to frustrate any casual intruder. When we arrived a number of suited men with thick, impenetrable faces were clustered importantly on the drive, like staff officers before a battle.

Inside, the house was spacious and, though Sir Terence Conran might have shuddered, the decor did not reek of the kind of vulgar ostentation so often favoured by the criminal fraternity. There was however something of a clash of styles. Maureen had gone in for prettiness of the glazed chintz variety. The drawing room was in light pastel shades and the porcelain figurines on the mantelpiece were complemented by the pink Dresden shepherdesses on the wallpaper. Reg's study and other parts of the house showed his more manly taste for dark oak and cherry-coloured leather. He owned one or two genuinely good pictures and antiques; in particular a magnificent blue and white Ming vase, about four feet high, decorated with dragon motifs. I had once expressed my admiration for it.

"You're not going to ask me where I got it or how much I paid, are you?" he said.

"My dear Reg, I wouldn't dream of asking such sensitive questions," I answered. For some reason Reg found my reply extremely funny. I think he found *me* extremely funny sometimes. I don't resent that, but I am slightly baffled. Very few of us are good at finding ourselves funny.

Our stretch limousine was one of the first vehicles to arrive at the house, but very soon people were coming thick and fast for the wake, and Reg's mansion began to feel uncomfortably small. Cups of tea were being drunk, sweet sherry sipped, sandwiches devoured. My nephews were very soon engulfed by the crowd. I had tea accidentally spilled over me by a huge man with a shaven head. Almost immediately after the accident he was being berated by a little black-eyed woman in spectacles who then turned to me.

"I'm so sorry, Professor." She appeared to know who I was. "My hubby can be very clumsy sometimes," she said. "Now you apologise nicely to the professor."

I accepted a mumbled apology from the man.

"Introduce yourself properly, Horace," she said to him. "You know what I keep telling you about manners. This is my husband Horace, and I'm his better half, Enid."

"I'm the Hoxton Strangler," said the man.

"That's right, Horace," said his wife, "you're the Hoxton Strangler, aren't you? But that's just, like, his stage name. He's a wrestler, you see: professional. We decided to call him the Hoxton Strangler."

I shook a warm, sweaty, hand that felt like a padded leather glove, and would have liked to talk to him about the world of professional wrestling, but it was not to be. The Hoxton Strangler had a very rudimentary grasp of the art of conversation and soon the tide of people tore us apart.

I wanted to go home, but my nephews were nowhere to be seen. To escape the noise and the heat I decided to take refuge if possible in some less crowded part of the house. I peered into various rooms, only to find them noisily occupied. Eventually I tried the door of Reg's study, which I had expected to be locked. It was not.

It looked like the study of a cabinet minister. The furnishings were rich and sombre, the books on the shelves were mostly leather bound, doubtless bought (or stolen) by the yard. I had been in this room before but I had never before realised how pretentious it all was. Reg had been fooling himself that he was a man of consequence, a statesman of some kind; though probably he had kept up the pretence as much to impress others as for his own egotistical benefit.

"Hello! What the fuck are you doing here?"

I started and looked round to see that Den was sitting at the desk in the window bay. He had been sorting through papers. Naturally he was not pleased to see me.

He said: "I suppose you've come for your vase, have you?"

"I beg your pardon?"

"The vase, that bloody blue thing." He pointed to a shelf where stood the exquisite Ming vase, innocent, untainted by the surrounding vulgarity and deception.

"I have no idea what you're talking about."

"Don't give me that! You know perfectly well Reg left it to you in his will. Here," he said, waving a sheaf of papers in his hand. "It says so here."

"How very generous of him. I had no idea."

"Yes...well...just take the thing and eff off, will you."

"I can't do that. It should go through probate and...so on..."

"Look, mate, what do you want?"

I was beginning to find my ex-brother-in-law extremely irritating. I said: "I don't want anything. I just want to find my nephews and take them back to their mother as soon as possible."

"Well, they're not here. And I've got work to do."

There was a knock on the door.

"Bloody Hell!" said Den. This was apparently taken as an invitation to enter because the door opened and in came Mr. Pigsny. He was carrying a black portfolio case which had not been with him in the limo.

"Oh, it's you, is it, short-arse," said Den. "What do you want?"

"I'll leave you gentlemen to it," I said, making for the door. But Mr. Pigsny barred my way, holding up his hand palm outwards, like an old-fashioned traffic policeman. Though small, there was a curious air of solidity and authority about the man.

"If you don't mind, Professor Chibnall, I would prefer you to stay," said Mr. Pigsny. "After all you are, as I understand, co-executor of the late Mr. McCall's will with Mr. Dennis here?"

I looked at Den in amazement. He made a face.

"Yeah. Yeah. That's right. I was going to tell you, only I didn't think you'd want to be bothered with all the detail." I sat down in one of Reg's masculine leather armchairs, too astonished to say anything.

"I also understand," went on Mr. Pigsny, "that I am mentioned in the will."

"If you're expecting any money," said Den aggressively, "you're out of luck, chummybum." Mr. Pigsny sat down uninvited in the chair opposite Den.

"I was not expecting any remuneration. Mr. McCall and I agreed about that before his decease."

"All right," said Den. "There's something in the will about retaining you as an adviser and that, but it's not legally binding. I could have my brief overturn it just like that—" he snapped his fingers. "And you'd be out on your arse, mate."

Mr. Pigsny sat quite still for a moment, apparently quite unmoved by Den's threat; then he said: "I have something to show you gentlemen."

He opened the portfolio and took out what looked like an unframed and unmounted black and white engraving, printed on heavy art paper roughly the size of an A3 sheet. He then rose from his chair and walked over to a circular table in the centre of the room. Having swept the books and papers on it unceremoniously to the floor he laid out the print on it with almost reverential care.

Den and I had been too astonished to move until Mr. Pigsny beckoned us over to examine the item. For a good thirty seconds we both looked at it in silence. I doubt if we so much as breathed. From behind Reg's thick study door came the faint lugubrious murmur of the wake.

It was indeed a monochrome print of some kind, though whether it was an engraving, an etching or even a lithograph I am simply not qualified to say. The style of it was vaguely antique, possibly Victorian, but no particular artist sprang to mind. Perhaps there was a hint of Gustave Doré about it, but it was certainly not by him. Whoever had done it possessed an extraordinary skill and power. All these reflections I give as afterthoughts because what possessed me at the time was the image itself.

Under a lowering sky of thick, dirty cloud was stretched a vast frozen lake. Its distant edges were fringed with jagged pitiless mountains whose peaks and ridges were laced with snow. In the middle distance a number of figures were skating aimlessly about on the surface of the lake. They were human apart from their heads, which were those of birds, reptiles or insects. The foreground was dominated by a single figure standing rather unsteadily on the ice in his bare feet. He wore a shapeless, baggy overall that vaguely resembled an ancient prison uniform. What shocked us most was the face of the man, because it was Reg McCall to the life.

The expression on his face was not so much of horror as of resentful despair. He looks out of the picture directly at us. Perhaps he pleads.

"What is this shit?" said Den. "Who did it?" There was menace in his voice, as if he were threatening to punish the artist responsible.

"I wonder if you gentlemen could be seated once more," said Mr. Pigsny. I obeyed and so, to my surprise, did Den.

Mr. Pigsny said: "The picture was commissioned by Mr. McCall before his death. It depicts his present existence in Hell."

I saw Den's mouth gape. I am sure he wanted to say something, but he was as incapable of speech as I was. He looked at me and I felt a tiny spark of fellow feeling pass between us.

"Naturally, this is not a precise and naturalistic depiction. That would be impossible given the circumstances, but it does represent a reality. Was it not Picasso who told us that art is a lie which tells us the truth?"

"Piss off, Pigsny," said Den, and again I felt at one with him. I could not have put it better myself. "Who's the little shit who drew that crap? I'll ring his bastard neck for him."

"The artist in question is beyond even your reach, Mr. McCall," said Pigsny, putting the print back into his portfolio and preparing to leave the room. Den barred his way.

He said: "What's the point of all this, Pigsny? Tell me what you want. Come on, out with it, and don't mess me about. I warn you, I don't like being messed about."

"Surprisingly few people do, in my experience, Mr. McCall. As to what I want, *I* want nothing. It was your late brother who wanted you to see the picture. You may wish to reflect on it, as he intended you to do. Good afternoon, gentlemen. I will be calling on you both in due course." With that Pigsny left the room unhindered by Den, who seemed shattered by the whole experience.

"Fuck me!" he said eventually, after a long silence. As I could not contribute anything more cogent myself I remained silent until my nephews Robert and Arthur burst into the room.

"Is it okay if we go now, Dad?" said Arthur. "We've said our goodbyes to Auntie Maureen and she's now gone into a huddle with that ghastly Piggy man who was in the limo with us."

Den waved us away wearily, almost graciously.

II

Within a month or so my rooms at Cambridge were graced by the Ming vase. I rang to thank Den for its safe delivery. He dismissed my gratitude quickly.

"Has that Pigsny been onto you?" he asked.

"No. Have *you* seen him, then?"

"No! So, what's the fucker up to?"

"I can't say I'm bothered."

"Yeah. Right. But that's all very well. I mean…He must be up to something. I mean, who is he? Where's he come from? What's his bloody game?"

I had no answers for him, so the conversation ended inconclusively, but by the end of it he had managed to infect me with some of his unease.

It was May, and in the gardens of King's College some undergraduates were performing the *Orestes* in its original language. I like to keep my acquaintance with Greek literature in good repair, and encourage it in others, so I went. It was a warm evening, and I must admit my attention wandered. The diction of the actors, somewhat hampered by masks, was not good enough to hold me, and I began to lose the thread of the Greek. The words transformed themselves from meaningful sentences into an alien music.

The wooden seating for the audience was tiered and in a horseshoe shape, like an ancient auditorium. I was seated near to the bottom of one extremity of the horseshoe so that I had as good a view of the audience as I did of the action on stage. I began to watch the watchers.

About halfway up the other side of the auditorium, almost directly oppo-site me, but higher, sat a man I thought I recognised. I had spotted him first because he was dressed differently from the rest of us. Instead of loose summery clothes he wore a dark suit and a tie. He was short and he covered his baldness with a rather nasty "comb-over" of greasy reddish hair. It was Mr. Pigsny.

His appearance at such an event seemed to me so bizarre that it took me quite some time before my mind would authorise what my senses told me. After that I ignored the play completely and divided my time between taking furtive glances at him and speculating on his possible motives in attending an undergraduate performance of a play in Greek.

His whole attention was fixed on the action on stage, and it did not look as if he had noticed me. Eventually there was another chorus about vengeance and the guilt of the house of Atreus, and an interval was declared. I toyed with the idea of leaving, but I was too curious about Mr. Pigsny.

I found him over by the makeshift bar in the cloisters, sipping tomato juice.

"Hello, Professor Chibnall. Fancy seeing you here!" He spoke to me with a condescension I had expected to use towards him.

"I didn't know you were a devotee of classical drama," I said.

"Oh, yes. These olden-time Greeks, they knew a thing or two, didn't they?"

"You're finding the Euripides easy to follow?"

"Oh, not so bad," he said, and he proceeded to quote in Greek from the chorus we had just heard, those lines about blood upon blood, murder upon murder not leaving go of the two sons of Atreus. There was something odd about his pronunciation. It was far from barbarous—all the quantities were correct—but I had never heard anything quite like it before. He spoke in a hieratic tone, as if pronouncing a liturgy. His style reminded me most of a performance I had once seen in Tokyo of the Nō drama.

I was too astounded to react in any other way than to bow respect-fully. After a moment of silence I said: "Were you wanting to see me about something?"

"I left an envelope for you with the porter at your college," Mr. Pigsny said and then, quite pointedly, turned his back on me.

On returning to my own college, St. Jude's, I asked at the porter's lodge if there was anything for me, and our porter, George, handed me a large manilla envelope. Usually George has plenty to say for himself but on this occasion, for some reason, loquaciousness had deserted him.

In my rooms I opened the envelope and took out a print similar, but not identical, to the one Mr. Pigsny had shown us on the day of the funeral.

There was the lowering sky of dirty cloud, the frozen lake, the distant horned peaks. The figure of Reg was still on the ice in the foreground, but something had happened to him. The lower part of his body had begun to deliquesce into a dark, slug-like shape that seemed fixed by frozen bonds to the lake. The body's dark viscosity was beginning to extend into the features of the face, stretching and distorting them in strange ways. The head was still recognisably Reg's, and his expression was that of a drowning man just about to go under for the last time, and knowing it.

As before, the scene was depicted with a meticulous graphic accuracy, and a touch of genuine artistic flair which only made it more obscene. I could not bear to look at it, but at the same time I felt somehow that to destroy it would amount to a betrayal of the trust Reg had placed in me. I rolled up the print and placed it carefully in Reg's Ming vase.

My bedroom in college looks over one of the quads, and usually I sleep soundly, but that night I was restless. I did eventually fall asleep, but, it seemed to me, I woke up again almost immediately. I listened. Was it a noise that had woken me? No, all was silent.

Then the silence was disturbed by a faint sound. It was not one of the usual ones that occasionally afflict a Cambridge quadrangle late at night, like drunken laughter or argument, or a sudden blast of pop music. It was the sound of a single flute playing a lively dance tune. Its note sequences were vaguely familiar: sometimes Irish in feel, sometimes gypsy-like or mid-European, perhaps even Middle Eastern at moments, but ultimately belonging to none of these cultures. The rhythm was a kind of jig, I think, but I am no musical expert. Its tone was cold, as if blown not through reed and wood, but granite and cold steel, and it was compelling enough to make me get up to look out of my window and into the quad.

The world outside my window was flooded with moonlight and on the grass at the centre of the quadrangle was a short man in a suit, dancing and blowing on some sort of instrument. I knew it at once to be Pigsny, even though his strange coppery hair was not lying flat on his cranium but sticking up from it in ragged peaks. They shimmered slightly as if he had covered them with gel.

Because he was on grass it was only to be expected that his leaps and capers should be entirely silent, but still it seemed strange. He had a grace, and an extraordinary vitality for a little fat man.

The flute music stopped, Mr. Pigsny made one final leap into the air, landed with a kind of pirouette and then bowed low in my direction, as if he had known all along that I was watching. I hurried down from my rooms to catch him, but, as I had expected, he had gone when I reached the quad. The college gates had been locked for well over an hour. Who had given him a key?

The following day I rang Den to ask if he had seen Mr. Pigsny and found myself on the receiving end of a torrent of bad language at the conclusion of which he said:

"What is that fucker playing at, eh? Eh? Went to the Dog and Gibbet the other night. Need to show my face there now and again to stop them getting out of order. Horace—you know, the Hoxton Strangler—and Enid were having a knees-up to celebrate their silver, and there was a ceilidh band, and bugger me if that Pigsny bastard wasn't in it playing the flute. Then he did one of those Irish step dance things. Doing a fucking step dance at my effing pub! If it wasn't for Horace and Enid, I'd have had him slung out on his arse. Did you put him up to this?"

"Of course not!"

"Then what are you calling me for?"

I briefly told him of my recent experiences. Den said: "Yeah, I had one of those stupid prints. I mean, what's it all about? It must be some kind of a wind-up. I mean what is this Hell crap? Eh? What the bloody Hell is all that about. Eh? When you're dead, you're bloody dead. End of story. It's all a piss-take and I seriously do not like having the piss taken."

Den was not going to be of help to me; I could see that. My irritation with Mr. Pigsny was no less than his but I needed some kind of explanation. As an epigraphist I am, in my own way, a man of science. Mr. Pigsny may have been a madman, but even madness has its reasons. I rang up my sister to see if she could help me.

Once a wayward and slender beauty, Gwen had grown over the years into a rather solid woman, a stalwart on all the committees in the Buckinghamshire village where she lived. She came to the phone rather breathlessly.

"Hello! Sorry about that. We're in the middle of a garden crisis. I've called in Parker who does our garden on Fridays usually. There's a slug invasion, so it's all hands to the pumps. I've even got the boys setting beer traps."

She sounded hearty and conventional. Marriage to a merchant banker had undoubtedly changed her, but not necessarily for the better. I told her what I wanted, which was the telephone number of Reg's widow, Maureen.

"Oh, really, Lawrence! Can't you get it off Den? Frankly, Lawrence, I do not want to know. That wretched little Maureen woman has been ringing me up and saying that I should meet a friend of hers called Mr. Piggy or something. He sounds perfectly dreadful. Apparently he's a kind of spiritualist. I couldn't really understand what she was saying. Well, I told her very firmly that we were all Church of England here, which shut her up, but I mean, really!"

Patiently, I asked her again for the number and she went off to get it. When she had given it to me she said: "Don't you get me involved again with that awful little woman; I have quite enough to contend with, what with these slugs. What they have done to my courgettes is quite literally unspeakable."

III

It took me some days before I had the courage to ring Maureen. It was not her I was afraid of, naturally, but what she might tell me. And what might she tell me? I had no idea. That was the problem: fear is the shadow of the unknown. When I finally got round to phoning her, I came straight to the point and asked her about Mr. Pigsny.

Maureen is one of those people who finds it hard to answer any question directly. I had to disentangle the information she gave me from a litany of complaints about Den's handling of Reg's estate; how so few people had been in touch with her after Reg's death; how she was not receiving the respect she felt she was owed. Apparently the one person who had behaved himself to her satisfaction had been Mr. Pigsny; though, like Den, and for that matter myself, she was not at all sure what he was "up to."

She told me that about a year before he died Reg had begun to take an interest in spiritualism and the afterlife. Ostensibly his main object was to get in touch with their daughter, Janet, who had died in a car crash, though Maureen suspected that the knowledge of his own impending death had played a part. He had visited various psychics and spiritualist churches and it was at one of these meetings that he had encountered Mr. Pigsny. As far as she knew, Pigsny was not an established psychic, or a medium with a following; but he had impressed Reg with his wide understanding of occult matters. Reg had once told her that Mr. Pigsny knew more about the spirit world than "all those other bullshit artists put together." For the last few months of Reg's life the two men had been virtually inseparable. Mr. Pigsny had come to stay in their house, though he had always made himself scarce when other people, like Den, came visiting. As far as she knew there had been no financial transactions between Reg and Pigsny, though she did think that Reg had "signed some sort of document." Maureen said that after Reg's death, Mr. Pigsny had continued to come to the house. He was able to reassure her that Reg was "doing all right" in the afterlife and had met up with his daughter, Janet.

"I don't know though," said Maureen finally. "I mean, I don't hold with this afterlife business, do you? It's so—like—unnecessary, isn't it? I mean this life's bad enough really, you don't want any more of it after. Do you know what I mean? The whole thing gives me the creeps. I told him straight. He seemed to understand and he told me he was arranging things so I wouldn't have to worry. Then he wanted me to sign something, so he could guarantee no worries."

"Sign what exactly?"

"Well, I don't know really. It was all in funny writing, like the olden times. I said I wasn't sure about this signing business. Anyway he took the paper away, saying he'd come back another time."

I said: "Before you sign anything, tell Mr. Pigsny I want to see him and talk to him."

She agreed at once to this, and appeared to be relieved that I had taken the matter out of her hands.

A few days later I was taking a short cut across the Fellows' Garden on my way to a seminar. There was enough time, I thought, to greet Nickolds, the college gardener, who I thought was looking rather disconsolate. I asked him what was the matter.

"We've been invaded, that's what," he said in his distinctive, laconic fashion. He pointed to the bed of gloxinias and hostas in which he took a special pride. Even I could tell they were in a bad way. The leaves had been gnawed into shreds by some creature or other.

"Slugs," said Nickolds, pointing to an unusually large specimen, dark and glutinous. With one neat thrust he bisected it with a spade.

"I've put down beer traps and caught dozens, but they keep coming. Where are they from?"

I expressed bewilderment and sympathy in the best way I could and began to move off to my seminar.

"If you see one of them bastards, Professor, you bloody well smash 'im," said Nickolds. I said I would not fail him, hoping devoutly that the eventuality would not arise.

As I was returning from my seminar across the main quad, our porter, George, approached and informed me that there was someone at the lodge asking to see me. Something about his look told me he was more than usually troubled. I was therefore not surprised to find little Mr. Pigsny pretending to study a notice board under the great entrance arch of St. Jude's.

"Come to my rooms," I said.

As we walked there Mr. Pigsny trotted beside me, chatting inconsequentially about the weather and other trivial topics. I was conscious of him deliberately keeping the talk light and free of significance, perhaps to tease or torment me in some way. One thing he said, however, struck a different note.

"Your college here, St. Jude's. It's always been a favourite of mine."

"Really?" I said. "In what way?"

"Oh, I've been familiar with it over the years. Did you know about Dr. Barnsworth committing suicide in your rooms?"

I was shocked. Yes, I had heard about Barnsworth, but it was well before my time, over sixty years ago. "What about Barnsworth?" I said angrily.

"Oh, nothing," said Mr. Pigsny. "Some people have claimed it was some sort of erotic strangulation, but it wasn't, you know." After that we walked to my rooms in silence.

It was a bright hot day and the windows of my rooms were open, so that the faint murmur of normality could be distinctly heard from the quad below. I offered Mr. Pigsny a sherry, the only drink I had available, but he refused, so I then asked him for an explanation. Of what? he asked. I repeated the catalogue, from his appearance in my quad and at the Greek play to the prints and the paper he was wanting Maureen to sign.

"You people always want an explanation, don't you?" said Mr. Pigsny. "Well, what if there isn't an explanation? Or what if there is one, but I couldn't make you understand it, not in a million years? What if there just aren't words in the poxy English language to express a meaning, you bone-headed little shit?"

I think there was a long silence after this, or perhaps it was the shock I felt which made it long in my memory. When he began again, his speech was low and level again, almost too quiet to hear, but not quite.

"Your friend Reg wanted an explanation, so I gave him what he wanted. He wanted to know if there was life beyond death, so I told him that he might never die. But he wanted a guarantee that he would never die, so I gave it to him. He signed and he had it. He wanted folks here to go on worrying and thinking about him. He wanted people to go on saying he was a diamond geezer, so I gave it to him. What a muppet! What a moron! As if anybody gives a damn!"

"I do!" I said.

"No, you don't. You're like the rest! You couldn't give a toss. All you care about is that stupid Ming vase he gave you. Anyway, what's it to you? He got what he wanted, didn't he? Got what he deserved. He'll never die! He'll never never die! He'll crawl on his knees through shit, begging for death, fucking begging for it, but he'll never, never bloody die!"

By this time Mr. Pigsny's voice had risen to a shrill scream and he was dancing about the room, thundering on the floorboards so that I could feel them bowing under his weight.

"Stop!" I shouted. He did so, and for a long time we stood staring at each other without speaking while the breath went rasping in and out of Mr. Pigsny's stunted little body.

Then Mr. Pigsny opened his mouth wide but this time out of it came no speech or noise, only a vast writhing darkness. His mouth widened still further and I saw that it was filled with slugs, boiling and wriggling like the tormented souls they were. Soon they were spilling onto one of my precious rugs in great vomited legions, some great, some small, all of a blackish colour but carrying a faint iridescent sheen of red and green and blue. The larger slugs had faces which bore the semblance of humanity, traces of the cruelty and lust they had once fondled in life. There was no sound but the rustling, seething sound of Mr. Pigsny's possessed souls, as he belched them into my Cambridge study.

Did I really see this? Or did I see it with the eyes of madness and illusion? I only know that I saw and nothing else. I only know that what I saw filled me with white rage and the strength of seven men, so that I picked up little Mr. Pigsny almost without effort and threw him out of my open window into the quad.

For some seconds I was in a daze, horrified at what I had done. I did not dare look out of the window but stared only at the floor where the writhing slugs were slowly evaporating into foul-smelling smoke, leaving behind several dark, glutinous stains on my lovely Bokhara rug. The college servant who cleans my rooms has complained to me bitterly about it several times, but I have offered him neither apology nor explanation.

When finally I looked out of the window I saw that a crowd of curious undergraduates had gathered round the place where Mr. Pigsny must have fallen. It was onto the flagstone path that surrounded the grass of the quad-rangle and not onto the soft earth. Mr. Pigsny could not have survived the fall without, at the very least, suffering very serious injuries.

The crowd looked up and saw me, and, as they did so, I caught a glimpse of what they were surrounding. It was not the body of Mr. Pigsny at all. On the pavement lay the shattered fragments of the Ming vase that Reg had left me in his will.

"Dear me," I said fatuously for the benefit of the spectators. "What a ter-rible thing," and hurried down stairs to clear away the shards.

By the time I reached the quad most of the crowd had dispersed. Cambridge takes eccentricity in its stride, and if my conduct in throwing a priceless vase out of my window was regarded as odd, no one, happily, thought it warranted more than a raised eyebrow. I began to pick up the fragments of the vase and put them in a plastic bag I had thoughtfully grabbed on the way out of my rooms. As I did so I heard flute music. My heart seemed to stop, but then I noticed that it was coming from the open window of our organ scholar. I could even see him innocently playing, a tall thin young man with incipient baldness. I returned to my gathering of the shards. It was then that I discov-ered a roll of paper lying on the grass beside the shattered Ming. It was the print that I had put inside the vase, the print which Mr. Pigsny had left for me at the porter's lodge after the Greek play.

I took it up with me to examine at leisure in my rooms. The picture was in many ways as before. Under a lowering sky of thick, dirty cloud was stretched a vast frozen lake. Its distant edges were fringed with jagged pitiless mountains whose peaks and ridges were laced with snow. But there were no figures on the frozen lake, neither in the foreground nor the middle distance. Nothing now relieved the perfect desolation and loneliness of the scene.

I might even have thought of framing it and hanging it up as a curiosity; but the condition of the print was marred irrevocably. It was criss-crossed by lines of some dark viscous, oily substance which looked to me like the trails of slugs.

Ray Cluley's work has appeared in various magazines and anthologies. It has been reprinted in Ellen Datlow's *Best Horror of the Year* as well as Steve Berman's *Wilde Stories 2013: The Year's Best Gay Speculative Fiction* and has been translated into French and Polish. He won the British Fantasy Award for Best Short Story in 2013 and was nominated for Best Novella in 2015. His collection *Probably Monsters* is available now from ChiZine Press.

At Night, When the Demons Come
Ray Cluley

You'll notice these records have no dates. I don't think anyone really knows what the year is these days anyway. The last one I remember is 2020. Everyone remembers 2020, but my point is I didn't keep track after. Why bother? I only write this because of what happened recently, because someone taught me that others might learn if only I provided the opportunity.

There were four of us when Cassie came and she made six because she didn't come alone and naturally we counted her last. She was female, next to useless, and a little girl at that, so totally useless. But the man she was with, he was worth having around. We had a couple of guys on our college football team, back when things like that mattered, who were as big as this man. A couple, as in put them together and you had the right size. Fuck knows where he got his clothes. If he wasn't on your side, your side was going to lose, and I'm not talking football anymore. His name was Frances, can you believe that? Jones called him a walking Johnny Cash song. I was never a fan, but I knew what he meant.

If it hadn't been for the demon we probably would have hidden like we usually did and waited for the strangers to move on. We probably missed out on a lot of good people that way, but we sure missed out on a lot of bad ones too and that was fine with all of us. This time, though, we came out and stood in the road until they were near enough to talk to. Not that we knew they were a they at that time. We thought it was just him. Frances.

"Hello traveller," Jones said. It sounded stupid, like he was pretending to be someone else. We'd not had much practice talking to anyone but each other, and there was never much need for hello with us.

The man who would later tell us he had a girl's name just stood, assessing the situation. He made no effort to hide it. He looked Jones up and down, then Frank next to him. He saw me easy enough, over by the pump, and he took in both windows, looking for others. There was only George, who he saw up on the roof. George knew he'd been seen. He stood up, put one foot on the wall, leaned over and spat. Then he raised his rifle, just enough for it to be visible. George always acted like he was cool and calm, like some kind of movie hero. He did it with us even though we knew better. Even though nobody gave a shit about movies anymore.

"Just the four of you?" the big man asked.

Frank seemed surprised. "Yeah."

"So no trouble."

"That's right," Frank said, but I reckon he misunderstood. Frances meant he'd find the four of us no trouble, that's what I reckon.

"What does he want?" George called down.

"Water, if you have it. Food, if you can spare it. Somewhere to sleep, either way." He said it quietly, addressing those who had spoken to him directly. "The wind's picking up and this place looks like it might have a storm cellar."

"It does," said Jones. "Only we haven't been in there yet."

The man waited for more but neither Jones nor Frank were eager to spill it. They looked at each other instead, then looked over to me. I was already heading over, breaking the shotgun open to show myself harmless.

"There was a demon," I told him.

I swear he didn't move, yet suddenly his empty hands weren't empty anymore. It was like the guns just appeared there. Both were cylinder loaders and looked to be full, unless he'd fashioned fakes to make it seem that way. Fakes wouldn't be much good against a winged bitch, though, which said to me the bullets were real.

"Quiet," he said. Not to us. Then I thought I heard something else but he covered it with words of his own.

"When was it here?" he asked.

Me, I put my hand up to shield my eyes from the sun he was walking from and said, "Still is."

Just like that, one of the guns was gone. "Dead?"

I nodded. Heard that something else again.

"Shh," said the giant. Then, "You?"

I was flattered he'd think so. I was also glad George couldn't hear else there'd be some preening and showmanship before we could cut to the honest answer. "No. She was dead when we got here."

There was no need to ask if we were sure. We wouldn't still be here otherwise.

"Show me," he said.

"Alright," said Jones, "but do you want to put that gun away first?"

"No. Not yet."

"It's dead."

I thought I heard an echo of that, and judging from Jones and Frank and the way they frowned, so did they.

"Who you got with you?" I asked.

He said nothing, so it was up to her to make the introductions.

"I'm Cassie," she called out from behind him. Her voice was high, with the enthusiasm of someone about to play. "This man is my friend. He's called Frances."

Frances squatted down in the road. There was the sound of metal on metal, the sound buckles make, and he stood again. From behind him emerged Cassie. A little girl about six years old. She reached up and his hand was there for her.

I stepped behind the man Frances but he recoiled to keep his back facing away from me. It was only a reflex action. He turned back after and I could see a system of harnesses strapped around him. The girl had been fixed in, completely out of our sight back there and protected by the mass of muscle that was Frances in front.

"This is Jones, Frank, that there's George," I said. "My name's Charlie."

Nobody shook hands.

We'd found the place at around twelve. It took the best part of an hour to get close enough to see it seemed empty, and another hour on that to make sure it was. A two-pump gas station, dust-blown and sun-baked, with a workshop and store and a single Shell sign squeaking in a building breeze. That building breeze was why we'd risked an approach in the first place. Oklahoma was not a nice place to be out in the open, unless you liked flying kites. Tornado Valley, this stretch used to be called. I doubt there's much of anyone left to call it anything anymore, but that wouldn't stop the tornados from coming.

"Empty," Frank had said and we'd all hushed him immediately.

George slapped him across the back of his head. "Idiot."

"Sorry."

Frank said empty last time, right before three women popped up from behind the sofa and started shooting. Lucky for us we were quicker, though Jones got some splinters from an exploding picture frame. The time before that, someone was hiding in the refrigerator. I got a gun rammed into my mouth because of that, which is why the front teeth aren't pretty. I drew my knife and that stopped things getting worse. I knew I could save my bullets because I knew he had none, and I knew *that* because there was still a gun in my mouth and not my brains on the wall. After two seconds he was backing away with his hands up and I was feeling in my bloody mouth to straighten my teeth. When Frank said empty it meant it wasn't and that someone who wasn't Frank was going to get hurt. To be fair, though, there was food or water to be had both times.

"You go first," Jones said to Frank.

And to be fair, Frank always did.

He backed out from behind the building. His gun was out but he wasn't really pointing it at anything.

"Frank?"

"You should come and see," he said. He pointed with his weapon. It trembled in his hand.

He showed us a demon nailed to a door.

She was an ugly bitch. None of us had ever seen one up close before. Obviously, because we were still alive. But we'd all seen them in the skies at some point, and I saw the carcass of one once in a ditch at the roadside but its wings had been pulled off and taken and so had the head and claws, so it wasn't much more than a mutilated female torso. Seen that way the purple skin isn't much different to mottled bruising. This one, the one Frank found, its skin still had a vibrant brightness even though it was dead, the pale lavender color of its body darkening into violet at the arms and legs. The wings were stretched out to full span and pinned to the door with knives, railroad spikes, and even a couple of forks. They were a rich purple. The claws, two big scoops where the hands should be, were a plum color so dark it was almost black. She was the colors of dusk given fleshy form, hairless and vile.

"Nice tits," said George, trying to sound like the movie star tough guy he wanted to be.

The tits were plump and round and firm-looking but they were hellish in that they were hers. All that suckled there was demon or doomed.

"She looks like your momma," said Jones. I guess he was tired of George's shit.

George knew better than to fight with Jones, though. "She's got better teeth." Its teeth were like a shark's, sharp triangles folding back from the gums in double rows. Too many teeth.

"What should we do with it?" Frank asked.

The door it had been impaled on had long ago been torn from its hinges and rested now against the sloping hatch of a storm cellar, maybe as some kind of warning, maybe as some kind of victory mark. Jones and I took a side each and pulled it face down into the dirt.

George jumped on it and we heard her bones crack. He lost his balance and fell on his ass and something else broke in the bitch under him. It was pretty funny.

"How did it die?" the big man asked, following us round.

"Various shots to the chest," Jones was telling him. "A couple very close range."

"You showing him our demon?" George called down from the roof, trying to take credit.

"Yeah."

I waved him down.

"Here she is," said Frank. He took hold of one edge and flipped it over, though that makes it sound easier than it was.

A bone stuck from its flank and its nose was broken flat; otherwise it looked much as it had. The skin had picked up some of the sandy dust from the ground. I thought the stranger might shelter the girl from the sight, but he actually steered her towards it. They looked at it together.

"See," said Jones, pointing to the chest area. Just beneath the breasts was a mess of bullet holes of different calibres. He pointed to where the skin was puffed and scorched. "Close range."

George was with us by then. "Nice tits, huh?"

Everybody ignored him. He spat on the body. He liked to spit. "Give you nightmares, little girl."

Frances pointed to the cellar doors. "You've not been in there?"

Frank shook his head.

"The demon was on it," I said.

"You think there's another one in there?"

It sounded ridiculous when he said it. "Maybe."

George pulled back the slide of what he liked to call his piece, just for the dramatic impact of the noise. "Only one way to find out, eh?"

Jones said, "You weren't so eager before."

"If it's loaded you can come," said the giant. He was checking the barrels of his weapons, spinning them, snapping them shut. "That shotgun would be handy close range, too."

I offered it to him.

"Going to have my hands full," he said, raising his revolvers.

"God damn it," I muttered, but I went to the doors.

"I'll stay with the girl," said Frank.

"Me too," said Jones.

"Good," said Frances. "Stick close to her down there, but keep her behind us."

Frank looked at Jones. "She's going too?"

Jones merely shrugged and turned the cylinder of his own thirty-eight, lining it up so the four shots he had left were ready to fire.

"I have to," said the girl. "Frances might need me."

Frank went to the left door, Jones to the right. Each grabbed a handle. Frances stood in the middle, both guns pointing down at where the stairs would be. George and I were on either side of him doing the same. The girl was behind us.

"Alright," Frances said, "on three."

But they were already opening the doors.

"Shit." I brought the barrel close to aim, panicked by the sudden opening, and caught myself in the cheek with the stock.

Stairs led down into gloom. Nothing came out. Nothing moved. There was no noise.

Frances went in.

"Shit," I said again and followed him down into the dark.

There were beds. About a dozen of them. We stood in the slant of sunlight that had come down with us, but the room went way back into a darkness black as oil. The beds we could see clearly were occupied. There was a woman bound to each of them.

"Penitentary," Frances said.

"What?"

We walked slowly, inspecting each bed just enough to tell us the person on it was dead. I said, "What?" again but nobody else said anything.

The women were drawn and wasted, skin over bone, dressed only in shadows where the flesh was sunken. They'd starved down here. All of them were manacled with homemade cuffs and chains, and all of them had deep dry lacerations that spoke of attempts to escape. One woman I saw had scraped her flesh down to the bone trying to pull her way out and I stopped looking at the others after that.

The girl was muttering prayers for them.

Pushed against one wall was a plastic crate filled with bottled water, the huge types that refilled office coolers. I hadn't seen one in years and here there was four of them, plus one half empty on its stand. Or half full, depending on your philosophy.

"Whoo!" George cried, and he did a little dance step. "Jackpot! Look at all that!"

At that moment we were attacked.

A woman leapt up from the foot of the cooler, not at all hidden but missed because of the distraction water is to thirsty men. I yelled for George. Jones grabbed at him, pulling him round just as the woman's nails raked at his face. She'd been going for the eyes but thanks to Jones only managed to scratch thin strips across his cheeks.

"Fuck!"

"Don't!" Frances called. I'm not sure who to.

I barrelled forward, pushed the shotgun firm into her stomach, and fired. Her back splashed against the wall and she flopped down in two pieces near enough.

"Was it one of them?" George cried. "Was it a demon?" He was patting at his wounds, probably hoping he weren't poisoned.

"No," said Frances, slipping his guns away and rubbing his face with his hands. "Just a woman."

"Oh. Good."

"Just a woman," Cassie repeated, looking at me where I leaned against the wall taking shaky breaths.

Fucked if I was going to feel guilty.

The cellar doors had a place to slide a bar across but no bar. Up in the store section of the gas station we took down a regular door to saw into pieces the right size. The wind had picked up some by then. I'd started to clean up the mess I'd made but Frances pushed me away and said he'd do it. He was very firm about it. I think he was pissed at me for some reason.

"What if they're taking the water?" George asked, laying the door in place across the counter. The slices down his face had dried into crusty lines.

"They're not taking the water," I said.

"He's got that harness, he'd get one in that alright."

"I don't think even a guy his size would want to carry one of those on his back," said Jones. "And Frank's with him."

"Oh, Frank. Great. Everything will be fine then."

Just a woman. I kept hearing that in my head. The way the girl said it.

"She must have been crazy," said Jones. "Down in the dark like that when she could have come out. Doors weren't locked."

"The demon was leaning against them." George pushed and pulled at the saw. It bit its way through the wood reluctantly. It was old, that saw. We'd been carrying it around awhile, blunt teeth and all.

"It don't weigh so much you can't push it down opening them doors out."

"Maybe she was too weak," I said, holding the door steady. "They looked starved."

"She was just a woman," George said. As if that explained everything. Or as if it didn't matter so why keep talking about it.

These last unnumbered years have been hard for everyone of course, but the women got it hardest once the demons came. Maybe before then.

There was a group I used to belong to. They stuck together like we did, safety in numbers, and they gathered up women they found along the way. Mostly it was the purpose I alluded to earlier, but sometimes it wasn't only that. There were other ways to fuck a woman, like calling her demon. They were always female, see, the demons, so it made sense that they were once women. Women who turned into hellish carnivores that flew with the wind-blown ash. Accuse a woman of turning, smack her around a bit for some convincing purple, and you had Salem all over again. I've seen women strung up worse than the demon we found on the door. Shit, I even believed it once.

"Hey, Charlie, where you going?"

I ignored George, but I told Jones on the way out I was going to speak with Frances.

Frances had seen places like this before but he wouldn't tell me anything more until we had the place secure. That meant tossing the bodies outside, making barricades of the rusty metal bed frames, and taking an inventory of remaining ammunition. I thought that was a little pointless. I was the only one who'd fired.

"He does it every time we stop," Cassie told me.

George and Jones managed to make a sturdy beam for the doors, halving the door from the store and binding the pieces together. I helped them carry it.

"Oh, now you decide to help," said George.

"I've been busy," I said. I pointed to the pile of bodies as Frances shrugged another two from his shoulders. We were going to burn them, the best funeral we could manage and more than most people got these days. The wind tossed his hair back with the tail of his long coat in a way I knew George must have envied. It was getting so we had to shout to be heard or our voices were snatched away too quickly. The gas sign rocked back and forth, screeching a rusty protest.

"How many more?" I called, but Frances ignored it. He stood looking up at the sky, letting the wind do its thing, and I thought oh shit, another George.

Cassie came up out of the cellar. She was dragging one of the bodies (just a woman). I heard it bump up the steps. Jesus, she was six years old.

"Frances," she said.

"I know."

All of us turned to see.

"Oh. Shit." Jones wasted nothing, not even words.

Back the way we'd come from, criss-crossing the road in angry sweeps, was a twister. It spun its dust with quiet violence for now but it was going to be on us quick and then we'd hear it scream.

I ran to the girl and took the ankles from her hands. I dragged the corpse up the last steps and dropped it to the side of the doors.

"No, over here. We don't want them feeding that close to the door."

"What?"

Frances pointed again.

"Oh shit. Shit."

Sailing in the winds of the storm were two demons. They dived and arced as if the cyclone was a large pet they played with.

I dragged the body over at a run. "Have they seen us?"

"Not yet."

Frances grabbed me by the shoulder and ran me back to the doors.

"How can you tell?" I yelled against the wind.

"They're still over there instead of here."

George was feeding the door-block down into the cellar. "Quickly, quickly."

Cassie was standing and clutching herself like she needed to pee. She stepped from one foot to the other in the rising dust, looking to where hell flew at us.

"Inside, little heart," Frances said.

We followed her down and George pulled the doors shut behind us.

Sitting in the dark, we listened to the wind howl. It wasn't long before the howls were those of the things flying with it.

"I thought they only came at night," Frank whispered. We all shushed him quiet.

Above us, something landed on the roof with a heavy thump. We heard it even in the cellar. It screamed, and the winds pulled the sound round and round in echo. To me it sounded like a woman in labour, giving birth to something stillborn. Jones said later it sounded like the slaughterhouse. I guess we hear what we can relate to.

"Maybe the other one will—"

Jones, whispering so quiet it was like I was thinking the words, was cut off by the sound of something landing on the dry ground outside. It, too, screamed. It screamed in short sharp shreds. This was no bestial cry of the hunt. It was communicating with the one on the roof. It was scratching its way around the pile we'd made out there.

The doors shook. I cried out but my throat was parched and the noise I made was only a cracked nothing. Frank stifled a yelp. The doors thumped. It was only the wind, lifting and dropping them in its frantic wrath.

There came next a wailing shriek I never in whatever life I've got left ever want to hear again. If that rooftop scream was a woman birthing death, this one sounded like the demon clawed her own abortion. The shards of it went through me like jagged porcelain and as it trailed off it thinned to a fiery hot needle in my ears. The way the wind whipped it into a ricochet pulled it through me like infected thread, yanking the line tight till I clutched my head against the pain. When the other one joined in I wished for death just so the chorus would end.

It stopped eventually, though the reverberations of those screams will be with me forever as a tortured background noise as permanent as thought. I can still hear it now when I close my eyes, finding myself in the same darkness.

"They've found their sister," said Frances.

When the doors thundered again in their frames it was not the wind.

"Oh Jesus," Jones moaned.

"Shh," said Frances. "They don't know we're here."

"Sounds like they know," said George.

"Shh."

Sure enough, after a while of pounding the doors we heard them demolishing the store above.

"They'll tear the place apart just in case, but those doors are strong and we have water, even some tinned food. If we keep quiet, we can wait them out if we have to."

"You know what else we got?" I said. I pointed to the bodies we hadn't shifted yet. "Think they smell good now, wait a few days."

"Good," said Frances. "They'll smell it too and figure the only humans down here are dead ones."

The destruction above ceased. The only sounds we heard then were those of the wind as it tore its way over us.

"Think they've gone?"

"Maybe," said Frances, but we could tell he didn't think so.

"No," whispered Cassie. "They're still here."

They stayed long after the cyclone had passed. The new quiet allowed us to hear the occasional heavy dragging outside. When the sounds became wet, thick, and guttural we knew they were feeding.

"There's plenty bodies out there," Frank whispered. "They could eat here for weeks."

Nobody liked that idea.

Frances nodded his agreement and pointed across the room. We trod our way silently to the far end and huddled so we could talk quietly.

"There are only two of them," Frances said.

"Only?"

He spared me a glance but otherwise ignored my comment.

"There are six of us," he said. "If we're quick, we can take them."

Six. He'd counted the girl.

"Frances, you're a big man," said Jones. "You've probably survived by being a big man. Quick, too. But me, us, we've survived by keeping low, hiding out. Playing it safe, you could say, as safe as this new world allows. We're not about to go at it with two demon bitches."

It was a speech for Jones.

"Shit, Jones, you're chicken."

"Yeah, George, I am. Only a stupid person wouldn't be."

"I'm not," George replied, apparently missing the implication.

Frances counted off our advantages on his fingers. "They're feeding, so they're distracted. They're close, so we won't miss. There's only two of them, so they're outnumbered. There's a few hours of sun left, so they're weak."

I think he may have been making up the sunlight bit.

"Good enough for me," said George, already moving to the doors.

Frances saw an opportunity for visual emphasis and moved over with him, the girl going too, leaving just three of us cowering in the shadows. Frank said, "I go where the big man goes," and went.

"What about you, Charlie?"

I shrugged. "You make more sense," I said.

"But you want to take them down," Jones added.

"Yeah."

Jones sighed. "Yeah," he repeated, "me too."

We joined the others. It took only a minute to plan our tactics.

Frank checked his gun in the light that slanted down from between the doors. "We're all going to die," he said.

He was wrong about that. They only got two of us.

Four days after that fight at the gas station, Frances told me about the demon he and Cassie had seen in Colorado. We were camping at the side of the road, eating beans from a can.

"Her parents were still with us then," he said.

Cassie nodded to herself, scraping at the sides of her tin.

"What happened to them?"

"People on the road," said Cassie. "They tried to take my mom for their penitentary."

"Penitentiary," I said, pronouncing the "sh."

Frances said, "No, she's right. They call it a penitentary."

I remembered he'd said the word in the cellar. Back when the others were still with us.

"Places where women are kept prisoner," Frances explained. "Sometimes by religious nuts, sometimes by men who are scared. Sometimes by those who just like an excuse to hurt women."

I nodded and put my can aside. Frances pointed at it with his spoon.

"Not hungry," I said.

He gave the rest of my beans to the girl.

"Anyway, we'd crossed the Rockies hoping things would be different on this side of the mountains. They weren't. We found a scrap yard, figured we might find a car. What we found was one of those things. It was flapping only in bursts, wings beating against the ground and hiding most of what it was hunched over."

"It was Brenda," said Cassie, as if I should know who she meant. I could guess why she wasn't with them now. "She looked like she was having a bad dream with her eyes open."

"We thought it was eating her at first but it wasn't."

"Was it turning her into a demon?" I asked.

The girl shook her head. "It was doing what adults do."

I looked to Frances but he only nodded.

"It was fucking her?"

The girl sucked in a breath.

"What?" I reached for my gun.

"You said a bad word."

"Oh. Yeah. Sorry."

Frances smiled and nodded again. "It was doing what adults do."

"But…"

"They're not all women," Frances said. "Whatever you've heard, or maybe even seen, there's at least one out there that isn't female."

"If we tell people they'll stop hurting each other," Cassie said. "They'll be nice again and just hate demons if someone tells them."

"You sure?"

Cassie misunderstood. "I saw its thing," she said.

Frances held his hands out about a foot apart. He shook his head, either appalled or impressed.

"What did you do?"

"We hid and it flew away."

"With the woman?"

"No, she came with us."

Before I could ask, Cassie said, "She died having a baby." She burped and covered her mouth.

Frances told Cassie to bury the cans a little way off and added quietly, "We did what we had to when we saw what was coming out of her."

I thought of my poor Beth. All that futile pushing, a labour of pain that brought only death.

"Do you think we should give him something to eat?" Cassie asked, coming back before I could ask any questions.

We all looked at where Frank lay, his broken body strapped as tight as he could bear it. He was asleep, the only retreat he had from the pain.

"Wait until he wakes," I said, knowing that he wouldn't.

Cassie simply nodded. Maybe she knew it too.

"Why didn't he shoot?" Frances asked, but I still didn't have an answer for him.

We'd burst out of the cellar as one, but that was as much of the plan we stuck to. After that, all tactics were abandoned in our response to the horror before us. We knew what we'd see, but confronted by it we could only react. Our reaction was to fire, fire, and fire again. We fired until our guns were empty, which didn't take long. We all fired at the same one.

She was standing over a body, one clawed foot buried in the cavity of its chest whilst the other clawed at what flesh remained of the stomach. A line of entrails stretched up from the corpse to the creature's mouth, its talon hands hooking more and more into a gathered mouthful as if balling twine. Its leathery wings beat just enough to add strength to its pulling.

We surprised it; that bit went to plan. Its mouth was a bloody slop of guts and when it screamed at us, chewed stinking mouthfuls dropped down its chest. It released the corpse anchoring it and took to the sky, managing only one sweep of its wings before we hit it. I ran to it firing and was satisfied to see a good chunk of purple thigh vanish in a spray of blood, the rest of the leg severed by the creature's own attempts to flee, hooked as it was in the cadaver that had been its meal. Shots from George and Jones and Frank peppered the demon's torso, each round a splash of blood and bile that hammered it back. Frances was more deliberate with his guns, hitting it three times in the head. Another blast from my shotgun blew its wing into tatters but it was already falling then.

The other one had been scooping handfuls of flesh from higher up the body pile and retreated behind the corpses the moment we started firing. Part of me registered that. Part of me knew it was there even as part of me knew the one on the ground was dead, yet that was the one I approached. I broke the shotgun open and reloaded as the demon body jumped and shivered with wasted rounds from the others. They were clicking empty when I put the barrel against the head and burst it like a melon.

"Charlie!"

I dropped, turned, and fired all in one action but missed as the other one sailed over my head. It caught a tangle of my hair by chance, even short as it was, and tore it from my scalp as it passed.

Frances dropped his gun behind him and Cassie crouched to reload it whilst he fired with the other. It was a smooth operation that suggested practice and I wondered how many fire fights this little girl had been in. Her hands weren't even shaking.

The demon wheeled in the air. A hole appeared in its wing but that seemed to be the only hit and it didn't slow it down none. It dove towards us screaming.

That was enough to send me and George back to the cellar. We crouched on the steps and saw Jones fumble for his knife. He raised it quick enough to lunge once and then the demon had him, lifting him up with her talons as she shredded his legs and bowels with clawed feet. He screamed his agony till something broke in his throat. She cast him away, flying back and up as Jones flew forwards. He smacked into the corner of the building with a crack that broke his spine.

"Come here, you bitch!" George yelled, then ran out to her before she could take him up on the offer. He fired all the way, quick for a man with a rifle, but she only soared higher, a twisting shape in silhouette against the darkening sky.

"Reload!" Frances shouted. "While it's up there, quick, reload!" He swapped his gun for the one Cassie offered.

Frank stood, shielding his eyes from the dying sun, watching as the creature hovered.

"Reload, Frank!" I told him, pushing two cartridges into mine. When that was done I ran to him and snatched his weapon from a limp grip. I ejected the magazine and slapped his arm for a fresh one.

"We made them," he said, "when we did what we did to ourselves. They were born from the ashes that came after." He pointed. "We made it."

It was something I'd heard before, but not from Frank. Religious bullshit, like we didn't have enough to feel guilty about. I shook him, keeping an eye on the demon. It arced left and right but remained distant.

"Get some more fucking bullets in this and unmake it then," I said.

When he looked at me his eyes were empty, but he did as he was told.

"Spread out," Frances called. He'd shrugged out of his coat and harness. If the demon grabbed any of us, I hoped it grabbed him. With his bulk he wasn't being thrown anywhere, and with those arms he could tear this thing apart. Maybe that was why he only used crappy revolvers.

I put distance between me and Frank. George, for reasons known only to him, scrambled up the pile of corpses. He stood atop them with his arms out, daring the bitch to attack.

It did. It dived for Frank.

Frank levelled his gun at it calmly and had plenty of time to fire. But he didn't. He faced his doom as it flew down at him. George popped a few shots, making more tiny holes in the membrane of its wing. Frances took one careful shot but only clipped it as far as I could tell. I didn't dare from where I stood. It hurtled straight and hard, hitting Frank across the upper body and tugging him into the sky as it pulled up and away. I saw it rake a claw across his gun hand. The other sank into Frank's fleshy shoulder and he swung one arc of a pendulum before the creature's momentum took them both high.

I ran to where Frank had dropped his gun. A few of his fingers lay scattered around it like bloody commas.

Above us the demon screamed in play and tossed Frank away. He cartwheeled and fell a short distance but the bitch snatched him up again before he really began any descent, clutching him sharply around the ankle. A line of blood splashed down across my upturned face.

"Fucking shoot it!" I yelled. My own weapon was useless at this range.

"Might hit Frank," said George. He was taking aim.

"I don't think it matters now," said Frances, also lining up for a steady shot. "Might be better."

The demon swooped low, dragging Frank so he hit the ground and broke somewhere. Then it was diving away in an abrupt turn and Frank was thrown into our midst. He struck George across the legs and the two of them fell in a tumble of female corpses.

I fired both barrels as it passed me. A chunk of its hip blew out and it spun, only for Frances to hit it once, twice, three times in the side and breast. It crashed down into the dirt and flopped in a writhing mass of purple flesh.

I was reloading as I ran. Frances was still shooting as he came at it.

The creature was rolling and flapping and spraying its blood, clouds of dust billowing in the gusts of its attempted flight. Part of its sleek violet skull erupted, then another as Frances aligned his second shot by the success of his first.

I raised the shotgun to my shoulder but Frances, beside me, lowered it with his hand. "Save your ammunition," he said.

We watched it twitch and spasm until it was still. Then Frances tore it to pieces with only his hands.

George, taken down by the thrown body of Frank, had fired another shot as he fell. It went in under his chin and opened the top of his head. Not the movie-star end he would have wanted. Not the end many would have wanted, though I've known a few that have taken a similar route. I've thought about it myself from time to time. Only my fear that the demons will still come has kept me from that darkness.

George was dead. Jones was dead. Frank had lost a lot of one hand, which we bandaged, and most of one foot, which we amputated. Didn't take much but a snip here and there. He was a crooked tangle of limbs, each one broken more than once. His chest rose and fell in an awkward shape as he made rasping shallow breaths. He only screamed once with the pain of moving him and that pain was enough to make him pass out. He was easier to handle after that.

"He's my friend," I said, "but he's gone, Frances."

"That's not up to us," he said.

We made a stretcher for Frank. It was agreed without conversation that we'd leave the gas station behind as soon as we could.

Cassie gathered our supplies. When the stretcher was done I went through the pockets of the dead and said my goodbyes.

We didn't bury anybody.

Four days later they told me about demons with dicks, devil babies, and a mercy killing. I took a moral from the tale and smothered Frank that same night and in the morning we left him by the road still strapped to his stretcher.

We travelled south all morning. I learnt that Frances was a mechanic, and that for a short while he and Cassie had travelled by car. I learnt that Cassie had owned sixteen dolls and teddies and I was told each of their names. I learnt her father had been a school teacher and her mother a police officer, back when we needed such things.

I didn't tell them anything about me other than a few stories about the others I'd travelled with. They figured it out on their own, though. Well, Cassie did. I'd travelled with Jones, George, and Frank for the best part of a year and they never found out. Five days with this little girl and I'm asked, "Is Charlie short for Charlotte?"

Frances was as surprised as I was, and after the surprise it was too obvious to deny.

"Yeah."

"Charlotte is pretty," she said.

"Charlotte doesn't want to be pretty," I said back.

Which was why I'd cropped my hair right down to my scalp and let it grow everywhere else. I farted, belched, and scratched my crotch. Strapping down my chest wasn't much of a problem because there wasn't much there to begin with.

"Why don't you want to be pretty?" Cassie asked. "My mom was pretty."

Frances knew the answer. He told Cassie not to pry. Already he was looking at me different.

I didn't know what these penitentary places were, but I knew places like them, and probably a few places worse. Before Jones and George and Frank I belonged to a group who used me by night and called me demon by day to feel better about it. Sometimes, when we met others, I'd be loaned out in exchange for food, water, ammunition. It wasn't until I got pregnant that it stopped. Poor little Beth, spat from my poisoned loins in a flood of blood, reluctant to live in the world we'd given her.

They left me to die with her, and so I did.

And then Cassie came and reminded me of how things were, and how they could be.

"Left corner," said Frances.

Another fucking gas station. Like the one where we'd met, this one had a store and a bay for vehicle repair and two pumps out front, though one had been knocked down and lay like a blocky corpse in a dusty shroud. Unlike the other gas station, this one had people in it that were alive. One of them was leaning in the corner of the walled roof, a rifle pointing to where we stood in the road. The sun shone from his weapon in little winks of light, otherwise it was a good position.

"Seen," I said, though there wasn't much I could do about it from here.

Cassie was strapped in behind Frances, unseen. "We could move on," she said softly.

"There's another one in the repair well," I said, watching the man carefully adjust the angle of his rifle so it pointed up for a head shot if he needed it.

"Charlotte, we could move on."

I hissed at Cassie. "Shh."

From behind the standing pump emerged a bearded man. He held a pistol down by his knee and raised his other hand slowly in greeting.

"What do you think?"

Frances looked around. "I think there's a few more, maybe laying in ditches we can't see. I think the ones we can see are distractions. But we'll see what he has to say. Maybe they're just careful, like us."

"We ain't careful if we stick around."

"We need food."

"And what are you thinking of trading for it?"

He met my stare. "Guns. We got empty guns they probably have bullets for. Even if they don't, a man will miss a meal or two for another gun."

"Hello!" the man called, nearing. His beard grew to the left as if blown by a wind we couldn't feel. His shirt was open, his scrawny chest the canvas for a large drawn cross. Jesus sagged in tattooed crucifixion and behind him rose the purple form of a demon, wings open to full span creating a bruised background for Christ's death.

"Not a word, little heart," Frances warned.

From where I stood I saw her mime a lip-zipping gesture. She smiled at me. I'll always remember that.

"I'll talk to him, keep him away from you and the girl."

I broke open my weapon and approached with it hooked over one arm. I could snap it closed quick enough if I had to. It was a gesture, that was all.

The tattooed man responded by holstering his.

"Dangerous road to be travelling in twos," the man said, "unless you're seeking some Noah I know nothing about." He laughed, though he'd clearly thought it up on his walk over.

"It is," I said. I gestured to my waist pocket and he nodded, making a lowering motion with one hand which I hoped was a signal to the others not to panic. I reached in and showed him what I had.

"Impressive," he said, "You must walk the righteous path."

"I do."

I returned the talons to my pocket.

"So do we," he said. "Got one of the bitches back there a way. She'd sniffed us out, found our haven."

"Too bad."

"Inevitable. What do you want, you want shelter?"

"Food, if you have spare."

"No such thing, but we can spare some of what we have. What you got to spare us?"

I had something better than guns.

The food he traded took me into Texas and there I hooked up with some people heading east. I'll go at least as far as Mississippi with them, depending how things go. They have paper and pens and keep leaving messages for others along the way, telling people where they're going. I started writing this down so others might learn the truth when they got there, only I'm not sure what truth it is I want to tell. That some demons are men, there's that, though I doubt you'll believe me. I never seen one of those things that weren't a bitch with wings, and I've seen a few now. Not all women are demons, but some are. I should admit that.

The men at that gas station thought so. They took me to the cellar and showed me.

"You have to whip them," the man with the tattoo explained. "It stops the wings from growing."

The women were tied face down over boards, their backs laced with red lines that ran in ribbons. He showed me what they'd done to stop demons being born, and then he showed me where the food was, piled high in tin towers. I began stuffing my pack with it, not sure how long I'd have before Frances tried something.

"They'll find us again," the bearded man said. "Sniff us out. When you take their chicks, the mothers come hunting. But people need to learn, and we provide the opportunity here. We can't stop in our work."

No, I didn't think he could. And all the time there were groups like this, the person who Cassie called Charlotte would be in danger. It was only a matter of time before Frances saw me as a means to feed and clothe his adopted daughter, and who knew what he'd do to her when she got older.

"He's going to be trouble, isn't he?" the man with me said.

"If you give him time to be."

He hadn't believed me at first, this man, when I told him Frances was my prisoner. "He looks a little big for you to manage," he'd said, "and he looks armed."

"He is. But so am I and I walk behind."

"And he carries his demon on his back," the man added, liking the symbolism.

"You don't need to take it," the man said now as I forced my bag closed and hefted it over my shoulder. "You could stay."

They'd had enough from me already.

"No. Thanks. I need to keep moving."

"Alright."

He walked me outside where Frances stood patient, trusting and careful.

"Want to say anything?" the man asked me.

"No."

"Forgive him, Lord," said the man. He signalled and Frances fell, for a moment looking as if the man's quick point had thrown him down. Then came the crack of the roof man's rifle.

Cassie called for Frances from where she lay under him. The men around me heard a girl's voice calling a man a girl's name. If she later called me Charlotte they'd dismiss it as something the same.

"You want to stay for her cleansing at least?"

I shook my head, more to clear it of its images than as answer.

"Alright," said the man, and clasped my hand.

I made sure my grip was hard and firm, then walked away.

There are demons everywhere. That's what I've seen. That's what the clarity of post-2020 vision shows me. You don't need a harness to carry them, either. They come at night, tormenting my darkest hours and screaming when I try to sleep. I have a strip of wire for when they come and I whip my back to keep the wings away, lashing at my skin, scouring my flesh until they're satisfied by the pain. They come and they scream and they know me for what I am, and they know it's not just a woman.

Before earning her MFA from Vermont College of Fine Arts, Mary Rickert worked as a kindergarten teacher, a coffee shop barista, a balloon vendor at Disneyland, and in the personnel department of Sequoia National Park, where her time off was spent "bagging" peaks. She has published numerous short stories.

Her first novel, *The Memory Garden*, was published in 2014 and won the Locus Award for Best First Novel. She is the winner of the Crawford Award and the World Fantasy Award for her collection *Map of Dreams*. She also won the World Fantasy Award for her short story "Journey into the Kingdom" and the Shirley Jackson Award for her short story "The Corpse Painter's Masterpiece."

Her newest collection, *You Have Never Been Here*, was published in 2015. For more information, visit her website at WWW.MRICKERT.NET.

Was She Wicked? Was She Good?
M. Rickert

SHE LEAVES THE small creatures in tortured juxtapositions. Her mother and I find them on the porch steps, in the garden, drowning in small puddles, the green hose dripping water from the copper nozzle, guilty as blood. For a few weeks we are able to believe that these tragedies have nothing to do with our little girl whose smile breaks each morning like the sun. We scrape them up, gently, with the edge of leaves or blades of grass (once I cut one in half that way, a horrible accident and it bled while Sheilah laughed, I thought at some imaginary play), but we save none. Sometimes, we have to take them out of their misery, the slow agony of dying they suffer; we step on them, hard, and later scrape their squashed remains from the soles of our shoes.

It has been a long, hot summer. The flowers wither on exhausted stems. We almost regret our stance against air conditioning. We place fans throughout the house; the hum is as annoying as the insidious hum of hornets that occasionally circle over us in the garden, like a threat.

Sheilah runs through the summer days in her nightgown, pale pink and ethereal, her white limbs and moon-white face protected by slatherings of coconut-scented sunscreen. At night, when she finally falls asleep, tiny beads of sweat dotting her pink lips, heat emanates from her blonde curls as if she, herself, were a season.

Had there been earlier signs that we ignored? Certainly, we tried to believe it was all accident and coincidence until, at last, she brought her game into the house. We found them in gruesome cups of strange concoctions in the kitchen, combinations of balsamic vinegar, Worcester sauce, and food coloring, their tiny bodies floating in the noxious liquid; we found them in the ice cubes, fingers splayed against their frozen death; finally we find them in Sheilah's bedroom, pinned alive to a bulletin board that displays her kindergarten graduation certificate, her blue ribbon for good citizenship, and a drawing of a horse. They are screaming but they are beyond being saved; we unpin them and hit them with the bottoms of our shoes, feeling worst about the one who survived our repeated attempts at mercy killing only to die in agony. From this upstairs window we watch Sheilah. She is, once again, dressed in the silky pink sleeveless nightgown, sitting on a quilt under the oak tree. One second we are looking down at the golden-haloed head of our child, her murmured voice rising up to us, pretty as the cardinal's morning song, and the next, we are running out of the room, down the wooden stairs, through the meditation room, into the kitchen (with its bright windows and spider plants), down the concrete steps lined with terra-cotta pots filled with geraniums, awkwardly running across the lawn to Sheilah, who sits on the old quilt beneath the ancient tree, plucking wings and severing limbs, the damaged and wounded writhing in agony while she sings.

With a moan, Anne scoops Sheilah up and runs back into the house, as though escaping a tornado, which leaves me to take care of the mess. I apologize to each and every one. I beg forgiveness. Their eyes lock into mine, infinitesimal eyes filled with the infinite suffering my daughter has caused. Later, when I go inside, I find Anne closing all the windows. "What are you doing?" I ask. "Isn't this why we moved to the country? It'll be a hundred degrees in here."

She looks at me with bright eyes, as though she suffers a fever. "They aren't going to let her get away with this," she says. "You know they won't."

"You're right," I nod. "We need to punish her."

Anne turns from the closed window, the air around us charged, like the feeling before a storm. "What are you saying?"

I step toward her but stop when I see the stone of her face, once beautiful, now set into the hard lines first etched three years ago. "Maybe we should reconsider. Maybe a little punishment—"

She turns away from me, she whirls out of the room. I stand there and listen to the sound of windows being slammed shut.

This is a difficult time for all of us. Anne makes jewelry in the basement studio, which Sheilah is forbidden to enter, while I work on my second book (*The Possibilities for Enchantment in a World at War with the Self, the Other, and the Infinite*) in my upstairs office, also forbidden. Sheilah follows this rule so completely that, one morning, I find her lying curled against the door, like a good dog.

"Why don't you go play?"

She looks up at me, her eyes bright and wide as pennies. "You mean outside?" she asks.

I shake my head. Sadly. "No, Sheilah, not outside."

She purses her lips into rosebud shape. "I wanna go outside."

Every time she mentions the outdoors I picture the little bodies, the dark eyes, the strange combination of her singing and their small screams. "We've already talked about this, Sheilah. No."

"Why not why not why not?" she wails.

"You know why," I say, and am surprised by how mean I sound. She stops her whining. She stares at me. I can't tell if her expression is one of insolence, or horror. I step around her, carefully shutting the door behind me. My office window overlooks the backyard. I press up on the sash, hard. These are old windows, with screens and stormers that we change each spring and fall, a massive undertaking we had not considered when we bought the place, frantic to make our escape. I breathe in the scent of dirt, roses, leaves, grass, the green, loamy scent of summer, but my reverie is interrupted by droning, low and near. Hanging from the eave, like some dark tumor, is the hornet's nest.

I am both repelled and fascinated by the hornets, their golden wings quivering as they work their way around the orb. Sheilah is no longer screaming, perhaps she's gone to bother Anne, or maybe she's actually playing with her crystals or her chemistry set. I breathe in until I become restless and can't stand still any longer, then I pull down the sash. The effect is immediate; stifled in my own home. I inspect the room carefully, checking the corners, the ceiling, the hiding places behind the furniture.

We are striving for something like normal. The thought of having a "normal" child would once have struck us as a failing. Now it is our hope. The honey butter melts across the biscuits and we wash our hands under the tap as we stare out the closed window, remembering how we used to lick each other's sticky fingers. When she comes into the kitchen, wearing that nightgown, her hair a wild cloud around her sleep-pink face, we greet her joyfully. She pushes us away with her tiny, dangerous hands. She sighs like an old woman. She demands white bread (who knows where she was introduced to this vile concoction), toasted and slathered with sugary peanut butter. She chews with her mouth open, her pearled teeth coated with oily brown, and squints at us. "I wanna go outside."

We shake our heads.

"Why not why not why not," she cries and flings the toast to the floor, where she follows it in a spectacular display of temper. "Why not why not why not?" We sit in the rays of morning sun, sealed in with her screams and the heavy moaning heat, and it does not escape me that, in a way, we have become her victims.

Many nights, after Sheilah falls asleep in mid-protest, Anne goes outside, only to return streaked with dirt and grass, her blue eyes bereft of even the memory of joy. She does not invite me to join her, but one night I follow, allowing myself the freedom we must deny our daughter. Anne sits in the garden on a rock large enough, just barely, for one. She does not acknowledge me. Once my eyes adjust, I see what she has done. Miniature tombstones stand in neat rows, flowers in acorn cups arranged before them. I glance at Anne, then lean closer. Each stone is carved with a symbol; a star, a moon, a little shoe, a feather, a clock.

"I didn't know their names."

"Anne, listen, we—"

"Don't. Don't try to make this right with words."

What else do I have? I stand there at the foot of the fairies' graveyard for a long time, hoping that Anne will speak, but she doesn't. Finally, I turn around and walk back inside, immediately assaulted by the hot air, the droning fans, and Sheilah's screams, wild with terror. I take the steps, two at a time, slipping on the braided rug, pushing against the floor as I call, "I'm coming! Daddy's here."

She is sitting in bed, tears streaming down her face, her mouth open, her hair blowing up and back as though she is possessed, but before I can take her in my arms, Anne swoops past. She turns to me, her eyes wide, her own hair blowing in the hot fan wind. "What happened?"

I shrug. Anne frowns as if I have failed her with this answer. (I have failed her with this answer.) She is holding Sheilah, swaying side to side. The room is stifling, too hot with its shut windows, and too stuffy with a vague, sour odor. Suddenly, I feel nauseous. I step into the hall to catch my breath. Anne follows. "You can't do this right now. You have to make sure the room is safe." Reluctantly, I step back into the bedroom. The windows are closed and locked. I check behind the door, look in the closet. I even look under the bed.

Finished with my search, I follow the sound of Anne's cooing, downstairs into the living room, where the standing fan gently hums, its great unwieldy head turning slowly in repeated surveyance of mother and daughter sitting in the flowered chair. The windows are locked against the black night as though it is something that will creep in and destroy us if we give it any quarter.

"Can you tell me what frightened you? Can you tell Daddy?"

Sheilah sits in her mother's lap, her curls damp at the back of her neck. She glances up at me with her copper eyes and I see in them, for just a moment, the look of murder before her long lashes flutter down. "Wings," she says.

"Wings?" her mother and I repeat.

She nods, and, sniffling loudly, wraps her small arms around Anne's neck. The fan blows over us while Anne gently rocks. "I told you they would come after her."

"It was just a dream. A nightmare. Kids—"

"No. It was them. Do something, Michael."

"We need to punish her."

Anne holds Sheilah closer, as if I have suggested releasing her into the dark yard where those who seek revenge could have their way.

"We've already discussed this."

"I'm not saying we do anything corporal, I'm just saying that we need to show her that what she's doing is wrong. They won't bother her if she stops hurting them."

"No."

"Anne, listen to me—"

"Why should I? Do you listen to me? Do you ever listen to me? I told you we should have taken her to a different doctor. I told you he didn't understand people like us. I told you—"

"When? No. You didn't. You never said..."

Sheilah stirs against Anne, turning her head to reveal her profile, damp with sweat, wet curls plastered against her cheek.

"We're not going to punish her," Anne hisses. "She's already been through enough." She scoots to the edge of the chair and stands up, her eyes sharp on my face. "You're obsessed with vengeance."

"Don't be ridiculous."

"Ridiculous," she says as she passes me. It's only when I hear the creaking of the stairs that I realize she was calling me a name.

The fissures have formed beneath us, and I am not so far gone that I don't recognize we are falling. I stand there, I don't know for how long, as if any movement would collapse the careful arc that keeps us suspended. The fan drones; how I hate that sound.

Sheilah is sleeping with Anne in our bed. I try to move quietly, but they both stir when I crawl in beside them. For a while I just lay there, watching them breathe.

Bright light streams through the lace curtains of the humming room, and I awake to the sound of Anne weeping. I wrap her in my arms. She tries to explain but the words are swallowed by her tears. I pat her gently on the back. Over her shoulder I see Sheilah standing in the doorway in her favorite night-gown. She watches with a cold, calculated expression, holding in her dimpled fingers a fairy, so small it is almost invisible. Careful to cover the tiny mouth with her pinky she pulls one wing off the poor creature, and then the other. I take a deep breath and hold Anne closer.

We've had this problem with windows before, when we lived in the city. I begged Anne to lock them at night but she "couldn't feel closed in" and "had to have fresh air." Eventually, I had boards cut to size so that the windows could be left partially open, but safe. She used them for a while, but then one night she "forgot," or so she's always said, and I never had the heart to confront her about it. Whether she forgot to close the windows or not, her intention had been to let in the breeze, not the night creatures, with their masks and guns.

"This happens every year. It's like we're all stuck in some kind of cycle."

"We're not stuck," she says. "We moved. That's one thing. I'm making jewelry again. You're working on your book. We are making progress. Give me some credit."

Over Anne's shoulder, Sheilah pulls one leg off the poor fairy and then the other.

"No."

Anne pulls away from me, her face hard. Behind her Sheilah tosses wings, legs, and corpse to the floor, then walks down the hall, humming.

"I mean, you're right. Of course. We're not stuck, we're just, this is just a hard time of year for us and I was thinking that it might be nice for you to take a break."

"But how can I leave her, so close to the anniversary?"

"She'll be fine. She'll be with me. Besides, we don't even know if she remembers anything about that night."

Anne shakes her head. "It doesn't matter whether she remembers," she says. "What do you think this is all about?"

It is disturbing, how eagerly she leaves. Sheilah and I wave from the open doorway, the scent of summer dying in the morning air, the brown lilacs withered on the bush, the squirrels scampering wildly through the yard, which is overgrown and dried out. Anne waves from the open car window, the graceful arc of her hand the last we see of her as she turns the corner. Sheilah starts walking across the porch, she turns and looks at me, wonder and fear in her small face. I nod. She breaks into that brilliant smile and, with a shout, runs free, a wild thing released. Later, I lay the quilt under the tree, and bring out a thermos of lemonade, and peanut butter and jelly sandwiches. She gulps the lemonade, and tears into the sandwich. With her mouth full, she looks up at me, smiles, and plants peanut butter kisses all over my face.

She plays outside all day, and into the evening. When I call her in, she comes, tired and happy. She sits at the kitchen table and stares at the macaroni and cheese, her favorite food, but she cannot eat, instead she slumps forward, falling asleep, right there at the table. I carry her upstairs, and put her to bed in the clothes she played in.

I go from room to room opening all the windows and turning off the fans. The damp night air smells sweet, and reminds me of the scented candle Anne had in her bedroom when we first met. I stand at the open window of my office, breathing in the memory of those wild nights of limb and skin, when we discovered each other so thoroughly it was as though we were created by touch. I lean into the screen and it pops. I press just a little harder; it comes loose but doesn't fall. I pound it with my fist, remembering, as I do, how I hammered the corners to make it secure. It's an old house and we often found the screens fallen or dangling.

"What are you doing?"

"Go back to bed, Sheilah. I'm fixing something."

"I'm thirsty."

"Go back to bed. I'll bring you a glass of water as soon as I'm finished."

She looks at the open window. "Mommy's going to be mad."

"Yes, she is. If she calls and finds out that you are still awake she's going to be very angry at you."

Sheilah's face contorts. I have confused her, taken advantage of her logic skills, rooted, as they are, in her six-year-old mind. "Go on now."

Her eyes narrow as she glances from me to the window and back again. "Go on."

She shuffles out of the room, like a little old lady, weary with the wrongs of the world.

I hit the screen three more times, wincing with pain until, at last, it loosens, only to dangle by the bottom left corner. The hornet nest is silent, two hornets, the night guards, cling to its side.

"Daddy? I'm ready for my water now."

It takes both hands to wrench the thing free. My knuckles are bleeding.

"Daddy!"

Finally it comes undone. I shove it away, approximating a throw; it crashes to the ground, followed by a sound of brush scattered, twigs broken. I have frightened some creature down there, a deer, or perhaps something more dangerous.

"Daddy!"

When I walk into Sheilah's room her eyes widen. I hand her the glass of water. "Drink it," I say, and then I say it again, in a gentle tone. "Drink it, honey."

She shakes her head vigorously. "Don't wanna," she says.

I snatch the glass from her. Water slops out. "Go to sleep, now." I lay my hand on her head, bend down to kiss her. As I leave the room I prop open the door with the big book of Grimm, the one with the fake gold edging on all the pages.

Downstairs, the rich scented summer air flows through the rooms. I sit in the flowered chair, sipping last year's clover wine. It was on just such a night as this that we were ruined. I fall asleep remembering the screams, the terror, the open windows. Screams. I wake to her screams, my heart pounding like a trapped creature. She screams, and I run through the rooms brightened by morning sun. "I'm coming," I shout, "Daddy's here." I race up the stairs and do not hesitate as I approach her room, abuzz with dark noise and screams. She is sitting up, covered by them as if she were made of honey, their golden wings trembling. I can see her halo of hair, though some alight there as well, her mouth, open but blackened by their writhing. I grab a blanket and swing it but this only heightens their attack; she screams and they sting me without mercy. "Daddy's here, Daddy's here," I say even as I run out of the room, down the sunlit hall (but wait, what was that scurrying to hide in the corner) to the bathroom where I draw the water, which comes out languidly. I run back to the room, "Daddy's here," I say over and over again, wrapping her in the blanket. She screams at their new assault. Through the blanket I feel their squirming, their soft bodies, their stings. I rush down the hall to the bathroom, set her in the bath; she screams. I tear the blanket off; it is alive with wings; I press it, and her, under the water, releasing her just long enough for screams and breath before I hold her under again. They fly at me, as if they understand what I am doing. The water is black with them. She struggles against my grasp, her mouth wide with screams; I dunk her one more time, then I carry her, heavy and wet and screaming, down the hall, slipping but not falling, down the stairs (and there, what was that behind the potted plant, and what just flew overhead). I hold her close even as they continue to sting. I grab my car keys from the kitchen counter, I run down the crooked path. They follow us, stinging again and again; she screams and I scream too as I set her in the car. A few of them follow, but only a few. I kill them with a rolled up atlas. At least now she understands, I think, now she knows not to harm a creature with wings.

Although it is late fall we are making up for lost time and spend much of our evenings outdoors. Anne is sitting in the garden, painting a small portrait of a fairy. She has never accused me of doing anything more than opening all the windows on a hot summer night. Why has she stayed, knowing even this? Well, why did I stay three years ago? I like to think it is love, this tendency to believe in each other's innocence, but maybe it's something else. I sit here, on the porch, writing in this notebook, sipping dandelion wine we bought from an old German fellow at the Farmer's Market. Sheilah sits on the blanket beneath the oak. She is almost entirely recovered though she moves strangely at times, with an odd, careful slowness that you would expect from someone wounded, or very old. They had to shave her head. Her hair has grown in strange, bristly and sharp. The doctors say that it will likely fall out, this sort of thing happens sometimes as a result of trauma, and already there are a few patches of soft hair coming in behind her ears, no longer blonde, but pure white. She sits on her quilt, dressed in jeans and a cotton sweater, playing some sort of game with fallen leaves; they are scolding each other, their leafy voices brittle.

As the amber evening closes in around us, and the night fairies come out, carrying their tiny lanterns, whispering their dark thoughts, Sheilah continues playing; even when a parade of them crosses the patches of her blanket, even when several fly right past her, she pays them no mind at all. Anne and I have begun to suspect she no longer sees them, which is sad in a way, but given the choices we had, and what life made of us, we think we have done well by Sheilah. Now that we have a normal child, she will be safe in her normal world, and we will be safe in ours. We can hope, we can dream, we believe.

John Langan is the author of three collections, *Sefira and Other Betrayals* (Hippocampus 2016), *The Wide, Carnivorous Sky and Other Monstrous Geographies*, and *Mr. Gaunt and Other Uneasy Encounters*.

He's one of the founders of the Shirley Jackson Award and served as a juror during its first three years.

He lives in New York's Hudson Valley with his wife, younger son, and a growing collection of swords.

The Shallows
John Langan

"Il faut cultiver notre jardin."—Voltaire, *Candide*

"I COULD CALL you Gus," Ransom said.

The crab's legs, blue and cream, clattered against one another. It did not hoist itself from its place in the sink, though, which meant it was listening to him. Maybe. Staring out the dining room window, his daily mug of instant coffee steaming on the table in front of him, he said, "That was supposed to be my son's name. Augustus. It was his great-grandfather's name, his mother's father's father. The old man was dying while Heather was pregnant. We... I, really, was struck by the symmetry: one life ending, another beginning. It seemed a duty, our duty, to make sure the name wasn't lost, to carry it forward into a new generation. I didn't know old Gus, not really; as far as I can remember, I met him exactly once, at a party at Heather's parents' a couple of years before we were married."

The great curtain of pale light that rippled thirty yards from his house stilled. Although he had long since given up trying to work out the pattern of its changes, Ransom glanced at his watch. 2:02 p.m., he was reasonably sure. The vast rectangle that occupied the space where his neighbor's green-sided house had stood, as well as everything to either side of it, dimmed, then filled with the rich blue of the tropical ocean, the paler blue of the tropical sky. Waves chased one another toward Ransom, their long swells broken by the backs of fish, sharks, whales, all rushing in the same direction as the waves, away from a spot where the surface of the ocean heaved in a way that reminded Ransom of a pot of water approaching the boil.

(Tilting his head back, Matt had said, *How far up do you think it goes? I don't know,* Ransom had answered. Twenty feet in front of them, the sheet of light that had descended an hour before, draping their view of the Pattersons' house and everything beyond it, belled, as if swept by a breeze. *This is connected to what's been happening at the poles, isn't it?* Matt had squinted to see through the dull glare. *I don't know,* Ransom had said, *maybe. Do you think the Pattersons are okay?* Matt had asked. *I hope so,* Ransom had said. He'd doubted it.)

He looked at the clumps of creamer speckling the surface of the coffee, miniature icebergs. "Gus couldn't have been that old. He'd married young, and Heather's father, Rudy, had married young, and Heather was twenty-four or -five…call him sixty-five, sixty-six, tops. To look at him, though, you would have placed him a good ten, fifteen years closer to the grave. Old… granted, I was younger, then, and from a distance of four decades, mid-sixty seemed a lot older than it does twenty years on. But even factoring in the callowness of youth, Gus was not in good shape. I doubt he'd ever been what you'd consider tall, but he was stooped, as if his head were being drawn down into his chest. Thin, frail: although the day was hot, he wore a long-sleeved checked shirt buttoned to the throat and a pair of navy chinos. His head… his hair was thinning, but what there was of it was long, and it floated around his head like the crest of some ancient bird. His nose supported a pair of horn-rimmed glasses whose lenses were white with scratches; I couldn't understand how he could see through them, or maybe that was the point. Whether he was eating from the paper plate Heather's uncle brought him or just sitting there, old Gus's lips kept moving, his tongue edging out and retreating."

The coffee was cool enough to drink. Over the rim of the mug, he watched the entire ocean churning with such force that whatever of its inhabitants had not reached safety were flung against one another. Mixed among their flailing forms were parts of creatures Ransom could not identify, a forest of black needles, a mass of rubbery pink tubes, the crested dome of what might have been a head the size of a bus.

He lowered the mug. "By the time I parked my car, Gus was seated near the garage. Heather took me by the hand and led me over to him. Those white lenses raised in my direction as she crouched beside his chair and introduced me as her boyfriend. Gus extended his right hand, which I took in mine. Hard…his palm, the undersides of his fingers, were rough with calluses, the yield of a lifetime as a mechanic. I tried to hold his hand gently…politely, I guess, but although his arm trembled, there was plenty of strength left in his fingers, which closed on mine like a trap springing shut. He said something, *Pleased to meet you, you've got a special girl, here,* words to that effect. I wasn't paying attention; I was busy with the vise tightening around my fingers, with my bones grinding against one another. Once he'd delivered his pleasantries, Gus held onto my hand a moment longer, then the lenses dropped, the fingers relaxed, and my hand was my own again. Heather kissed him on the cheek, and we went to have a look at the food. My fingers ached on and off for the rest of the day."

At the center of the heaving ocean, something forced its way up through the waves. The peak of an undersea mountain, rising to the sun: that was still Ransom's first impression. Niagaras poured off black rock. His mind struggled to catch up with what stood revealed, to find suitable comparisons for it, even as more of it pushed the water aside. Some kind of structure—structures: domes, columns, walls—a city, an Atlantis finding the sun, again. No—the shapes were off: the domes bulged, the columns bent, the walls curved, in ways that conformed to no architectural style—that made no sense. A natural formation, then, a quirk of geology. No—already, the hypothesis was untenable: there was too much evidence of intentionality in the shapes draped with seaweed, heaped with fish brought suffocating into the air. As the rest of the island left the ocean, filling the view before Ransom to the point it threatened to burst out of the curtain, the appearance of an enormous monolith in the foreground, its surface incised with pictographs, settled the matter. This huge jumble of forms, some of which appeared to contradict one another, to intersect in ways the eye could not untangle, to occupy almost the same space at the same time, was deliberate.

Ransom slid his chair back from the table and stood. The crab's legs dinged on the stainless steel sink. Picking up his mug, he turned away from the window. "That was the extent of my interactions with Gus. To be honest, what I knew of him, what Heather had told me, I didn't much care for. He was what I guess you'd call a functioning alcoholic, although the way he functioned… he was a whiskey-drinker, Jack Daniel's, Jim Beam, Maker's Mark, that end of the shelf. I can't claim a lot of experience, but from what I've seen, sour mash shortcuts to your mean, your nasty side. That was the case with Gus, at least. It wasn't so much that he used his hands—he did, and I gather the hearing in Rudy's left ear was the worse for it—no, the whiskey unlocked the cage that held all of Gus's resentment, his bitterness, his jealousy. Apparently, when he was younger, Rudy's little brother, Jan, had liked helping their mother in the kitchen. He'd been something of a baker, Jan; Rudy claimed he made the best chocolate cake you ever tasted, frosted it with buttercream. His mother used to let him out of working with his father in the garage or around the yard so he could assist her with the meals. None of the other kids—there were six of them—was too thrilled at there being one less of them to dilute their father's attention, especially when they saw Gus's lips tighten as he realized Jan had stayed inside again.

"Anyway, this one night, Gus wandered into the house after spending the better part of the evening in the garage. He passed most of the hours after he returned from work fixing his friends' and acquaintances' cars, Hank Williams on the transistor radio, Jack Daniel's in one of the kids' juice glasses. In he comes, wiping the grease off his hands with a dish towel, and what should greet his eyes when he peers into the refrigerator in search of a little supper but the golden top of the cherry pie Jan made for the church bake sale the next day. Gus loves cherry pie. Without a second thought, he lifts the pie from the top shelf of the fridge and deposits it on the kitchen table. He digs his clasp-knife out of his pants pocket, opens it, and cuts himself a generous slice. He doesn't bother with a fork; instead, he shoves his fingers under the crust and lifts the piece straight to his mouth. It's so tasty, he helps himself to a second, larger serving before he's finished the first. In his eagerness, he slices through the pie tin to the table. He doesn't care; he leaves the knife stuck where it is and uses his other hand to free the piece.

"That's how Jan finds him when he walks into the kitchen for a glass of milk, a wedge of cherry pie in one hand, red syrup and yellow crumbs smeared on his other hand, his mouth and chin. By this age—Jan's around twelve, thirteen—the boy has long since learned that the safest way, the only way, to meet the outrages that accompany his father's drinking is calmly, impassively. Give him the excuse to garnish his injury with insult, and he'll take it.

"And yet, this is exactly what Jan does. He can't help himself, maybe. He lets his response to the sight of Gus standing with his mouth stuffed with half-chewed pie flash across his face. It's all the provocation his father requires. *What?* he says, crumbs spraying from his mouth.

"*Nothing*, Jan says, but he's too late. Gus drops the slice he's holding to the floor, scoops the rest of the pie from the tin with his free hand, and slaps that to the floor as well. He raises one foot and stamps on the mess he's made, spreading it across the linoleum. Jan knows enough to remain where he is. Gus brings his shoe down on the ruin of Jan's efforts twice more, then wipes his hands on his pants, frees his knife from the table, and folds it closed. As he returns it to his pocket, he tells Jan that if he wants to be a little faggot and wear an apron in the kitchen, that's his concern, but he'd best keep his little faggot mouth shut when there's a man around, particularly when that man's his father. Does Jan understand him?

"Yes, Pa, Jan says.

"Then take your little faggot ass off to bed, Gus says.

"What happened next," Ransom said, "wasn't a surprise; in fact, it was depressingly predictable." He walked into the kitchen, deposited his mug on the counter. "That was the end of Jan's time in the kitchen. He wasn't the first one outside to help his father, but he wasn't the last, either, and he worked hard. The morning of his eighteenth birthday, he enlisted in the Marines; within a couple of months he was on patrol in Vietnam. He was cited for bravery on several occasions; I think he may have been awarded a medal. One afternoon, when his squad stopped for a rest, he was shot through the head by a sniper. He'd removed his helmet...to tell the truth, I'm not sure why he had his helmet off. He survived, but it goes without saying, he was never the same. His problems...he had trouble moving, coordinating his arms and legs. His speech was slurred; he couldn't remember the names of familiar objects, activities; he forgot something the second after you said it to him. There was no way he could live on his own. His mother wanted Jan to move back home, but Gus refused, said there was no way he was going to be saddled with an idiot who hadn't known enough to keep his damn helmet on. Which didn't stop him from accepting the drinks he was bought when Jan visited and Gus paraded him at the V.F.W."

Behind him, a pair of doors would be opening on the front of a squat stone box near the island's peak. The structure, whose rough exterior suggested a child's drawing of a Greek temple, must be the size of a cathedral, yet it was dwarfed by what squeezed out of its open doors. While Ransom continued to have trouble with the sheer size of the thing, which seemed as if it must break a textbook's worth of physical laws, he was more bothered by its speed. There should have been no way, he was certain, for something of that mass to move that quickly. Given the thing's appearance, the tumult of coils wreathing its head, the scales shimmering on its arms, its legs, the wings that unfolded into great translucent fans whose edges were not quite in focus, its speed was hardly the most obvious detail on which to focus, but for Ransom, the dearth of time between the first hint of the thing's shadow on the doors and its heaving off the ground on a hurricane-blast of its wings confirmed the extent to which the world had changed.

(*What was that?* Matt had screamed, his eyes wide. *Was that real? Is that happening?* Ransom had been unable to speak, his tongue dead in his mouth.)

Like so many cranes raising and lowering, the cluster of smaller limbs that rose from the center of the crab's back was opening and closing. Ransom said, "I know: if the guy was such a shit, why pass his name on to my son?" He shrugged. "When I was younger—at that point in my life, the idea of the past…of a family's past, of continuity between the present and that past, was very important to me. By the time Heather was pregnant, the worst of Gus's offenses was years gone by. If you wanted, I suppose you could say that he was paying for his previous excesses. He hadn't taken notice of his diabetes for decades. If the toes on his right foot hadn't turned black, then started to smell, I doubt he ever would have returned to the doctor. Although…what that visit brought him was the emergency amputation of his toes, followed by the removal of his foot a couple of weeks later. The surgeon wanted to take his leg, said the only way to beat the gangrene that was eating Gus was to leap ahead of it. Gus refused, declared he could see where he was headed, and he wasn't going to be jointed like a chicken on the way. There was no arguing with him. His regular doctor prescribed some heavy-duty antibiotics for him, but I'm not sure he had the script filled.

"When he returned home, everyone said it was to die—which it was, of course, but I think we all expected him to be gone in a matter of days. He hung on, though, for one week, and the next, and the one after that. Heather and her mother visited him. I was at work. She said the house smelled like spoiled meat; it was so bad, she couldn't stay in for more than a couple of minutes, barely long enough to stand beside Gus's bed and kiss his cheek. His lips moved, but she couldn't understand him. She spent the rest of the visit outside, in her mother's truck, listening to the radio."

Ransom glanced out the window. The huge sheet of light rippled like an aurora, the image of the island and its cargo gone. He said, "Gus died the week after Heather's visit. To tell the truth, I half expected him to last until the baby arrived. Heather went to the wake and the funeral; I had to work. As it turned out, we settled on Matthew—Matt, instead."

His break was over. Ransom exited the kitchen, turned down the hallway to the front door. On the walls to either side of him, photos of himself and his family, his son, smiled at photographers' prompts years forgotten. He peered out one of the narrow windows that flanked the door. The rocking chair he'd left on the front porch in a quixotic gesture stood motionless. Across the street, the charred mound that sat inside the burned-out remains of his neighbor's house appeared quiet. Ransom reached for the six-foot pole that leaned against the corner opposite him. Careful to check that the butcher knife duct-taped to the top was secure, he gripped the improvised spear near the tape and unlocked the door. Leveling the weapon, he stepped back as the door swung in.

In two months of maintaining the ritual every time he opened any of the doors into the house, Ransom had yet to be met by anything. The precaution was one on which his son had insisted; the day of his departure north, Matt had pledged Ransom to maintaining it. With no intention of doing so, Ransom had agreed, only to find himself repeating the familiar motions the next time he was about to venture out to the garden. Now here he was, jabbing the end of the spear through the doorway to draw movement, waiting a count of ten, then advancing one slow step at a time, careful not to miss anything dangling from the underside of the porch roof. Once he was satisfied that the porch was clear, that nothing was lurking in the bush to its right, he called over his shoulder, "I'm on my way to check the garden, if you'd like to join me."

A chorus of ringing announced the crab's extricating itself from the sink. Legs clicking on the wood floors like so many tap shoes, it hurried along the hall and out beside him. Keeping the spear straight ahead, he reached back for one of the canvas bags piled inside the door, then pulled the door shut. The crab raced down the stairs and to the right, around the strip of lawn in front of the house. Watching its long legs spindle made the coffee churn at the back of his throat. He followed it off the porch.

Although he told himself that he had no desire to stare at the remnants of his neighbor Adam's house—it was a distraction; it was ghoulish; it was not good for his mental health—Ransom was unable to keep his eyes from it. All that was left of the structure was fire-blackened fragments of the walls that had stood at the house's northeast and southwest corners. Had Ransom not spent ten years living across the road from the white, two-story colonial whose lawn had been chronically overgrown—to the point that he and Heather had spoken of it as their own little piece of the rain forest—he could not have guessed the details of the building the fire had consumed. While he was no expert at such matters, he had been surprised that the flames had taken so much of Adam's house; even without the fire department to douse it, Ransom had the sense that the blaze should not have consumed this much of it. No doubt, the extent of the destruction owed something to the architects of the shape the house's destruction had revealed.

(*There's something in Adam's house*, Matt had said. The eyes of the ten men and women crowded around the kitchen table did not look at him. *They've been there since before…everything. Before the Fracture. I've heard them moving around outside, in the trees. We have to do something about them.*)

About a month after they had moved into their house, some ten years ago, Ransom had discovered a wasps' nest clinging to a light on the far side of the garage. Had it been only himself, even himself and Heather, living there, he would have been tempted to live and let live. However, with an eight-year-old factored into the equation, one whose curiosity was recorded in the constellations of scars up his arms and down his legs, there was no choice. Ransom called the exterminator, and the next day the nest was still. He waited the three days the woman recommended, then removed the nest by unscrewing the frosted glass jar to which it was anchored. He estimated the side stoop the sunniest part of the property; he placed the nest there to dry out. His decision had not pleased Heather, who was concerned at poison-resistant wasps emerging enraged at the attack on their home, but after a week's watch brought no super-wasps, he considered it reasonable to examine it with Matt. It was the first time he had been this near to a nest, and he had been fascinated by it, the gray, papery material that covered it in strips wound up and to the right. Slicing it across the equator had disclosed a matrix of cells, a little less than half of them chambering larvae, and a host of motionless wasps. Every detail of the nest, he was aware, owed itself to some physiological necessity, evolutionary advantage, but he'd found it difficult to shake the impression that he was observing the result of an alien intelligence, an alien aesthetic, at work.

That same sensation, taken to a power of ten, gripped him at the sight of the structure that had hidden inside Adam's house. Its shape reminded him of that long-ago wasps' nest, only inverted, an irregular dome composed not of gray pulp but a porous substance whose texture suggested sponge. Where it was not charred black, its surface was dark umber. Unlike the house in which it had grown up, Ransom thought that the fire that had scoured this dwelling should have inflicted more damage on it, collapsed it. In spots, the reddish surface of the mound had cracked to reveal a darker substance beneath, something that trembled in the light like mercury. Perhaps this was the reason the place was still standing. What had been the overgrown yard was dirt-baked and burnt brittle by the succession of fires. At half a dozen points around the yard, the large shells of what might have been lobsters—had each of those lobsters stood the size of a small pony—lay broken, split wide, the handles of axes, shovels, picks spouting from them.

(Matt had been so excited, his cheeks flushed in that way that made his eyes glow. The left sleeve of his leather jacket, of the sweatshirt underneath it, had been sliced open, the skin below cut from wrist to shoulder by a claw the size of a tennis racket. He hadn't cared, had barely noticed as Ransom had washed the wound, inspected it for any of the fluid [blood?] that had spattered the jacket, and wrapped it in gauze. Outside, whoops and hollers of celebration had filled the morning air. *You should have come with us,* Matt had said, the remark less a reproach and more an expression of regret for a missed opportunity. *My plan worked. They never saw us coming. You should have been there.* Despite the anxiety that had yet to drain from him, pride had swelled Ransom's chest. Maybe everything wasn't lost. Maybe his son...*Yes, well,* Ransom had said, *someone has to be around to pick up the pieces.*)

Ransom continued around the front lawn to what they had called the side yard, a wide slope of grass that stretched from the road up to the treeline of the rise behind the house. If the wreckage across the street was difficult to ignore, what lay beyond the edge of the yard compelled his attention. Everything that had extended north of the house: his next door neighbor Dan's red house and barn, the volunteer fire station across from it, the houses that had continued on up both sides of the road to Wiltwyck, was gone, as was the very ground on which it all had been built. As far ahead as Ransom could see, to either side, the earth had been scraped to bare rock, the dull surface of which bore hundred-yard gouges. Somewhere beyond his ability to guesstimate, planes of light like the one on the other side of his house occulted the horizon. Ransom could not decide how many there were. Some days he thought at least four, staggered one behind the other; others he was certain there was only the one whose undulations produced the illusion of more. Far off as the aurora(e) was, its sheer size made the figures that occasionally filled it visible. These he found it easier to disregard, especially when, as today, they were familiar: a quartet of tall stones at the top of a rounded mountain, one apparently fallen over, the remaining three set at irregular distances from one another, enough to suggest that their proximity might be no more than a fluke of geology; from within the arrangement, as if stepping down into it, an eye the size of a barn door peered and began to push out of it. Instead, he focused on the garden into which he, Matt, and a few of his neighbors had tilled the side yard.

While Ransom judged the crab capable of leaping the dry moat and clambering up the wire fence around the garden, it preferred to wait for him to set the plank over the trench, cross it, and unlock the front gate. Only then would it scuttle around him, up the rows of carrots and broccoli, the tomatoes caged in their conical frames, stopping on its rounds to inspect a leaf here, a stalk there, tilting its shell forward so that one of the limbs centered in its back could extend and take the object of its scrutiny in its claw. In general, Ransom attributed the crab's study to simple curiosity, but there were moments he fancied that, prior to its arrival in his front yard the morning after Matt's departure, in whatever strange place it had called home, the crab had tended a garden of its own.

Latching but not locking the gate behind him, Ransom said, "What about Bruce? That was what we called our dog…the only dog we ever had. Heather picked out the name. She was a huge Springsteen fan. The dog didn't look like a Bruce, not in the slightest. He was some kind of weird mix, Great Dane and greyhound, something like that. His body…it was as if the front of one dog had been sewed to the back of another. He had this enormous head—heavy jowls, brow, huge jaws—and these thick front legs, attached to a skinny trunk, back legs like pipe cleaners. His tail—I don't know where that came from. It was so long it hung down almost to his feet. I kept expecting him to tip over, fall on his face. I wanted to call him Butch, that or something classical, Cerberus. Heather and Matt overruled me. Matt was all in favor of calling him Super Destroyer, or Fire Teeth, but Heather and I vetoed those. Somehow, this meant she got the final decision, and Bruce it was."

The beer traps next to the lettuce were full of the large red slugs that had appeared in the last week. One near the top was still moving, swimming lazily around the PBR, the vent along its back expanding and contracting like a mouth attempting to speak. The traps could wait another day before emptying; he would have to remember to bring another can of beer with him tomorrow. He said, "Heather found the dog wandering in the road out front. He was in pretty rough shape: his coat was caked with dirt, rubbed raw in places; he was so thin, you could've used his ribs as a toast rack. Heather was a sucker for any kind of hard case; she said it was why she'd gone out with me in the first place. Very funny, right? By the time Matt stepped off the school bus, she'd lured the dog inside with a plateful of chicken scraps (which he devoured), coaxed him into the downstairs shower (after which, she said, he looked positively skeletal), and heaped a couple of old blankets into a bed for him. She tried to convince him to lie down there, and he did subject the blankets to extensive sniffing, but he refused to allow Heather out of his sight. She was...at that point, she tired easily—to be honest, it was pretty remark-able that she'd been able to do everything she had—so she went out to the front porch to rest on the rocking chair and wait for Matt's bus. When she did, the dog—Bruce, I might as well call him that; she'd already settled on the name—Bruce insisted on accompanying her. He plopped down beside her and remained there until Matt climbed the front steps. I would have been worried...concerned about how Bruce would react to Matt, whether he'd be jealous of Heather, that kind of thing. Not my wife: when Matt reached the top of the stairs, the dog stood, but that was all. Heather didn't have to speak to him, let alone grab his collar."

The lettuces weren't ready to pick, nor were the cabbages or broccoli. A few tomatoes, however, were sufficiently red to merit plucking from the plants and dropping into the canvas bag. The crab was roaming the top of the gar-den, where they'd planted Dan's apple trees. Ransom glanced over the last of the tomatoes, checked the frames. "That collar," he said. "It was the first thing I noticed about the dog. Okay, maybe not the first, but it wasn't too long before it caught my eye. This was after Matt had met me in the driveway with the news that we had a guest. The look on his face...he had always been a moody kid—Heather and I used to ask one another, *How's the weather in Mattsville?*—and adolescence, its spiking hormones, had not improved his temperament. In all fairness, Heather being sick didn't help matters any. This night, though, he was positively beaming, vibrating with nervous energy. When I saw him running up to the car, my heart jumped. I couldn't con-ceive any reason for him to rush out the side door that wasn't bad: at the very best, an argument with his mother over some school-related issue; at the very worst, another ambulance ride to the hospital for Heather."

A blue centipede the size of his hand trundled across the dirt in front of him. He considered spearing it, couldn't remember if it controlled any of the other species in the garden. Better to err on the side of caution—even now. He stepped over it, moved on to the beans. He said, "Matt refused to answer any of my questions; all he would say was, *You'll see.* It had been a long day at work; my patience was frayed to a couple of threads and they weren't looking any too strong. I was on the verge of snapping at him, telling him to cut the crap, grow up, but something, that grin, maybe, made me hold my tongue. And once I was inside, there was Heather sitting on the couch, the dog sprawled out beside her, his head in her lap. He didn't so much as open an eye to me.

"For the life of me, I could not figure out how Heather had gotten him. I assumed she had been to the pound, but we owned only the one car, which I'd had at work all day. She took the longest time telling me where the dog had come from. I had to keep guessing, and didn't Matt think that was the funniest thing ever? It was kind of funny…my explanations grew increasingly bizarre, fanciful. Someone had delivered the dog in a steamer trunk. Heather had discovered him living in one of the trees out front. He'd been packed away in the attic. I think she and Matt wanted to hear my next story."

Ransom had forgotten the name of the beans they had planted. Not green beans: these grew in dark purple, although Dan had assured him that they turned green once you cooked them. The beans had come in big, which Dan had predicted: each was easily six, seven inches long. Of the twenty-five or thirty that were ready to pick, however, four had split at the bottom, burst by gelid, inky coils that hung down as long again as the bean. The ends of the coils raised toward him, unfolding petals lined with tiny teeth.

"Shit." He stepped back, lowering the spear. The coils swayed from side to side, their petals opening further. He studied their stalks. All four sprang from the same plant. He swept the blade of the spear through the beans dangling from the plants to either side of the affected one. They dinged faintly on the metal. The rest of the crop appeared untouched; that was something. He adjusted the canvas bag onto his shoulder. Taking the spear in both hands, he set the edge of the blade against the middle plant's stem. His first cut drew viscous green liquid and the smell of spoiled eggs. While he sawed, the coils whipped this way and that, and another three beans shook frantically. The stem severed, he used the spear to loosen the plant from its wire supports, then to carry it to the compost pile at the top of the garden, in the corner opposite the apple trees. There was lighter fluid left in the bottle beside the fence; the dark coils continued to writhe as he sprayed them with it. The plant was too green to burn well, but Ransom reckoned the application of fire to it, however briefly, couldn't hurt. He reached in his shirt pocket for the matches. The lighter fluid flared with a satisfying *whump*.

The crab was circling the apple trees. Eyes on the leaves curling in the flames, Ransom said, "By the time Heather finally told me how Bruce had arrived at the house, I'd been won over. Honestly, within a couple of minutes of watching her sitting there with the dog, I was ready for him to move in. Not because I was such a great dog person—I'd grown up with cats, and if I'd been inclined to adopt a pet, a kitten would have been my first choice. Heather was the one who'd been raised with a houseful of dogs. No, what decided me in Bruce's favor was Heather, her...demeanor, I suppose. You could see it in the way she was seated. She didn't look as if she were holding herself as still as possible, as if someone were pressing a knife against the small of her back. She wasn't relaxed—that would be an overstatement—but she was calmer.

"The change in Matt didn't hurt, either." Ransom squeezed another jet of lighter fluid onto the fire, which leapt up in response. The gelid coils thrashed as if trying to tear themselves free of the plant. "How long had that boy wanted a dog...By now, we'd settled into a routine with Heather's meds, her doctors' visits—it had settled onto us, more like. I think we knew...I wouldn't say we had given up hope; Heather's latest tests had returned better than expected results. But we—the three of us were in a place we had been in for a long time and didn't know when we were going to get out of. A dog was refreshing, new."

With liquid pops, the four coils burst one after the other. The trio of suspect beans followed close behind. "That collar, though..." Bringing the lighter fluid with him, Ransom left the fire for the spot where the affected plant had been rooted. Emerald fluid thick as honey topped the stump, slid down its sides in slow fingers. He should dig it out, he knew, and probably the plants to either side of it, for good measure, but without the protection of a pair of gloves he was reluctant to expose his bare skin to it. He reversed the spear and drove its point into the stump. Leaving the blade in, he twisted the handle around to widen the cut, then poured lighter fluid into and around it. He wasn't about to risk dropping a match over here, but he guessed the accelerant should, at a minimum, prove sufficiently toxic to hinder the plant from regrowing until he could return suitably protected and with a shovel.

There was still the question of whether to harvest the plants to either side. Fresh vegetables would be nice, but prudence was the rule of the day. Before they'd set out for the polar city with Matt, his neighbors had moved their various stores to his basement, for safe keeping; it wasn't as if he were going to run out of canned food anytime soon. Ransom withdrew the spear and returned to the compost, where the fire had not yet subsided. Its business with the apple trees completed, the crab crouched at a safe remove from the flames. Ransom said, "It was a new collar, this blue, fibrous stuff, and there was a round metal tag hanging from it. The tag was incised with a name, 'Noble,' and a number to call in case this dog was found. It was a Wiltwyck number. I said, *What about the owner? Shouldn't we call them?*

"Heather must have been preparing her answer all day, from the moment she read the tag. *Do you see the condition this animal is in?* she said. *Either his owner is dead, or they don't deserve him.* As far as Heather was concerned, that was that. I didn't argue, but shortly thereafter I unbuckled the collar and threw it in a drawer in the laundry room. Given Bruce's state, I didn't imagine his owner would be sorry to find him gone, but you never know.

"For five days Bruce lived with us. We took turns walking him. Matt actually woke up half an hour early to take him out for his morning stroll, then Heather gave him a shorter walk around lunchtime, then I took him for another long wander before bed. The dog tolerated me well enough, but he loved Matt, who couldn't spend enough time with him. And Heather... except for his walks, he couldn't bear to be away from her; even when we had passed a slow half-hour making our way up Main Street, Bruce diligently investigating the borders of the lawns on the way, there would come a moment he would decide it was time to return to Heather, and he would leave whatever he'd had his nose in and turn home, tugging me along behind him. Once we were inside and I had his leash off, he would bolt for wherever Heather was—usually in bed, asleep—and settle next to her."

He snapped the lighter fluid's cap shut and replaced it beside the fence. The crab sidled away along the rows of carrots and potatoes on the other side of the beans and tomatoes. Ransom watched it examine the feathery green tops of the carrots, prod the potato blossoms. It would be another couple of weeks until they were ready to unearth, though after what had happened to the beans, a quick check was in order. "On the morning of the sixth day, Bruce's owner arrived, came walking up the street the same way his dog had.

William Harrow: that was the way he introduced himself. It was a Saturday. I was cooking brunch; Matt was watching TV; Heather was sitting on the front porch, reading. Of course, Bruce was with her. September was a couple of weeks old, but summer was slow in leaving. The sky was clear, the air was warm, and I was thinking that maybe I'd load the four of us into the car and drive up to the Reservoir for an afternoon out."

On the far side of the house, the near curtain of light, on which he had watched the sunken island rise for the twentieth, the thirtieth time, settled, dimmed. With the slow spiral of food coloring dropped into water, dark pink and burnt orange spread across its upper reaches, a gaudy sunset display that was as close as the actual sky came to night anymore. A broad concrete rectangle took up the image's lower half. At its other end, the plane was bordered by four giant steel and glass boxes, each one open at the top. To the right, a single skyscraper was crowned by an enormous shape whose margins hung over and partway down its upper stories. Something about the form, a handful of scattered details, suggested an impossibly large toad.

The first time Ransom had viewed this particular scene, a couple of weeks after Matt and their neighbors had embarked north, a couple of days after he had awakened to the greater part of Main Street and its houses gone, scoured to gray rock, he had not recognized its location. *The polar city?* Only once it was over and he was seated on the couch, unable to process what he had been shown, did he think, *That was Albany. The Empire State Plaza. Those weren't boxes: they were the bases of the office buildings that stood there. Fifty miles. That's as far as they got.*

He was close enough to the house for its silhouette to block most of the three figures who ran onto the bottom of the screen, one to collapse onto his hands and knees, another to drop his shotgun and tug a revolver out of his belt, the third to use his good hand to drag the blade of his hatchet against his jeans' leg. The crab paid no more attention to the aurora's display than it ever did; it was occupied in withdrawing one of the red slugs from a beer trap. Ransom cleared his throat. "Heather said she never noticed William Harrow until his work boots were clomping on the front stairs. She looked up from her book, and there was this guy climbing to meet her. He must have been around our age, which is to say, late thirties. Tall, thin, not especially remarkable looking one way or the other. Beard, mustache…when I saw the guy, he struck me as guarded; to be fair, that could have been because he and Heather were already pretty far into a heated exchange. At the sound of the guy's feet on the stairs, Bruce had stood; by the time I joined the conversation, the dog was trembling.

"The first words out of Harrow's mouth were, *That's my dog.* Maybe things would have proceeded along a different course...maybe we could have reached, I don't know, some kind of agreement with the guy, if Heather hadn't said, *Oh? Prove it.* Because he did; he said, *Noble, sit,* and Bruce did exactly that. *There you go,* Harrow said. I might have argued that that didn't prove anything, that we ourselves had trained the dog to sit, and it was the command he was responding to, not the name; but Heather saw no point in ducking the issue. She said, *Do you know what shape this animal was in when we found him? Were you responsible for that?* and the mercury plummeted.

"Matt came for me in the kitchen. He said, *Mom's arguing with some guy. I think he might be Bruce's owner.*

"*All right,* I said, *hold on.* I turned off the burners under the scrambled eggs and home fries. As I was untying my apron, Matt said, *Is he gonna take Bruce with him?*

"*Of course not,* I said.

"But I could see...as soon as I understood the situation, I knew Bruce's time with us was over, felt the same lightness high in the chest I'd known sitting in the doctor's office with Heather a year and a half before, which seems to be my body's reaction to bad news. It was...when Matt—when I..."

From either end of the plaza, from between two of the truncated buildings on its far side, what might have been torrents of black water rushed onto and over the concrete. There was no way for the streams to have been water: each would have required a hose the width of a train, pumps the size of houses, a score of workers to operate it, but the way they surged toward the trio occluded by the house suggested a river set loose from its banks and given free rein to speed across the land. The color of spent motor oil, they moved so fast that the objects studding their lengths were almost impossible to distinguish; after his initial viewing, it took Ransom another two before he realized that they were eyes, that each black tumult was the setting for a host of eyes, eyes of all sizes, shapes, and colors, eyes defining strange constellations. He had no similar trouble identifying the mouths into which the streams opened, tunnels gated by great cracked and jagged teeth.

Ransom said, "Heather's approach...you might say that she combined shame with the threat of legal action. Harrow was impervious to both. As far as he was concerned, the dog looked fine, and he was the registered owner, so there was nothing to be worried about. *Of course he looks good,* Heather said, *he's been getting fed!*

"If the dog had been in such awful shape, Harrow wanted to know, then how had he come all the way from his home up here? That didn't sound like a trip an animal as severely abused as Heather was claiming could make.

"He was trying to get as far away as he could, she said. Had he been in better condition, he probably wouldn't have stopped here.

"This was getting us nowhere—had gotten us nowhere. *Look,* I said. *Mr. Harrow. My family and I have become awfully attached to this dog. I understand that you've probably spent quite a bit on him. I would be willing to reimburse you for that, in addition to whatever you think is fair for the dog.* Here I was, pretty much offering the guy a blank check. Money, right? It may be the root of all evil, but it's solved more than a few problems.

"William Harrow, though…he refused my offer straightaway. Maybe he thought I was patronizing him. Maybe he was trying to prove a point. I didn't know what else to do. We could have stood our ground, insisted we were keeping Bruce, but if he had the law on his side, then we would only be delaying the inevitable. He could call the cops on us, the prospect of which made me queasy. As for escalating the situation, trying to get tough with him, intimidate him…that wasn't me. I mean, really."

With the house in the way, Ransom didn't have to watch as the trio of dark torrents converged on the trio of men. He didn't have to see the man who had not risen from his hands and knees scooped into a mouth that did not close so much as constrict. He didn't have to see the man with the pistol empty it into the teeth that bit him in half. And he did not have to watch again as the third figure—he should call him a man; he had earned it—sidestepped the bite aimed at him and slashed a groove in the rubbery skin that caused the behemoth to veer away from him. He did not have to see the hatchet, raised for a second strike, spin off into the air, along with the hand that gripped it and most of the accompanying arm, as the mouth that had taken the man with the pistol sliced away the rest of the third man. Ransom did not have to see any of it.

(At the last moment, even though Ransom had sworn to himself he wouldn't, he had pleaded with Matt not to leave. *You could help me with the garden,* he had said. *You'll manage,* Matt had answered. *Who will I talk to?*

Ransom had asked. *Who will I tell things to? Write it all down,* Matt had said, *for when we get back.* His throat tight with dread, Ransom had said, *You don't know what they'll do to you.* Matt had not argued with him.)

Its rounds of the garden completed, the crab was waiting at the gate. Ransom prodded the top of a carrot with the blunt end of the spear. "I want to say," he said, "that, had Heather been in better health, she would have gone toe-to-toe with Harrow herself...weak as she was, she was ready to take a swing at him. To be on the safe side, I stepped between them. *All right,* I said. *If that's what you want to do, then I guess there isn't any more to say.* I gestured at Bruce, who had returned to his feet. From his jeans pocket, Harrow withdrew another blue collar and a short lead. Bruce saw them, and it was as if he understood what had happened. The holiday was over; it was back to the place he'd tried to escape from. Head lowered, he crossed the porch to Harrow.

"I don't know if Harrow intended to say anything else, but Heather did. Before he started down the stairs with Bruce, Heather said, *Just remember, William Harrow: I know your name. It won't be difficult finding out where you live, where you're taking that dog. I'm making it my duty to watch you—I'm going to watch you like a hawk, and the first hint I see that you aren't treating that dog right, I am going to bring the cops down on you like a hammer. You look at me and tell me I'm lying.*

"He did look at her. His lip trembled; I was sure he was going to speak, answer her threat with one of his own...warn her that he shot trespassers, something like that, but he left without another word.

"Of course Heather went inside to track down his address right away. He lived off Main Street, on Farrell Drive, a cul-de-sac about a quarter of a mile that way." Ransom nodded toward the stone expanse. "Heather was all for walking up there after him, as was Matt, who had eavesdropped on our confrontation with Harrow from inside the front door. The expression on his face...It was all I could do to persuade the two of them that chasing Harrow would only antagonize him, which wouldn't be good for Bruce, would it? They agreed to wait a day, during which time neither spoke to me more than was absolutely necessary. As it turned out, though, Heather was feeling worse the next day, and then the day after that was Monday and I had work and Matt had school, so it wasn't until Monday evening that we were able to visit Farrell Drive. To be honest, I didn't think there'd be anything for us to see.

"I was wrong. William Harrow lived in a raised ranch set back about fifty yards from the road, at the top of a slight hill. Ten feet into his lawn, there was a cage, a wood frame walled and ceilinged with heavy wire mesh. It was maybe six feet high by twelve feet long by six feet deep. There was a large doghouse at one end with a food and water dish beside it. The whole thing... everything was brand new. The serial numbers stenciled on the wood beams were dark and distinct; the mesh was bright; the doghouse—the doghouse was made out of some kind of heavy plastic, and it was shiny. Lying half in the doghouse was Bruce, who, when he heard us pull up, raised his head, then the rest of himself, and trotted over to the side of the cage, his tongue hanging out, his tail wagging.

"Heather and Matt were desperate to rush out of the car, but none of us could avoid the signs, also new, that lined the edge of the property: NO TRESPASSING, Day-Glo orange on a black background. Matt was all for ignoring them, a sentiment for which Heather had not a little sympathy. But—and I tried to explain this to the two of them—if we were going to have any hope of freeing Bruce, we had to be above reproach. If there were a record of Harrow having called the police on us, it would make our reporting him to the cops appear so much payback. Neither of them was happy, but they had to agree, what I was saying made sense.

"All the same, the second we were back home, Heather had the phone in her hand. The cop she talked to was pretty agreeable, although she cautioned Heather that as long as the dog wasn't being obviously maltreated, there wasn't anything that could be done. The cop agreed to drive along Farrell the next time she was on patrol, and Heather thanked her for the offer. When she hung up the phone, though, her face showed how satisfied she was with our local law enforcement."

Beyond the house, the scene at the Empire State Plaza had faded to pale light. Finished checking the carrots and potatoes, Ransom crossed to the gate. The crab backed up to allow him to unlatch and swing it in. As the crab hurried out, he gave the garden a final look-over, searching for anything he might have missed. Although he did not linger on the apple trees, they appeared quiet.

On the way back around the yard, the crab kept pace with him. Ransom said, "For the next month, Heather walked to Farrell Drive once a day, twice when she was well enough. During that time, Bruce did not leave his cage.

Sometimes, she would find him racing around the place, growling. Other times, he would be leaping up against one wall of the pen and using it to flip himself over. As often as not, he would be lying half in the doghouse, his head on his paws. That she could tell—and believe you me, she studied that dog, his cage, as if his life depended on it (which, as far as she was concerned, it did)—Harrow kept the pen tidy and Bruce's dishes full. While she was careful not to set foot on the property, she stood beside it for half an hour, forty-five minutes, an hour. One afternoon, she left our house after lunch and did not return till dinner. When Bruce heard her footsteps, he would stop whatever he was doing, run to the nearest corner of the cage, and stand there wagging his tail. He would voice a series of low barks that Heather said sounded as if he were telling her something, updating the situation. *No change. Still here.*

"She saw Harrow only once. It was during the third-to-last visit she made to Bruce. After a few minutes of standing at the edge of the road, talking to the dog, she noticed a figure in the ranch's doorway. She tensed, ready for him to storm out to her, but he remained where he was. So did Heather. If this guy thought he could scare her, he had another thing coming. Although she wasn't feeling well, she maintained her post for an hour, as did Harrow. When she turned home, he didn't move. The strange thing was, she said to me that night, that the look on his face...granted, he wasn't exactly close to her, and she hadn't wanted him to catch her staring at him, but she was pretty sure he'd looked profoundly unhappy."

The crab scrambled up the stairs to the porch. His foot on the lowest step, Ransom paused. "Then Heather was back in the hospital, and Matt and I had other things on our minds beside Bruce. Afterwards...not long, actually, I think it was the day before the funeral, I drove by William Harrow's house, and there was the cage, still there, and Bruce, still in it. For a second, I was as angry as I'd ever been; I wanted nothing more than to stomp the gas to the floor and crash into that thing, and if Bruce were killed in the process, so be it. Let Harrow emerge from his house, and I would give him the beating I should have that September morning.

"I didn't, though. The emotion passed, and I kept on driving."

Ransom climbed the rest of the stairs. At the top, he said, "Matt used to say to me, *Who wants to stay in the shallows their whole life?* It was his little dig at his mother and me, at the life we'd chosen. Most of the time, I left his question rhetorical, but when he asked it that afternoon, I answered him; I said, *There are sharks in the shallows, too.* He didn't know what to make of that. Neither did I." Ransom went to say something more, hesitated, decided against it. He opened the door to the house, let the crab run in, followed. The door shut behind them with a solid *thunk.*

At the top of the garden, dangling from the boughs of the apple trees there, the fruit that had ripened into a score, two, of red replicas of Matt's face, his eyes squeezed shut, his mouth stretched in a scream of unbearable pain, swung in a sudden breeze.

Anna Taborska is a British filmmaker and horror writer. She has written and directed two short fiction films, two documentaries, and an award-winning TV drama. She has also worked on more than twenty other film and television productions, including the BBC TV series *Auschwitz: The Nazis and the Final Solution* and *World War Two: Behind Closed Doors—Stalin, the Nazis and the West*.

Taborska's short stories have appeared in a number of Year's Best anthologies, and her debut short-story collection, *For Those Who Dream Monsters*, published by Mortbury Press in 2013, won the Dracula Society's Children of the Night Award and was nominated for a British Fantasy Award. A new collection of novelettes and short stories (working title: *Bloody Britain*) is planned for release soon.

You can watch clips from Taborska's films and view her full résumé here: ANNATABORSKA.WIX.COM/HORROR.

Little Pig
Anna Taborska

PIOTR WAITED NERVOUSLY in the International Arrivals Hall of Heathrow Airport's Terminal 1. Born and bred in London, Piotr had never thought of himself as the type of guy who would import a wife from Poland. His parents had made sure that he'd learnt Polish from an early age; while his English friends had played football or watched *Swap Shop* on Saturday mornings, Piotr had been dragged kicking and screaming to Polish classes in Ealing. But it had all paid off in the end when he went to Poland one summer and met Krystyna. Since that time, Krystyna had moved to London and moved in with Piotr. They were engaged to be married, and it seemed to Piotr that all the members of Krystyna's family had already visited London and stayed with them—all, that is, except Krystyna's grandmother, and that was who Piotr was now waiting for. Krystyna had not been able to get the day off work, and Piotr was now anxiously eyeing every elderly woman who came through the arrival gate, in the hope that one of them would match the tattered photograph that Krystyna had given him.

Eventually a little old lady came out alone. Piotr recognised her immediately and started to walk towards her, stopping abruptly as he saw the woman slip, drop her glasses and, in a desperate effort to right herself, step on them, crushing them completely. Upset for the woman, Piotr began to rush forward, only to halt as she started to laugh hysterically. She muttered something under her breath and, had he not known any better, Piotr could have sworn that what she said was "little pig!"

The sleigh sped through the dark forest, the scant moonlight reflected by the snow lighting up the whites of the horse's eyes as it galloped along the narrow path, nostrils flaring and velvet mouth spitting foam and blood into the night. The woman cried out as the reins cut into her hands, and screamed to her children to hang on.

The three little girls clung to each other and to the sides of the sleigh, their tears freezing onto their faces as soon as they formed. The corner of the large blanket in which their mother had wrapped them for the perilous journey to their grandparents' house had come loose and was flapping violently in the icy air.

"Hold on to Vitek!" the woman screamed over her shoulder at her eldest child, her voice barely audible over the howling wind. But the girl did not need to be told; only two days away from her seventh birthday, she clung onto her baby brother, fear for her tiny sibling stronger than her own terror. The other two girls, aged two and four, huddled together, lost in an incomprehensible world of snow and fear and darkness.

The woman whipped the reins against the horse's heaving flanks, but the animal was already running on a primal fear stronger than pain. The excited yelps audible over the snowstorm left little doubt in the woman's mind: the pack was gaining on the sleigh—the hungry wolves were getting closer.

That winter had been particularly hard on the wolf pack. The invading Russian army had taken the peasants' livestock, and with no farm animals to snatch, the wolves had been limited to seeking out those rabbits and wild fowl that the desperate peasants and fleeing refugees had not killed and eaten. Driven half-mad with starvation, the wolves had already invested an irrevocable amount of energy in chasing the horse, and instinct informed them that it was too late to give up now—they had to feed or had to die.

The horse was wheezing, the blood freezing in its nostrils as it strained through the snow. Its chestnut coat was matted with sweat whipped up into a dirty foam. Steam rose off its back like smoke, giving the bizarre impression that the animal was on fire.

The woman shouted at the horse, willing it on, and brought the reins down against its flanks. She had only been fending for herself for three days—since the soldiers had tied her husband to a tree, cut off his genitals and sawn him in half with a blunt saw—but she knew instinctively that without the horse she and her children would die. If the starving wolves did not kill them, the cold would. They still had many miles to travel—and they would never make it on foot. The time had come to resort to the last hope her children had left.

The woman pulled on the reins, slowing the horse to a more controlled pace. She tied the reins to the sleigh, the horse running steadily along the forest path. She tried not to look at her shaking, crying children, clinging onto each other as they were thrown around the sleigh—the pitiful sight would break her, and she must not break. She must not lose the battle to keep her children alive.

"Good girls," she muttered, without looking back, "hold on to your brother." She stood up carefully in the speeding sleigh and reached over the side, unfastening the buckles on the wicker basket attached there. She opened the lid as slowly and as carefully as the shaking sleigh would allow. The sight that greeted her made her stomach turn, as fear for her children gave way to shock and panic. She howled in despair. A sudden jerky movement sent her sprawling back into the sleigh. She pulled herself up and clawed at the basket again, tearing the whole thing off in an effort to change the unchangeable.

"Little pig!" screamed the woman, her eyes wild and unseeing. The children screamed too, the madness in their mother's voice destroying the last remnant of safety and order in their world. "Little pig!" she screamed. "They took the little pig!"

The woman fell back onto her seat. The horse was slowing. An expectant howl pierced the darkness behind the sleigh. The woman grabbed the reins and struck at the horse's flanks again. The animal snorted and strained onwards, but even in her panic the woman knew that if she tried to force any more speed out of it, she would kill it, and all her children with it.

The howling and snarling grew closer, forcing the horse's fear onto a new level. It reared and tried to bolt, almost overturning the sleigh, but its exhaustion and the snow prevented its escape from the hungry pack.

The wolves were beginning to fan out on either side of the sleigh, still behind it, but not far off. One of the beasts—a battle-scarred individual with protruding ribs and cold yellow eyes—broke away from the others and made a dash for the horse, nipping at its heels. The horse screamed and kicked out, catching the wolf across the snout and sending it tumbling into the trees. It pulled itself up in seconds and started back after its companions.

The reins almost slipped from the woman's bleeding, freezing hands. She tightened her grip, wrapping the reins around her wrists. If only they were closer to her parents' village, she could let the wolves have the horse—it was the horse that they were after. But without the horse they would all freeze in the snow long before they reached safety.

The pack was catching up with the sleigh now; the wolves spilled forward, biting at the horse. The woman shouted at the wolves, whipped at them and at the horse with the reins, but there was nothing she could do. She cast a glance at her daughters: the two little ones pale as sheets, Irena holding onto Vitek as if he were life itself. And Vitek—her perfect little boy. The woman remembered her husband's face when she first told him he had a son. His face had lit up; he had taken the little boy from her and held him in his big, strong arms…her husband…then an image of the last time she had seen him—seen his mutilated corpse tied to the old walnut tree in the orchard…

She was back in the present, fighting to save her children—losing the fight to save her children. The little pig was gone—she had put it in the wicker basket at the side of the sleigh and fastened the straps when the soldiers were getting drunk inside her house. She had gone back to the barn to get the children, to flee with them under cover of darkness to what she hoped would be the relative safety of her parents' village. Someone must have seen her put the piglet in the basket, someone cruel enough to take the time to do up the straps after sentencing her children to death in the wolf-infested forest.

The little pig was gone and another sacrifice was needed in its place to pro-tect the horse. The woman prepared to jump out of the sleigh. She turned to Irena and shouted, "Give Vitek to Kasia!" Irena stared at her mother blankly. "Give your brother to Kasia!" The woman's voice rose to a hysterical pitch. Four-year-old Kasia clung onto her two-year-old sister, and Irena began to cry, clutching her brother even tighter. "Give him to her!" screamed the woman, "I need you to hold the reins!" But even as she said it, she knew that the six-year-old would never be able to control the terrified horse. Her own hands were a bloody ruin and she wondered how she was able to hang on as the frantic animal fought its way forward.

"Irena! Give Vitek to Kasia—now!" But Irena saw something in her mother's eyes that scared her more than the dark and the shaking sleigh and even the wolves. She clutched her brother to her chest and shook her head, fresh tears rolling down her face and freezing to her cheeks.

A large silver wolf clamped its jaws onto the horse's left hind leg. The horse stumbled, but managed to right itself and the wolf let go, unable to keep up with the horse in the deep snow—but not for long. As the chestnut reeled, the sleigh lurched and the woman panicked. She had to act now or lose all her children. She could not give her life for them because they would never make it to safety without her. But a sacrifice had to be made. If she could not die to save her children, then one of them would have to die to save the others. She would not lose them all. One of them would have to die and she would have to choose. The delicate fabric of the woman's sanity was finally stretched to its limits and gave way. She threw back her head and howled her anguish into the night. All around her the night howled back.

The woman turned and looked into the faces of her children. A sharp intake of breath—like that taken by one about to drown. She took the reins in one hand, and with the other she reached out for her beloved son—her husband's greatest joy; the frailest of her children, half-frozen despite his sister's efforts to keep him warm, too exhausted even to cry, and the least likely to survive the journey.

"Give him to me!" she screamed at Irena. The girl struggled with her mother. The woman wrenched her baby out of her daughter's grasp and held him to her, gazing for a moment into his eyes. The woman smiled through her tears at her son. Snow was falling on the baby's upturned face, the frost had tinged his lips a pale blue, but in the woman's fevered mind, her baby smiled back at her.

Two of the wolves had closed in on the horse and were trying to bring it down. The woman screamed and threw Vitek as far from the sleigh as she could. There was a moment's silence, then a triumphant yelping as the wolves turned their attention away from the horse, and rushed away into the night. Irena cried out, and her little sisters stared uncomprehendingly at their mother, who screamed and screamed as she grabbed the reins in both hands and whipped the horse on into the dark.

As the first light of dawn broke across the horizon, an eerie sight greeted the sleepy village. The sleigh rolled in slowly, as the exhausted horse made it within sight of the first farmhouse. It stood for a moment, head drooping, blood seeping from its nostrils, its mouth, from open wounds along its flanks. Then it dropped silently to the ground and lay still. In the sleigh sat a wild-eyed woman, staring but unseeing, her black hair streaked with white, reins clenched tightly in her bloody hands. Behind her were three little girls. Two were slumped together, asleep. The third girl, the eldest of the three, was awake—she sat very still, eyes wide, silent as her mother.

"Irena?" Piotr reached the old lady and touched her arm. "I'm Piotr." He bent down and picked up what was left of Irena's glasses. "I'm sorry about your glasses," he told her, handing the crushed frames back to her.

"No need to be sorry," said Irena. "It's just a little pig."

Piotr was taken aback. It was bad enough taking care of Krystyna's relatives, but she had never said that her grandmother was senile.

Irena read Piotr like an open book.

"A little pig," she explained, "a small sacrifice to make sure nothing really terrible happens...during my visit."

"I understand," said Piotr. He did not understand, but at least there was some method in the old lady's madness, and that was good enough for him. He paid the parking fee at the ticket machine, and they left the building: a tall young man pushing a trolley and a little old lady clutching a pair of broken glasses.

Livia Llewellyn is a writer of horror, dark fantasy, and erotica, whose fiction has appeared in *ChiZine*, *Subterranean*, *Apex Magazine*, *Postscripts*, and *Nightmare Magazine* as well as numerous anthologies. Her first collection, *Engines of Desire: Tales of Love & Other Horrors*, was published in 2011 by Lethe Press and received two Shirley Jackson Award nominations, for Best Collection and Best Novelette (for "Omphalos"). Her story "Furnace" received a 2013 SJA nomination for Best Short Fiction. Her second collection, titled *Furnace*, was recently published by Word Horde. You can find her online at LIVIALLEWELLYN.COM.

Omphalos
Livia Llewellyn

VACATION DOESN'T BEGIN when Father pulls the Volkswagen camper out of the driveway, and speeds through the sleepy Tacoma streets toward Narrows Bridge. It doesn't begin on the long stretches of Route 16 through Gig Harbor, Port Orchard, and Bremerton, your twin brother Jamie fast asleep beside you on the warm back seat, his dark blond hair falling over his eyes. It doesn't begin with the hasty lunch at the small restaurant outside Poulsbo, where your father converses with the worn folds of the Triple-A map as your mother slips the receipt into a carefully labeled, accordioned envelope. 16 whittles down to 3, blossoms into 104 as the camper crosses Hood Canal onto the Olympic Peninsula, and still your vacation does not begin. Discovery Bay, Sequim, Dungeness: all the feral playgrounds of vacations and summers past: no. It is in Port Angeles, under a storm-whipped sky, against the backdrop of Canada-bound ferries gorging their wide, toothless mouths on rivers of slow-moving cars, when Father turns away from your mother, thin-lipped and tearful from the forced confession that another envelope holding four passports sits on the quiet kitchen counter back in Tacoma. You roll your eyes. Why do they go to such trouble of pretense? Oh, yes: for the neighbors. For the pastor, for colleagues and relatives, for all the strangers and passers-by who wouldn't understand, who want to hear only the normal. Father sees the look on your face, and takes you aside as his large flat thumb rubs against your cotton-clad arm in that old familiar way, that way you've known all of your fifteen long and lonely years, the way that always sends your mind into the flat black void. Old Spice tickles your nose, and you rub the itch away as Jamie scowls, the color fading from his perfect face like the sun.

"Don't worry, June-Bug. I know a place. Better than Victoria. No distractions, no tourists. Where there's nothing at all. You know the place. You've been there, before. It's where you always go." He places his calloused finger at the center of your forehead, and you almost piss yourself in fear: does he know?

"Where we can—you know."

Your mother takes Jamie aside, her fingers sliding around his slender waist as she spins her own version of the same tale. Father winks and parts his lips, coffee and cigarette breath drifting across your face as he whispers in your ear.

"Be alone."

Vacation has begun.

Salt ocean air and the cries of gulls recede as Father guides the camper through Port Angeles. You wish you could stay, walk through the postcard-pretty gingerbread-housed streets with Jamie, shop for expensive knick-knacks you don't need, daydream of a life you'll never have. Father drives on. Office buildings and shopping districts give slow way to industrial parks and oversized construction sheds surrounded by rusting bulldozers and dump trucks. None of it looks permanent, not even the highway. 101 lengthens like overworked taffy into a worn, three-lane patchwork of blacktop and tar. Campers and flat-beds, station wagons and Airstreams all whoosh across its surface, with you and against you. Port into town, town into suburbs, suburbs into the beyond. The sun has returned in vengeance, and all the grey clouds have whipped away over the waters, following the ferry you were never meant to take.

"Once we're off the highway, we can follow the logging roads," Father shouts over the roaring wind as he steers the camper down the Olympic Highway. He sounds excited, almost giddy. "They'll take us deep into the Park, past the usual campgrounds and tourist spots, past the Ranger Stations, right into the heart of the forest. And then, once the logging roads have ended—well, look at the map. Just see how far we can go."

You stare at the silhouette of his head, dark against the dirty brilliance of the window shield. One calloused hand rests on the steering wheel, one hand on your mother's shoulder. His fingers play with the gold hoop at her ear, visible under the short pixie cut of gray-brown hair. She turns to him, her cheek rising as she smiles. They remind you of how you and Jamie must look together: siblings, alike and in love, always together. Father and you used to look like that. Now you and he look different. You clench your jaw, look away, look down.

"It's not even noon, we should be able to make it to Lake Mills by this afternoon—"

Your mother interrupts him. "That far? We'll never make it to Windy Arm by then, it's too far." So that's your destination. You've been there before, you know how much she loves the lake, the floating, abandoned logs, the placid humming of birds.

"Not this time, remember? We're taking Hot Springs Road over to the logging roads. Tomorrow we'll start out early, and we should be there by sundown."

"But there's nothing—wait, isn't Hot Springs closed? Or parts of it? I thought we were going down Hurricane Ridge." Your mother looks confused. Evidently, they didn't make all the vacation plans together. Interesting.

"It's still drivable, and there won't be any traffic—that's the point. To get away from everyone. Don't worry."

"Aren't we going back home?" Jamie asks. "Where are we going?"

"We're not going all the way to the end of Hot Springs, anyway," Father continues over Jamie. "I told you we're taking the logging roads, they go deeper into the mountains. We already mapped this all out, last week."

"We didn't discuss this." Your mother has put on her "we need to speak in private" voice.

"Take a look at the map. June has it," Father says.

"I don't need to look at the map, I know where we planned on going. I mean, this is ridiculous—where in heaven's name do you think you're taking us to?"

"I said we're going all the way." His hand slides away from her shoulder, back to the wheel.

"All the way to where?"

"All the way to the end."

The map Father gave you to hold is an ordinary one, a rectangular sheaf of thick paper that unfolds into a table-sized version of your state. Jamie scoots closer to you as you struggle with the folds, his free hand resting light on your bare thigh, just below your shorts. His hands are large and gentle, like the paws of a young German shepherd. You move your forehead close, until your bangs mingle with his, and together you stare down at the state you were born in, and all its familiar nooks and crevices. In the upper corner is your small city—you trace your route across the water and up the right hand side of the peninsula to Port Angeles, then down. The park and mountains are a blank green mass, and there are no roads to be seen.

You lift the edge of the map that rests on your legs, and dark markings well up from the other side. "Turn it over to the other side," you say.

"Just a minute." He holds his side tight, so you lift your edge up as you lower your head, peering. The other side of the paper is the enlarged, fang-shaped expanse of the Olympic Mountain Range. Small lines, yellow and pink and dotted and straight, fan around and around an ocean devoid of the symbols of cartography, where even the logging roads have not thrust themselves into. You can see where your father has circled small points throughout various squares, connecting each circle with steady blue dashes that form a line. Underneath his lines, you see the lavender ink of your mother's hand, a curving line that follows Whiskey Road to its end just before Windy Arm. Over all those lines, though, over all those imagined journeys, someone has drawn another road, another way to the interior of the park. It criss-crosses back and forth, overlapping the forests like a net until it ends at the edges of a perfect circle—several perfect circles, in fact, one inside another inside another, like a three-lane road. Like a cage. The circles enclose nothing—nothing you can see on the map, anyway, because nothing is in the center except mountains and snow, nothing the mapmakers thought worth drawing, nothing they could see. The circles enclose only a single word:

Χάος

Someone has printed it in the naked center of the brown-inked circles, across the mountains you've only ever seen as if in a dream, as smoky gray ridges floating far above the neat rooftops of your little neighborhood, hundreds of miles away. Letters of brown, dark brown like dried-up scratches of blood—not Father's handwriting, and not your mother's.

"Do you see that?" you ask Jamie. "Did you write that?"

"Write what?" He's still on the other side of the state. He doesn't see anything. He doesn't care.

You brush a fingertip onto the word. It feels warm, and a bit ridged. "Help me," you whisper to it, even though you're not sure to who or what you're speaking, or why. The words come out of your mouth without thought. They are the same words you whisper at night, when Father presses against you, whispering his own indecipherable litany into your ears. Your finger presses down harder against the paper, until it feels you'll punch a hole all the way through the mountains. "Save me. Take me away. Take it all away."

The word squirms.

Goosebumps cascade across your skin, a brushfire of premonition. As you lower your edge of the map, Jamie's fingers clench down onto your thigh. Perhaps he mistakes the prickling heat of your skin for something else. You don't dissuade him. Under the thick protection of the paper, hidden from your parents' eyes, your fingers weave through his, soaking up his heat and sweat; and your legs press together, sticking in the roaring heat of engine and sun-soaked wind. Your hand travels onto his thigh, resting at the edge of his shorts where the whorls of your fingertips glide across golden strands of hair, until you feel the start, the beginning of him, silky soft, and begin to rub back and forth, gently. His cock twitches, stiffens, and his breath warms your shoulder in deep bursts, quickening. You know what he loves.

"Do you see where we're headed to?" Father asks.

Hidden and unseen, Jamie's hand returns the favor, traveling up your leg. You feel the center of yourself unclench, just a little. Just enough. Raising the map again, you peek at the word. After all these years and so many silent pleas, has something finally heard? Face flush with shock, you bite your lower lip so as not to smile. You stare out the window, eyes hidden behind sticky sunglasses, watching the decayed ends of Port Townsend dribble away into the trees, watching the woods rise up to meet the road, the prickly skin of an ancient beast, slumbering and so very, very ready to awaken.

You want to believe, but you shouldn't. Belief is an empty promise. Belief just leads back to the void. You shouldn't want to believe, but you will. This time, just this once, you will.

"Yes," you say. "Yes, I do."

The beginning of a journey is always deception. The beginning always appears beautiful, as a mirage. Once you fold the map away, there's laughter and music, jokes and gentle pinches, and the heady anticipation of traveling someplace new, all of you together, a family like any other family in the world. Sunlight drenches the windows and you laugh at the sight—so many prisms and prickles of color, glitter-balling the camper's dull brown interior into a jewelry box. After half an hour, your mother unbuckles her seat belt and makes her way across the porta-potty, wedged in between the small refrigerator and the tiny bench with its fake leather cushions that hide the bulk of the food.

"Something to eat—a snack? We had lunch so early." Your mother raises the folding table up, fixing the single leg to the camper's linoleum floor, then pulls sandwiches and small boxes of juice from the fridge, passing them up to Father. She's a good wife, attentive. Jamie drinks a Coke, wiping beads of sweat from its bright red sides onto his T-shirt. You pick at your bread, rolling it into hard balls before popping them into your mouth. The camper is traveling at a slight incline, and the right side of the highway peels away, revealing sloping hills that form the eastern edge of the Peninsula. You think of the ferry, of all that cool, wide ocean, waters without end, in which all things are hidden, in which all things can be contained.

"Can we stop?" You point to a small grocery stand and gas station coming up ahead to the right, overlooking a rest stop and lookout point.

Your mother points to the porta-potty. "You need to go?"

"No." You feel yourself recoil. "No, I just—I just thought we could stop for a while. I'm getting a little queasy." It's true, you get carsick, sometimes. You think of the curved slope beyond the rest stop, and how easy it'd be to slip over the guard rail as you pretend to be sick. You think of the water, so close you can almost see it. "While we can."

Your father doesn't slow the camper. "Sorry, June-Bug. We need to keep going."

You nod your head. "Sure. No problem." You think about what you've just said, and decide that it's not a lie. Running away would mean you didn't really believe that the word moved, that something out there in the mountains is weaving its way to you, some beautiful, dangerous god coming to save the queen. You want to stay. Just this once, you want to see your miracle.

Outside, 101 splits off, part of it flying off and up the coast to Neah Bay as the newly-formed 112. Now the landscape morphs, too, sloughing off yet more buildings and houses. A certain raw, ugly quality descends all around. The highway curves away, and with it, the store, the land. You're going in a different direction now. No use to think of ferries and guard rails anymore.

Jamie pulls out a deck of cards. They fan out and snap back into themselves as he shuffles them again and again. Your mother leans back against the small bench, watching him deal the cards. Go Fish—their favorite game. You've never liked games. You don't believe in luck or chance. You believe in fate.

Reaching to the floor, you pull a fat book out of your backpack, and turn the pages in an absentminded haze, staring at nothing as words and illustrations flow past. Ignore her, you say, ignore the two small feet, bare and crowned with nails painted a pretty coral, that appear between you and

Jamie, and nestle in cozy repose at his thigh. You press yourself against the edge of the seat, forehead flat against the window, legs clamped tight, ignoring the low hum of their voices calling out the cards. It's not as if you hate your mother—you have long talks with her sometimes, she's a good listener. And she's never touched you, never like that. Sometimes, she even comes to your defense, when you can't—just can't do it anymore, when you're tired or sick or just need a break, just need an evening to yourself, to sit in your pink-ruffled bedroom and pretend you're a normal girl in a normal world. Still, though. She's your mother, not your friend, and Jamie is her favorite, just as you are Father's favorite. Sometimes you wonder if Jamie might love her more than you. That would kill you. It would be like, she's rejecting one half of you for the other, without any real reason why.

"Where did you get the map?" Why did you ask her that? You curse yourself silently. Always too curious, always wanting to know everything, and more. Like father, like daughter.

Your mother looks up from her cards, mouth pursed. Clearly she doesn't like being reminded of the map, and doesn't want to answer—or she's going to answer, but she's buying a bit of time. It's her little not-so-secret trick, her way of rebelling. Jamie does the same. Like mother, like son.

"It's just a regular map," she finally says, adjusting her hand as she speaks. "I don't know where your father got it. Maybe the car dealership? Or the 76 station on Bridgeport." She lays down a card, as you wait for the shoe to drop. Your mother is often more predictable than she'd care to admit.

"Why do you want to know?" she asks.

"Never mind."

Your mother sighs. "You know I hate it when you say that. Why did you ask?"

Jamie looks up from his cards. "She wants to know who drew the third map and the circle on it."

"The third *what*?"

"Jamie." Your voice is calm, but the biting pinch of your fingers at his thigh tells him what he needs to know. "Nothing, I meant nothing," Jamie says, but it's too late, he's said too much.

"Did you draw on the map?" Your mother's voice is hushed, conspiratorial. Together, your heads lean toward each other, voices dropping so that Father won't hear.

"No, I swear. I thought *someone* had drawn on it. That's all. That Father drew over it, where we were going to go, and someone else drew another map over those two."

"Juney, there's no third map—there's no second map. What are you talking about?"

"I—"

Now you're the one who's said too much. She places her cards on the table, and holds out one hand. The diamond on her wedding ring catches the light, hurling tiny rainbow dots across your face. "Let me see it." Her voice is low. You realize she's not just angry but afraid, and it unsettles you. Your mother is often cautious, but never afraid.

"I didn't write on it, I swear."

"I hope to God you didn't. He'll kill you—"

"What's going on back there?" Father, up in the driver's seat.

"Nothing, honey. We're playing Go Fish." She motions for the map. You pull it out from underneath your jacket, and hand it over. Your mother opens it up, spreading it across the table. Cards flutter to the floor. She stares down, hands aloft as if physically shaping her question with the uplift of her palms. From where you sit, you can see what she sees, upside down. You look up at the front of the camper. Father's sea green eyes stare back from the mirror, watching.

"Sonavu*bitch*," she whispers.

"What do you see?" I don't want to know, but I have to know. What map does she see?

"June." She throws up her hands, as if exasperated. "I have no idea what you're talking about. I see my map, which obviously your father can't see because he obviously is ignoring everything we've been planning for the last two months, but there is no second or third set of drawings here."

"How can you not see that?" You know you see the lines, drawn over her directions and Father's. You know you see the word in the circular void. It's right there, on the paper, right in front of her. And, you know you don't want her to see, you want it to be *your* destination, the secret place only you can travel to. But you place a trembling finger onto the middle of the circle, just below the word. You have to confirm it, that your map is unseen, safe. "All these new roads, leading to this circle in the middle, leading to this word—"

Your mother raises her hand, and your voice trails away. She stares down, her brow furrowing as if studying for a test. You want to believe that the small ticks and movements of her lips, her eyelids, are the tiny cracks of the truth, seeping up from the paper and through her skin. Her fingers move just above the lines, and then away, as if deflected from the void in the middle. She moves her fingers again, her eyes following as she touches the paper. Again, deflection, and confusion drawing lazy strokes across her face, as her fingers slide somewhere north. Relief flares inside you, prickly cold, followed by hot triumph. She does not see your map. She sees the route and destination only meant for her.

"June, honey." She leans back, thrusting the map toward you as if anxious to be rid of it. "It's just coffee stains. It's a stain from the bottom of a coffee cup. See how it's shaped? Probably from your father's thermos."

"Yeah, you're right. I didn't see it until now."

"All that fuss for nothing. What were you talking about, anyway—what, did you think it was some mysterious, magical treasure map?" She laughs in that light, infectious tone you loathe so much—although, the way she rubs at the small blue vein in her right temple reveals a hidden side to her mood. "Come on, now. You're not five anymore, you're too old for this."

"Ah," you say, cheeks burning with sudden, slow anger. She's done this before, playing games with you. Long ago, like when she'd hide drawings you'd made and replace them with white paper, only to slide them out of nowhere at the last minute, when you'd worked yourself into an ecstatic frenzy of conspiracies about intervening angels or gods erasing what you'd drawn. You'd forgotten about that part of her. You'd forgotten about that part of yourself.

"It just looked like," you grasp for an explanation, "it just looked like you'd drawn your own map of our vacation, and Father drew another, and the circles looked—I mean, look..." The explanation fades.

"Sweetie, calm down." Your mother tousles your hair, cropped like hers. She appears bemused now, with only a touch of concern. She doesn't believe in miracles or the divine, and sometimes she thinks you're a bit slow. "Honestly. You read too much into everything, and you get so overexcited. That's your father's fault, not yours. All those damn books he gives you—"

"I'm sorry," you stutter. "It was stupid, I know—it's so bright in here. The sun."

"Are you feeling alright?" She places a cool palm against your forehead. She does love you, as best she can, in her own way. "Maybe we should have stopped. Do you want some water? Let me get you some water."

"Don't tell Father," you say, touching her arm with more than a little urgency. She pats your hand, then squeezes it.

"Of course." A flicker of fear crosses her face again. "Absolutely not."

As your mother busies herself in the fridge with the tiny ice cube tray, you fold the map back up, turning it around as you collapse it into itself. Your hand brushes the surface, casually, and you close your eyes. The paper is smooth to your touch. It's just our secret, the circle, you tell yourself. It's between us, between me and the void. That's what you call it: the void, that black, all-enveloping place you go to whenever Father appears in your doorway, the place where you don't have to think or remember or be. After all these years of traveling to it, perhaps now it is coming to you.

"Are you OK?" Jamie touches your arm. You shrug.

"I'm fine. Help me pick up the cards. I want to play Old Maid."

"June, it's getting dark. How can you read that—scoot your chair over here before you hurt your eyes."

"It's OK. I can read it just fine," you lie.

If there's a sun left in the sky, you can't see it from the makeshift campsite, a small flat spot Father found just off the one of the dead-ended offshoots of Hot Springs Road. He says that according to the map—his version of it—there's a lake nearby, but it's hidden from view—wherever it is Father has parked the camper, you get no sense of water or sloping hills, of the space a lake carves for itself out of hilly land. The earth is hard and flat, and piles of stripped logs lie in jumbled heaps at the edges, as though matchsticks tossed by a giant. The woods here seems weak and tired, as if it never quite recovered from whatever culling happened decades ago. You sit on a collapsible camp stool, watching Father set up a small table for the Coleman stove and lanterns. No fire tonight, this time. Father says there isn't time, they have to be to bed early and up early. "It's ready," he says to your mother, as he lights the small stove. "I'll be back in a bit." He turns and walks off with the lighter, disappearing between tree trunks and the sickly tangle of ferns. His job is finished, and he's off to smoke a cigarette or two, an ill-kept secret no one in the family is supposed to notice. There are so many other secrets to keep track of, he can afford to let slip one. Besides, it calms him down. You note that the map is in his back pocket, sticking out like a small paper flag.

Your mother has become thin-lipped and subdued over the past hour—you know what she's thinking, even if she doesn't. No matter where the family goes, a vacation for all of you is never a vacation for her, only the usual cooking and serving and cleaning without any of the comforts of home. Jamie knows how she feels, and as usual, he helps her. Beef stew and canned green beans tonight, and store-bought rolls with margarine. Chocolate pudding cups for dessert. If she was in the mood, she'd make drop biscuits from the box, or cornbread. She's not in the mood tonight. It's more than just cooking, this time. Father and your mother are divided over the vacation, over the destination. This is a first for them, and a first for you. Usually they are united in all things, as you and Jamie are, because so much is always at stake for all of you, because everything must be done in secret, away from the eyes of those who wouldn't understand, which is everyone in the world. But things are off-balance, tonight. You stare up at the trees, trying to see past them to the heart of the mountains. Your mother couldn't see the brown ink lines, the map within the map. Does he? You think you know the answer. Otherwise, why would he ignore his own vacation plans, his own map and dotted blue lines, why would he take you all here?

"June." Your mother, her voice clipped and tired. "Go get your father. Dinner's ready."

You stand up, looking around. Nothing but trees. It's peaceful here without him, brooding over everyone. You don't see the need to change that.

"I don't know where he went…"

"June, please. It's been a long day. Just go get him."

"I don't even know where he went to!"

"Just follow the smoke," Jamie says.

"Hush!" Your mother slaps at his arm, a playful smile on her face. For a moment, her dour mood has lifted. You use it, slipping into the woods unnoticed. You'll follow the smoke only as far as you need to, before going in the opposite direction. He can come back on his own.

Five feet in, and the darkness seals up the space behind you, as though the cozy camper and the soft lights never existed at all. Up above, the sky is still blue, but starless and without light. There are no paths or trails here, only ground thick with fallen pine needles and cones, and large ferns that brush at your face as you push through them. No trace of smoke is in the air, you smell only wet earth and pitch and leaves. You should have grabbed a flashlight, but you've never been afraid of the dark before, so you push forward. After several thick strands of webbing lash your face, you raise your arm, holding the book up high before you like a shield. It's a crumbling cloth-bound volume Father gave you years ago, for your seventh birthday. *Mythology of Yore.* "Mythology of your what?" you'd joked when you unwrapped the book. Father stopped smiling; later, when you started reading, you stopped smiling as well. The stories are old, very old, and deliciously cruel, and when you touch the illustrations, red and silver bleeds off onto your skin. "This will explain everything," Father had said when he gave it to you. "This will explain why we do what we do, and why it is not wrong. Why it is as old as mankind itself, beautiful, divine."

He must not have read all the stories in the book.

"You know where we're going, don't you?" Father appears from behind the trees, and you let out a small gasp as you lower the book. He's barely visible in the gloom, the red tip of the cigarette the only real part of him you can fix your sight on. Yet, you can tell, even in the dark, even from a distance, that some strange mood has seized him, morphing his face into a mask. He wants something, he's seeking something. You remember what he told you on the piers at Port Angeles. Now is not the time for a smart-ass reply.

"We're going to the mountains. Into the center of the Olympics, like you said."

"We're going into the center." Smoke billows from his mouth as he speaks, and he crushes the remains of the cigarette with his finger and thumb, carefully so as not to create stray sparks. You watch him slip the butt into his front pocket—Father never approved of littering—and his hand is upon your throat, lifting you up and back into the solid wall of a tree. The book tumbles from your grasp, away into the dense brush. It's gone, you'll never find it in the dark. Once again, he places a finger at the center of your forehead. Small coughs erupt from your lips, wet with spittle, as you struggle to breathe, as your feet slide up and down the rough bark, trying to find some place to come to rest.

"And where are you going, where do you go?" Father asks. His voice is a whispered snarl, hard and tight. What little air your lungs clutch at is tinged with warm smoke and rank sweat. "Where do you go when I'm with you?

Where are you when the light leaves your eyes and all that darkness pools out of them as you beg me to take you away? What do you see?"

"I—don't—know." The words are little more than croaks.

"You don't know? You don't know? I treat you like a goddess, like a queen, and you slip away like some backstabbing little whore?"

"No—never."

The finger at your forehead disappears, and you hear the rustle of paper. The map. "Is it here? Oh yes, I see it. I don't know how you did it, when you drew it, but there it is. I drew my road to where I wanted to go, and she drew hers, and then your little web appeared, shitting itself all over our destinations. Except, I couldn't figure out how to get my road to the center of your map, to that nice big space inside you, no matter how many roads there were, no matter how many times the lines crossed. I always lost the way to the center of your little Tootsie Pop. *And it's just a fucking piece of paper!*"

"Guess—it's not—you stupid—fuck."

The map slams against your face, and there's a *crunch*. Blood streams from your nose, and pain explodes like lightning through your skull. And then Father wrenches your shorts and panties down and off your legs in a single motion and his zipper is down and your legs up as he parts them wide and he's against you and inside you in a single painful thrust, his cock spearing you against the tree like a butterfly.

For a moment he doesn't move, only breathes hard against your face as the branches rustle overhead, catching the evening wind. It's true night now, and there is no moon and there are no stars. What is he waiting for? You realize the map is still stuck against your face, stuck in the sweat and tears and blood. You move, listening to the rustling of paper so close to your open eyes, your open eyes that see only liquid primordial night, and he begins to thrust. Long, hard strokes slamming your back and head against the rough bark, in and out, again, again, and you can feel it but you can't help it but you can feel it the old familiar vortex of pleasure forming somewhere deep down inside your traitorous thrusting body and you would give anything to not go there to not feel that and the words form silent in your blood-filled mouth *take me away take it away take it all away*, and even though you can't see, you feel it, you feel the blood-brown word expanding, burning through the layers of map, burning through bone and skin. Somewhere, a chain is being pulled, a hole unplugged, and your muscles slacken as the dark of night whorls around, thickens and deepens, as the flat black void opens wide to take you back in, even as something begins to spill out—

The map disappears, and the hand comes down hard against your cheek. You're back.

"I go everywhere with you. *Everywhere!* Do you hear me?" Your father's grip tightens, and you spasm against the tree, struggling as he pins your arms back against the trunk with his hands. Tears and snot drip down your face, plop onto your breasts.

"I go *everywhere*," he says. "You don't get to leave me behind. And the next time, the next time?—I go with you. The next time, I see everything you see." He leans in, kissing you hard as he thrusts deeper, harder, his tongue pushing into your mouth, filling it up until all you taste is him, all you breathe is the air from his lungs, all you feel is what he feels, what he wants.

He lets go.

You fall, choking on your spit and pain, into the roots of the tree, your shorts and panties bunched at your feet. Father walks away, thin branches snapping under his feet as he zips up his pants. Then the metal rasp of his lighter, followed by the solitary blue-orange flame singeing the tobacco into red. "Tomorrow night, when we get there, I'll be with you. All the way to the end." A moment of silence as he takes a deep drag, and exhales. You stay huddled in the knotted arms of the tree, hand at your throat, afraid to breathe.

"Dinner's waiting, June-Bug. Hurry up." He walks away, crashing and cursing as he tries to find his way. It would be funny, if—When you no longer hear the sound of his footsteps, you crawl to your feet, clinging to the bark of the tree for support, then pull your shorts back on with trembling hands. The map is stuck to the bottom of your right sandal. You wipe the blood and dirt off with great care, then fold it small enough to tuck into your panties, small enough to not be noticed by anyone. He's done for the night, and you're not touching Jamie again tonight, not with your mother's smell all over him.

Off to your left, that's where the campsite was supposed to be, except, you don't know what left is anymore, or where it used to be. You walk forward, toes curled and back hunched, as if worried that a single noise will bring him flying out of the darkness at you again. Your sandals slide over blacktop, flat and smooth. Overhead, the stars, and a sudden feeling of space and distance: the road. It's the same road Father drove down two hours ago, before he turned off onto the dirt road into the woods. You turn, looking back into the woods. All of the trees look the same, you can't tell which one Father pressed you against. All you know is that when he first did, you and he were not at the side of the road, there was no road at all. You closed your eyes and you traveled. You escaped, but you took him with you, and only this far.

Is this what he was waiting for?

How much farther can you go?

Dinner is a dream. Your mother pinches your nose and wipes the blood away without a word, then gives you cold water with miniature ice cubes from the tiny freezer, saying nothing as she hands you the glass. She must know what Father did. Maybe she made him do it. Father has two beers, and your mother doesn't hesitate in bringing them to him. He's mad at her, which is when he drinks. She's subservient when she's mad, which makes him angrier, because he knows she's just pretending. Jamie's eyes look a bit puffy, not enough for anyone except you to notice. Your mother did or said something to him, that he didn't like. He touches his bangs constantly, keeps his head down. You eat your beef stew in small bites, careful to grind it down to a paste your tender throat can swallow. It all tastes the same. And as you force down your meal, you realize that all the things you know about your world, the normal things, aren't the right things. They aren't the things that are going to save you. You think of the book, lonely and cold, heroes and gods already festering in the damp of the undergrowth.

But the map…The map is folded into a tiny square, shoved deep into your underwear. It's your map now, it's not his or hers, he threw it away, and besides, it was never his map anyway. It was never his journey, his destination. He had his own, and besides—isn't what he gets from you enough? Does he have to go everywhere, see everything? Is there no place left for you and you alone? You bite down on the lip of the plastic tumbler. There's nothing you can do, really. It's not your fight, what they fight about. You, like any good map, can only point any number of ways. But if he wants to see everything, he's going to be surprised. Everything is not where you're headed. Everything is never where you go.

After dinner, it's quick to washing up and then to bed. You and Jamie each get five minutes alone in the camper to change before clambering up into the camper's upper bed. Father and your mother argue quietly in the front of the camper, behind a small plaid curtain your mother sewed. I can't believe you lost the map, she says. We don't need a map, I know where we are, and I'll know when we get there, he says. That doesn't even make sense, she says. We agreed to go to Windy Arm, we agreed to go where I wanted to go for once, she says. Wherever we go, we go together, he says. We do it for the family. That's how Mom and Dad taught us, it's how we survive. We do it as one.

Jamie and you lay on your sides in a shallow imitation of spooning, his arm draped across your waist. At first you didn't want him touching you, afraid they'd stick their heads up into the pop-top for a last good-night— you've long suspected that they know what you and Jamie do, what you are to each other. Still. You don't need them to have it confirmed. Finally, the lights click out: the night is so dark in contrast, for a second it seems bright as noon. You slide your hand across Jamie's, bring it up to between your breasts, as if to shield your heart. Your breath is shallow. Father and your mother zip themselves into their sleeping bags, and the camper settles into the ground, little creaks and ticks sounding out like metal insects. You wait. And, after what seems like half the night, gentle snores and deep breathing fill the small space. They're asleep. Nothing more will be needed of you and your brother tonight.

Your lips part, and you close your eyes, letting anxiety sieve out through the netting into the cool night air. Still, though, you don't move a muscle, and neither does Jamie. Let them fall asleep peacefully below, undisturbed. Let them lay together, like they should. Sometimes, after the school day was over, Jamie would whisk you into one of the crumbling old portable classrooms, unused for years since the new additions were built. There in the soft of the chalky air, he'd press you against the plaster walls, his body fitting neatly against and into yours. It was so different than with Father, it felt so good, so right. There was no need for the void with Jamie, no need to escape, because you wanted to be there, you wanted to remember every sigh, every moan. It's like Jamie was made for you, made to fit you, made to taste and smell exactly how you like. He *was* made for you, though, he was a part of you once, inside your mother's womb. Making love to him was the only way you could love yourself.

Jamie's hand opens, slides down around your right breast, cupping it gently. You feel protected, safe. And yet. And yet.

Another hour passes, and another. Jamie drifts off, you can hear it in the rhythm of his breath, feel it in the dead weight of his limbs. Below, Father and your mother are lost in sleep. Do you dare? Even as your mind asks the question, your body is answering, your hands slipping up to zip, inch by careful inch, the hard mesh that surrounds the pop-top of the camper. Jamie stirs, turns over and away. You stop, listening. Somewhere in the woods, a branch cracks, sharp like a gunshot, and silky rustling follows. Here, in this part of the world, the moon is of little use to you, and the stars are nothing. Here nothing can penetrate the blanket of wood and branch and needles. You move forward, sticking your face outside. You see nothing. You are blind as a worm.

The zipper moves again, and now your entire upper body is exposed to the night. If you try to climb down the camper's slick sides, you'll only fall, and that will mean noise, unnatural human noise, the kind that wakens other humans. This is the most you can do, the most you can be free. Hidden at the bottom of your sleeping bag is the map. Your toes grasp the folds of paper, and you bend your knees up, reaching down at the same time. Slowly the map travels into your hands. You hold it out into the open air, outside in the world, your finger brushing across the bumpy ridges of the circles and into the center, where it once again rests on that strange, lone word. Is this truly the place you travel toward, when Father visits you in the night? Do you really hold the map to that invisible place, and if so, how and when did you draw it? Or was it you? Perhaps there is more in the flat black void than sublime nothingness. You move your finger back and forth, coaxing the letters to respond.

The brownish ink, invisible in the night, leaps against the whorls of your fingertip, as if tracing a route, an escape from the center and into the world. The paper crackles, and you stiffen, holding your breath in. Again, you listen. Silence. For a wild second, you imagine Father and your mother, awake and perched at the edge of the bunk, pupils wide and oily-black as owls as they stare down at you and your sleeping twin, younger versions of themselves, when they were brother and sister, before they were husband and wife. You ignoring the cold fear as you send your plea, your command, out into the mountains, wherever in the night they are. *Save me. Take me away.*

But nothing happens, and your arms become stiff and cold. Soft hooting punctuates the silence, followed by another passage of the wind through the ferns and trees. Resisting the temptation to sigh, you curl your arms back into the camper, and fumble for the zipper. As you close the mesh screen, the wind picks up, and small cracks sound throughout the clearing. It's a familiar sound, but you can't place it. Something flaps against the screen then whooshes away: startled, you shiver and slide back from the netting, images of insects and bats filling your mind. Jamie stirs, turns away. Another object hits the mesh and slides away—this time you recognize the sound for what it is. Stretching one hand out, you press against the mesh as hard as possible, fingers outstretched, wiggling as if coaxing. When the page hits the flat of your hand, you grab and reel it back in. The wind dies down, and the flapping of loose paper fades. What's left of the book is gone for good, scattered into the sky. You take the page and insert it into the folds of the map. You fall into restless sleep, paper clutched against your chest like a rag doll. In the early morning before everyone else awakens, when the sky is the color of ash, you'll wake up and study the pen-and-ink drawing of an ancient maelstrom, its nebulous center leading somewhere you cannot see.

The road Father drives down while you fall asleep is smooth as silk compared to the road you wake up to. It had been beautiful before—unbroken lanes of blacktop, with perfect rows of evergreens lining each side, wildflowers of crimson red and white crowding at their roots. The magazine slipping from your hands, you'd grabbed a pillow from the storage area behind the bench and snuggled against the window, bare feet resting flat against Jamie's legs. You slept hard, so hard you didn't feel the vibration in your bones as the road shifted to gravel and dirt, pitted with potholes and large rocks. You didn't see the forest fall away, dissolve into ragged sweeps of ravaged land, green only in the brush and grasses sprouting around stumps of long-felled trees. You didn't see the land itself fall away, until all that remained of the road was a miserly ledge, barely wide enough for any car, clinging to the steep sides of barren hills. You only woke up when you heard your mother screaming.

"Don't ask," Jamie says, before you can. He's sitting on the porta-potty, ashen-faced and shoulders hunched over, methodically placing one green grape after another in his mouth. You rub your eyes, trying to make sense of the ugly, unexpected landscape. To your right, the hill rises in a steep incline, tree stumps clinging for their lives to the dirt like severed hands. To your left: nothing. There is more desolation in the distance, but right beside the camper, there is nothing but jagged space.

The camper lurches down and shoots up, sending books and backpacks sliding across the floor. Your mother screams again. "Turn around, goddammit!" Tears stain her face in shining streaks.

"I can't turn around," Father shouts. "There's nowhere to turn!"

"Where are we?"

Jamie shrugs. "A logging road, somewhere. It's not on the map. Dad says it is, but—" He shrugs again, and shoves several more grapes in his mouth, barely chewing before they're gone. He always eats mindlessly when he's stressed out.

"When did we leave the real road?"

"I don't know—an hour ago? It didn't get really bad until about twenty minutes ago. I can't believe you slept through all that. I thought you were dead." The camper lurches again, swaying wildly. Jamie stares out the window, a grape at his lip. "Yeah, I don't want to talk anymore. I just want to be quiet for a while, OK? I need to not—I need to be quiet."

"Yeah. Sure." Reaching for the grapes, you start to rise, and Jamie shoots out his hand to block you. "Stop, OK? Just—don't. Fucking. Move. Sit down." The camper lurches again, and for a wild second, you get the impression that there is nothing under the wheels, that you're all about to topple over and fall. The shriek is out of your mouth before you can stop it.

"Goddammit." Father, at the wheel. "Sit down, June, both of you sit down and shut up!" Your mother covers her face with her hands. You've never seen her cry. You've never seen her lose control of her emotions, or of Father. They've always done things as one. Now she's sobbing like a child. Father turns back to you, motioning.

"Come up here."

"I—" You're paralyzed.

"Look at the road—" your mother shrieks. Father's hand lashes out like a snake. You can't hear the slap of his hand over the roar of gravel and rock under spinning wheels.

"June, get up here *now*. Jamie, get off the goddamn toilet and help your mother to the back. Everybody, now!"

Jamie stands up, legs shaking, and grabs your mother's hand as she sidles out of the passenger seat. Mascara coats her face in wet streaks, except for where Father slapped it away, and her lipstick has bled around the edges, making her mouth voracious and wide. Jamie helps her across the porta-potty, while you stand to the side, fingernails biting into your palms. There'll be raw red crescents in the skin when you finally unclench your hands.

"Come on," Father snaps, and you crawl across the toilet, hitting your head against the edge of the refrigerator as the camper slams over a log. Father

curses under his breath, but doesn't slow down. Sweat the color of dust drib-
bles down his face, collects at the throat of his T-shirt and under his arms. If
his jaw was clenched any tighter, his teeth would break. "Sit down. Open up
the map."

Up here, in your mother's seat, you see now how bad it is. The road before
you is barely there, crumbling on the right side back into the mountain,
gouged with giant potholes—more like depressions where the road simply
dropped away. No guard rails or tree line, just a straight drop hundreds of
yards down, the kind of fall the camper would never survive. And the road
curves, so steep and sharp that you can't see more than ten or twenty yards
ahead, assuming there's even a road ten or twenty yards beyond that. No
wonder your mother was hysterical. Father's going to kill you all.

"June, the map."

"You threw it away in the woods, I don't have it—"

"Never mind the fucking seat belt. Take out the fucking map!"

Reaching into your blouse, you pull out the warm square of paper.

"Open it up."

You do as he says, refolding it so that only the folds showing the Olympic
Peninsula show. It fits perfectly in your lap, the land and the void.

"Tell me where we are."

"OK, I—" Your finger traces over the hand-drawn roads, so many of the
brown-red roads that start and end with each other as abrupt as squares of
netting. Below them, somewhere, is Father's dotted blue ink line, along with
your mother's wishful scrawl of lavender road. Frantic, you move your fingernail along Father's road, following, following—You lost it. No: it's simply
gone.

"Where are we, June-Bug?" Father manages a tight smile. "How much
further do we have to go? I'm counting on you to help us."

"I'm looking—it's hard to see, it's like a furnace up here." Panic sharpens
your voice. Again, you find the start of Father's road, and you follow, follow—
it disappears. And it's not like it simply stops and you can see the end. The
road is there and then it's not, and your gaze is somewhere else on the map, on
another map altogether, on the one that was meant for you.

"I'm sorry." The words barely leave your dry mouth. "I just can't find it. It's
not on here. I'm looking and I see all these lines but there aren't any logging
roads, and I can't find the road you drew—"

Father puts his foot on the brake, and the camper grinds to a hard halt. When he cuts the engine, the silence almost makes you groan with pleasure. Only the ticking of the engine now, and the whisper of wind and rolling gravel outside. Father places a hand on your shoulder. It sits there like some cancerous growth, hot and heavy, pressing down until the bones grind together. "You can do better than that," he says. "You know what map I'm talking about." He leans toward you, his eyes still on the ever-thinning road ahead. "Look at your map, June-Bug. I want you to tell me where we are on *your* map, not mine. Because, every time I try to read it, I can't quite make out the roads. You know what I mean. Read your map, and tell me where we are. How far we are from the center."

You look back at your mother. She holds Jamie in her arms. His face rests at her throat, lips on her skin, pressing gently, whispering words you cannot hear because they aren't meant for you. Those beautiful large hands, around her waist and thighs. He didn't love you most, after all.

"June-Bug." Father stares at you, and you return his glance. There can't be any lying now. He already knows, and you're so tired. You just want this all to be done.

"It's not my map. I didn't draw it, you know. I don't know how it got there."

"I know. We didn't draw those other maps, either, your mother and me."

"What?" You lean back in the seat, astonished and angry as you stare at the limp paper. You wanted divine intervention for yourself, not for him, because *you* were the one who needed it, not him. Did the void betray you? "Why didn't you tell me?"

"It doesn't matter."

"Do you know how it got there?"

"I don't know. I got it at a gas station, I didn't open it till I got home, and there it was." He stares at the dusty windshield, beads of sweat matting his brown-gray hair. "I think—I think they appeared because that's where we wanted to go more than anywhere else in the world; and I think something in the world heard us and showed us the way. To a place where we can be ourselves without anyone else's eyes on us, to where we can be free to do and act as we please."

As animals, you think. As monsters. But you remember Jamie in the same breath, curving over you in the quiet corners of the school. Like father, like daughter. Animal, monster, too.

"Why can you see my map? Why can't we both see yours?"

"Because your map, that's where we both most want to go now. Because I love you, and I want to be with you. We need to go there together."

"All of us, together?"

Father's hand moves from your shoulder, gliding over your breast as he lowers it onto your thigh, the fingers rubbing hard against your sore crotch. "Us, together. Just the two of us. That's how it's supposed to be."

The sun boils the fabric of the seat, searing your skin. You stare out your window at all the desolation, feeling his hand, working, working. You barely see a thing in the glare, but you don't need to. You don't need to see anything at all. The cool, black edges of the void nip at the edges of your conscious, small nudges that leave smears of black in your vision, as though ink is trickling into your tears.

"I know the way to the center," you say.

"Good girl." Father leans in, kissing you on the cheek, almost chaste in his touch. "Good girl."

The engines roar, and the wheels whine as Father shifts into first, sending the camper rattling back up the small ledge. It's not that much farther, you tell him, just a few more corners to round, and we'll be at the top, and the road will even out. You stare at the map as you speak, fingers moving back and forth as they trace the roads to the nothingness in the middle. Another corner comes and goes, and another, and you can see the anger in his face start to rise again, anger and impatience because he thinks *no he knows* that you lie, and you move your hand to his shoulder and squeeze it, then place it on his thigh. He smiles, takes your wrist and moves it in and down, wrenching the small bones in his haste. Repulsion fills your throat as you slide your hand past the folds of fabric, but you grab tight, grab as you slide to the edge of your seat, place your other hand on the wheel and your foot on the gas, down hard. And the road becomes a blur, the cliff is a blur and the screams and Father's fist against your face are mere blurs, and only the momentary silence under the wheels before the sharp weightless flip of the entire world strikes you as having any substance or weight, just the right weight and terror to send you into the flat black void, into the nothingness of the center, as you whisper to Father and Jamie and your mother and to anything else that can hear:

Can you see everything now?

You open your eyes.

You stand in an open field on a hill. Beyond this hill, more hills—small mountains bristling with dark green trees. Beyond those, the Olympics rise up from one end of the horizon to the other—endless, imperious, cold and white, their jagged peaks tearing through passing clouds like tissue. Until now, you never thought they were quite real. You never knew anything so colossal, so beautiful, could actually exist. Behind them, the sun is lowering, and long shadows are creeping toward you and the hill. The light is wrong: thin and pale. The air is cool, almost cold. It doesn't feel like summer anymore. It doesn't feel like June.

Both your hands are covered in clotted scars and blood—your right hand clutches a long, pitted bone. Many of your nails are gone, the rest have grown out hideous and sharp. It takes a moment to recognize the filthy strips hanging from your body as the remains of your pajamas. Your skin is deep blue: hands, arms, torso, legs, feet. Dye from the small septic tank in the porta-potty. You smell like shit and death.

An animal-like grunt sounds out. Startled, you turn. To your right, a small herd of elk graze on the short grass. They are large and thick-furred, the males with antlers high as tree branches. They pay no attention to you. To your left sits the camper, monstrously dented and mangled, windows shattered, sliding side door long gone. Inside, it's dark. There's no movement in or around it, save for several birds perched on the pop-top. Scattered all around you are bits of clothes, empty cans and boxes, plastic bags, with a larger pile by the front tire of the camper, like a large nest. The hill. The road. The fall. The camper should not be here. You should not be here, alive. This is not the remains of the logging road. This is the interior. This is the center. But of what, you do not know.

Turning to the camper again, you wait.

You wait for Jamie. You wait for anyone. You wait until the sun begins to lower behind the range. Waves of nausea roll through you, sending drool and bile spilling out from between your lips, and your muscles spasm and twitch. But you are not ill, and you are not hungry, and you hold a long clean bone in your hand. You raise the bone to your face. It's been scratched and scoured clean.

You know they will not appear. You know where they've gone.

As you lower your hand, you notice how rounded your belly is, like a little pillow, and how your naval sticks out like a round fat tongue. You're thin but not starved. Bending over slightly, you study your inner thighs: they, of all places on you that should be caked with blood, are clean. "Oh." It's the only word you can form. You know what this means, and you now know you've been on this mountainside longer than just three months. The tight, blue skin of your stomach is dotted with a latticework of markings as intricate as lace. You touch the blood, a road map of brown ink—it's the map, you realize, it's your map made flesh. You run your finger in a spiral around to your naval, circled three times in dried blood. Press at the soft nub of flesh, the place that still connects you to your mother's womb, and to all the women before her, to the beginning of time, the first woman, the first womb. It was always going to be like this. It has to end like this. It cannot begin again.

Behind the mountains, the clouds and skies deepen into vivid pinks and purples, rich and wonderful. A wind barrels down, sharp and stiff: the herd raise their heads from the grass in a single movement, then shoot off down the slope. You smell the change in the air, see the shimmering dark gather around the high peaks as the first thread of lightning splits down and away. Shivering, you sit down in the grass, balancing the bone at the crest of your mounded stomach, and carefully, firmly, run your wrists across the sharpened edges. And the sunset begins its slow dissolve, while lightning dances around the mountaintops, as all light fades from the world, and you start to cry. It's not a mirage, you see it: a separate, circular mass of black flowing up from the heart of the mountains, up and over the peaks like a tidal wave. Clouds and lightning curve toward the darkness, sliding into the mouth of the maelstrom and away. Near the edges of the whorl, uprooted trees begin to swarm into the air like locusts, disappearing with the earth itself. The ground beneath you shifts, and the entire hill jerks forward: the camper topples over and rolls out of sight. This is it. This is it. Raising your arms high, you inhale as much as your cracked ribs allow, and shout as hard as you can.

Take me. Save me.

It's not very loud, or hard, and your broken voice can barely be heard. But it doesn't matter. It's widening, consuming everything, and it doesn't even care or know that you exist because this is chaos, this is nothing and not nothing, and this is where you want to go more than anyplace else at all, because inside that, there is no sorrow, there is no pain. Only everything you ever were, waiting to be reborn.

And while you can still feel, you feel joy.

Within your belly, movement—a deep watery ping of a push, like someone beating down against a drum, over and over. You cover the mound of flesh with your weeping arms, and crouch before the rising winds. Everything's going, this time. Nothing will return. Cherry red ribbons cover the blue stains and black scars, erase the circles, the roads. No new map this time. Only a river rushing into itself, only a girl striking out on her own, with no directions left behind that anyone can follow.

Which is as it should be. Where a girl goes, the world is not meant to know.

Dan Chaon's most recent book is the short-story collection *Stay Awake* (2012), a finalist for the Story Prize. Other works include the national bestseller *Await Your Reply* and *Among the Missing*, the latter a finalist for the National Book Award. Chaon's fiction has appeared in *Best American Short Stories*, the *Pushcart Prize* anthologies, and *The O. Henry Prize Stories*. He has been a finalist for the National Magazine Award in Fiction and the Shirley Jackson Award, and he was the recipient of an Academy Award in Literature from the American Academy of Arts and Letters.

Chaon lives in Ohio and teaches at Oberlin College. A new novel, *Ill Will*, is due out in the spring of 2017.

How We Escaped Our Certain Fate
Dan Chaon

> "I think of you when I am dead, the way rocks
> think of earthworms and oak roots, tendrils
> that break down to loam and nutrients
> something growing out of every
> disappearance..."
> —Reginald Shepherd, "Also Love You"

THE ROBBERY WAS in progress when my son Peter came out of the back store-room. *Everything happened so quickly.* That's what we said to ourselves later.

I was on the floor by the cash register and the robber was pistol-whipping me and without thinking Pete took our gun from its hiding place beneath the counter. At that moment the robber looked up and Peter shot him in the face.

This robber, this young guy that Peter shot, was a normal living person, that was the weird part. He wasn't one of *them*, one of the infected—the zombies or whatever you want to call them.

In the last few years, we'd gotten used to having to kill a zombie or two every once in a while. If you weren't careful, they'd get in your backyard and attack your dog and trample your tomato plants; you'd come across them in parking garages late at night, or you'd accidentally hit one when it wandered out onto the interstate as you were driving home after staying late at work.

But this robber that Peter killed was just a regular kid. Maybe eighteen, nineteen years old.

"Where's the money?" he was snarling. "Where's the money, where's the money motherfucker?"—and then when he heard Peter behind him, he stopped hitting me with the butt of his revolver and started to turn, fumbling with his gun—

If he hadn't fumbled he would have killed Peter so I don't know why I should have to think about that expression on the robber's face when he realized that Peter was going to shoot him, the way he said

"…hey, wait…"

right before Peter pulled the trigger. Seeing the young robber's eyes widen you might have thought, *Why he's no more than a child, he could be my own baby,* something like that, a foolish and sentimental thing to think because of course this thug would have murdered us without a second thought, people like that will only use mercy to their advantage and in the end it was probably better that he was no longer walking the earth, though I guess I'm sorry that I didn't do it myself.

The pistol that Peter had in his hands was a compact .380 semi-automatic, a Beretta Cheetah with a black matte finish, lightweight and easy to use.

We took the robber's head off, just like you do with the zombies, and we hauled him out back and put him in the dumpster, just like you do with a zombie.

But this was the first living person we'd killed.

Afterwards, I had some trouble sleeping. Insomnia. Nightmares.

Peter seemed to be getting by okay, despite everything. He continued to eat with good appetite. He was doing well in school, got good grades, was involved in activities, came home and made supper for the two of us. He'd sit at the kitchen table finishing his homework while I did the dishes, and I would try to engage him in conversation. How was school? What were his plans for the weekend? And he answered respectfully, looked me in the eye, seemed perfectly stable and reasonable. Despite everything.

Still, I worried.

More than a few nights I lay awake listening to him moving from room to room in the house, checking all the locks, the creak of the boards as he went into the basement to check on the generator, the hum as he held open the refrigerator door and peered into it, wishing, I presume, that it was as full as it used to be. He turned on the television—even though, of course, they broadcast more and more rarely—and over the shushing static I could hear him taking the guns apart and cleaning them.

His mom had died before any of this began to happen. How horrified she would have been to imagine him so devoted to weaponry, to see him go off to school in his youth militia uniform, ammo belt on his shoulder. She had been in the hospital when the first reports of the infection began coming in, and I remember thinking that it was a hoax, some bizarre mass hysteria and media frenzy.

There was something on the news the day she died—some footage from Detroit that was playing over and over on CNN, and I remember pausing in one of the hospital waiting rooms to watch it, holding my bouquet of flowers, and then I turned and went down the hall to her room and she was no longer living; had died in those moments that I was standing there mesmerized by the television. When I told Peter later that she was gone, I pretended that I'd been there with her. I pretended that I'd been holding her hand, and she let out a sigh, and closed her eyes very peacefully.

I've repeated this scene so many times in my mind that most of the time it feels like a real memory.

For a time after the robbery, it seemed as if Peter was up at all hours, pacing and prowling, nearly every night. But then after a week or so, he began to calm down. Maybe he got worn out from so little sleep. In any case, when I woke in the night the house was quiet, and when I went into his bedroom I found him sound asleep in his bed, still in his clothes with his headphones on. The tinny specters of music wisped up as I detached the plastic branch of earpiece from his head.

Sitting there on his bed—untangling the cord from his neck, hushing him as he stirred for a moment—I couldn't help but think back to when he was a baby. I could picture him in his infant carrier in the back seat of our car, the way I would play those children's lullabies on the tape deck, over and over, driving around the neighborhood until his bottle or teething ring grew slack in his mouth and his head lolled and his eyes lost focus and shut—at last, at last, I used to think, it was so hard to get him down for the night when he was little.

Of course he was not a baby any longer. Not at all.

At sixteen, he was already bigger than I was. Six foot two, two hundred odd pounds. A real bruiser, as they say, which was taking some getting used to. For years he was small for his age. It was embarrassing to recall some of the gushing, diminutive nicknames my wife and I had for him. Peter Rabbit,

Mouse, Squeakie, Bunny. I loved to pick him up, to carry him in my arms or on my shoulders. I loved to rub his soft cheeks, tickle him, tousle his hair, and it may be that I kept him babified for too long after his mom died, because he was small for his age and I didn't recognize that he was growing up.

Now, of course, I'm getting my comeuppance. His physical affection can be alarming. I'll have to speak to him sharply at times: I don't want to wrestle, I don't care to have my back slapped, I don't enjoy being lifted off the ground in a bear hug. His strength is unnerving. Is this the way he felt once? The looming larger adult, the implied threat of being overpowered, suffocated, crushed?

"Enough!" I told him that night, when he was pestering me and rough-housing after dinner. *Enough!* It never seemed to sink in with him until I raised my voice. *Quit it right now, Peter! I mean it! Get off me!*

His face fell, then, and he dropped his arms abruptly to his sides, backing away. "Fine," he said petulantly. "Geez, I was just being affectionate...," and off he slumped to his room.

Then I felt bad, naturally. He had needed to be hugged, he had needed to be close to me, especially after all he had been through, after the robbery, etc. He had needed some comfort. How could I not realize that?

But there was no hugging him now. When I came to the doorway of his room, he barely looked at me. Headphones plugged into his ears, face hooded. Out came the solvents and lubricating oils, pipe cleaners and toothbrushes. Wordlessly, he began again to clean the guns.

So then, to make it up to him, I decided to take him out driving. He had been wanting to learn to drive—he couldn't wait to get behind the wheel, couldn't get enough of it—but there wasn't much opportunity for me to teach him, not much time in the day between work and chores, and of course it wasn't particularly wise to be out on the roads at night, especially with an inexperienced driver at the wheel.

But that night I saw that it was necessary. I had atoning to do, and when I came upstairs with the keys and held them out, he deigned to unplug a single ear from its headphone.

"Hey, buddy," I said. "Why don't we take the car out?" And it was better than an apology.

The power grid had become very spotty in recent years, and there were rolling blackouts all over the city. You'd see the lights shut down, streetlights fluttering dimmer and then dead, block by block vanishing and some of the house alarms setting up a wail—

But at the same time, the city could be very beautiful in the darkness, very mysterious. The tree boughs hung over the road in layers and the sky intensified with starlight, constellations, the sheets of headlights emerging from the distance, the corona of a police cruiser's flashers, red and blue sheen circling over the surface of the bushes and houses and wet asphalt.

We drove for quite a while before we began to catch glimpses of zombies. By the park, we saw a naked female on the edge of a ravine, her skin almost fluorescently pale as she bent there digging through the leaves, lifting her head as blankly and innocently as a deer, the headlights glinting in her eyes before she bolted. Behind the old Popeye's Chicken, we noted a bearded male emerging from an overturned dumpster, scrambling on his hands and knees toward a hole in a fence, still dressed in a ragged lumberjack shirt and jeans, one foot missing, the other wearing a boot. Over on Derbyshire Lane, where most of the houses were abandoned, an elderly female froze in the road as we approached. It was carrying a dead shih tzu in one hand as daintily as a purse, and for a moment it appeared as if it were trying to flag us down, as if it were waving. Then, it tottered with surprising speed off of the road and into a long-neglected yard overgrown with tall grass and butterfly weeds.

I watched as Peter straightened in the driver's seat, hands tightened on the wheel, face stern and alert, not reaching for the gun on the seat beside us, not over-reacting. "Just go slow," I said. "Keep your eyes on the road." I said, and his expression was pinched but nevertheless I felt that this moment was better than any other kind of driving we'd done together. This kind of focus. Down the pitch-dark streets our headlights pulled us across the surface of the road. We were as close to father and son as we'd ever be again, I thought. For a moment. For a second.

And then it was morning. I opened my eyes and my cheek was pressed against the passenger window and I could see, close-up, a smatter of rain droplets on the glass. We were pulling into the driveway and the garage door was folding open to receive us and waking I didn't for a moment know where I was being taken or who I was with. I blinked to see him behind the wheel, his big square head, his sideburns and chin hair, his stern eyes straight ahead as he settled the car gently into its place in the garage. Here was the grey dawn light, the sun spreading up into the sky and tracing along the branches of the trees.

"We drove all night," I said. "I can't believe I fell asleep."

"Yeah," he said, and smiled sheepishly. "I just didn't want to stop. I know it's a waste of gas, I hope…"

Then, abruptly, his eyes hardened. "Oh, crap," he said, and pointed to where our trash can lay overturned. Garbage was strewn about and clawed through. "Damn," Peter said. "Looks like they got into the backyard somehow last night!"

"I could have sworn I locked the gate," I said, and he frowned.

"Great," he said. "If they found any food in there, they're liable to come back, you know."

I slept for a little while and then got up around noon and went down to the store. Cleveland wasn't as bad as a lot of places—not like Atlanta or Chicago. The ratio of living to dead was still in our favor, and most of the basic services were still plugging along, police and firemen, water and electricity. I still had customers coming in—maybe more than usual. In such times, people needed a good liquor store.

The zombie problem had been spreading across the country for a while by that point—though not as exponentially as they first thought. It wasn't the end of the world, or at least that's what I kept telling myself. In most cases, a zombie was more like a pest than a threat. Of course, a bite would infect you, but they weren't terribly aggressive, in general. "They are more afraid of us than we are of them," people said; and they feared with good reason, since the militias and the National Guard and police shot them on sight, and took their heads off and burned the corpses down at the old foundry by the river.

The truth was, the military were so efficient about it that it seemed like they should have just about finished them all off. But they clung on stubbornly. They were nocturnal, and seemed to have an instinctual sense of self-preservation, since it was oddly difficult to discover their daylight hiding places—the narrow little burrows they would find to curl up in, like culverts and the crawlspaces under abandoned houses and piles of junkyard debris. Some were even said to dig nests for themselves under overgrown bushes and shrubs, and then cover themselves up with leaves.

We had been assured that they had no thoughts or feelings, but sometimes I wondered if there wasn't some tiny little spark of memory or emotion left inside their skulls, still flickering from time to time.

That evening, I was locking up the store and pulling down the security gate when I saw one in the alleyway. A boy, maybe thirteen or fourteen years old, eating a pigeon. The zombie went stock still when it saw me, its mouth full of feathers, its jaw working stupidly as it gazed at me. His eyes were wide and alert, and when I looked into them I thought he seemed scared and sad. As if there were a shudder of remembering: a house, an old room with a bunk bed and football posters, a mother and father: all lost.

"Shoo!" I said. "Shoo! Get out of here!" and he took off with a hunched, ambling gait, pigeon still clutched in his mouth, vanishing into the alley, the tunnel of garbage bags and rubble and abandoned buildings.

Driving home, I couldn't help but wonder if my sentimentality would be repaid one day—that zombie kid popping back one evening to give me a quick, nasty death with its sharp teeth and ragged fingernails.

"Stupid," I whispered to myself. "Stupid, stupid," and I mentioned nothing about it to Peter when I got home.

He was in the backyard when I pulled into the driveway, pacing along the perimeter. We had lined the top of the fence with razor wire, and I watched as he tapped the wire with an old golf club, testing the tautness.

"What's up?" I said, and he turned to regard me with that soldier-like gaze he'd been developing.

"Just trying to figure out how they got in here last night," he said. "I think we need to get a chain and padlock for that gate."

"Okay," I said—though it seemed doubtful to me that a zombie would be able to work the latch on our gate.

"Maybe it was something else," I said. "Like cats or raccoons or something..."—though this was equally unlikely, since most such animals had long ago been cleared out by roving, hungry zombies. You hardly saw squirrels anymore, let alone a skunk or an opossum.

"Anyway," I said, and showed him the bag I was carrying. "I got some ground beef! Pretty fresh, too! Some guy came in and traded it for a bottle of Absolut. You want to make some meatloaf?"

That was always his favorite when he was a kid, and his look brightened.

"Like Mom made it," I said. "With the carrots and onions chopped up in it."

"Yeah," he said softly.

Like a lot of things, meat is harder to come by these days, so dinner had a kind of celebratory quality. Our worries about the breach in the yard were forgotten momentarily, and we had the sort of cheerful, ordinary conversation I imagined fathers and sons used to have back in times past. Peter spoke enthusiastically about his day at school, where the kids were being taught to operate a flamethrower, and I listened and nodded, though of course a part of me was sad to think that this was the state of the world we lived in.

I didn't mention this, naturally. There were so many things we never talked about: that zombie kid with his puzzled, rueful expression; that dead robber, the way Peter had taken a hacksaw to his neck while I held the corpse steady on the plastic tarp in the back room; his mother in her hospital bed that last week of her life, the fitful way she drifted in and out of awareness, the way she tucked her face against her shoulder as she slept, frowning hard like an infant or an old, old woman.

For such things, what words could we find? These days, a whole species of language seemed to have gone extinct. But maybe that had always been so between teenaged boys and their fathers.

In general, I think, it has become more difficult to find words for the things we do and see.

Like the word "zombie" for example. At first, people tried to believe the official pronouncements—that it was an "infection," akin to rabies, that a cure was being actively sought, etc., etc. They were sick people, not "zombies," that was what the government and the news networks told us in the beginning.

But once you began to see them in real life, there was no way to deny that—whatever else they were—they were definitely dead. They came out of fatal car wrecks and morgues and graveyards and burbled up out of the bottoms of murky rivers. I had never seen an actual walking skeleton, but I'd come across plenty that were decayed or eviscerated or nearly limbless or essentially mummified, and it was clear that they hadn't been living creatures in a very long time.

Everyone had heard the stories. People swear that they have seen long-dead mothers, lost loved ones, people whose funerals were years and years past. One of my customers insisted that he had seen his son, Skittles—killed in a drunk-driving accident a decade ago. That Skittles, still young, still with his long hair and bright blue eyes, had come to their front porch late one night and tapped gently against the door, and they were afraid, the old man said, blinking quickly, as if still astonished. "We were afraid, my wife and I," he said. "We didn't let him in, and he never came back again." He put his hand to his mouth.

I nodded thoughtfully, though I didn't put much stock in it. Skittles had been in the ground for ten years, I thought; Skittles was dust.

I thought of the story again that night though. I had been asleep when I was awakened by a noise. I took out my little flashlight and looked at my watch. 2:30 a.m.

There was the sound of a rusty hinge—uncertain and irregular, an unlatched door opening and closing in the wind—and when I peered down from my second-floor window I could see her there in the backyard garden.

No, I'm not saying that it was my wife.

It was only that I was reminded of her in a powerful way. She was about the same height, and her hair was also blonde, though matted and tangled. She wore a hospital gown, and she—it—was walking in our garden in the moonlight, stepping carefully, barefoot, through the rows of green-bean vines and carrots and cabbage, toward the corner where our corn was almost shoulder-high, appearing to take care not to step on our plants. There was a kind of tenderness in its step, a sort of reverie or reverence in its movements.

Was this the way you would walk into a yard that was lost to you long ago? A place from your past that was changed a little, but still mostly the same: that old apple tree, that little statue of St. Francis with a bird alighting on his finger, that patch of garage wall where trumpet vine had rooted and spread?

I couldn't see her face, only the slow movement of her body and the white of the hospital gown, rustling in the wind of a summer night. Still, for at least a minute, every part of me believed. I stood there at the window, motionless, conscious even of the rising and falling of my chest as I breathed, fearing that any movement or sound would startle her and she would be gone. I just wanted her to linger a little while. Her face remained in shadows, turned away.

When someone we love is dead, it's common, I guess, to keep looking for them, to be willing to give anything to see them again, even just for a moment.

I wanted to tell her about how the world had changed since she left it. To find a barometer in her eyes and voice: *Be honest, how bad are things, really? It will get better, won't it?*

I thought about how it would be to explain to her about Peter. *I know I haven't been the best father, I know I've screwed things up, but I've tried, really I have, and he's a good boy, despite everything. Didn't he turn out okay?*

She wandered around the backyard, aimlessly, as I watched. They have no thoughts or feelings, I told myself. There is nothing human about them any more, I told myself, as the zombie female crept along the edge of our fence. She scratched in the dirt under the apple tree, picking out morsels from the upturned soil—earthworms, maybe, or grubs—and putting them into her mouth. For a moment, she paused, as if struck by a thought; she passed her hand through her hair.

As morning was nearing, she left. I watched as she pushed open the gate and hobbled down the driveway, and when I went to a front-facing window to see which way she was headed, she was already gone.

I went to the front door and peered out. A breeze rattled the geraniums and the maple trees, and moths swam around the porch light. The squat fire hydrant stood at attention on the corner, gazing back at me blankly as a guard.

At the table, sipping my weak, contraband coffee, I felt embarrassed and ashamed. Such stupid, indulgent sentimentality! How angry Peter would have been, if he'd known I'd willingly stood and watched a zombie traipse about our garden.

The first lesson everyone learned was not to anthropomorphize the dead. In the early days, the infection spread rapidly because we couldn't stop believing they were still human. Zombie mothers preyed on their children, biting them, often eating them. Zombie husbands sought out their wives, zombie neighbors would seem to be merely confused, and then they would rush at you, teeth bared. An infected person would go to work in the morning, and by mid-afternoon they'd have transformed, often managing to drag down and contaminate a good number of their co-workers in their wake.

After that first wave, we learned quickly that the infected would always first seek out those they knew, those they once loved. With strangers, they were far less aggressive. Almost shy, you might say.

After that first wave, most people learned quickly how to harden their hearts. It reminded me a little of the way, when I first moved to a city in my youth, I had to teach myself to ignore the homeless. No eye contact. No acknowledgement when they called out after you as you passed. Only fools would interact with them or give them money or linger on their condition, no matter how wretched or pathetic they might seem.

But I never perfected that thousand-yard stare of the true urbanite, never quite figured out how not to look, how to make your face and mind as blank as outer space, and it was in this way that even now I created problems for myself. Thus, watching silently as a zombie invaded my yard or crept around my place of business.

Thus, the last words of the young robber still vividly imprinted, right on the surface of my consciousness when I closed my eyes. *"...hey, wait..."*

When I got home from work that day, Peter was back out in the yard. He had a colander, and was working his way along a row of our green beans, but when he saw me drive up he stood and came to meet me.

"There was something in the yard again last night," he said, and he pointed over to a spot beneath the apple tree where it was clear that digging had occurred.

I recognized the spot, then. It was the place where, many years ago, we had buried Peter's pet turtle, Louisa. She had lived her life in a terrarium in Peter's room, swimming in circles around the edges of a plastic tub, or sunning herself on a rock in the middle of her enclosure. She had been unusually responsive for a turtle, we believed—she seemed to become eager and even playful when it was her time to be fed, and she would often stretch her neck out to its full length and regard us flirtatiously with her yellow reptile eyes. When she died, it was the first real death that Peter had experienced, and my wife had created a fairly elaborate ceremony for her funeral, with songs and flowers and a little cardboard coffin that she and Peter had decorated with crayons and ribbons and glued-on sequins.

The coffin, of course, had rotted long ago, but the turtle's shell and skeleton remained. This is what had been unearthed. We saw that Louisa's carapace had been dug up and broken open, and whatever had still been contained in it had been picked over.

I watched as Peter bent down and fit the pieces of the broken carapace together, as if they were shards of a smashed vase. He looked up at me grimly.

"I think we better start keeping a watch," he said. "We can just do it in shifts." He looked back down at the turtle shell and shook his head. "If one of them is getting in here, before long it's going to bring others. And then we could end up having some serious problems."

"Right," I said. "You're absolutely right."

There was a dinner of rice, with a few frozen peas and carrots thrown into it, and some of the green beans, which we stir fried with some hot pepper flakes and oil, and I sat there touching my plate with my fork, thinking for some reason about the boy we had killed, the robber. He might have been very hungry, I thought.

And I thought, *Should a hungry man be punished for stealing bread?* It was one of those old ethical riddles. Probably not applicable in this case, since it was a liquor store and the corpse of the perpetrator, when we dismembered him, was not the body of someone who was starving. And he probably would have killed us if we didn't kill him, I reminded myself.

"This is really good," I said, and put a green bean to my mouth. "I like the spices."

"Mm-hm," Peter said.

He was already deep in thought—thinking about killing, I assumed, thinking about his gun and the bead he would draw on the garden from the upstairs back landing, and the things they had taught him in school about crosshairs and accuracy.

When she arrived at our back gate, it was almost midnight. It was my shift—Peter was asleep, and I was sitting on our second-floor porch, staring down. Not really "keeping watch," I have to admit.

I was thinking about Peter. Peter, that little rabbit we had loved so much, the way he fit in my arms and nuzzled against my chest; the way he had walked between us, my wife and me, as we waded in the lake, the way we lifted him as the water got deeper, his little legs paddling along without touching bottom. The way we would sit on his bed, the two of us, singing softly together, taking turns stroking his hair until he fell asleep. It is not until much later that you realize that the child you once had is lost to you; you cannot even pinpoint the moment when it happens, when you understand that you will never see that little boy again, you will never again hold him in your arms. There is the other person that he has become, of course. But that baby, that child—that is something you will never get back.

It sent a kind of keen shudder through me, this thought. And then I looked down and the gate was opening. There was the familiar creak. She knew how to work the latch, I thought. How was that possible?

In any case, here she was again. White cotton hospital gown with periwinkle pattern. Long matted blonde hair. The old rifle was beside me, which my father had given me when we used to hunt deer, but I didn't pick it up.

As I watched her, I thought of my wife when she had been in the hospital right after Peter was born. She walked like a woman who had just given birth, that kind of dreamy, exhausted intensity. I watched her pale bare feet move through the grass toward our garden. I watched as she knelt down and began to dig in the soil.

If Peter had been there, he would have aimed and taken the headshot without a second thought; and after the zombie fell, he would have gone down and removed the head with an axe or a saw, and it wouldn't have perturbed him. It would have seemed like the right thing to do.

And it was. It *was* the right thing to do.

When I came to the back door, she didn't notice me at first, she was so involved. She ran her fingers along the garden soil as tenderly as a fortune teller reading a palm. As if she were searching for something fragile and precious. Or so it seemed.

"Hello?" I said. I took a cautious step forward. I couldn't say what I was thinking, really. I spoke more clearly. "Hello?"

And then she turned. Her pale, unnaturally cloudy eyes lit upon me, and it was not clear if she saw me, or smelled me, or sensed me in some other way, and she gave a low, trickling growl.

I put one foot, then another, down the back steps. "It's okay," I said, softly. "Hi, there." My flashlight ran across her face—which was so torn and ragged that little remained of the cheeks or nose. Perhaps the word "face" wasn't the right word, though she lifted her head and glared into the light. Looking at those eyes, those bared lipless teeth, I wouldn't have said that there was anything human about her. But she didn't rush to attack. She cocked her shoulder with a kind of dainty puzzlement. Then she stood.

"Come on," I said softly. "It's time to go. Let's go now."

And I began to step slowly toward the gate. "Come on," I said, and I made a little whistling, kissing sound, like you would do with a dog you were trying to lure.

I opened the gate wide, like a gentleman, and moved gently into the driveway, walking slowly backwards. "C'mon, baby," I whispered. "C'mon, sweetheart. Let's go. It's time to leave now."

And after a moment she began to follow me. She held her arms out, and tottered forward, the way that zombies do, a wet, thick sound whispering from her lungs, and I waited until she'd gotten close before I took another step back down the driveway.

"That's right," I whispered. "Here we go. Come on." And she followed.

There was something so gentle and hopeful about the way her hands groped forward. I thought of the way that we reach out to try to touch something insubstantial in the darkness. I thought of the way Peter had toddled forward toward me when he was first learning to walk, the way his arms stretched out for me to catch him. I thought of my wife the day she had gone into the hospital, the way her hands rose up, pleading and comforting, to touch my face. "I'll be all right," she said. "Don't worry."

By this time we had reached the street, she and I, me backing up and her following, and she was coming on faster, more determined and hungry. I could see Peter's darkened window above me.

"Come on," I whispered. "Come on."

What would it feel like to let her embrace me? I wondered. Would it be so bad?

Robert Shearman has written five short-story collections, and collectively they have won the World Fantasy Award, the Shirley Jackson Award, the Edge Hill Readers' Prize, and three British Fantasy Awards. He began his career in theater, both as a playwright and a director, and his work has won the Sunday Times Playwriting Award, the Sophie Winter Memorial Trust Award, and the Guinness Award for Ingenuity in association with the Royal National Theatre. His interactive series for BBC Radio Four, *The Chain Gang*, ran for three seasons and won two Sony Awards.

However, he may be best known as a writer for *Doctor Who*, reintroducing the Daleks for its BAFTA-winning first series, in an episode nominated for a Hugo Award.

That Tiny Flutter of the Heart
I Used to Call Love
Robert Shearman

KAREN THOUGHT OF them as her daughters, and tried to love them with all her heart. Because, really, wasn't that the point? They came to her, all frilly dresses, and fine hair, and plastic limbs, and eyes so large and blue and innocent. And she would name them, and tell them she was their mother now; she took them to her bed, and would give them tea parties, and spank them when they were naughty; she promised she would never leave them, or, at least, not until the end.

Her father would bring them home. Her father travelled a lot, and she never knew where he'd been, if she asked he'd just laugh and tap his nose and say it was all hush-hush—but she could sometimes guess from how exotic the daughters were, sometimes the faces were strange and foreign, one or two were nearly mulatto. Karen didn't care, she loved them all anyway, although she wouldn't let the mulatto ones have quite the same nursery privileges. "Here you are, my sweetheart, my angel cake, my baby doll," and from somewhere within Father's great jacket he'd produce a box, and it was usually gift-wrapped, and it usually had a ribbon on it—"This is all for you, my baby doll." She liked him calling her that, although she suspected she was too old for it now, she was very nearly eight years old.

She knew what the daughters were. They were tributes. That was what Nicholas called them. They were tributes paid to her, to make up for the fact that Father was so often away, just like in the very olden days when the Greek heroes would pay tributes to their gods with sacrifices. Nicholas was very keen on Greek heroes, and would tell his sister stories of great battles and wooden horses and heels. She didn't need tributes from Father; she would much rather he didn't have to leave home in the first place. Nicholas would tell her of the tributes Father had once paid Mother—he'd bring her jewellery, and fur coats, and tickets to the opera. Karen couldn't remember Mother very well, but there was that large portrait of her over the staircase, in a way Karen saw Mother more often than she did Father. Mother was wearing a black ball gown, and such a lot of jewels, and there was a small studied smile on her face. Sometimes when Father paid tribute to Karen, she would try and give that same studied smile, but she wasn't sure she'd ever got it right.

Father didn't call Nicholas "angel cake" or "baby doll," he called him "Nicholas," and Nicholas called him "sir." And Father didn't bring Nicholas tributes. Karen felt vaguely guilty about that—that she'd get showered with gifts and her brother would get nothing. Nicholas told her not to be so silly. He wasn't a little girl, he was a man. He was ten years older than Karen, and lean, and strong, and he was attempting to grow a moustache; the hair was a bit too fine for it to be seen in bright light, but it would darken as he got older. Karen knew her brother was a man, and that he wouldn't want toys. But she'd give him a hug sometimes, almost impulsively, when Father came home and seemed to ignore him—and Nicholas never objected when she did.

Eventually Nicholas would say to Karen, "It's time," and she knew what that meant. And she'd feel so sad, but again, wasn't that the point? She'd go and give her daughter a special tea party then, and she'd play with her all day; she'd brush her hair, and let her see the big wide world from out of the top window; she wouldn't get cross even if her daughter got naughty. And she wouldn't try to explain. That would all come after. Karen would go to bed at the usual time, Nanny never suspected a thing. But once Nanny had left the room and turned out the light, Karen would get up and put on her clothes again, nice thick woollen ones, sometimes it was cold out there in the dark. And she'd bundle her daughter up warm as well. And once the house was properly still she'd hear a tap at the door, and there Nicholas would be, looking stern and serious and just a little bit excited. She'd follow him down the stairs and out of the house, they'd usually leave by the tradesmen's entrance, the door was quieter. They wouldn't talk until they were far away, and very nearly into the woods themselves.

He'd always give Karen a few days to get to know her daughters before he came for them. He wanted her to love them as hard as she could. He always seemed to know when it was the right time. With one doll, her very favourite, he had given her only until the weekend—it had been love at first sight, the eyelashes were real hair, and she'd blink when picked up, and if she were cuddled tight she'd say, "Mama." Sometimes Nicholas gave them as long as a couple of months; some of the dolls were a fright, and cold to the touch, and it took Karen a while to find any affection for them at all. But Karen was a girl with a big heart. She could love anything, given time and patience. Nicholas must have been carefully watching his sister, just to see when her heart reached its fullest—and she never saw him do it; he usually seemed to ignore her altogether, as if she were still too young and too silly to be worth his attention. But then, "It's time," he would say, and sometimes it wasn't until that very moment that Karen would realise she'd fallen in love at all, and of course he was right, he was always right.

Karen liked playing in the woods by day. By night they seemed strange and unrecognisable, the branches jutted out at peculiar angles as if trying to bar her entrance. But Nicholas wasn't afraid, and he always knew his way. She kept close to him for fear he would rush on ahead and she would be lost. And she knew somehow that if she got lost, she'd be lost forever—and it may turn daylight eventually, but that wouldn't matter, she'd have been trapped by the woods of the night, and the woods of the night would get to keep her.

And at length they came to the clearing. Karen always supposed that the clearing was at the very heart of the woods, she didn't know why. The tight press of trees suddenly lifted, and here there was space—no flowers, nothing, some grass, but even the grass was brown, as if the sunlight couldn't reach it here. And it was as if everything had been cut away to make a perfect circle that was neat and tidy and so empty, and it was as if it had been done especially for them. Karen could never find the clearing in the daytime. But then, she had never tried very hard.

Nicholas would take her daughter, and set her down upon that browning grass. He would ask Karen for her name, and Karen would tell him. Then Nicholas would tell Karen to explain to the daughter what was going to happen here. "Betsy, you have been sentenced to death." And Nicholas would ask Karen upon what charge. "Because I love you too much, and I love my brother more." And Nicholas would ask if the daughter had any final words to offer before sentence was carried out; they never had.

He would salute the condemned then, nice and honourably. And Karen would by now be nearly in tears; she would pull herself together. "You mustn't cry," said Nicholas, "you can't cry, if you cry the death won't be a clean one." She would salute her daughter too.

What happened next would always be different.

When he'd been younger Nicholas had merely hanged them. He'd put rope around their little necks and take them to the closest tree and let them drop down from the branches, and there they'd swing for a while, their faces still frozen with trusting smiles. As he'd become a man he'd found more inventive ways to despatch them. He'd twist off their arms, he'd drown them in buckets of water he'd already prepared, he'd stab them with a fork. He'd say to Karen, "And how much do you love this one?" And if Karen told him she loved her very much, so much the worse for her daughter—he'd torture her a little first, blinding her, cutting off her skin, ripping off her clothes and then toasting with matches the naked stuff beneath. It was always harder to watch these executions because Karen really *had* loved them, and it was agony to see them suffer so, but she couldn't lie to her brother. He would have seen through her like glass.

That last time had been the most savage, though Karen hadn't known it would be the last time, of course—but Nicholas, Nicholas might have had an inkling.

When they'd reached the clearing he had tied Mary-Lou to the tree with string. Tightly, but not *too* tight—Karen had said she hadn't loved Mary-Lou especially, and Nicholas didn't want to be cruel. He had even wrapped his own handkerchief around her eyes as a blindfold.

Then he'd produced from his knapsack Father's gun.

"You can't use that!" Karen said. "Father will find out! Father will be angry!"

"Phooey to that," said Nicholas. "I'll be going to war soon, and I'll have a gun all of my own. Had you heard that, Carrie? That I'm going to war?" She hadn't heard. Nanny had kept it from her, and Nicholas had wanted it to be a surprise. He looked at the gun. "It's a Webley Mark IV service revolver," he said. "Crude and old-fashioned, just like Father. What I'll be getting will be much better."

He narrowed his eyes, and aimed the gun, fired. There was an explosion, louder than Karen could ever have dreamed—and she thought Nicholas was shocked too, not only by the noise, but by the recoil. Birds scattered. Nicholas laughed. The bullet had gone wild. "That was just a warm up," he said.

It was on his fourth try that he hit Mary-Lou. Her leg was blown off.

"Do you want a go?"

"No," said Karen.

"It's just like at a fairground," he said. "Come on."

She took the gun from him, and it burned in her hand, it smelled like burning. He showed her how to hold it, and she liked the way his hand locked around hers as he corrected her aim. "It's all right," he said to his little sister gently, "we'll do it together. There's nothing to be scared of." And really he was the one who pulled the trigger, but she'd been holding on too, so she was a *bit* responsible, and Nicholas gave a whoop of delight and Karen had never heard him so happy before, she wasn't sure she'd *ever* heard him happy. And when they looked back at the tree Mary-Lou had disappeared.

"I'm going across the seas," he said. "I'm going to fight. And every man I kill, listen, I'm killing him for you. Do you understand me? I'll kill them all because of you."

He kissed her then on the lips. It felt warm and wet and the moustache tickled, and it was hard too, as if he were trying to leave an imprint there, as if when he pulled away he wanted to leave a part of him behind.

"I love you," he said.

"I love you too."

"Don't forget me," he said. Which seemed such an odd thing to say—how was she going to forget her own brother?

They'd normally bury the tribute then, but they couldn't find any trace of Mary-Lou's body. Nicholas put the gun back in the knapsack, he offered Karen his hand. She took it. They went home.

They had never found Nicholas's body either; at the funeral his coffin was empty, and Father told Karen it didn't matter, that good form was the thing. Nicholas had been killed in the Dardanelles, and Karen looked for it upon the map, and it seemed such a long way to go to die. There were lots of funerals in the town that season, and Father made sure that Nicholas's was the most lavish, no expense was spared.

The family was so small now, and they watched together as the coffin was lowered into the grave. Father looking proud, not sad. And Karen refusing to cry—"Don't cry," she said to the daughter she'd brought with her, "you mustn't cry, or it won't be clean," and yet she dug her fingernails deep into her daughter's body to try to force some tears from it.

———

Julian hadn't gone to war. He'd been born just too late. And of course he said he was disappointed, felt cheated even, he loved his country and whatever his country might stand for, and he had wanted to demonstrate that love in the very noblest of ways. He said it with proper earnestness, and some days he almost meant it. His two older brothers had gone to fight, and both had returned home, and the younger had brought back some sort of medal with him. The brothers had changed. They had less time for Julian, and Julian felt that was no bad thing. He was no longer worth the effort of bullying. One day he'd asked his eldest brother what it had been like out there on the Front. And the brother turned to him in surprise, and Julian was surprised too, what had he been thinking of?—and he braced himself for the pinch or Chinese burn that was sure to follow. But instead the brother had just turned away; he'd sucked his cigarette down to the very stub, and sighed, and said it was just as well Julian hadn't been called up, the trenches were a place for real men. The whole war really wouldn't have been his bag at all.

When Julian Morris first met Karen Davison, neither was much impressed. Certainly, Julian was well used to girls finding him unimpressive: he was short, his face was too round and homely, his thighs quickly thinned into legs that looked too spindly to support him. There was an effeminacy about his features that his father had thought might have been cured by a spell fighting against Germans, but Julian didn't know whether it would have helped; he tried to take after his brothers, tried to lower his voice and speak more gruffly, he drank beer, he took up smoking. But even there he'd got it all wrong some-how. The voice, however gruff, always rose in inflection no matter how much he tried to stop it. He sipped at his beer. He held his cigarette too languidly, apparently, and when he puffed out smoke it was always from the side of his mouth and never with a good bold manly blast.

But for Julian to be unimpressed by a girl was a new sensation for him. Girls flummoxed Julian. With their lips and their breasts and their flowing contours. With their bright colours, all that perfume. Even now, if some aged friend of his mother's spoke to him, he'd be reduced to a stammering mess. But Karen Davison did something else to Julian entirely. He looked at her across the ballroom and realised that he rather despised her. It wasn't that she was unattractive, at first glance her figure was pretty enough. But she was so much older than the other girls, in three years of attending dances no man had yet snatched her up—and there was already something middle-aged about that face, something jaded. She looked bored. That was it, she looked bored. And didn't care to hide it.

Once in a while a man would approach her, take pity on her, ask her to dance. She would reject him, and off the suitor would scarper, with barely disguised relief.

Julian had promised his parents that he would at least invite one girl on to the dance floor. It would hardly be his fault if that one girl he chose said no. He could return home, he'd be asked how he had got on, and if he were clever he might even be able to phrase a reply that concealed the fact he'd been rejected. Julian was no good at lying outright, his voice would squeak, and he would turn bright red. But not telling the truth? He'd had to find a way of mastering it.

He approached the old maid. Now that she was close he felt the usual panic rise within him, and he fought it down—look at her, he told himself, look at how *hard* she looks, like stone; she should be *grateful* you ask her to dance. He'd reached her. He opened his mouth to speak, realised his first word would be a stutter, put the word aside, found some new word to replace it, cleared his throat. Only then did the girl bother to look up at him. There was nothing welcoming in that expression, but nothing challenging either— she looked at him with utter indifference.

"A dance?" he said. "Like? Would you?"

And, stupidly, opened out his arms, as if to remind her what a dance was, as if without her he'd simply manage on his own in dumbshow.

She looked him up and down. Judging him, blatantly judging him. Not a smile upon her face. He waited for the refusal.

"Very well," she said then, though without any enthusiasm.

He offered her his hand, and she took it by the fingertips, and rose to her feet. She was an inch or two taller than him. He smelled her perfume, and didn't like it.

He put one hand on her waist, the other was left gently brushing against her glove. They danced. She stared at his face, still quite incuriously, but it was enough to make him blush.

"You dance well," she said.

"Thank you."

"I don't enjoy dancing."

"Then let us, by all means, stop."

He led her back to her chair. He nodded at her stiffly, and prepared to leave. But she gestured towards the chair beside her, and he found himself bending down to sit in it.

"Are you enjoying the ball?" he asked her.

"I don't enjoy talking either."

"I see." And they sat in silence for a few minutes. At one point he felt he should get up and walk away, and he shuffled in his chair to do so—and at that she turned to look at him, and managed a smile, and for that alone he decided to stay a little while longer.

"Can I at least get you a drink?"

She agreed. So he went to fetch her a glass of fizz. Across the room he watched as another man approached and asked her to dance, and he suddenly felt a stab of jealousy that astonished him. She waved the man away, in irritation, and Julian pretended it was for his sake.

He brought her back the fizz.

"There you are," he said.

She sipped at it. He sipped at his the same way.

"If you don't like dancing," he said to her, "and you don't like talking, why do you come?" He already knew the answer, of course, it was the same reason he came, and she didn't bother dignifying him with a reply. He laughed, and hated how girlish it sounded.

At length she said, "Thank you for coming," as if this were *her* ball, as if he were *her* guest, and he realised he was being dismissed. He got to his feet.

"Do you have a card?" she asked.

Julian did. She took it, put it away without reading it. And Julian waited beside her for any further farewell, and when nothing came, he nodded at her once more, and left her.

The very next day Julian received a telephone call from a Mr. Davison, who invited him to have dinner with his daughter at his house that evening. Julian accepted. And because the girl had never bothered to give him her name, it took Julian a fair little time to work out who this Davison fellow might be.

Julian wondered whether the evening would be formal, and so overdressed, just for safety's sake. He took some flowers. He rang the bell, and some hatchet-faced old woman opened the front door. She showed him in. She told him that Mr. Davison had been called away on business, and would be unable to dine with him that evening. Mistress Karen would receive him in the drawing room. She disappeared with his flowers, and Julian never saw them again, and had no evidence indeed that Mistress Karen would ever see them either.

At the top of the staircase Julian saw there were two portraits. One was a giantess, a bejewelled matriarch sneering down at him, and Julian could recognise in her features the girl he had danced with the night before, and he was terrified of her, and he fervently hoped that Karen would never grow up to be like her mother. The other portrait, much smaller, was of some boy in army uniform.

Karen was waiting for him. She was wearing the same dress she had worn the previous night. "I'm so glad you could come," she intoned.

"I'm glad you invited me."

"Let us eat."

So they went into the dining room, and sat either end of a long table. The hatchet-face served them soup. "Thank you, Nanny," Karen said. Julian tasted the soup. The soup was good.

"It's a very grand house," said Julian.

"Please, there's no need to make conversation."

"All right."

The soup bowls were cleared away. Chicken was served. And, after that, a trifle.

"I like trifle," said Karen, and Julian didn't know whether he was supposed to respond to that, and so he smiled at her, and she smiled back, and that all seemed to work well enough.

Afterwards Julian asked whether he could smoke. Karen said he might. He offered Karen a cigarette, and she hesitated, and then said she would like that. So Julian got up, and went around the table, and lit one for her. Julian tried very hard to smoke in the correct way, but it still kept coming out girlishly. But Karen didn't seem to mind; indeed, she positively imitated him, she puffed smoke from the corner of her mouth and made it all look very pretty.

And even now they didn't talk, and Julian realised he didn't mind. There was no awkwardness to it. It was companionable. It was a shared understanding.

Julian was invited to three more dinners. After the fourth, Mr. Davison called Mr. Morris, and told him that a proposal of marriage to his daughter would not be unacceptable. Mr. Morris was very pleased, and Mrs. Morris took Julian to her bedroom and had him go through her jewellery box to pick out a ring he could give his fiancée, and Julian marvelled, he had never seen such beautiful things.

Julian didn't meet Mr. Davison until the wedding day, whereupon the man clapped him on the back as if they were old friends, and told him he was proud to call him his son. Mr. Morris clapped Julian on the back too; even Julian's brothers were at it. And Julian marvelled at how he had been transformed into a man by dint of a simple service and signed certificate. Neither of his brothers had married yet, he had beaten them to the punch, and was there jealousy in that back clapping? They called Julian a lucky dog, that his bride was quite the catch. And so, Julian felt, she was; on her day of glory she did nothing but beam with smiles, and there was no trace of her customary truculence. She was charming, even witty, and Julian wondered why she had chosen to hide these qualities from him—had she recognised that it would have made him scared of her? Had she been shy and hard just to win his heart? Julian thought this might be so, and in that belief discovered that he did love her, he loved her after all—and maybe, in spite of everything, the marriage might just work out.

For a wedding present the families had bought them a house in Chelsea. It was small, but perfectly situated, and they could always upgrade when they had children. As an extra present, Mr. Davison had bought his daughter a doll—a bit of a monstrosity, really, about the size of a fat infant, with blonde curly hair and red lips as thick as a darkie's, and wearing its own imitation wedding dress. Karen seemed pleased with it. Julian thought little about it at the time.

They honeymooned in Venice for two weeks, in a comfortable hotel near the Rialto.

Karen didn't show much interest in Venice. No, that wasn't true; she said she was fascinated by Venice. But she preferred to read about it in her guidebook. Outside there was noise, and people, and stink; she could better experience the city indoors. Julian offered to stay with her, but she told him he was free to do as he liked. So in the daytime he'd leave her, and he'd go and visit St Mark's Square, climb the basilica, take a gondola ride. In the evening he'd return, and over dinner he'd try to tell her all about it. She'd frown, and say there was no need to explain, she'd already read it all in her Baedeker. Then they would eat in silence.

On the first night he'd been tired from travel. On the second, from sight-seeing. On the third night Karen told her husband that there were certain manly duties he was expected to perform. Her father was wanting a grandson; for her part, she wanted lots of daughters. Julian said he would do his very best, and drank half a bottle of claret to give him courage. She stripped off, and he found her body interesting, and even attractive, but not in the least arousing. He stripped off too.

"Oh!" she said. "But you have hardly any hair! I've got more hair than you!" And it was true, there was a faint buzz of fur over her skin, and over his next to nothing—just the odd clump where Nature had started work, rethought the matter, given up. Karen laughed, but it was not unkind. She ran her fingers over his body. "It's so *smooth*, how did you get it so smooth?"

"Wait a moment," she then said, and hurried to the bathroom. She was excited. Julian had never seen his wife excited. She returned with a razor. "Let's make you perfect," she said.

She soaped him down, and shaved his body bald. She only cut him twice, and that wasn't her fault, that was because he'd moved. She left him only the hairs on his head. And even there, she plucked the eyebrows, and trimmed his fine wavy hair into a neat bob.

"There," she said, and looked over her handiwork proudly, and ran her hands all over him, and this time there was nothing that got in their way.

And at that he tried to kiss her, and she laughed again, and pushed him away.

"No, no," she said. "Your duties can wait until we're in England. We're on holiday."

So he started going out at night as well, with her blessing. He saw how romantic Venice could be by moonlight. He didn't know Italian well, and so could barely understand what the *ragazzi* said to him, but it didn't matter, they were very accommodating. And by the time he returned to his wife's side she was always asleep.

The house in Chelsea had been done up for them, ready for their return. He asked her whether she'd like him to carry her over the threshold. She looked surprised at that, and said he could try. She lay back in his arms, and he was expecting her to be quite heavy, but it went all right really, and he got her through the doorway without doing anything to disgrace himself.

As far as he'd been aware, Karen had never been to the house before. But she knew exactly where to go, walking straight to the study, and to the wooden desk inside, and to the third drawer down. "I have a present for you," she said, and from the drawer she took a gun.

"It was my brother's," she said.

"Oh. Really?"

"It may not have been his. But it's what they gave us anyway."

She handed it to Julian. Julian weighed it in his hands. Like his wife, it was lighter than he'd expected.

"You're the man of the house now," Karen said.

There was no nanny to fetch them dinner. Julian said he didn't mind cooking. He fixed them some eggs. He liked eggs.

After they'd eaten, and Julian had rinsed the plates and left them to dry, Karen said that they should inspect the bedroom. And Julian agreed. They'd inspected the rest of the house; that room, quite deliberately, both had left as yet unexplored.

The first impression that Julian got as he pushed open the door was pink, that everything was pink; the bedroom was unapologetically feminine, that blazed out from the soft pink carpet and the wallpaper of pink rose on pink background. And there was a perfume to it too, the perfume of Karen herself, and he still didn't much care for it.

That was before he saw the bed.

He was startled, and gasped, and then laughed at himself for gasping. The bed was covered with dolls. There were at least a dozen of them, all pale plastic skin and curls and lips that were ruby red, and some were wearing pretty little hats, and some carrying pretty little nosegays, all of them in pretty dresses. In the centre of them, in pride of place, was the doll Karen's father had given as a wedding present—resplendent in her wedding dress, still fat, her facial features smoothed away beneath that fat, sitting amongst the others like a queen. And all of them were smiling. And all of them were looking at him, expectantly, as if they'd been waiting to see who it was they'd heard climb the stairs, as if they'd been waiting for him all this time.

Julian said, "Well! Well. Well, we won't be able to get much sleep with that lot crowding about us!" He chuckled. "I mean, I won't know which is which! Which one is just a doll, and which one my pretty wife!" He chuckled. "Well."

Karen said, "Gifts from my father. I've had some since I was a little girl. Some of them have been hanging about for years."

Julian nodded.

Karen said, "But I'm yours now."

Julian nodded again. He wondered whether he should put his arms around her. He didn't quite like to, not with all the dolls staring.

"I love you," said Karen. "Or rather, I'm trying. I need you to know, I'm trying very hard." And for a moment Julian thought she was going to cry, but then he saw her blink back the tears, her face was hard again. "But I can't love you fully, not whilst I'm loving them. You have to get rid of them for me."

"Well, yes," said Julian. "I mean. If you're sure that's what you want."

Karen nodded grimly. "It's time. And long overdue."

She put on her woollen coat then, she said it would be cold out there in the dark. And she bundled up the dolls too, each and every one of them, and began putting them into Julian's arms. "There's too many," he said, "I'll drop them," but Karen didn't stop, and soon there were arms and legs poking into his chest, he felt the hair of his wife's daughters scratching under his chin. Karen carried just one doll herself, her new doll. She also carried the gun.

It had been a warm summer's evening, not quite yet dark. When they stepped outside it was pitch, only the moonlight providing some small relief, and that grudging. The wind bit. And Chelsea, the city bustle, the pavements, the pedestrians, the traffic—Chelsea had gone, and all that was left was the house. Just the house, and the woods ahead of them.

Julian wanted to run then, but there was nowhere to run to. He tried to drop the dolls. But the dolls refused to let go, they clung on to him, he could feel their little plastic fingers tightening around his coat, his shirt buttons, his skin, his own skin.

"Follow me," said Karen.

The branches stuck out at weird angles, impossible angles, Julian couldn't see any way to climb through them. But Karen knew where to tread and where to duck, and she didn't hesitate, she moved at speed—and Julian followed her every step, he struggled to catch up, he lost sight of her once or twice and thought he was lost for good, but the dolls, the dolls showed him the way.

The clearing was a perfect circle, and the moon shone down upon it like a spotlight on a stage.

"Put them down," said Karen.

He did so.

She arranged the dolls on the browning grass, set them in one long neat line. Julian tried to help, he put the new doll in her wedding dress beside them, and Karen rescued her. "It's not her time yet," she said. "But she needs to see what will one day happen to her."

"And what is going to happen?"

Her reply came as if the daughters themselves had asked. Her voice rang loud, with a confidence Julian had never heard from her before. "Chloe. Barbara. Mary-Sue. Mary-Jo. Suki. Delilah. Wendy. Prue. Annabelle. Mary-Ann. Natasha. Jill. You have been sentenced to death."

"But why?" said Julian. He wanted to grab her, shake her by the shoulders. He wanted to. She was his wife, that's what he was supposed to do. He couldn't even touch her. He couldn't even go near. "Why? What have they done?"

"Love," said Karen. She turned to him. "Oh, yes, *they* know what they've done."

She saluted them. "And you," she said to Julian, "you must salute them too. No. Not like that. That's not a salute. Hand steady. Like me. Yes. Yes."

She gave him the gun. The dolls all had their backs to him, at least he didn't have to see their faces.

He thought of his father. He thought of his brothers. Then, he didn't think of anything.

He fired into the crowd. He'd never fired a gun before, but it was easy, there was nothing to it. He ran out of bullets, so Karen reloaded the gun. He fired into the crowd again. He thought there might be screams. There were no screams. He thought there might be blood…and the brown of the grass seemed fresher and wetter and seemed to pool out lazily towards him.

And Karen reloaded his gun. And he fired into the crowd, just once more, please, God, just one last time. Let them be still. Let them stop twitching. The twitching stopped.

"It's over," said Karen.

"Yes," he said. He tried to hand her back the gun, but she wouldn't take it—it's yours now, you're the man of the house. "Yes," he said again.

He began to cry. He didn't make a sound.

"Don't," said Karen. "If you cry, the deaths won't be clean."

And he tried to stop, but now the tears found a voice, he bawled like a little girl.

She said, "I will not have you dishonour them."

She left him then. She picked up her one surviving doll, and went, and left him all alone in the woods. He didn't try to follow her. He stared at the bodies in the clearing, wondered if he should clear them up, make things tidier. He didn't. He clutched the gun, waited for it to cool, and eventually it did. And when he thought to turn about he didn't know where to go, he didn't know if he'd be able to find his way back. But the branches parted for him easily, as if ushering him fast on his way, as if they didn't want him either.

"I'm sorry," he said.

He hadn't taken a key. He'd had to ring his own doorbell. When his wife answered, he felt an absurd urge to explain who he was. He'd stopped crying, but his face was still red and puffy. He held out his gun to her, and she hesitated, then at last took it from him.

"Sorry," he said again.

"You did your best," she said. "I'm sorry too. But next time it'll be different."

"Yes," he said. "Next time."

"Won't you come in?" she said politely, and he thanked her, and did.

She took him upstairs. The doll was sitting on the bed, watching. She moved it to the dressing table. She stripped her husband. She ran her fingers over his soft smooth body, she'd kept it neat and shaved.

"I'm sorry," he said one more time; and then, as if it were the same thing, "I love you."

And she said nothing to that, but smiled kindly. And she took him then, and before he knew what he was about he was inside her, and he knew he ought to feel something, and he knew he ought to be doing something to help. He tried to gyrate a little. "No, no," she said, "I'll do it," and so he let her be. He let her do all the work, and he looked up at her face and searched for any sign of passion there, or tenderness, but it was so *hard*—and he turned to the side, and there was the fat doll, and it was smiling, and its eyes were twinkling, and there, there, on that greasy plastic face, there was all the tenderness he could ask for.

Eventually she rolled off. He thought he should hug her. He put his arms around her, felt how strong she was. He felt like crying again. He supposed that would be a bad idea.

"I love you," she said. "I am very patient. I have learned to love you."

She fetched a hairbrush. She played at his hair. "My sweetheart," she said, "my angel cake." She turned him over, spanked his bottom hard with the brush until the cheeks were red as rouge. "My big baby doll."

And this time he *did* cry, it was as if she'd given him permission. And it felt so good.

He looked across at the doll, still smiling at him, and he hated her, and he wanted to hurt her, he wanted to take his gun and shove the barrel right inside her mouth and blast a hole through the back of her head. He wanted to take his gun and bludgeon with it, blow after blow, and he knew how good that would feel, the skull smashing, the wetness. And this time he wouldn't cry. He would be a real man.

"I love you," she said again. "With all my heart."

She pulled back from him, and looked him in the face, sizing him up, as she had that first time they'd met. She gave him a salute.

He giggled at that, he tried to raise his own arm to salute back, but it wouldn't do it, he was so very silly.

There was a blur of something brown at the foot of the bed; something just out of the corner of his eye, and the blur seemed to still, and the brown looked like a jacket maybe, trousers, a uniform. He tried to cry out—in fear, or at least in surprise?—but there was no air left in him. There was the smell of mud, so much mud. Who'd known mud could smell? And a voice to the blur, a voice in spite of all. "Is it time?"

He didn't see his wife's reaction, nor hear her reply. His head jerked, and he was looking at the doll again, and she was the queen doll, the best doll, so pretty in her wedding dress. She was his queen. And he thought she was smiling even wider, and that she was pleased he was offering her such sweet tribute.

Caitlín R. Kiernan was recently hailed by the *New York Times* as "one of our essential authors of dark fiction." A two-time winner of both the World Fantasy and Bram Stoker awards, she has published ten novels, including *The Red Tree* and *The Drowning Girl: A Memoir*. She is also the recipient of the Locus and James Tiptree, Jr. awards.

Her short fiction has been collected in thirteen volumes, including *Tales of Pain and Wonder*, *The Ammonite Violin & Others*, *A Is for Alien*, and *The Ape's Wife and Other Stories*. Subterranean Press has released a two-volume set collecting the best of her short fiction, *Two Worlds and In Between* and *Beneath an Oil-Dark Sea*.

Interstate Love Song
(Murder Ballad No. 8)
Caitlín R. Kiernan

"The way of the transgressor is hard." —Cormac McCarthy

I.

THE IMPALA'S WHEELS singing on the black hot asphalt sound like frying steaks, USDA choice-cut T-bones, sirloin sizzling against August blacktop in Nevada or Utah or Nebraska, Alabama or Georgia, or where the fuck ever this one day, this one hour, this one motherfucking minute is going down. Here at the end, the end of one of us, months are a crimson thumb smudge across the bathroom mirror in all the interchangeable motel bathrooms that have come and gone and come again. You're smoking and looking for music in the shoebox filled with cassettes, and the clatter of protective plastic shells around spools of magnetically coated tape is like an insect chorus, a cicada symphony. You ask what I want to hear, and I tell you it doesn't matter, please light one of those for me. But you insist, and you keep right on insisting, "What d'you wanna hear?" And I say, well not fucking Nirvana again, and no more Johnny Cash, please, and you toss something from the box out the open passenger window. In the side-view mirror, I see a tiny shrapnel explosion when the cassette hits the road. Cars will come behind us, cars and trucks, and roll over the shards and turn it all to dust. "No more Nirvana," you say, and you laugh your boyish girl's laugh, and Jesus and Joseph and Mother Mary, I'm not going to be able to live in a world without that laugh. Look at me, I say. Open your eyes, please open your eyes and look at me, please. You can't fall asleep on me. Because it won't be falling asleep, will it? It won't be falling asleep at all. We are on beyond the kindness of euphemisms, and maybe we always were. So, don't fall asleep. Don't flutter the eyelashes you've always hated because they're so long and pretty, don't let them dance that Totentanz tarantella we've delighted at so many goddamn times, don't let the sun go down on me. You shove a tape into the deck. You always do that with such force, as if there's a vendetta grudge between you and that machine. You punch it in and twist the volume knob like you mean to yank it off and yeah, that's good, I say. That's golden, Henry Rollins snarling at the sun's one great demon eye. You light a Camel for me and place it between my lips, and the steering wheel feels like a weapon in my hands, and the smoke feels like Heaven in my lungs. Wake up, though. Don't shut your eyes. Remember the day that we, and remember the morning, and remember *that* time in—shit, was it El Paso? Or was it Port Arthur? It doesn't matter, so long as you keep your eyes open and look at me. It's hours until sunrise, and have you not always sworn a blue streak that you would not die in the darkness? That's all we've got here. In for a penny, in for a pound, but blackness, wall to wall, sea to shining sea, that's all we've got in this fluorescent hell, so don't you please fall asleep on me. Hot wind roars in through the Impala's windows, the stink of melting tar, roaring like an invisible mountain lion, and you point west and say take that next exit. We need beer, and we're almost out of cigarettes, and I want a pack of Starburst Fruit Chews, the tropical flavors, so the assholes better have those out here in the world's barren shit-kicker asshole. You'll just like always save all the piña colada ones for me. Then there's a thud from the trunk, and you laugh that laugh of yours all over again, only now with true passion. "And we need a bottle of water," I say. "No good to us and a waste of time and energy, and just a waste all the way round, if she ups and dies of heat stroke back there," and you shrug. Hey, keep your eyes open, love. Please, goddamn it. You can do that for me, I know you can. And I break open one of the ampules of ammonia and cruelly wave it beneath your nostrils so that both eyes pop open wide, opening up cornflower blue, and I think of startled birds bursting from their hiding places in tall grass. Tall grass, there's so much of tall grass here at the end, isn't there? I kiss your forehead, and I can't help thinking I could fry an egg on your skin, fry an egg on blacktop, fry an egg on the hood of the Impala parked in the dog-day sun outside a convenience store. You ask me to light a candle, your voice gone all jagged and broken apart like a cassette tape dropped on I-10 at 75 mph. I press my fingers and palm to the sloppy red mess of your belly, and I do not dare take my hand away long enough to light a candle, and I'm so sorry, I'm so, so sorry. I cannot even do that much for you. Just please don't close your eyes. Please don't you fall asleep on me.

2.

All these things you said to me, if not on this day, then surely on some other, and if not during this long Delta night, than surely on another. The blonde with one brown eye and one hazel-green eye, she wasn't the first, but you said to me she'll be the most memorable yet. She'll be one we talk about in years to come when all the rest have faded into a blur of delight and casual slaughter. We found her at a truck stop near Shreveport, and she'd been hitching down I-49 towards Baton Rouge and New Orleans. Sister, where you bound on such a hot, hot, sweltersome night? you asked. And because she was dressed in red, a Crimson Tide T-shirt and a red Budweiser baseball cap, you said, "Whither so early, Little Red Cap?" And she laughed, and you two shared a joint while I ate a skimpy dinner of Slim Jims, corn chips, and Mountain Dew. Eighteen-wheeled dinosaurs growled in and growled out and purred at the pumps. We laughed over a machine that sold multi-colored prophylactics and another that sold tampons. And would she like a ride? Would she? 'Cause we're a sight lot better than you're likely gonna find elsewhere, if you're looking for decent company and conversation, that is, and the weed, there's more where that came from. How old? Eighteen, she said, and you and I both knew she was adding years, but all the better. She tossed her knapsack in the back seat, and the extra pair of shoes she wore around her neck, laces laced together. She smelled of the road, of many summer days without a bath, and the world smelled of dinosaur trucks and diesel and dust and Spanish moss; and I love you so much, you whispered as I climbed behind the wheel. I love you so much I do not have words to say how much I love you. We set sail southwards, washed in the alien chartreuse glow of the Impala's dash, and she and thee talked while I drove, listening. That was enough for me, listening in, eavesdropping while my head filled up with a wakeful, stinging swarm of bees, with wasps and yellow jackets, courtesy those handy shrink-wrapped packets of dextroamphetamine and amphetamine, Black Beauties, and in the glove compartment there's Biphetamine-T and 40mg capsules of methaqualone, because when *we* drove all damn day and all damned night, we came prepared, didn't we, love? She's traveled all the way from Chicago, the red-capped backseat girl, and you and I have never been to Chicago and have no desire to go. She talks about the road as it unrolls beneath us, before me, hauling us towards dawn's early light. She tells you about some old pervert who picked her up outside Texarkana. She fucked him for twenty bucks and the lift to Shreveport. "Could'a done worse," you tell her, and she doesn't disagree. I watch you both in the rearview mirror. I watch you both, in anticipation, and the uppers and the prospect of what will come, the mischief we will do her in the wood, has me more awake than awake, has me ready to cum then and there. "You're twins," she said. It wasn't a question, only a statement of the obvious, as they say. "We're twins," you reply. "But she's my big sister. Born three minutes apart on the anniversary of the murder of Elizabeth Short," and she has no goddamn idea what you're talking about, but, not wanting to appear ignorant, she doesn't let on. When she asks where we're from, "Los Angeles," you lie. You have a generous pocketful of answers at the ready for that oft-asked question. "South Norton Avenue, midway between Coliseum Street and West 39th," you say, which has as little meaning to the heterochromatic blonde as does Glasgow smile and Leimert Park. I drive, and you spin our revolving personal mythology. She will be one for the books, you whispered back at the truck stop. Can't you smell it on her? Can't I smell what on her? Can't you smell happenstance and inevitability and fate? Can't you smell victim? You say those things, and always I nod, because, like backseat girl, I don't want to appear ignorant in your view. This one I love, this one I love, eating cartilage, shark-eyes, shark-heart, and black mulberry trees means I will not survive you, when the truth is I won't survive *without* you. Backseat girl, she talks about how she's gonna find work in New Orleans as a waitress, when you and I know she's cut out for nothing much but stripping and whoring the Quarter, and if this were a hundred years ago she'd be headed for fabled, vanished Storyville. "I had a boyfriend," she says. "I had a boyfriend, but he was in a band, and they all moved off to Seattle, but, dude, I didn't want to fucking *go* to fucking Seattle, you know?" And you say to her how it's like the California Gold Rush or something, all these musician sheep lemming assholes and would-be wannabe musician posers traipsing their way to the fabled Northwest in hopes of riding a wave that's already broken apart and isn't even sea foam anymore. That ship has *sailed*, you say. It's sailed and sunk somewhere in the deep blue Pacific. But that's not gonna stop anyone with stars in their eyes, because the lure of El Dorado is always a bitch, whichever El Dorado is at hand. "Do you miss him?" I ask, and that's the first thing I've said in over half an hour, more than happy just to listen in and count off the reflective mile markers with the help of anger and discord jangling from the tape deck. "Don't know," she says. And she says, "Maybe sometimes. Maybe." The road's a lonely place, you tell her, sounding sympathetic when I know so much better. I know your mind is full to the brim with red, red thoughts, the itch of your straight-razor lusts, the prospect of the coming butchery. Night cruising at 80 mph, we rush past the turnoff for Natchitoches, and there's a sign that says "Lost Bayou," and our passenger asks have *we* ever been to New Orleans. Sure, you lie. Sure. We'll show you round. We have friends who live in an old house on Burgundy, and they say the house is haunted by a Civil War ghost, and they'll probably let you crash there until you're on your feet. Sister, you make us sound like goddamn guardian angels, the best break she's ever had. I drive on, and the car reeks of pot and sweat, cigarette smoke and the old beer cans heaped on the back floorboard. "I've always wished I had a twin," she says. "I used to make up stories that I was adopted, and somewhere out there I had a twin brother. One day, I'd pretend, we'd find one another. Be reunited, you know." It's a pretty dream from the head of such a pretty, pretty red-capped girl in the backseat, ferried by you and I in our human masks to hide hungry wolfish faces. *I could turn you inside out,* I think at the girl. And we will. It's been a week since an indulgence, a week of aimless July motoring, letting peckish swell to starvation, taking no other pleasures but junk food and blue-plate specials, you and I fucking and sleeping in one another's arms while the merciless Dixie sun burned 101°F at motel-room rooftops, kerosene air gathered in rooms darkened and barely cooled by drawn curtains and wheezing AC. Strike a match, and the whole place woulda gone up. Cartoons on television, and watching MTV, and old movies in shades of black and white and grey. Burgers wrapped in meat-stained paper and devoured with salty fries. Patience, love, patience, you whispered in those shadows, and so we thrummed along back roads and highways waiting for just the right confection. And. My. Momma. Said. Pick the Very. Best One. And You. Are. It.

3.

Between the tall rustling corn-silk rows, ripening husks, bluebottles drone as the sun slides down from the greasy blue sky to set the horizon all ablaze, and you straddle Thin Man and hold his cheekbones so that he has no choice but to gaze into your face. He can't close his eyes, as he no longer has eyelids, and he screams every time I shake another handful of Red Devil lye across his bare thighs and genitals. Soft flesh is melting like hot wax, here beneath the fading Iowa day. I draw a deep breath, smelling chemical burns, tilled red-brown Bible Belt soil, and corn, and above all else, corn. The corn smells alive in ways I cannot imagine being alive, and when we are done with Thin Man,

349

I think I would like to lie down here, right here, in the dirt between the tall rows, and gaze up at the June night, at the wheeling twin dippers and bear twins and the solitary scorpion and Cassiopeia, what I know of summer stars. "You don't have to do this," the man blubbers, and you tell him no, we don't, but yes, we do. We very much actually do. And he screams, and his scream is the lonesome cry of a small animal dying alone so near to twilight. He could be a rabbit in a fox's jaws, just as easily as a thin man in our company. We found him standing alongside a pickup broken down miles and miles north of Ottumwa, and maybe we ought to have driven him farther than we did, but impatience wins sometimes, and so you made up that story about our uncle Joe who has a garage just a little ways farther up the road. What did he have to fear from two pale girls in a rust-bucket Impala, and so I drove, and Thin Man—whose name I still unto this hour do not know—talked about how liberals and niggers and bleeding hearts and the EPA are ruining the country. Might he have become suspicious of our lies if you'd not switched out the plates at the state line? Might he have paused in his unelicited screed long enough to think twice and think better? You scoop up fertile soil and dribble it into his open mouth, and he gags and sputters and chokes and wheezes, and still he manages to beg throughout. He's pissed himself and shat himself, so there are also those odors. Not too far away are train tracks, and not too far away there is a once-red barn, listing like a drunkard, and silver grain silos, and a whistle blows, and it blows, calling the swallows home. You sing to Thin Man, *Heed the curves, and watch the tunnels. Never falter, never fail.* Remember that? Don't close your eyes, and do not dare sleep, for this is not that warm night we lay together near Thin Man's shucked corpse and screwed in the eyes of approving Maggot Corn King deities thankful for our oblation. Your lips on my breasts, suckling, your fingers deep inside me, plowing, sewing, and by tomorrow we'll be far away, and this will be a pleasant dream for the scrapbooks of our tattered souls. More lye across Thin Man's crotch, and he bucks beneath you like an unbroken horse or a lover or an epileptic or a man being taken apart, piece by piece, in a cornfield north of Ottumwa. When we were children, we sat in the kudzu and live-oak shade near the tracks, waiting, waiting, placing pennies and nickels on the iron rails. You, spitting on the rails to cool them enough you would not blister your ear when you pressed it to the metal. I hear the train, you announced and smiled. Not much farther now, I hear it coming, and soon the slag ballast will dance and the crossties buck like a man dying in a cornfield. Soon now, the parade of clattering doomsday boxcars, the steel wheels that can sever limbs and flatten coins. Boxcars the color of rust—Southern Serves the South and CSX and a stray Wisconsin Central as good as a bird blown a thousand miles off course by hurricane winds. Black cylindrical tankers filled with corn syrup and crude oil, phenol, chlorine gas, acetone, vinyl chloride, and we spun tales of poisonous, flaming, steaming derailments. Those rattling, one-cent copper-smearing trains, we dreamed they might carry us off in the merciful arms of hobo sojourns to anywhere far, far away from home. *Keep your hand upon the throttle, and your eye upon the rail.* And Thin Man screams, dragging me back to the now of then. You've put dirt in his eyes, and you'd imagine he'd be thankful for that, wouldn't you? Or maybe he was gazing past you towards imaginary pearly gates where delivering angels with flaming swords might sweep down to lay low his tormentors and cast us forever and anon into the lake of fire. More Red Devil and another scream. He's beginning to bore me, you say, but I'm so busy admiring my handiwork I hardly hear you, and I'm also remembering the drive to the cornfield. I'm remembering what Thin Man was saying about fairy child-molesting atheist sodomites in all branches of the federal government and armed forces, and an international ZOG conspiracy of Jews running the USA into the ground, and who the *fuck* starts in about shit like that with total, helpful strangers? Still, you were more than willing to play along and so told him yes, yes, yes, how we were faithful, God-fearing Southern Baptists, and how our daddy was a deacon and our momma a Sunday school teacher. That should'a been laying it on too thick, anyone would've thought, but Thin Man grinned bad teeth and nodded and blew great clouds of menthol smoke out the window like a locomotive chimney. Open your eyes. I'm not gonna tell you again. Here's another rain of lye across tender meat, and here's the corpse we left to rot in a cornfield, and I won't be left alone, do you hear me? Here are cordials to keep you nailed into your skin and to this festering, unsuspecting world. What am I, what am I, what *am* I? he wails, delirious, as long cornstalk shadows crosshatch the field, and in reply do you say, A sinner in the hands of angry gods, and we'd laugh about that one for days. But maybe he did believe you, sister, for he fell to praying, and I half believe he was praying not to Father, Son, and Holy Ghost, but to you and me. You tell him, By your own words, mister, we see thou art an evil man, and we, too, are surely out and about and up to no good, as you'll have guessed, and we are no better than thee, and so there is balance. I don't know why, but you tack on something about the horned, moon-crowned Popess squatting between Boaz and Jachin on the porch of Solomon. They are pretty words, whether I follow their logic or not. Near, nearer, the train whistle blows again, and in that moment you plunge your knife so deeply into Thin Man's neck that it goes straight through his trachea and spine and out the other side. The cherry fountain splashes you. You give the Bowie a little twist to the left, just for shits and giggles. Appropriately, he lies now still as death. You pull out the knife and kiss the jetting hole you've made, painting sticky your lips and chin. Your throat. You're laughing, and the train shrieks, and now I want to cover my ears, because just every once and a while I do lose my footing on the winding serpent highway, and when I do the fear wraps wet-sheet cold about me. This, here, now, is one of those infrequent, unfortunate episodes. I toss the plastic bottle of lye aside and drag you off Thin Man's still, still corpse. Don't, I say. Don't you dare laugh no more, I don't think it's all that funny, and also don't you dare shut your eyes, and don't you dare go to sleep on me. *Till we reach that blissful shore*

Where the angels wait to join us

In that train

Forevermore.

I seize you, love, and you are raving in my embrace: *What the fuck are you doing? Take your goddamn filthy hands off me cunt, gash, bitch, traitor.* But oh, oh, oh I hold on, and I hold on tight for dear forsaken life, 'cause the land's tilting teeter-totter under us as if on the Last Day of All, the day of Kingdom Come, and just don't make me face the righteous fury of the Lion of Judah alone. In the corn, we rolled and wallowed like dust-bathing mares, while you growled, and foam flecked your bloody lips, and you spat and slashed at the gloaming with your dripping blade. A voyeuristic retinue of grasshoppers and field mice, crickets and a lone bull snake took in our flailing, certainly comedic antics while I held you prisoner in my arms, holding you hostage against my shameful fear and self-doubt. Finally, inevitably, your laughter died, and I only held you while you sobbed and Iowa sod turned to streaks of mud upon your mirthless face.

4.

I drive west, then east again, then turn south onto I-55, Missouri, the County of Cape Girardeau. Meandering like the cottonmouth, silt-choked Mississippi, out across fertile floodplain fields all night-blanketed, semisweet darkness to hide river-gifted loam. You're asleep in the backseat, your breath soft as velvet, soft as autumn rain. You never sleep more than an hour at a time, not ever, and so I never wake you. Not ever. Not even when you cry out from the secret nightmare countries behind your eyelids. We are moving along between the monotonous, barbarous topography and the overcast sky, overcast at sunset the sky looked dead, and now, well past midnight, there is still no sign of moon nor stars to guide me, and I have only the road signs and the tattered atlas lying open beside me as I weave and wend through the Indian ghosts of Ozark Bluff Dwellers, stalkers of shambling mastodon and mammoth phantoms along these crude asphalt corridors. I light cigarette after cigarette and wash Black Beauties down with peach Nehi. I do not often know loneliness, but I know it now, and I wish I were with you in your hard, hard dreams. The radio's tuned to a gospel station out of Memphis, but the volume is down low, low, low so you'll not be awakened by the Five Blind Boys of Alabama or the Dixie Hummingbirds. In your sleep, you are muttering, and I try not to eavesdrop. But voices carry, as they say, and I hear enough to get the gist. You sleep a walking sleep, and in dreams, you've drifted back to Wichita, to that tow-headed boy with fish and starfish, an octopus and sea shells tattooed all up and down his arms, across his broad chest and shoulders. "Because I've never seen the ocean," he said. "But that's where I'm headed now. I'm going all the way to Florida. To Panama City or Pensacola." "We've never seen the sea, either," you tell him. "Can we go with you? We've really nowhere else to go, and you really have no notion how delightful it will be when they take us up and throw us with the lobsters out to sea." The boy laughed. No, not a boy, not in truth, but a young man older than us, a scruffy beard growing unevenly on his suntanned cheeks. "Can we? Can we, please?" Hey, you're the two with the car, not me, he replied, so I suppose you're free to go anywhere you desire. And that is the gods' honest truth of it all, ain't it? We are free to drive anywhere we please, so long as we do not attempt to part this material plane of simply three dimensions. Alone in the night, in the now and not the then, I have to be careful. It would be too easy to slip into my own dreams, amphetamine insomnia helping hands or no, and I have so often imagined our Odyssey ending with the Impala wrapped around a telephone pole or lying wheels-up turtlewise and steaming in a ditch or head-on folded back upon ourselves after making love to an oncoming semi. I shake my head and open my eyes wider. There's a rest stop not too far up ahead, and I tell myself that I'll pull over there. I'll pull over to doze for a while in sodium-arc pools, until the sun rises bright and violent to burn away the clouds, until it's too hot to sleep. The boy's name was Philip—one L. The young man who was no longer a boy and who had been decorated with the cryptic nautical language of an ocean he'd never seen, and, as it came to pass, never would. But you'd keep all his teeth in a Mason jar, just in case we ever got around to the Gulf of Mexico or an Atlantic shoreline. You kept his teeth, promising him a burial in salt water. Philip told us about visiting a museum at the university in Lawrence, where he saw the petrified skeletons of giant sea monsters that once had swum the vanished inland depths. He was only a child, ten or eleven, but he memorized names that, to my ears, sounded magical, forbidden, perilous Latin incantations to call down fish from the clear blue sky or summon bones burrowing upwards from yellow-gray chalky rocks. You sat with your arms draped shameless about his neck while he recited and elaborated—*Tylosaurus proriger, Dolichorhynchops bonneri, Platecarpus tympaniticus, Elasmosaurus platyurus,* birds with teeth and giant turtles, flying reptiles and the fangs of ancient sharks undulled by eighty-five million years, give or take. Show off, you said and laughed. That's what you are, a show off. And you said, Why aren't you in college, bright boy? And Philip with one L said his parents couldn't afford tuition, and his grades had not been good enough for a scholarship, and he wasn't gonna join the army, because he had a cousin went off to Desert Storm, right, and did his duty in Iraq, and now he's afraid to leave the house and sick all the time and constantly checks his shoes for scorpions and land mines. The military denies all responsibility. Maybe, said Philip with one L, I can get a job on a fishing boat, or a shrimping boat, and spend all my days on the water and all my nights drinking rum with mermaids. We could almost have fallen in love with him. Almost. You even whispered to me about driving him to Florida that he might lay eyes upon the Gulf of Mexico before he died. But I am a jealous bitch, and I said no, fuck that sentimental horseshit, and he died the next day in a landfill not far from Emporia. I did that one, cut his throat from ear to ear while he was busy screwing you. He looked up at me, his stark blue irises drowning in surprise and confusion, and then he came one last time, coaxed to orgasm, pumping blood from severed carotid and jugular and, too, pumping out an oyster stream of jizz. It seemed all but immaculate, the red and the silver-gray, and you rode him even after there was no more of him left to ride but a cooling cadaver. You cried over Philip, and that was the first and only one you ever shed tears for, and Jesus I am sorry but I wanted to slap you. I wanted to do something worse than slap you for your mourning. I wanted to leave a scar. Instead, I gouged out his lifeless eyes with my thumbs and spat in his face. You wiped your nose on your shirt sleeve, pulled up your underwear and jeans, and went back to the car for the needle-nose pair of pliers in the glove compartment. It did not have to be that way, you said, you pouted, and I growled at you to shut up, and whatever it is you're doing in his mouth, hurry because this place gives me the creeps. Those slumping, smoldering hills of refuse, Gehenna for rats and maggots and crows, coyotes, stray dogs and strayer cats. We *could* have taken him to the sea, you said. We *could* have done that much, and then you fell silent, sulking, taciturn, and not ever again waking have you spoken of him. Besides the teeth, you peeled off a patch of skin, big as the palm of your hand and inked with the image of a crab, because we were born in the sign of Cancer. The rest of him we concealed under heaps of garbage. *Here you go, rats, here's something fresh. Here's a banquet, and we shall not even demand tribute in return. We will be benevolent rat gods, will we two, bringing plenty and then taking our leave, and you will spin prophecies of our return. Amen. Amen. Hosannah.* Our work done, I followed you back to the Impala, stepping superstitiously in your footsteps, and that is what I am doing when—now—I snap awake to the dull, gritty noise of the tires bumping off the shoulder and spraying dry showers of breakdown-lane gravel, and me half awake and cursing myself for nodding off; fuck me, fuck me, I'm such an idiot, how I should have stopped way the hell back in Bonne Terre or Fredericktown. I cut the wheel left, and, just like that, all is right again. Doomsday set aside for now. In the backseat, you don't even stir. I turn up the radio for companionship. If I had toothpicks, I might prop open my eyes. My hands are red, love. Oh god, my hands are so red, and we have not ever looked upon the sea.

5.

Boredom, you have said again and again, is the one demon might do you in, and the greatest of all our foes, the *one* demon, Mystery Babylon, the Great Harlot, who at the Valley of Josaphat, on the hill of Megiddo, wraps chains about our porcelain slender necks and drags us down to dust and comeuppance if we dare to turn our backs upon the motherfucker and give it free fucking rein. I might allow how this is the mantra that set us to traveling on the road we are on and has dictated our every action since that departure, your morbid fear of boredom. The consequence of this mantra has almost torn you in half, so that I bend low over my love, only my bare hands to keep your insides from spilling outside. Don't you shut your eyes. You don't get out half that easy. Simple boredom is as good as the flapping wings of butterflies to stir the birth throes of hurricanes. Tiresome recitations of childhood traumas and psychoses be damned. As are we; as are we.

6.

We found her, or she was the one found us, another state, another county, the outskirts of another slumbering city. Another truck-stop diner. Because we were determined to become connoisseurs of everything that is fried and smothered in lumpy brown gravy, and you were sipping a flat Coke dissolute with melting ice. You were talking—I don't know why—about the night back home when the Piggly Wiggly caught fire, so we climbed onto the roof and watched it go up. The air smelled like burning groceries. We contemplated cans of Del Monte string beans and pears and cans of Grapico reaching the boiling point and going off like grenades, and the smoke rose up and blotted out the moon, which that night was full. You're talking about the fire, and suddenly she's there, the coal-haired girl named Haddie in her too-large Lollapalooza T-shirt and black jeans and work boots. Her eyes are chipped jade and honey, that variegated hazel, and she smiles so disarming a smile and asks if, perhaps, we're heading east towards Birmingham, because she's trying to get to Birmingham, but—insert here a woeful tale of her douche-bag boyfriend—and now she's stranded high and dry, not enough money for bus fare, and if we're headed that way, could she please, and would we please? You scoot over and pat the turquoise sparkle vinyl upholstery, inviting her to take a Naugahyde seat, said the spider to the fly. "Thank you," she says. "Thank you very much," and she sits and you share your link sausage and waffles with her, because she says she hasn't any money for food, either. We're heading for Atlanta, you tell her, and we'll be going right straight through Birmingham, so sure, no problem, the more the goddamn merrier. We are lifesavers, she says. Never been called that before. You chat her up, sweet as cherry pie with whipped cream squirted from a can, and, me, I stare out the plate-glass partition at the gas pumps and the stark white lighting to hide the place where a Mississippi night should be. "Austin," she says, when you ask from whence she's come. "Austin, Texas," she volunteers. "I was born and raised there." Well, you can hear it, plain as tits on a sow, in her easy, drawling voice. I take in a mouthful of lukewarm Cheerwine, swallow, repeat, and do not let my attention drift from the window and an idling eighteen-wheeler parked out there with its cab all painted up like a Santería altar whore, gaudy and ominous and seductive. Smiling Madonna and cherubic child, merry skeletons dancing joyful round about a sorrowful, solemn Pietà, roses and carnations, crucifixions, half-pagan *orichá* and weeping bloody Catholic Jesus. Of a sudden, then, I feel a sick coldness spreading deep in my bowels, ice water heavy in my guts, and I want to tell this talkative Lone-Star transient that no, sorry, but you spoke too soon and, sorry, but we *can't* give her a ride, after all, not to Birmingham or anywhere else, that she'll have to bum one from another mark, which won't be hard, because the night is filled with travelers. I want to say just that. But I don't. Instead, I keep my mouth shut tight and watch as a man in dirty orange coveralls climbs into the cab of the truck, him and his goddamn enormous shaggy dog. That dog, it might almost pass for a midget grizzly. In the meanwhile, Ms. Austin is sitting there feeding you choice slivers of her life's story, and you devour it, because I've never yet seen you not hungry for a sobby tale. This one, she's got all the hallmarks of a banquet, doesn't she? Easy pickings, if I only trust experience and ignore this inexplicable wash of instinct. Then you, love, give me a gentle, unseen kick beneath the table, hardly more than an emphatic nudge, your right foot insistently tapping, tap, tap, at my left ankle in a private Morse. I fake an unconcerned smile and turn my face away from the window and that strange truck, though I can still hear its impatient engines. "A painter," says Ms. Austin. "See, I want to be a painter. I've got an aunt in Birmingham, and she knows my mom's a total cunt, and she doesn't mind if I stay with her while I try to get my shit together. It was supposed to be me and him both, but now it's just gonna be me. See, I shut my eyes, and I see murals, and that's what I want to paint one day. *Wallscapes.*" And she talks about murals in Mexico City and Belfast and East Berlin. "I need to piss," I say, and you flash me a questioning glance that Ms. Austin does not appear to catch. I slide out of the turquoise booth and walk past other people eating other meals, past shelves grounded with motor oil, candy bars, and pornography. I'm lucky and there's no one else in the restroom, no one to hear me vomit. *What the fuck is this? Hunh? What the fuck is wrong with me now?* When the retching is done, I sit on the dirty tile floor and drown in sweat and listen to my heart throwing a tantrum in my chest. Get up and get back out there. And you, don't you even think of shutting your eyes again. The sun won't rise for another two hours, another two hours at least, and we made a promise one to the other. Or have you forgotten in the gauzy veils of hurt and Santísima Muerte come to whisper in your ear? Always have you said you were hers, a demimondaine to the Bony Lady, *la Huesuda.* So, faithless, I have to suffer your devotions as well? I also shoulder your debt? The restroom stinks of cleaning fluid, shit and urine, my puke, deodorant cakes and antibacterial soap, filth and excessive cleanliness rubbing shoulders. I don't recall getting to my feet. I don't recall a number of things, truth be told, but then we're paying the check, and then we're out in the muggy Lee County night. You tow Ms. Austin behind you. She rides your wake, slip-streaming, and she seems to find every goddamn thing funny. You climb into the backseat with her, and the two of you giggle and titter over private jokes to which I have apparently not been invited. What all did I miss while I was on my knees, praying to my Toilet Gods? I put in a Patsy Cline tape, *punch* it into the deck as you would, and crank it up loud so I don't have to listen to the two of you, not knowing what you (not her, just *you*) have planned, feeling like an outsider in your company, and I cannot ever recall that having happened. Before long, the lights of Tupelo are growing small and dim in the rearview, a diminishing sun as the Impala glides southeast along US 78. My foot feels heavy as a millstone on the gas pedal. So, I have "A Poor Man's Roses" and "Back in Baby's Arms" and "Sweet Dreams" and a fresh pack of Camels and you and Ms. Austin spooning at my back. And still that ice water in my bowels. She's talking about barbeque, and you laugh, and what the fuck is funny about barbeque. "Dreamland," she says, "just like what those UFO nuts call Area 51 in Nevada, where that dead Roswell alien and shit's supposed to be hidden." Me, I smoke and chew on bitter cherry-flavored Tums tablets, grinding calcium carbonate and corn-starch and talc between my teeth. "Those like you," says Ms. Austin, "who've lost their way," and I have no god-damn idea what she's going on about. We cross a bridge, and if it's a river below us, I do not see any indication that it's been given a name. But we're entering Itawamba County, says a sign, and that sounds like some mythologi-cal world serpent or some place from a William Faulkner novel. Only about twenty miles now to the state line, and I'm thinking how I desire to be shed of the bitch, how I want her out of the car before Tuscaloosa, wondering how I can signal you without making Ms. Austin Texas Chatterbox suspicious. We pass a dozen exits to lonely country roads where we could take our time, do the job right, and at least I'd have something to show for my sour stomach. I'm thinking about the couple in Arkansas, how we made him watch while we took our own sweet time with her, and you telling him it wasn't so different from skinning catfish, not really. A sharp knife and a pair of pliers, that's all you really need, and he screamed and screamed and screamed. Hell, the pussy bastard son of a bitch screamed more than she did. In the end, I put a bullet in his brain just to shut him the fuck up, please. And we'd taken so long with her, hours and hours, well, there wasn't time remaining to do him justice, anyway. After that we've made a point of avoiding couples. After that, it became a matter of policy. Also, I remember that girl we stuck in the trunk for a hundred miles, and how she was half dead of heat prostration by the time we got around to ring around the rosies, pockets full of posies time. And you sulked for days. Now, here, I watch you in the rearview, and if you notice that I am, you're purposefully ignoring me. I have to take a piss, I say, and she giggles. Fuck you, Catfish. Fuck you, because on this road you're traveling, is there hope for tomorrow? On this Glory Road you're traveling, to that land of perfect peace and endless fucking day, that's my twin sister you've got back there with you, my one and true and perfect love, and this train is bound for Glory, ain't nobody ride it, *Catfish*, but the righteous and the holy, and if this train don't turn around, well, I'm Alabama bound. You and me and she, only, we ain't going that far together. Here's why God and all his angels and the demons down under the sea made detours, *Catfish*. The headlights paint twin high-beam encouragement, luring me on down Appalachian Corridor X, and back there behind me you grumble something about how I'm never gonna find a place to piss here, not unless it's in the bushes. I'm about to cut the wheel again, because there's an unlit side road like the pitchy throat of evening wanting to swallow us whole, and right now, I'm all for that, but... Catfish, née Austin Girl, says that's enough, turn right around and get back on the goddamn highway. And whatever I'm supposed to say, however I'm about to tell her to go fuck herself, I don't. She's got a gun, you say. Jesus, Bobbie, she's got a gun, and you laugh a nervous, disbelieving laugh. You laugh a stunned laugh. She's got a goddamn gun. *What the fuck,* I whisper, and again she instructs me to retrace my steps back to 78. Her voice is cold now as the Arctic currents in my belly. I look in the rearview, and I can't *see* a gun. I want to believe this is some goddamn idiot prank you and she have cooked up, pulling the wool for whatever reason known only to thee. What do you want? I ask, and she says we'll get to that, in the sweet by-and-by, so don't I go fretting my precious little head over what she wants, okay? Sure, sure. And five minutes later we're back on the highway, and you're starting to sound less surprised, surprise turning to fear, because this is not how the game is played. This is *not* the story. We don't have shit, I tell her. We ain't got any money, and we don't have shit, so if you think—and she interrupts, Well, you got this car, don't you? And that's more than me, so how about you just shut up and drive, Little Bird. That's what she calls me, *Little Bird*. So, someone's rewriting the fairy tale all around us; I know that now, and I realize that's the ice in the middle of me. How many warnings did we fail to heed? The Santería semi, that one for sure, as good as any caution sign planted at the side of any path. Once upon a time, pay attention, you and you who have assumed that no one's out there hunting wolves, or that all the lost girls and boys and men and women on the bum are defenseless lambs to the slaughter. Wrong. Wrong. Wrong, and it's too late now. But I push those thoughts down, and I try to focus on nothing but your face in the mirror, even though the sight of you scares the hell out of me. It's been a long time since I've seen you like that, and I thought I never would again. You want the car? I ask Catfish. Is that it? Because if you want the car, fuck it, it's yours. Just let me pull the fuck over, and I'll hand you the goddamn keys. But no, she says. No, I think you should keep right on driving for a while. As for pulling over, I'll say when. I'll say when, on that you can be sure.

7.

Maybe, you say, *it wouldn't be such a bad idea to go home now,* and I nod, and I wipe the blood off your lips, the strawberry life leaking from you freely as ropy cheesecloth, muslin ectoplasm from the mouth, ears, nostrils of a 1912 spiritualist. I wipe it away, but I hold it, too, clasping it against the loss of you. So long as I can catch all the rain in my cupped hands, neither of us shall drown. You just watch me, okay? Keep your eyes on my eyes, and I'll pull you through. It looks a lot worse than it is, I lie. I know it hurts, but you'll be fine. All the blood makes it look terrible, I know, but you'll be fine. Don't you close your goddamn eyes. Oh, sister, don't you die. Don't speak. I cannot stand the rheumy sound of the blood in your throat, so please do not speak. But you say, *You can hear the bells, Bobbie, can't you? Fuck, but they are so red, and they are so loud, how could you not? Take me and cut me out in little stars....*

8.

So fast, my love, so swift and sure thy hands, and when Catfish leaned forward to press the muzzle of her 9mm to my head and tell me to shut up and drive, you drew your vorpal steel, and the razor folded open like a silver flower and snicker-snacked across coal-haired Haddie's throat. She opened up as if she'd come with a zipper. Later, we opened her wide and sunk her body in a marshy maze of swamp and creek beds and snapping-turtle weeds. Scum-green water, and her guts pulled out and replaced with stones. You wanted to know were there alligators this far north, handy-dandy helpful gator pals to make nothing more of her than alligator shit, and me, I said, hey this is goddamn Mississippi, there could be crocodiles and pythons for all I know. Afterwards, we bathed in the muddy slough, because cutting a bitch's throat is dirty goddamn business, and then we fucked in the high grass, then had to pluck off leeches from our legs and arms and that one ambitious pioneer clinging fiercely to your left nipple. *What about the car? The car's a bloody goddamn mess.* And yeah, I agreed, what about the car? We took what we needed from the Impala, loaded our scavenged belongings into a couple of backpacks, knapsacks, a pillowcase, and then we shifted the car into neutral and pushed it into those nameless waters at the end of a nameless dirt road, and we hiked back to 78. You did so love that car, our sixteenth-birthday present, but it is what it is and can't be helped, and no way we could have washed away the indelible stain left behind by treacherous Catfish's undoing. That was the first and only time we ever killed in self-defense, and it made you so angry, because her death, you said, spoiled the purity of the game. What have we got, Bobbie, except *that* purity? And now it's tainted, sullied by one silly little thief—or what the hell ever she might have been. We have us, I reply. We will always have us, so stop your worrying. My words were, at best, cold comfort, I could tell, and that hurt more than just a little bit, but I kept it to myself, the pain, the hollow in the pit of my soul that had not been there only the half second before you started in on purity and being soiled by the thwarted shenanigans of Catfish. Are you all right? you asked me, as we marched up the off-ramp. I smiled and shook my head. Really, I'm thinking, let's not have that shoe's on the other foot thing ever again, love. Let's see if we can be more careful about who we let in the car that we no longer have. There was a moon three nights past full, like a judgmental god's eye to watch us on our way. We didn't hitch. We just fucking walked until dawn, and then stole a new car from a driveway outside of Tremont. You pulled the tag and stuck on our old Nebraska plates, amongst that which we'd salvaged from the blooded Impala. The new ride, a swank fucking brand-new '96 Saturn the color of Granny Smith apples, it had all-electric windows, but a CD player when all he had was our box of tapes, so fuck that; we'd have to rely on the radio. We hooked onto WVUA 90.7 FM outta Tuscaloosa, and the DJ played Soundgarden and Beck and lulled us forward on the two-lane black-racer asphalt rails of that river, traveling dawnwise back to the earliest beginnings of the world, you said, watching the morning mist burning away, and you said, *When vegetation rioted on the earth, and the big trees were kings.* Read that somewhere? Yeah, you said, and shortly thereafter we took Exit 14, stopping just south of Hamilton, Alabama, because there was a Huddle House, and by then we were both starving all over again. There was also a Texaco station, and good thing, too, as the Saturn was sitting on empty, running on fumes. So, in the cramped white-tile fluorescent drenched restroom, we washed off the swamp water we'd employed to wash away the dead girl's blood. I used wads of paper towels to clean your face as best I could, after the way the raw-boned waitress with her calla-lily tattoo stared at you. I thought there for a moment maybe it was gonna be her turn to pay the ferryman, but you let it slide. There's another woman's scabs crusted in your hair, stubborn clots, and the powdery soap from the powdery soap dispenser on the wall above the sink isn't helping all that much. I need a drink, you say. I need a drink like you would not believe. Yeah, fine, I replied, remembering the half-full, half-empty bottle of Jack in the pillowcase, so just let me get this spot here at your hairline. You go back to talking about the *river*, as if I understand—often I never truly understood you, and for that did I love thee even more. The road which is the river, the river which is the road, mortality, infinity, the grinding maw of history; *An empty stream, a great goddamn silence, an impenetrable forever forest. That's what I'm saying,* you said. *In my eyes, in disposed, in disgrace.* And I said it's gonna be a scorcher today, and at least the Saturn has AC, not like the late beloved lamented Impala, and you spit out what the fuck ever. I fill the tank, and I mention how it's a shame Ms. Austin Catfish didn't have a few dollars on her. We're damn near busted flat. Yeah, well, we'll fix that soon, you say. We'll fix that soon enough, my sweet. You're sitting on the hood, examining the gun she'd have used to lay us low. Make sure the safety is on, I say. And what I think in the split second before the pistol shot is *Please be careful with that thing, the shit our luck's been,* but I didn't say it *aloud.* An unspoken thought, then bang. No. Then BANG. You look nothing in blue blazes but surprised. You turn your face towards me, and the 9mm slips from your fingers and clatters to the oil- and antifreeze-soaked tarmac. I see the black girl behind the register looking our way, and Jesus motherfucking-fucking-fuck-fuck-fucking-motherfucker-oh fuck me this *cannot* be goddamn happening, no way can *this* be happening, not after everything we've done and been through and how there's so much left to do and how I love you so. Suddenly, the air is nothing if not gasoline and sunlight. I can hardly clear my head, and I'm waiting for certain spontaneous combustion and the grand *whump* when the tanks blow, and they'll see the mushroom cloud for miles and miles around. My head fills with fire that isn't even there, but, still, flash-blind, I somehow wrestle you into the backseat. Your eyes are muddy with shock, muddy with perfect incredulity. I press your left hand against the wet hole in that soft spot below your sternum, and you gasp in pain and squeeze my wrist so hard it hurts. *No, okay, you gotta let go now, I gotta get us the fuck outta here before the cops show up. Let go, but keep pressure on it, right? But we have to get out of here now.* Because, I do not add, that gunshot was louder than thunder, that gunshot cleaved the morning apart like the wrath of Gog and Magog striding free across the Armageddon land, Ezekiel 38:2, or wild archangel voices and the trumpet of Thessalonians 4:16. There's a scattered handful of seconds, and then I'm back on the highway again, not thinking, just driving south and east. I try not to hear your moans, 'cause how's that gonna help either of us, but I do catch the words when you whisper, *Are you all right, Bobbie? You flew away like a little bird,* and isn't that what Catfish called me? *So how about you just shut up and drive, Little Bird.* And in my head I do see a looped serpent made of fire devouring its own tail, and I know we cheated fate only for a few hours, only to meet up with it again a little farther down the road. I just drive. I don't even think to switch on the AC or roll down the window or even notice how the car's becoming as good as a kiln on four wheels. I just fucking *drive.* And, like agate beads strung along a rosary, I recite the prayer given me at the End of Days, the end of one of us: Don't you fucking shut your eyes. Please, don't you shut your eyes, because you do not want to go there, and I do not want to be alone forever and forever without the half of me that's you. In my hands, the steering wheel is busy swallowing its own tail, devouring round and round, and we, you and I, are only passengers.

Garth Nix was born in Melbourne, Australia. A full-time writer since 2001, he has worked as a literary agent, marketing consultant, book editor, book publicist, book sales representative, bookseller, and part-time soldier in the Australian Army Reserve.

Nix's books include the bestselling Old Kingdom fantasy series comprising *Sabriel, Lirael, Abhorsen, Clariel,* and a new book due out in late 2016; the Regency romance *Newt's Emerald*; and the science-fiction novels *Shade's Children* and *A Confusion of Princes*. His fantasy novels for children include *The Ragwitch*; the six books of *The Seventh Tower* sequence; *The Keys to the Kingdom* series; and the *Troubletwisters* books (with Sean Williams). His short fiction has appeared in numerous publications and has been collected in two volumes so far, *Across the Wall* and *To Hold the Bridge*.

More than five million copies of Nix's books have been sold around the world. His books have appeared on the bestseller lists of the *New York Times*, *Publishers Weekly*, the *Guardian*, and the *Australian*, and his work has been translated into forty-one languages. He lives in Sydney, Australia.

Shay Corsham Worsted
Garth Nix

THE YOUNG MAN came in one of the windows, because the back door had proved surprisingly tough. He'd kicked it a few times, without effect, before looking for an easier way to get in. The windows were barred, but the bars were rusted almost through, so he had no difficulty pulling them away. The window was locked as well, but he just smashed the glass with a half brick pried out of the garden wall. He didn't care about the noise. He knew there was only the old man in the house, the garden was large and screened by trees, and the evening traffic was streaming past on the road out front. That was plenty loud enough to cloak any noise he might make.

Or any quavering cries for help from the old man, thought the intruder, as he climbed through. He went to the back door first, intending to open it for a quick getaway, but it was deadlocked. More afraid of getting robbed than dying in a fire, thought the young man. That made it easier. He liked the frightened old people, the power he had over them with his youth and strength and anger.

When he turned around, the old man was standing behind him. Just standing there, not doing a thing. It was dim in the corridor, the only light a weak bulb hanging from the ceiling, its pallid glow falling on the bald head of the little man, the ancient slight figure in his brown cardigan and brown corduroy trousers and brown slippers, just a little old man that could be picked up and broken like a stick and then whatever pathetic treasures were in the house could be—

A little old man whose eyes were silver.

And what was in his hands?

Those gnarled hands had been empty, the intruder was sure of it, but now the old bloke held long blades, though he wasn't exactly holding the blades… they were growing, growing from his fingers, the flesh fusing together and turning silver…silver as those eyes!

The young man had turned half an inch towards the window and escape when the first of those silvery blades penetrated his throat, destroying his voice box, changing the scream that rose there to a dull, choking cough. The second blade went straight through his heart, back out, and through again.

Pock! Pock!

Blood geysered, but not on the old man's brown cardigan. He had moved back almost in the same instant as he struck and was now ten feet away, watching with those silver eyes as the young man fell writhing on the floor, his feet drumming for eighteen seconds before he became still.

The blades retreated, became fingers once again. The old man considered the body, the pooling blood, the mess.

"Shay Marazion Velvet," he said to himself, and walked to the spray of blood farthest from the body, head-high on the peeling wallpaper of green lilies. He poked out his tongue, which grew longer and became as silver as the blades.

He began to lick, tongue moving rhythmically, head tilted as required. There was no expression on his face, no sign of physical excitement. This was not some fetish.

He was simply cleaning up.

"You'll never guess who I saw walking up and down outside, Father," said Mary Shires, as she bustled in with her ludicrously enormous basket filled with the weekly tribute of home-made foods and little luxuries that were generally unwanted and wholly unappreciated by her father, Sir David Shires.

"Who?" grunted Sir David. He was sitting at his kitchen table, scrawling notes on the front page of the *Times*, below the big headlines with the latest from the war with Argentina over the Falklands, and enjoying the sun that was briefly flooding the whole room through the open doors to the garden.

"That funny little Mister Shea," said Mary, putting the basket down on the table.

Sir David's pencil broke. He let it fall and concentrated on keeping his hand still, on making his voice sound normal. He shouldn't be surprised, he told himself. It was why he was here, after all. But after so many years, even though every day he told himself this could be *the* day, it was a terrible, shocking surprise.

"Really, dear?" he said. He thought his voice sounded mild enough. "Going down to the supermarket like he normally does, I suppose? Getting his bread and milk?"

"No, that's just the thing," said Mary. She took out a packet of some kind of biscuit and put it in front of her father. "These are very good. Oatmeal and some kind of North African citrus. You'll like them."

"Mister Shea," prompted Sir David.

"Oh, yes. He's just walking backwards and forwards along the footpath from his house to the corner. Backwards and forwards! I suppose he's gone ga-ga. He's old enough. He must be ninety if he's a day, surely?"

She looked at him, without guile, both of them knowing he was eighty himself. But not going ga-ga, thank god, even if his knees were weak reeds and he couldn't sleep at night, remembering things that he had forced himself to forget in his younger days.

But Shay was much older than ninety, thought Sir David. Shay was much, much older than that.

He pushed his chair back and stood up.

"I might go and...and have a word with the old chap," he said carefully. "You stay here, Mary."

"Perhaps I should come—"

"No!"

He grimaced, acknowledging he had spoken with too much emphasis. He didn't want to alarm Mary. But then again, in the worst case...no, not the worst case, but in a quite plausible minor escalation...

"In fact, I think you should go out the back way and get home," said Sir David.

"Really, Father, why on—"

"Because I am ordering you to," snapped Sir David. He still had the voice, the tone that expected to be obeyed, deployed very rarely with the family, but quite often to the many who had served under him, first in the Navy and then for considerably longer in the Department, where he had ended up as the deputy chief. Almost fifteen years gone, but it wasn't the sort of job where you ever completely left, and the command voice was the least of the things that had stayed with him.

Mary sniffed, but she obeyed, slamming the garden gate on her way out. It would be a few years yet, he thought, before she began to question everything he did, perhaps start bringing brochures for retirement homes along with her special biscuits and herbal teas she believed to be good for reducing the chance of dementia.

Dementia. There was an apposite word. He'd spent some time thinking he might be suffering from dementia or some close cousin of it, thirty years ago, in direct connection to "funny old Mister Shea." Who was not at all funny, not in any sense of the word. They had all wondered if they were demented, for a time.

He paused near his front door, wondering for a moment if he should make the call first, or even press his hand against the wood paneling just so, and flip it open to take out the .38 Colt police revolver cached there. He had a 9mm Browning automatic upstairs, but a revolver was better for a cached weapon. You wouldn't want to bet your life on magazine springs in a weapon that had sat too long. He checked all his armament every month, but still…a revolver was more certain.

But automatic or revolver, neither would be any use. He'd learned that before, from direct observation, and had been lucky to survive. Very lucky, because the other two members of the team hadn't had the fortune to slip in the mud and hit themselves on the head and be forced to lie still. They'd gone in shooting, and kept shooting, unable to believe the evidence of their eyes, until it was too late…

Sir David grimaced. This was one of the memories he'd managed to push aside for a long, long time. But like all the others, it wasn't far below the surface. It didn't take much to bring it up, that afternoon in 1953, the Department's secure storage on the fringe of RAF Bicester…

He did take a walking stick out of the stand. A solid bog oak stick, with a pommel of bronze worked in the shape of a spaniel's head. Not for use as a weapon, but simply because he didn't walk as well as he once did. He couldn't afford a fall now. Or at any time really, but particularly not now.

The sun was still shining outside. It was a beautiful day, the sky as blue as a bird's egg, with hardly a cloud in sight. It was the kind of day you only saw in films, evoking some fabulous summertime that never really existed, or not for more than half an hour at a time.

It was a good day to die, if it came to that, if you were eighty and getting tired of the necessary props to a continued existence. The medicines and interventions, the careful calculation of probabilities before anything resembling activity, calculations that Sir David would never have undertaken at a younger age.

He swung out onto the footpath, a military stride, necessarily adjusted by age and a back that would no longer entirely straighten. He paused by the kerb and looked left and right, surveying the street, head back, shoulders close to straight, sandy eyebrows raised, hair no longer quite so regulation short, catching a little of the breeze, the soft breeze that added to the day's delights.

Shay was there, as Mary had said. It was wearing the same clothes as always, the brown cardigan and corduroy. They'd put fifty pairs in the safe house, at the beginning, uncertain whether Shay would buy more or not, though its daily purchase of bread, milk and other basics was well established. It could mimic human behavior very well.

It looked like a little old man, a bald little man of some great age. Wrinkled skin, hooded eyes, head bent as if the neck could no longer entirely support the weight of years. But Sir David knew it didn't always move like an old man. It could move fluidly, like an insect, faster than you ever thought at first sighting.

Right now Shay was walking along the footpath, away from Sir David. Halfway to the corner, it turned back. It must have seen him, but as usual, it gave no outward sign of recognition or reception. There would be no such sign, until it decided to do whatever it was going to do next.

Sir David shuffled forward. Best to get it over with. His hand was already sweating, slippery on the bronze dog handle of his stick, his heart hammering in a fashion bound to be at odds with a cardio-pulmonary system past its best. He knew the feeling well, though it had been an age since he'd felt it more than fleetingly.

Fear. Unalloyed fear, that must be conquered, or he could do nothing, and that was not an option. Shay had broken free of its programming. It could be about to do anything, anything at all, perhaps reliving some of its more minor exploits like the Whitechapel murders of 1888, or a major one like the massacre at Slapton Sands in 1944.

Or something greater still.

Not that Sir David was sure he *could* do anything. He'd only ever been told two of the command phrases, and lesser ones at that, a pair of two-word groups. They were embossed on his mind, bright as new brass. But it was never known exactly what they meant, or how Shay understood them.

There was also the question of which command to use. Or to try and use both command phrases, though that might somehow have the effect of one of the four-word command groups. An unknown effect, very likely fatal to Sir David and everyone for miles, perhaps more.

It was not inconceivable that whatever he said in the next two minutes might doom everyone in London, or even the United Kingdom.

Perhaps even the world.

The first command would be best, Sir David thought, watching Shay approach. They were out in public, the second would attract attention, besides its other significant drawback. Public attention was anathema to Sir David, even in such dire circumstances. He straightened his tie unconsciously as he thought about publicity. It was a plain green tie, as his suit was an inconspicuous grey flannel, off the rack. No club or regimental ties for Sir David, no identifying signet rings, no ring, no earring, no tattoos, no unusual facial hair. He worked to look a type that had once been excellent camouflage, the retired military officer. It still worked, though less well, there being fewer of the type to hide amongst. Perhaps the Falklands War would help in this regard.

Shay was drawing nearer, walking steadily, perfectly straight. Sir David peered at it. Were its eyes silver? If they were, it would be too late. All bets off, end of story. But the sun was too bright, Sir David's own sight was not what it once was. He couldn't tell if Shay's eyes were silver.

"Shay Risborough Gabardine," whispered Sir David. Ludicrous words, but proven by trial and error, trial by combat, death by error. The name it apparently gave itself, a station on the Great Western Line, and a type of fabric. Not words you'd ever expect to find together, there was its safety, the cleverness of Isambard Kingdom Brunel showing through. Though not as clever as how IKB had got Shay to respond to the words in the first place. So clever that no one else had worked out how it had been done, not in the three different attempts over more than a hundred years. Attempts to try to change or expand the creature's lexicon, each attempt another litany of mistakes and many deaths. And after each such trial, the fear that had led to its being shut away. Locked underground the last time, and then the chance rediscovery in 1953 and the foolishness that had led it to being put away here, parked and forgotten.

Except by Sir David.

Shay was getting very close now. Its face looked innocuous enough. A little vacant, a man not too bright perhaps, or very short of sleep. Its skin was pale today, matching Sir David's own, but he knew it could change that in an instant. Skin colour, height, apparent age, gender…all of these could be changed by Shay, though it mostly appeared as it was right now.

Small and innocuous, old and tired. Excellent camouflage among humans.

Ten paces, nine paces, eight paces…the timing had to be right. The command had to be said in front of its face, without error, clear and precise—

"Shay Risborough Gabardine," barked Sir David, shivering in place, his whole body tensed to receive a killing blow.

Shay's eyes flashed silver. He took half a step forward, putting him inches away from Sir David, and stopped. There was a terrible stillness, the world perched on the brink. Then it turned on its heel, crossed the road and went back into its house. The old house, opposite Sir David's, that no one but Shay had set foot in for thirty years.

Sir David stood where he was for several minutes, shaking. Finally he quelled his shivering enough to march back inside his own house, where he ignored the phone on the hall table, choosing instead to open a drawer in his study to lift out a chunkier, older thing that had no dial of any kind, push-button or rotary. He held the handset to his head and waited.

There were a series of clicks and whines and beeps, the sound of disparate connections working out how they might after all get together. Finally a sharp, quick male voice answered on the other end.

"Yes."

"Case Shay Zulu," said Sir David. There was a pause. He could hear the flipping of pages, as the operator searched through the ready book.

"Is there more?" asked the operator.

"What!" exploded Sir David. "Case Shay Zulu!"

"How do you spell it?"

Sir David's lip curled almost up to his nose, but he pulled it back.

"S-H-A-Y," he spelled out. "Z-U-L-U."

"I can spell Zulu," said the operator, affronted. "There's still nothing."

"Look up my workname," said Sir David. "Arthur Brooks."

There was tapping now, the sound of a keyboard. He'd heard they were using computers more and more throughout the Department, not just for the boffins in the back rooms.

"Ah, I see…I've got you now, sir," said the operator. At least there was a "sir," now.

"Get someone competent to look up Shay Zulu and report my communication at once to the duty officer with instruction to relay it to the Chief," ordered Sir David. "I want a call back in five minutes."

The call came in ten minutes, ten minutes Sir David spent looking out his study window, watching the house across the road. It was 11 a.m., too late for Shay to go to the supermarket like it had done every day for the last thirty years. Sir David wouldn't know if it had returned to its previous safe routine until 10:30 a.m. tomorrow. Or earlier, if Shay was departing on some different course…

The insistent ringing recalled him to the phone.

"Yes."

"Sir David? My name is Angela Terris, I'm the duty officer at present. We're a bit at sea here. We can't find Shay Zulu in the system at all—What was that?"

Sir David had let out a muffled cry, his knuckles jammed against his mouth.

"Nothing, nothing," he said, trying to think. "The paper files, the old records to 1977, you can look there. But the important thing is the book, we…I must have the notebook from the Chief's safe, a small green leather book embossed on the cover with the gold initials IKB."

"The Chief's not here right now," said Angela brightly. "This Falklands thing, you know. He's briefing the cabinet. Is it urgent?"

"Of course it's urgent!" barked Sir David, regretting it even as he spoke, remembering when old Admiral Puller had called up long after retirement, concerned about a suspicious new postman, and how they had laughed on the Seventh Floor. "Look, find Case Shay Zulu and you'll see what I mean."

"Is it something to do with the Soviets, Sir David? Because we're really getting on reasonably well with them at the moment—"

"No, no, it's nothing to do with the Soviets," said Sir David. He could hear the tone in her voice, he remembered using it himself when he had taken Admiral Fuller's call. It was the calming voice that meant no immediate action, a routine request to some functionary to investigate further in days, or even weeks, purely as a courtesy to the old man. He had to do something that would make her act, there had to be some lever.

"I'm afraid it's something to do with the Service itself," he said. "Could be very, very embarrassing. Even now. I need that book to deal with it."

"Embarrassing as in likely to be of media interest, Sir David?" asked Angela.

"Very much so," said Sir David heavily.

"I'll see what I can do," said Angela.

"We were really rather surprised to find the Department owns a safe house that isn't on the register," said the young, nattily dressed and borderline rude young man who came that afternoon. His name, or at least the one he had supplied, was Redmond. "Finance were absolutely delighted, it must be worth close to half a million pounds now, a huge place like that. Fill a few black holes with that once we sell it. On the quiet, of course, as you say it would be very embarrassing if the media get hold of this little real estate venture."

"Sell it?" asked Sir David. "Sell it! Did you only find the imprest accounts, not the actual file? Don't you understand? The only thing that stops Shay from running amok is routine, a routine that is firmly embedded in and around that house! Sell the house and you unleash the...the beast!"

"Beast, Sir David?" asked Redmond. He suppressed a yawn and added, "Sounds rather Biblical. I expect we can find a place for this Shea up at Exile House. I daresay they'll dig his file up eventually, qualify him as a former employee."

They could find a place for Sir David too, were the unspoken words. Exile House, last stop for those with total disability suffered on active service, crippled by torture, driven insane from stress, shot through both knees and elbows. There were many ways to arrive at Exile House.

"Did you talk to the Chief?" asked Sir David. "Did you ask about the book marked 'IKB'?"

"Chief's very busy," said Redmond. "There's a war on you know. Even if it is only a little one. Look, why don't I go over and have a chat to old Shea, get a feel for the place, see if there's anything else that might need sorting?"

"If you go over there you introduce another variable," said Sir David, as patiently as he could. "Right now, I've got Shay to return to its last state, which may or may not last until ten-thirty tomorrow morning, when it goes and gets its bread and milk, as it has done for the last thirty years. But if you disrupt it again, then who knows what will happen."

"I see, I see," said Redmond. He nodded as if he had completely understood. "Bit of a mental case, hey? Well, I did bring a couple of the boys in blue along just in case."

"Boys in blue!"

Sir David was almost apoplectic. He clutched at Redmond's sleeve, but the young man effortlessly withdrew himself and sauntered away.

"Back in half a mo'," he called out cheerfully.

Sir David tried to chase him down, but by the time he got to the front door it was shut in his face. He scrabbled at the weapon cache, pushing hard on a panel till he realized it was the wrong one. By the time he had the revolver in his hand and had wrestled the door open, Redmond was already across the road, waving to the two policemen in the panda car to follow him. They got out quickly, large men in blue, putting their hats on as they strode after the young agent.

"Not even Special Branch," muttered Sir David. He let the revolver hang by his side. What could he do with it anyway? He couldn't shoot Redmond, or the policemen.

Perhaps, he thought bleakly, he could shoot himself. That would bring them back, delay the knock on the door opposite…but it would only be a delay. And if he was killed, and if they couldn't find Brunel's book, then the other command words would be lost.

Redmond went up the front steps two at a time, past the faded sign that said, "Hawkers and Salesmen Not Welcome, Beware of the Vicious Dog," and the one underneath it that had been added a year after the first, "No Liability for Injury or Death, You Have Been Warned."

Sir David blinked, narrowing his eyes against the sunshine that was still streaming down, flooding the street. It was just like the afternoon, that afternoon in '43 when the sun had broken through after days of fog and ice, but even though it washed across him on the bridge of his frigate he couldn't feel it, he could only see the light, he was so frozen from the cold Atlantic days the sunshine couldn't touch him, there was no warmth that could reach him…

He felt colder now. Redmond was knocking on the door. Hammering on the door. Sir David choked a little on his own spit, apprehension rising. There was a chance Shay wouldn't answer, and the door was very heavy, those two policemen couldn't kick it down, there would be more delay—

The door opened. There was the flash of silver, and Redmond fell down the steps, blood geysering from his neck as if some newfangled watering system had suddenly switched on beside him, drawing water from a rusted tank.

A blur of movement followed. The closer policeman spun about, as if suddenly inspired to dance, only his head was tumbling from his shoulders to dance apart from him. The surviving policeman, that is the policeman who had survived the first three seconds of contact with Shay, staggered backwards and started to turn around to run.

He took one step before he too was pierced through with a silver spike, his feet taking him only to the gutter where he lay down to die.

Sir David went back inside, leaving the door open. He went to his phone in the hall and called his daughter. She answered on the fourth ring. Sir David's hand was so sweaty he had to grip the plastic tightly, so the phone didn't slip from his grip.

"Mary? I want you to call Peter and your girls and tell them to get across the Channel now. France, Belgium, doesn't matter. No, wait, Terence is in Newcastle, isn't he? Tell him...listen to me...he can get the ferry to Stavanger. Listen! There is going to be a disaster here. It doesn't matter what kind! I haven't gone crazy, you know who I know. They have to get out of the country and across the water! Just go!"

Sir David hung up. He wasn't sure Mary would do as he said. He wasn't even sure that the sea would stop Shay. That was one of the theories, never tested, that it wouldn't or couldn't cross a large body of water. Brunel almost certainly knew, but his more detailed papers had been lost. Only the code book had survived. At least until recently.

He went to the picture window in his study. It had been installed on his retirement, when he'd moved here to keep an eye on Shay. It was a big window, taking up the place of two old Georgian multi-paned affairs, and it had an excellent view of the street.

There were four bodies in full view now. The latest addition was a very young man. Had been a young man. The proverbial innocent bystander, in the wrong place at the wrong time. A car sped by, jerking suddenly into the other lane as the driver saw the corpses and the blood.

Shay walked into the street and looked up at Sir David's window.

Its eyes were silver.

The secure phone behind Sir David rang. He retreated, still watching Shay, and picked it up.

"Yes."

"Sir David? Angela Terris here. The police are reporting multiple 999 calls, apparently there are people—"

"Yes. Redmond and the two officers are dead. I told him not to go, but he did. Shay is active now. I tried to tell you."

Shay was moving, crossing the road.

"Sir David!"

"Find the book," said Sir David wearily. "That's the only thing that can help you now. Find the leather book marked 'IKB.' It's in the Chief's safe."

Shay was on Sir David's side of the street, moving left, out of sight.

"The Chief's office was remodeled last year," said Angela Terris. "The old safe…I don't know—"

Sir David laughed bitter laughter and dropped the phone.

There was the sound of footsteps in the hall.

Footsteps that didn't sound quite right.

Sir David stood at attention and straightened his tie. Time to find out if the other command did what it was supposed to do. It would be out of his hands then. If it worked, Shay would kill him and then await further instructions for twenty-four hours. Either they'd find the book or they wouldn't, but he would have done his best.

As always.

Shay came into the room. It didn't look much like an old man now. It was taller, and straighter, and its head was bigger. So was its mouth.

"Shay Corsham Worsted," said Sir David.

Nathan Ballingrud is the author of *North American Lake Monsters: Stories* and *The Visible Filth*, a novella from This Is Horror.

His work has appeared in numerous Year's Best anthologies, and he has twice won the Shirley Jackson Award. He lives with his daughter in Asheville, North Carolina.

The Atlas of Hell
Nathan Ballingrud

"HE DIDN'T EVEN know he was dead. I had just shot this guy in the head and he's still standing there giving me shit. Telling me what a big badass he works for, telling me I'm going to be sorry I was born. You know. Blood pouring down his face. He can't even see anymore, it's in his goddamn eyes. So I look down at the gun in my hand and I'm like, what the fuck, you know? Is this thing working or what? And I'm starting to think maybe this asshole is right, maybe I just stepped into something over my head. I mean, I feel a twinge of real fear. My hair is standing up like a cartoon. So I look at the dude and I say, 'Lay down! You're dead! I shot you!'"

There's a bourbon and ice sitting on the end-table next to him. He takes a sip from it and puts it back down, placing it in its own wet ring. He's very precise about it.

"I guess he just had to be told, because as soon as I say it? Boom. Drops like a fucking tree."

I don't know what he's expecting from me here. My leg is jumping up and down with nerves. I can't make it stop. I open my mouth to say something but a nervous laugh spills out instead.

He looks at me incredulously, and cocks his head. Patrick is a big guy; but not doughy, like me. There's muscle packed beneath all that flesh. He looks like fists of meat sewn together and given a suit of clothes. "Why are you laughing?"

"I don't know, man. I don't know. I thought it was supposed to be a funny story."

"No, you demented fuck. That's not a funny story. What's the matter with you?"

It's pushing midnight, and we're sitting on a coffee-stained couch in a darkened corner of the grubby little bookstore I own in New Orleans, about a block off Magazine Street. My name is Jack Oleander. I keep a small studio apartment overhead, but when Patrick started banging on my door half an hour ago I took him down here instead. I don't want him in my home. That he's here at all is a very bad sign.

The bookstore is called Oleander. I sell used books, for the most part, and I serve a very sparse clientele: mostly students and disaffected youth, their little hearts love-drunk on Kierkegaard or Salinger. That suits me just fine. Most of the books have been sitting on their shelves for years, and I feel like I've fostered a kind of relationship with them. A part of me is sorry whenever one of them leaves the nest.

The bookstore doesn't pay the bills, of course. The books and documents I sell in the back room take care of that. Few people know about the back room, but those who do pay very well indeed. Patrick's boss is one of those people. We parted under strained circumstances a year or so ago. I was never supposed to see him again. His presence here makes me afraid, and fear makes me reckless.

"Well if it's not a funny story, then what kind of story is it? Because we've been drinking here for twenty minutes and you haven't mentioned business even once. If you want to trade war stories it's going to have to wait for another time."

He gives me a sour look and picks up his glass, peering into it as he swirls the ice around. He'd always hated me, and I knew that his presence here pleased him no more than it did me.

"You don't make it easy to be your friend," he says.

"I didn't know we were friends."

The muscles in his jaw clench.

"You're wasting my time, Patrick. I know you're just the muscle, so maybe you don't understand this, but the work I do in the back room takes up a lot of energy. So sleep is valuable to me. You've sat on my couch and drunk my whiskey and burned away almost half an hour beating around the bush. I don't know how much more of this I can take."

He looks at me. He has his work face on now, the one a lot of guys see just before the lights go out. That's good; I want him in work mode. It makes him focus. The trick now, though, is to keep him on the shy side of violence. You have to play these guys like marionettes. I got pretty good at it back in the day.

"You want to watch that," he says. "You want to watch that attitude."

I put my hands out, palms forward. "Hey," I say.

"I come to you in friendship. I come to you in respect."

This is bullshit, but whatever. It's time to settle him down. These guys are such fragile little flowers. "Hey. I'm sorry. Really. I haven't been sleeping much. I'm tired, and it makes me stupid."

"That's a bad trait. So wake up and listen to me. I told you that story for two reasons. One, to stop you from saying dumb shit like you just did. Make you remember who you're dealing with. I can see it didn't work. I can see maybe I was being too subtle."

"Patrick, really. I—"

"If you interrupt me again I will break your right hand. The second reason I told you that story is to let you know that I've seen some crazy things in my life, so when I tell you this new thing scares the shit out of me, maybe you'll listen to what the fuck I'm saying."

He stops there, staring hard at me. After a couple seconds of this, I figure it's okay to talk.

"You have my full attention. This is from Eugene?"

"You know this is from Eugene. Why else would I drag myself over here?"

"Patrick, I wish you'd relax. I'm sorry I made you mad. You want another drink? Let me pour you another drink."

I can see the rage still coiling in his eyes, and I'm starting to think I pushed him too hard. I'm starting to wonder how fast I can run. But then he settles back onto the couch and a smile settles over his face. It doesn't look natural there. "Jesus, you have a mouth. How does a guy like you get away with having a mouth like that?" He shakes the ice in his glass. "Yeah, go ahead. Pour me another one. Let's smoke a peace pipe."

I pour us both some more. He slugs it back in one deep swallow and holds his glass out for more. I give it to him. He seems to be relaxing.

"All right, okay. There's this guy. Creepy little grifter named Tobias George. He's one of those little vermin always crawling through the city, getting into shit, fucking up his own life, you don't even notice these guys. You know how it is."

"I do." I also know the name, but I don't tell him that.

"Only reason we know about him at all is because sometimes he'll run a little scheme of his own, kick a percentage back to Eugene, it's all good. Well one day this prick catches a case of ambition. He robs one of Eugene's poker games, makes off with a lot of money. Suicidal. Who knows what got into the guy. Some big dream climbed up his butt and opened him like an umbrella. We go hunting for him but he disappears. We get word he went further south, disappeared into the bayou. Like, not to Port Fourchon or some shit, but literally on a goddamn boat into the swamp. Eugene is pissed, and you know how he is, he jumps and shouts for a few days, but eventually he says fuck it. We're not gonna go wrestle alligators for him. After a while we just figured he died out there. You know."

"But he didn't."

"That he did not. We catch wind of him a few months later. He's in a whole new ballgame. He's selling artifacts pulled from Hell. And he's making a lot of money doing it."

"It's another scam," I say, knowing full well it isn't.

"It's not."

"How do you know?"

"Don't worry about it. We know."

"A guy owes money and won't pay. That sounds more like your thing than mine, Patrick."

"Yeah, don't worry about that either. I got it covered when the time comes. I won't go into the details, 'cause they don't matter, but what it comes down to is Eugene wants his own way into the game. Once this punk is put in the ground, he wants to keep this market alive. We happen to know Tobias has a book that he uses for this set-up. An atlas that tells him how to access this shit. We want it, and we want to know how it works. And that's *your* thing, Jack."

I feel something cold spill through my guts. "That's not the deal we had."

"What can I tell you."

"No. I told…" My throat is dry. My leg is bouncing again. "Eugene told me we were through. He told me that. He's breaking his promise."

"That mouth again." Patrick finishes his drink and stands. "Come on. You can tell him that yourself, see how it goes over."

"Now? It's the middle of the night!"

"Don't worry, you won't be disturbing him. He don't sleep too well lately either."

I've lived here my whole life. Grew up just a regular fat-white-kid schlub, decent parents, a ready-made path to the gray fields of middle-class servitude. But I went off the rails at some point. I was seduced by old books. I wanted to live out my life in a fog of parchment dust and old glue. I apprenticed myself to a bookbinder, a gnarled old Cajun named Rene Aucoin, who turned out to be a fading necromancer with a nice side business refurbishing old grimoires. He found in me an eager student, which eventually led to my tenure as a librarian at the Camouflaged Library at the Ursulines Academy. It was when Eugene and his crew got involved, leading to a bloody confrontation with a death cult obsessed with the Damocles Scroll, that I left the Academy and began my career as a book thief. I worked for Eugene for five years before we had our falling out. When I left, we both knew it was for good.

Eugene has a bar up in Midcity, far away from the T-shirt shops, the fetish dens and goth hangouts of the French Quarter, far away too from the more respectable veneer of the Central Business and Garden Districts. Midcity is a place where you can do what you want. Patrick drives me up Canal and parks out front. He leads me up the stairs and inside, where the blast of cold air is a relief from a heat which does not relent even at night. A jukebox is playing something stale, and four or five ghostlike figures nest at the bar. They do not turn around as we pass through. Patrick guides me downstairs, to Eugene's office.

Before I even reach the bottom of the stairs, Eugene starts talking to me.

"Hey fat boy! Here comes the fat boy!"

No cover model himself, he comes around his desk with his arms outstretched, what's left of his gray hair combed in long, spindly fingers over the expanse of his scalp. Drink has made a red, doughy wreckage of his face. His chest is sunken in, like something inside has collapsed and he's falling inward. He puts his hands on me in greeting, and I try not to flinch.

"Look at you. Look at you. You look good, Jack."

"So do you, Eugene."

The office is clean, uncluttered. There's a desk and a few padded chairs, a couch on the far wall underneath a huge Michalopoulos painting. Across from the desk is a minibar and a door which leads to the back alley. Mardi Gras masks are arranged behind his desk like a congress of spirits. Eugene is a New Orleans boy right down to his tapping toes, and he buys into every shabby lie the city ever told about itself.

"I hear you got a girl now. What's her name, Locky? Lick-me?"

"Lakshmi." This is already going badly. "Come on, Eugene. Let's not go there."

"Listen to him now. Calling the shots. All independent, all grown up now. Patrick give you any trouble? Sometimes he gets carried away."

Patrick doesn't blink. His role fulfilled, he's become a tree.

"No. No trouble at all. It was like old times."

"Hopefully not too much like old times, huh?" He sits behind his desk, gestures for me to take a seat. Patrick pours a couple of drinks and hands one to each of us, then retreats behind me.

"I guess I'm just trying to figure out what I'm doing here, Eugene. Someone's not paying you. Isn't that what you have guys like him for?"

Eugene settles back, sips from his drink, and studies me. "Let's not play coy, Jack. Okay? Don't pretend you don't already know about Tobias. Don't insult my intelligence."

"I know about Tobias," I say.

"Tell me what you know."

I can't get comfortable in my chair. I feel like there are chains around my chest. I make one last effort. "Eugene. We had a deal."

"Are you having trouble hearing me? Should I raise my voice?"

"He started selling two months ago. He had a rock. It was about the size of a tennis ball but it was heavy as a television set. Everybody thought he was full of shit. They were laughing at him. It sold for a little bit of money. Not much. But somebody out there liked what they saw. Word got around. He sold a two-inch piece of charred bone next. That went for a lot more."

"I bought that bone."

"Oh," I say. "Shit."

"Do you know why?"

"No, Eugene, of course I don't."

"Don't 'of course' me. I don't know what you know and what you don't. You're a slimy piece of filth, Jack. You're a human cockroach. I can't trust you. So don't get smart."

"I'm sorry. I didn't mean it like that."

"He had the nerve to contact me directly. He wanted me to know what he was offering before he put it on the market. Give me first chance. Jack, it's from my son. It's part of a thigh bone from my son."

I can't seem to see straight. The blood has rushed to my head, and I feel dizzy. I clamp my hands on the armrests of the chair so I can feel something solid. "How...how do you know?"

"There's people for that. Don't ask dumb questions. I am very much not in the mood for dumb questions."

"Okay."

"Your thing is books, so that's why you're here. We tracked him to this old shack in the bayou. You're going to get the book."

I feel panic skitter through me. "You want me to go there?"

"Patrick's going with you."

"That's not what I do, Eugene!"

"Bullshit! You're a thief. You do this all the time. Patrick there can barely read a *People* magazine without breaking a sweat. You're going."

"Just have Patrick bring it back! You don't need me for this."

Eugene stares at me.

"Come on," I say. "You gave me your word."

I don't even see Patrick coming. His hand is on the back of my neck and he slams my face onto the desk hard enough to crack an ashtray underneath my cheekbone. My glass falls out of my hand and I hear the ice thump onto the carpet. He keeps me pinned to the desk. He wraps his free hand around my throat. I can't catch my breath.

Eugene leans in, his hands behind his back, like he's examining something curious and mildly revolting. "Would you like to see him? Would you like to see my son?"

I pat Patrick's hand; it's weirdly intimate. I shake my head. I try to make words. My vision is starting to fry around the edges. Dark loops spool into the world.

Finally, Eugene says, "Let him go."

Patrick releases me. I slide off the desk and land hard, dragging the broken ashtray with me, covering myself in ash and spent cigarette butts. I roll onto my side, choking.

Eugene puts his hand on my shoulder. "Hey, Jack, you okay? You all right down there? Get up. God damn you're a drama queen. Get the fuck up already."

It takes a few minutes. When I'm sitting up again, Patrick hands me a napkin to clean the blood off my face. I don't look at him. There's nothing

I can do. No point in feeling a goddamn thing about it.

"When do I leave?" I say.

"What the hell," Eugene says. "How about right now?"

We experience dawn as a rising heat and a slow bleed of light through the cypress and the Spanish moss, riding in an airboat through the swamp a good thirty miles south of New Orleans. Patrick and I are riding up front while an old man more leather than flesh guides us along some unseeable path. Our progress stirs movement from the local fauna—snakes, turtles, muskrats—and I'm constantly jumping at some heavy splash. I imagine a score of alligators gliding through the water beneath us, tracking our movement with yellow, saurian eyes. The airboat wheels around a copse of trees into a watery clearing, and I half expect to see a brontosaurus wading in the shallows.

Instead I see a row of huge, bobbing purple flowers, each with a bleached human face in the center, mouths gaping and eyes palely blind. The sight of them shocks me into silence; our guide fixes his stare on the horizon, refusing even to acknowledge anything out of the ordinary. Eyes perch along the tops of reeds; great kites of flesh stretch between tree limbs; one catches a mild breeze from our passage and skates serenely through the air, coming at last to a gentle landing on the water, where it folds in on itself and sinks into the murk.

Our guide points, and I see a shack: a small, single-room architectural catastrophe, perched on the dubious shore and extending over the water on short stilts. A skiff is tied to a front porch which doubles as a small dock. It seems to be the only method of travel to or from the place. A filthy Rebel flag hangs over the entrance in lieu of a door. At the moment, it's pulled to the side and a man I assume is Tobias George is standing there, naked but for a pair of shorts that hang precariously from his narrow hips. He's all bone and gristle. His face tells me nothing as we glide in toward the dock.

Patrick stands before we connect, despite a word of caution from our guide. He has some tough-guy greeting halfway out of his mouth when the airboat's edge lightly taps the dock, nearly spilling him into the swamp, arms pinwheeling.

Tobias is unaffected by the display, but our guide is easy with a laugh and chooses not to hold back.

Patrick recovers himself and puts both hands on the dock, proceeding to crawl out of the boat like a child learning to walk. I'm grateful to God for the sight of it.

Tobias makes no move to help.

I take my time climbing out. "You wait right here," I tell the guide.

"Oh, *wye*," he says, shutting down the engine and fishing a pack of smokes from his shirt.

"What're you guys doing here?" Tobias says. He hasn't looked at me once but he can't peel his gaze from Patrick. He knows what Patrick's all about.

"Tobias, you crazy bastard. What the hell do you think you're doing?"

Tobias turns around and goes back inside, the Rebel flag falling closed behind him. "Come on in I guess."

We follow him inside, where it's even hotter. The air doesn't move in here, probably hasn't moved in twenty years, and it carries the sharp tang of marijuana. Dust motes hang suspended in spears of light, coming in through a window covered over in ratty, bug-smeared plastic. The room is barely furnished: there's a single mattress pushed against the wall to our left, a cheap collapsible table with a plastic folding chair, and a chest of drawers. Next to the bed is a camping cooker with a little sauce pot and some cans of Sterno. On the table is a small pile of dull green buds, with some rolling papers and a Zippo.

There's a door flush against the back wall. I take a few steps in its direction and I can tell right away that there's some bad news behind it. The air spoils when I get close, coating the back of my throat with a greasy, evil film that feels like it seeps right into the meat. Violent fantasies sprout along my cortex like a little vine of tumors. I try to keep my face still, as I imagine coring the eyeballs out of both these guys with a grapefruit spoon.

"Stay on that side of the room, Patrick," I say. I don't need him feeling this.

"What? Why?"

"Trust me. This is why you brought me."

Tobias casts a glance at me now, finally sensing some purpose behind my presence. He's good, though: I still can't figure his reaction.

"Y'all here to kill me?" he says.

Patrick already has his gun in hand. It's pointed at the floor. His eyes are fixed on Tobias and he seems to be weighing something in his mind. I can tell that whatever is behind that door is already working its influence on him. It has its grubby little fingers in his brain and it's pulling dark things out of it. "That depends on you," he says. "Eugene wants to talk to you."

"Yeah, that's not going to happen."

The violence in this room is alive and crawling. I realize, suddenly, why he stays stoned. I figure it's time we get to the point. "We want the book, Tobias."

"What? Who are you?" He looks at Patrick. "What's he talking about?"

"You know what he's talking about. Go get the book."

"There is no book!"

He looks genuinely bewildered, and that worries me. I don't know if I can go back to Eugene without a book. I'm about to ask him what's in the back room when I hear a creak in the wood beyond the hanging flag and someone pulls it aside, flooding the shack with light. I spin around and Patrick already has his gun raised, looking spooked.

The man standing in the doorway is framed by the sun: a black shape against the sun, a negative space. He's tall and slender, his hair like a spray of light around his head. I think for a moment that I can smell it burning. He steps into the shack and you can tell there's something wrong with him, though it's hard to figure just what. Some malformation of the aura, tele-graphing a warning blast straight to the root of my brain. To look at him, as he steps into the shack and trades direct sunlight for the filtered illumina-tion shared by the rest of us, he seems tired and gaunt but ultimately not unlike any other poverty-wracked country boy, and yet my skin ripples at his approach. I feel my lip curl and I have to concentrate to keep the revul-sion from my face.

"Toby?" he says. His voice is young and uninflected. Normal. "I think my brother's on his way back. Who are these guys?"

"Hey, Johnny," Tobias says, looking at him over my shoulder. He's plainly nervous now, and although his focus stays on Johnny, his attention seems to radiate in all directions, like a man wondering where the next hit is coming from.

I could have told him that.

Fear turns to meanness in a guy like Patrick, and he reacts according to the dictates of his kind: he shoots.

It's one shot, quick and clean. Patrick is a professional. The sound of the gun concusses the air in the little shack and the bullet passes through Johnny's skull before I even have time to wince at the noise.

I blink. I can't hear anything beyond a high-pitched whine. I see Patrick standing still, looking down the length of his raised arm with a flat, dead expression. It's his true face. I see Tobias drop to one knee, his hands over his ears and his mouth working as though he's shouting something; and I see Johnny, too, still standing in the doorway, as unmoved by the bullet's passage through his skull as though it had been nothing more than a disappointing argument. Dark clots of brain meat are splashed across the flag behind him.

He looks from Patrick to Tobias and when he speaks I can barely hear him above the ringing in my head. "What should I do?" he says.

I step forward and gently push Patrick's arm down.

"Are you shitting me?" he says, staring at Johnny.

"Patrick," I say.

"Am I fucking cursed? Is that it? I shot you in the face!"

The bullet-hole is a dime-sized wound in Johnny's right cheekbone. It leaks a single thread of blood. "Asshole," he says.

Tobias gets back to his feet, his arms stretched out to either side like he's trying to separate two imaginary boxers. "Will you just relax? Jesus Christ!" He guides Johnny to the little bed and sits him down, where he brushes the blond hair out of his face and inspects the bullet hole. Then he cranes his head around to examine the damage of the exit wound. "God damn it!" he says.

Johnny puts his own hand back there. "Oh man," he says.

I take a look. The whole back of his head is gone; now it's just a red bowl of spilled gore. What look like little blowing cinders are embedded in the mess, sending up coils of smoke. Most of Johnny's brains are splashed onto the flag hanging in the doorway.

"Patrick," I say. "Just be cool."

He's still in a fog. You can see him trying to arrange things in his head. "I need to kill them, Jack. I need to. I never felt it like this before. What's happening here?"

Tobias pipes up. "I had a job for this guy all lined up at The Fry Pit! Now what!"

"Tobias, I need you to shut up," I say, keeping my eyes on Patrick. "Patrick, are you hearing me?" It's taking a huge effort to maintain my own composure. I have an image of wresting the gun from his hand and hitting him with it until his skull breaks. Only the absolute impossibility of it keeps me from trying.

My question causes the shutters to close in his eyes. Whatever tatter of human impulse stirred him to try to explain himself to me, to grope for reason amidst the bloody carnage boiling in his head, is subsumed again in a dull professional menace. "Don't talk to me like that. I'm not a goddamn kid."

I turn to the others. The bed is now awash in blood. Tobias is working earnestly to mitigate the damage back there, but I can't imagine what it is he thinks he can do. Brain matter is gathered in a clump behind them; he seems to be scooping everything out. Johnny sits there forlornly, shoulders slumped. "I thought it would be better out here," he said. "Shit never ends."

"The atlas," I say.

"Fuck yourself," Tobias says.

I stride toward the closed door. If there's anything I need to know before I open it, I guess I'll just find out the hard way. A hot pulse of emotion blasts out at me as I touch the handle: fear, rage, a lust for carnage. It's overriding any sense of self-preservation I might have had. I wonder if a fire will pour through the door when it's opened, a furnace exhalation, and engulf us all. I find myself hoping for it.

Tobias shouts at me: "Don't!"

I pull it open.

A charred skull, oily smoke coiling from its fissures, is propped on a stool in an otherwise bare room no bigger than a closet. Black mold has grown over the stool, and is creeping up the walls. A live current jolts my brain. Time dislocates, jumping seconds like an old record, and the world moves in jerky, stop-motion lurches. A language is seeping from the skull—a viscous, cracked sound like breaking bones and molten rock. My eyes sting and I squeeze them shut. The skin on my face blisters.

"Shut it! Shut the door!"

Tobias is screaming, but whatever he's saying has no relation to me. It's as though I'm watching a play. Blood is leaking from his eyes. Patrick is grinning widely, his own eyes like bloody headlamps. He's violently twisting his right ear, working it like an apple stem. Johnny is sitting quietly, holding his gathered brains in his hands, rocking back and forth like an unhappy child. My upper arms are hurting, and it takes me a minute to realize that

I'm gouging them with my own fingernails. I can't make myself stop.

Outside a sound rolls across the swamp like a foghorn: a deep, answering bellow to the language of Hell spilling from the closet.

Tobias lunges past me and slams the door shut, immediately muffling the skull's effect. I stagger toward the chair but fall down hard before I make it, banging my shoulder against the table and knocking Tobias's drug paraphernalia all over the floor. Patrick makes a sound, half gasp and half sob, and leans back against the wall, cradling his savaged ear. The left side of his face is painted in blood. He's digging the heel of his hand into his right eye, like he's trying to rub something out of it.

"What the fuck was that!"

I think it's me who says that. Right now I can't be sure.

"That's your goddamn 'atlas,' you prick," Tobias says. He comes over to where I am and drops to the floor, scooping up the scattered buds and some papers. He begins to assemble a joint; his hands are shaking badly, so this takes some doing.

"A skull? The book is a skull?"

"No. It's a tongue inside the skull. Technically."

"What the Christ?"

"Just shut up a minute." He finishes the joint, lights it, and takes a long, deep pull. He passes it over to me.

For one surreal moment I feel like we're college buddies sitting in a dorm. It's like there's not a scorched, muttering skull in the next room, corroding the air around it. It's like there's not a man with a blown-out skull moping quietly on the bed. I start to laugh, and I haven't even had a toke.

He exhales explosively, the sweet smoke filling the air between us. "Take it, man. I'm serious. Trust me."

So I do. Almost immediately I feel an easing of the pressure in the room. The crackle of violent impulse, which I had ceased to even recognize, abates to a low thrum. My internal gauge ticks back down to highly frightened, which, in comparison to a moment before, feels like a monastic peace.

I gesture for Patrick to do the same.

"No. I don't pollute my body with that shit." He's touching his ear gingerly, trying to assess the damage.

"Patrick, last night you single-handedly killed half a bottle of ninety-proof bourbon. Let's have some perspective here."

He snatches it from me and drags hard on it, coughing it all back out so violently I think he might throw up.

Johnny laughs from his position on the bed. It's the first bright note he's sounded since his head came apart. "Amateur!"

I notice that Johnny's head seems to be changing shape. The shattered bone around the exit wound has smoothed over and extended upward an inch or so, like something growing. A tiny twig of bone has likewise extended from the bullet wound beneath his eye.

"We need to get out of here," I say. "That thing is pretty much a live feed to Hell. We can't handle it. It's time to go."

"We're taking it with us," Patrick says.

"No. No we're not."

"Not up for debate, Jack."

"I'm not riding with that thing. If you take it you're going back alone."

Patrick nods and takes another pull from the joint, handling it much better this time. He passes it back to me. "Okay, but you gotta know that I'm leaving this place empty. You understand me, right?"

I don't, at first. It takes me a second. "You can't be serious. You're going to kill me?"

"Make up your mind."

For the first time since his arrival at my shop last night, I feel genuine despair. Everything to this point has had some precedence in my life. Even this brush with Hell isn't my first, though it's the most direct so far. But I've never seen my own death staring back at me quite so frankly. I always thought I'd confront this moment with a little poise, or at least a kind of stoic resignation. But I'm angry, and I'm afraid, and I feel tears gathering in my eyes.

"God damn it, Patrick. That doesn't make any sense."

"Look, Jack. I like you. You're weak and you're a coward, but you can't help those things. I would rather you come with me. We take this skull back to Eugene, like he wanted. We deliver Tobias to his just reward. You go back to your little bookstore and all is right with the world. But I can't leave this place with anybody in it."

Tobias doesn't seem to be paying attention. He's leaning back against the bed, a new joint rolled up and kept all to himself. I can't tell if he's resigned to his own death or if he's so far away he doesn't even know it's being discussed.

I can't think of anything to say. Maybe there isn't anything more to be said. Maybe language is over. Maybe everything is, at last, emptied out. I still feel the skull's muted influence crawling through my brain. It craves the bullet. I anticipate the explosion of the gun with a terrible relish. I wonder, idly, if I'll hold on to myself long enough to feel myself flying.

The bellow from the swamp sounds again. It's huge and deep, like the ululating call of a mountain. It just keeps on going.

Johnny smiles. "Brother's home," he says.

Patrick looks toward the flag-covered doorway. "What?"

Tobias holds his hand aloft, finger extended, announcing his intention to orate. His eyelids are heavy. The joint he'd made for himself is spent. "There's a hell monster. Did I forget to tell you?"

I start to laugh. I can't stop myself. It doesn't feel good.

Johnny smiles at me, mistaking my laughter for something else. "It appeared the same time I did. Toby calls it my brother." He sounds wistful.

Patrick uses the gun barrel to open the flag a few inches. He peers outside for a few moments, then lets it fall closed again. He looks at me. "We're stuck. The boat's gone."

"What? He left us?"

"Well…it's mostly gone."

I take a look for myself.

The airboat is a listing heap of bent scrap metal, the cage around its huge propeller a tangled bird's nest. Our guide's arm, still connected to a hunk of his torso, rests on the deck in a black puddle. The thing that did this is swimming in a lazy arc some distance away, trackable by the rolling surge of water it creates as it trawls along. Judging by the size of its wake, it's at least as big as a city bus. It breaches the surface once, exposing a mottled gray hide and an anemone-like thistle of eye stalks lifting skyward. The thing barrel-rolls until a deep black fissure emerges, and from this suppurated tear comes that stone-cracking bellow, the language of deep earth that curdles something inside me, springs tears to my eyes, brings me hard to my knees.

I scramble weakly away from the door. Patrick is watching me with a sad, desperate hope, his intent to murder momentarily forgotten, as though by some trick known only to me this thing might be banished back to its home, as though I might fix this scar that Tobias George, that mewling, incompetent little thief, has cut into the world.

I cannot fix this. There is no fixing this.

Behind us both, locked in its little room, the skull cooks the air.

It's the language that hurts. The awful speech. While that thing languishes in the waters out front, we're trapped inside. It seems to stay quiet unless it's provoked by some outrage to its senses: an appearance by one of us, or—we believe, since none of us heard the attack on the airboat and our guide—the effects of the skull in the room. As long as we're quiet and hidden, we seem to be safe.

"Why would you do that to a man?" Patrick says. We're all sitting in a little huddled circle, passing the joint around. We might have been friends, to someone who didn't know us. "Why would you send him a piece of his own dead son?"

"Are you serious? No one deserves it more than Eugene. He humiliated me. He made me feel small. All those years sending him a cut from money I earned, or doing errands for him, or tipping him off when I hear shit I think he should know. Never a 'thank you.' Never a 'good job.' Just grief. Just mockery. And his son was even worse. He would lay hands on me. Slap the back of my head. Slap my face, even. What am I going to do, challenge Eugene's son? So I became everybody's bitch. The laughing stock."

Patrick shakes his head. "You didn't, though. Truth is we barely ever thought about you. I didn't even know your name until you knocked over that poker game. Eugene had to remind me."

This is hard for Tobias to hear. He stares hard at the floor, the muscles in his jaw working. He looks at me. "See what I mean? Nothing. You just have to take it from these guys, you know? Just take it and take it and take it. It was one of the happiest days of my life when that kid finally got wasted."

He goes on. We have nothing but time. He robbed the poker game in a fit of deranged anger and then fled south, hoping to disappear into the bayou. The reality of what he'd just done was starting to sink in. He's of the vermin class in criminal society, and vermin come in multitudes. One of his vermin friends told him about this shack where his old granddaddy used to live. He gets a boat and comes out here, only to find a surprise waiting for him.

"The skull was in a black, iron box," he says, "sitting on its side in the corner. There's a hole in the bottom of the box, like the whole thing was meant to fit around someone's head. It had a big gouge in the side of it, like someone had chopped it with something. I don't know what cuts through metal like that though. And inside, this skull…talking."

"It's one of the astronauts," Johnny says.

I rub my fingers in my eyes. "Astronauts? What?"

Johnny leans in, grateful for his moment. He tells us that there are occasionally men and women who wander through Hell in thin processions, wearing heavy gray robes and bearing lanterns to light their way. They are invariably chained together, and led through the burning canyons by a loping demon: some malformed, tooth-spangled pinwheel of limbs and claws. They tour safely because they are shuttered against the sights and sounds of Hell by the iron boxes around their heads, which gives them the appearance of strange, prison-skulled astronauts on a pilgrimage through fire.

"I recognized the box," Johnny says. "This is one of those guys. The box was broken, so I guess something bad happened to him."

"Where is it?"

Tobias shrugs. "I threw it out in the bayou. What do I need a broken box for? I started asking for things, and it sent them. The rock, the shard of bone."

"Hold on. How did you know to ask it for things? You're leaving something out."

Tobias and Johnny exchange a look. The burning embers in the back of Johnny's head seem to have gathered more life: little tongues of flame spit into the air from time to time, as though a small fire has kindled. The extending bone around his head has grown further, opening out as though a careful hand has begun to fashion a wide, smooth bowl. The bone growing from his face has grown little offshoots, like a delicate branch.

Patrick picks up on their glance, and retrieves his gun from the floor, holding it casually in his lap.

"Everything that's brought here has a courier," Tobias says. "That's how Johnny got here. He brought the bone. And there was one already here when I found the skull. It told me."

"It?"

"Well…it was a person at first. Then it changed. They change over time. Evolve."

Patrick gets it before I do. "The thing in the water."

"Holy Christ. You mean Johnny's going to turn into something like *that*?" I look again at the fiery bowl his head is turning into.

"No no no!" Tobias holds out his hands, as if he could ward off the very idea of it. "I mean, I don't know. I'm pretty sure that's only because the other one never went away. I think it's the proximity of the skull that does it. There was one other courier, the girl who brought me the rock. I sent her away."

"Jesus. Where?"

"Just..." He waves, vaguely. "Away. Into the bayou."

"You're a real sweetheart, Tobias."

"Well come on, I didn't know what to do! She was just—there! I didn't know anybody was going to be coming with it! I freaked out and told her to get out! But the important thing is I never saw any sign that she changed into anything. I haven't seen or heard anything from her since. You notice how the plants get weird as you get close to this place? It's gotta be the skull's influence."

"That's not exactly airtight logic, Tobias," I say. "What if it's not just from the skull? What if it comes from them too? I could tell something was fucked up about Johnny as soon as I saw him."

"Well I'm taking the fucking chance! If there are going to be people coming out, they need to have a chance at a better life. That's why I got Johnny here a job. He'll be far away from that skull, so maybe he won't change into anything." He looks at his friend and at the lively fire that's crackling inside his head. "Well, he wouldn't have if you guys hadn't fucked it all up. I've got this all worked out. I'm going to find them jobs in little places, in little towns. I got money now, so I can afford to get them set up. Buy them some clothes, rent them out a place until they can start earning some money of their own. A second chance, you know? They deserve a second chance."

He's getting all worked up again, like he's going to break down into tears, and I'm struck with a revelation: Tobias is using this skull as a chance to redeem himself. He's going to funnel of people out of Hell and back into the world of sunlight and cheeseburgers.

Tobias George may be the only good man in a fifty-mile radius. Too bad it's the most doomed idea I've ever heard in a life rich with them. But there are several possibilities for salvaging this situation. One thing is clear: Eugene cannot have the atlas. The level of catastrophe he might cause is incalculable. I need to get it back to my bookstore and to the back room. There are books there that will provide protections; at least I hope so.

All I need is something to carry it in.

I know just where to get it.

"Patrick. You still want to bring this thing to Eugene?"

"He's the boss. You change your mind about coming?"

"I think so, yeah. Tobias, we're going into the room."

He goes in gratefully. I think he feels in control in this room in way that he doesn't out there with Patrick. It's almost funny.

The skull sits on the moss-blackened stool, greasy smoke seeping from its fissures and polluting the air. The broken language of Hell is a physical pressure. A blood vessel ruptures in my right eye and my vision goes cloudy and pink. Time fractures again. Tobias moves next to me, approaching the skull, but I can't tell what it's doing to him: he skips in time like I'm watching him through strobe lights, even though the light in here remains a constant, sizzling glare. I try not to vomit. Things are moving around in my brain like maggots in old meat.

The air seems to bend into the skull. I see it on the stool, blackening the world around it, and I try to imagine who it once belonged to: the chained Black Iron Monk, shielded by a metal box from the burning horrors of the world he moved through. Until something came along and opened the box like a tin can, and Hell poured inside.

Who was it? What order would undertake such a pilgrimage? And to what end?

Tobias is saying something to me. I have to study him to figure out what.

The poor scrawny bastard is blistering all over his body. His lips peel back from his bloody teeth.

"Tell it what you want," he says.

So I do.

The boy is streaked with mud and gore. He is twelve, maybe thirteen. Steam rises from his body like wind-struck flags. I don't know where he appears from, or how; he's just there, two iron boxes dangling like huge lanterns from a chain in his hand. I wonder, briefly, what a child his age had done to be consigned to Hell. But then, it doesn't really matter.

I open one of the boxes and tell the boy to put the skull inside. He does. The skin bubbles on his hands where he touches it, but he makes no sign of pain.

I close the door on it, and it's like a light going out. Time slips back into its groove. The light recedes to a natural level. My skin stops burning, the desire to commit violence dissipates like smoke. I can feel where I've been scratching my own arms again. My eye is gummed shut with blood.

When we stumble back into the main room, Patrick is on his feet with the gun in his hand. Johnny is sitting on the bed, the bony rim of his open skull grown further upward, elongating his head and giving him an alien grace. The fire in the bowl of his head burns briskly, crackling and shedding a warm light. Patrick looks at me, then at the boy with the iron boxes. "You got them," he says. "Where's the skull?"

I take the chain from the boy. The boxes are heavy together; the boy must be stronger than he looks. Something to remember. "In one of these. If it can keep that shit out, I'm betting it can keep it locked in, too. I think it's safe to move."

"And those'll get us past the thing outside?"

"If what Johnny said is true."

"It is," Johnny says. "But now there's only one extra box."

"That's right," I say, and swing them with every vestige of my failing strength at Patrick's head, where they land with a wet crunch. He staggers to his right a few steps, the left side of his face broken like crockery, and he puts a hand into the rancid scramble of his own brain. "I'll go get it," he says, "I'll go."

"You're dead," I tell him gently. "You stupid bastard."

He accepts this gracefully and collapses to his knees, and then onto his face. Dark blood pours from his head as though from a spilled glass. I scoop up the gun, which feels clumsy in my hand. I never got the hang of guns.

Tobias stands in shock. "I can't believe you did that," he says.

"Shut up. Are there any clothes in that dresser? Put something on the kid. We're going back to the city." While he's doing that, I look at Johnny. "I'm not going to be able to see. Will you be able to guide me out?"

"Yes."

"Good," I say, and shoot Tobias in the back of the head.

For once, somebody dies without an argument.

I don't know much about the trip back. I open a slot on the base of the box and fit it over my head. I am consumed in darkness. I'm led out to the skiff by Johnny and the boy. The boy rides with me, and Johnny gets into the water, dragging us behind him. Fire unfurls from his head, the sides of which are developing baroque flourishes. His personality is diminished, and I can't tell if it's because he mourns Tobias, or because that is changing too, developing into something cold and barren.

The journey takes several hours. I know we pass the corpse flowers, the staring eyes and bloodless faces pressing from the foliage. I am sure that the creature unleashes its earth-breaking cry, and that any living thing that hears it hemorrhages its life away, into the still waters. I know that night falls. I know the flame of our new guide lights the undersides of the cypress, runs out before us across the water, fills the dark like the final lantern in a fallen world.

I make a quiet and steady passage there.

Eugene is in his office. The bar is closed upstairs and the man at the door lets us in without a word. He makes no comment about my companions, or the iron boxes hanging from a chain. The world he lives in is already breaking from its old shape. The new one has space for wonders.

Eugene is sitting behind his desk in the dark. I can tell he's drunk. It smells like he's been here since we left, almost twenty-four hours ago now. The only light comes from the fire rising from Johnny's empty skull. It illuminates a pale structure on Eugene's desk: a huge antler, or a tree made of bone. There are human teeth protruding along some of its tines, and a long crack near the wider base of it reveals a raw, red meat, where a mouth opens and closes.

"Where's Patrick?" he says.

"Dead," I say. "Tobias, too."

"And the atlas?"

"I burned it."

He nods, as though he'd been expecting that very thing. After a moment he gestures at the bone tree. "This is my son," he says. "Say hi, Max."

The mouth shrieks. It stops to draw in a gasping breath, then repeats the sound. The cry is sustained for several seconds before stuttering into a sob, and then going silent again.

"He keeps growing. He's going to be a big boy before it's all over."

"Yeah. I can see that."

"Who're your friends, Jack?"

I have to think about that before I answer. "I really don't know," I say, finally.

"So what do you want? You want me to tell you you're off the hook? You want me to tell you you're free to go?"

"You told me that before. It turned out to be bullshit."

"Yeah, well. That's the world we live in, right?"

"You're on notice, Eugene. Leave me alone. Don't come to my door anymore. I'm sorry things didn't work out here. I'm sorry about your son. But you have to stay away. I'm only going to say it once."

He smiles at me. He must have to summon it from far away, but he smiles at me. "I'll take that under advisement, Jack. Now get the fuck out of here."

We turn and walk back up the stairs. It's a long walk back to my bookstore, where I'm anxious to get to work on the atlas. But I have a light to guide me, and I know this place well.

Richard Kadrey is the *New York Times* bestselling author of the Sandman Slim supernatural noir books. The eighth book in the series, *The Perdition Score*, has recently been published. His other books include *The Everything Box*, *Metrophage*, *Butcher Bird*, *Dead Set*, and the graphic novel *ACCELERATE*. Sandman Slim was included in Amazon's "100 Science Fiction & Fantasy Books to Read in a Lifetime" and is in development as a feature film.

Ambitious Boys Like You
Richard Kadrey

WITT PULLED HIS father's '71 Malibu to a stop down the block from the derelict house. The car coughed a couple of times. It wasn't vintage. It was just old.

Sonny was riding shotgun. He said, "There it is."

"I've been driving by this place my whole life," said Witt. "Didn't ever think I'd have a reason to go inside. Didn't ever want to."

"Why's that?"

"When we was young, we figured it was haunted."

"Haunted? How come?" asked Sonny.

"Well, look."

"At what?"

"The bodies."

"Jesus fucking Christ."

Sonny, his cousin, was from Houston, but being from the city isn't why Witt found him interesting. It was that while Witt believed in everything—God, the Devil, spooks, not spilling salt without throwing some over your shoulder—Sonny believed in absolutely nothing. Not 9/11 or the Kennedy assassination, not Heaven or Hell. The way he talked, Witt sometimes wondered if Sonny believed in him.

"Those are dolls, you psycho hillbilly."

"They don't look it at night," said Witt. "At night it looks like a whole cemetery in those trees."

Sonny had to give him that. There were at least a hundred small dolls nailed to the apple trees around the old man's yard. There were even a few on the porch and the low picket fence that surrounded the property.

"It's called hoarding," said Sonny. "These old assholes, their dog or their wife dies and their brains turn to Swiss cheese. They can't let go of anything. That's why we're here, right?"

Witt nodded.

"I know. I'm just all of a sudden amused that after all these years, I'll finally see inside the place for real. You know, we wouldn't ride our bikes by here at night. We'd go clear around the block to avoid it."

"What a great story. Promise me you'll write a memoir. You ready to go?"

"Hell yeah," said Witt, trying to sound more ready than he was.

It was just after 2 a.m. Witt had set the interior light on the Malibu to not come on when they opened the doors. Sonny carried the bag with their tools. They wore sneakers and latex gloves from the Walmart by the freeway. Sonny pulled on his ski mask. Witt kept his in his windbreaker's pocket. The night was hot and humid and the mask itched like a son of a bitch when he tried it on in the store. He'd put it on once they got inside.

Sonny was the first through the picket fence. He held the gate open for Witt, not because he was polite, but because he didn't want it to slam shut. That's the other thing Witt liked about Sonny. He was a thinker.

It was only about thirty feet from the fence to the porch, and even though it was night and he was wearing a mask, Sonny kept his head down. Witt followed him, covering the side of his face with his hand. Witt stepped onto the front porch gently. He didn't want the old boards to squeak. Sonny turned and looked at him.

"Where's your fucking mask?"

"In my pocket."

"Put it on."

"There's no one here."

"What if he has automatic lights or security cameras?"

"Cameras? You think this old son of a bitch is James Bond?"

Sonny sighed.

"Just put the damned mask on."

While Sonny got out his lock pick tools, Witt took the mask from his pocket and pulled it down over his face. He was sweating and itching in seconds. There better be something inside worth stealing, he thought. Gold coins or silver candlesticks or a goddamn treasure map from back when the hovel had been the nicest house in town, eighty some odd years ago. The old man had lived there by himself for as long as Witt could remember. No one had ever seen him take anything but the trash out, and even that was a rare thing. Witt hoped it was cash inside. He wasn't a pirate. He wouldn't know what the hell to do with a bunch of gold. When it was over, maybe he could buy his dad's Malibu and get it fixed up. That would be sweet. He was about to ask Sonny what he thought about the idea when Sonny said, "Well, damn."

"What?"

"You were right. The old man isn't exactly security-minded."

Sonny put the picks back in the bag and turned the knob on the door. It opened.

"The hayseed doesn't even lock the place."

"I told you," said Witt. "Folks don't like it here. There's no reason they'd want to go inside."

"But we're not just folks, are we?"

Witt smiled. Sonny reached up and pulled down a doll held with wire over the door frame. He handed it to Witt. The doll was about eight inches long. Its body was straw and the head was made of rough, untanned leather, with button eyes.

"Toss it," said Sonny. "Time to grow up. This is no cemetery. It's a flophouse."

Witt threw the doll into the yard and it felt like a hundred pounds of bullshit lifted off his back. He'd been afraid of the house for so long, he took it for granted that he'd be spooked forever. And now he wasn't. The old wreck, with its rotten gables and broken windows covered with cardboard, wasn't *Dr. Terror's House of Horrors*. It was just a prison for a pathetic old man. Witt all of a sudden sort of felt kind of sorry for him, but sorry didn't mean that he and Sonny weren't down for business.

Sonny pushed the front door open and Witt followed him inside.

The stink hit Witt hard, an overpowering combination of mildew, spoiled meat, and something like copper, with a sour sting that bought tears to his eyes.

"Jesus. Does this old fuck ever flush his toilet?" said Sonny.

"Sometimes in these old places, rats or raccoons will get in the walls and die there."

"Smells like it was Noah's whole goddamn ark."

Sonny flicked on a small LED flashlight and Witt did the same as they went deeper into the place.

They were in a wide foyer. The floor was covered with a carpet turned black with grime and mold. To the left was a parlor. Wallpaper peeled from the walls like burned skin. To the right was a dining room. A hallway led off from the foyer. A door to the kitchen in the distance. A closet. Another door under the stairs that Witt thought led to a basement. The place was even worse than he'd imagined.

"You sure there's anything left in here worth taking?" he said. "I mean, it smells like the damned dump."

"Spend a lot of time out there, do you?" said Sonny. "You said the family were bankers. People like that, they know what to squirrel away for a rainy day."

"I suppose."

"Damn right you do. Now, let's get to work. Don't forget what I told you. Slow and steady wins the race. Take your time, but don't get lazy. Don't make noise, but don't go so fast you're going to miss valuables."

Witt nodded. He wanted to breathe through his mouth, but he didn't want to look like a pussy in front of Sonny. He swung his light into the parlor.

"As good a place to start as any," Sonny said and they went inside.

They went to opposite ends of the room. The plan was to work their way in and meet in the middle. It sounded good when they'd talked it over, but now Witt wasn't so sure. What the hell was he looking for exactly? He was sure they weren't going to find a pile of hundreds just lying around the place.

He looked at the dusty paintings. Generations of the old man's family, each more mean and joyless than the last. It eased Witt's conscience a little.

Witt checked the bookcase and drawers on rickety old end tables. Picking up some old books, he wondered if they were worth something. Or one of the lamps. His grandma had an old gilt lamp from France that she swore was worth more than his granddad's soul. Witt shook his head. No. They weren't there for lamps or shit like that. He checked around the cushions on a sofa that kicked up enough dust that it looked like a west Texas sandstorm.

"What are you doing?" said Sonny.

"Searching. What do you think?"

"What are you looking for, bus fare? Leave the sofa alone."

Sonny played his light over the room. Witt checked his watch. They'd been in the room for fifteen minutes, but it felt like an hour. I might not be cut out for this life, he thought, but he kept his mouth shut.

Sonny pursed his lips like he was going to spit.

"There's nothing in here. Let's check the dining room."

They went across the hall and inspected the room the same way they'd done the other. The dining room was even less interesting than the parlor. Just a big table, some chairs, and a sideboard. There was a crystal chandelier in the center of the room, covered in cobwebs. That was probably worth something, thought Witt, but how would they get it out of there?

"Nice."

It was Sonny's voice. Witt went and looked over his shoulder. He had one of the sideboard drawers open and was holding up a shiny butter knife. Sonny handed it to Witt.

"You know what that is?"

Witt shook his head.

"Gold-plated silver. Old too."

Witt turned the knife over. It was pretty and it reflected a buttery light onto his jacket where the flashlight caught it. It was nice, but it didn't seem like a fortune.

"Is this what we came for?" he asked.

Sonny took the knife back and shook his head.

"It's a start. We've got a few thousand dollars here easy. I know people who love this kind of shit. They sell it to antique dealers and designer fags for a fortune."

Sonny put the knife back in the drawer.

"Aren't we going to take it?" said Witt.

"It's heavy. We'll get it on the way out. But this is exactly what we're looking for right now. Smalls. The old man will know where the big ticket stuff is, but for now remember to keep your eyes out for cash or watches or rings. We'll finish down here and go upstairs to roust granddad."

A few thousand dollars already, thought Witt. Maybe I am cut out for this after all.

Sonny went ahead down the hall and Witt followed him inside an old office. There was a heavy wooden desk with an old-fashioned typewriter on top. To the side, an office chair with bad springs. It sat low and leaned back at a funny angle. There was a hat rack with a moldy fedora and ancient lacquered file cabinets so swollen with moisture that some of the drawers were twisted and wedged tight. Sonny started to work on them while Witt looked through the desk.

It was one of the old kind you see in movies, with lots of cubbyholes on top. He shone his light in each one and stuck a finger in the holes where he saw something. All he found were a few dead roaches, some rusted paperclips, and mouse turds. The drawers weren't any better. Letterhead stationery, old pens, and a rusty letter opener. In one of the bottom drawers he found a dusty bottle of bourbon. He was tempted take it until he saw that the seal had been broken. Did whiskey go bad like beer? He didn't want to take a chance, so he put the bottle back and opened the top middle drawer.

There was a doll inside, like the ones in the trees. A goddamn funny place for one, Witt thought. He reached in the drawer and picked it up. It hung for a second, like it was caught on a nail, but it came free with a little tug.

Something black boiled out from the drawer, spread across the desktop, up the walls and down onto the floor. Witt almost shouted, but kept himself under control. Some of what writhed on the desk hopped off and landed on the legs of his jeans. He pointed his light down.

There were spiders, pouring out of the desk and trying to crawl up his legs.

"Fuck!" he yelled, and shook his legs like he was barefoot dancing on coals. Someone grabbed his jacket collar and pulled him into the hall.

Sonny turned him around and looked him over.

"Spiders," whispered Witt.

Without missing a beat, Sonny bent and brushed the spiders away with his sleeve. When they hit the floor, he stepped on them like it wasn't anything at all.

"Thanks," said Witt. "I'm scared shitless of those things."

Sonny slapped him across the face.

"Don't you make another goddamn noise, you hear me?" he said.

Witt was still trying to catch his breath. His cheek stung, but he nodded. Sonny walked over and closed the office door. Seeing the spiders locked inside, Witt relaxed a little.

"You got a thing about those bugs?" said Sonny.

Witt nodded.

"So did my old man. Turned to jelly at the sight of 'em. That's okay. You just better hope the old man didn't hear you and call the cops."

"Maybe we should leave?" said Witt.

Sonny shook his head. Stood quiet for a minute, listening for footsteps or a phone.

"No. We're just getting started," Sonny said.

Witt looked around.

"This place is huge," he said. "It could take all night."

"No. When you've got a big place like this what you do is hurt somebody. In this case, the old man."

"Why?"

. "Because he's obviously crazy and we're going to want him back on planet Earth for a while. Don't sweat it. I'll handle things. You just watch and learn."

Witt waited while Sonny walked down the hall. He wasn't sure how he felt about what Sonny wanted to do. Witt had been in plenty of fights over the years, but they were always stand up man-to-man things, not slapping an old cuss around. Still, the gold up front was awfully pretty and he didn't think Sonny was the kind of man who was going to be talked out of a plan once he'd set his mind to it. Witt knuckled his cheek where Sonny slapped him. Better the old man getting hurt than him.

He realized that he was still holding the doll. It was like the others. A few inches long and with a leather head. There was a piece of string around its waist, trailing off to a frayed end. Witt remembered the feeling of the doll getting snagged on something in the drawer. Then he thought of something else.

Sonny was halfway down the hall, headed for the kitchen. Witt came up behind him and grabbed his shoulder.

"I think it was a trick," he said.

"What?"

"The spiders. Look." He held up the doll so Sonny could see the string. "They could have been in a bag of a net or something and when I picked up the doll it let 'em loose."

Sonny looked at him and a smile crept across his face.

"Be cool, man. You're just spooked. We're about done down here. We've got the kitchen and if there's a basement, maybe give the downstairs a quick once over. Then we go upstairs and we're out. Okay?"

Witt wanted to agree. He didn't want Sonny mad at him, but he didn't want spiders even more.

"I still think it was a trick," he said. "Something the old man set up."

Sonny glanced upstairs.

"I doubt this old guy can find his way down to the shitter. Stay focused and do the job."

Sonny started away and Witt wanted to say something, but knew it wouldn't do any good. He played his flashlight over the walls and floor.

"Stop," he said.

Up ahead, Sonny stopped. He dropped his head a little. His shoulders were tense like he was about to hit something.

"What?" he said.

Witt didn't get any closer to him. He kept his light pointed at the floor a few feet in front of Sonny.

"Look down there."

Sonny took a couple of steps forward and stood for a moment, then went down on one knee.

"I'll be goddamned," he said.

Witt came to where Sonny knelt. Their lights illuminated a length of monofilament fishing line across the hall about six inches off the ground. Sonny grinned up at Witt.

"What do you think? More spiders? Maybe ninjas'll fall from the ceiling?"

"Don't touch it," said Witt as Sonny hooked a finger around the wire and pulled. It snapped. Witt froze. Nothing happened. Sonny looked up at him, then stood.

"I've got to give you points, man. You were right. Grandpa has been up to some funny games. But he's still an addled old man. This one didn't work."

Witt looked around the hall, expecting more spiders to come raining down. But nothing happened. He pointed at something shiny near the ceiling.

"What's that?" he said.

Sonny saw it too. He moved closer, pulling a pistol from his jeans. He used the barrel to brush the tiny specks of light above his head. They made a small sound swinging against each other, like tiny wind chimes. It was fishhooks. Dozens of them hanging at eye level on more monofilament.

Sonny swept the gun barrel through the hooks, sending them swinging.

"This is good news. Know why?"

Witt shook his head.

"Because it means there's something in this house worth protecting. We're going to make ourselves some money tonight."

Sonny walked under the hooks and stood when he reached the other side. He turned all the way around, checking the floor and walls for wires. When he was done, he motioned for Witt to follow him.

Witt hated creeping under the hooks almost as much as the spiders. He darted through and didn't stand again until he was past Sonny.

"We do the job just like we planned," he said. "Just keep your eyes open for any more pranks."

"Yeah. Okay," said Witt.

"And get rid of that fucking doll. You look like an idiot."

Witt looked down. He was still holding the doll with the string. He tossed it back down the hall the way they'd come and flinched, afraid it might set off another trap. But nothing happened.

"There's another wire up ahead," said Sonny. "I'll go that way. You check the closet."

As Sonny moved off, Witt looked over the closet door. He checked the ceiling for hooks, and moved his light slowly over, around, and below the frame. Ran his fingers around the doorknob feeling for a tripwire. He didn't find one. He looked down at Sonny, wondering if he could just say he'd checked the closet. But Witt knew he wasn't a good liar. There was nothing he could do.

He put his hand on the closet doorknob and turned. It opened. Nothing happened. He swung the door opened the rest of the way and shone his flashlight inside.

The closet was full of rotting coats and rain boots, some umbrellas and a couple of canes with silver tops. Those could be worth something, he thought. There were boxes on the floor and more on a shelf above the coats. He checked around for more lines, but didn't see any signs of them. The canes first, he thought, and reached for one.

A board under his foot sank a couple of inches. Witt froze. There was a metal-on-metal squeak. He pointed his flashlight at the floor. A board with long butcher knives pushed through it hung a foot away from his legs. It was supposed to swing out when he stepped on the board and hit him in the knees, but the house had betrayed the old man. The hinge the board hung from was caked with rust. Witt was so happy he wanted to laugh, but he didn't want to piss Sonny off by making noise. He grabbed one of the canes and stepped back. The board under his foot rose back up into place.

And another board swung out, this one chest-high. Witt jumped back, slamming his head into the wall opposite the closet. He went blind for a second as light exploded behind his eyes. When it cleared, he saw the second knife board, embedded in the closet door. It had missed him by a few inches. The doll he'd thrown away earlier lay by his side. He kicked it into the closet.

Footsteps pounded down the hall.

Sonny grabbed his shoulder and pushed him out of the way. He looked over the scene and then at Witt.

"You okay?"

Witt nodded, but he was still a little light-headed from the fall. Sonny grabbed his shoulders and pulled him to his feet.

"Fuck this," said Sonny. "Let's find him."

He was already on the stairs when Witt saw it.

"Stop!" he yelled.

Too late.

He ducked as Sonny's foot broke the fishing line.

A shotgun blast ripped across the hall, right by Sonny's head. It looked like an old sawed-off was inside the wall, hidden behind a flap of wallpaper, now scorched and torn by the blast. Sonny stumbled down the stairs, holding a hand over one ear. He pulled his hand away and checked it. There was blood on the palm.

Witt came over.

"You okay?" he said.

Sonny looked at him for a second, then snapped out of it.

"I think I'm fucking deaf in this ear. I think that fucker blew out my eardrum."

"Maybe we should get the knives and forks and just go," said Witt.

Sonny took out his pistol.

"We're not going anywhere. I'm going to find out what that old fuck has and kill him."

Under normal circumstances, Witt would argue about something like killing a person, but these circumstances were damned far from normal and the old bastard was kind of asking for it, Witt thought. He followed Sonny up the stairs. They weren't quiet as they went. The old man had to have heard the shotgun. There wasn't any point in being quiet anymore.

"Careful," Witt said.

A few steps up Sonny said, "There's another doll and another wire. Duck."

Sonny bent over and when he was through, Witt followed him. As Sonny stood Witt saw the other line, the one strung so if you missed the first, you'd hit the second. Witt closed his eyes and what felt like a thousand pounds crashed down on them.

They were pinned to the steps. Sonny cursed and thrashed. Witt tried to push the weight off, but every time he moved the net ripped into his skin. He managed to get his flashlight turned around and finally understood what had happened. The net they were trapped in was made of barbed wire. And they weren't alone. There was a body with them. A bag of bones and rags. Some other poor asshole who'd wandered into the old man's house and never left. Behind him, Sonny cursed and growled about all the ways he was going to murder the old man.

"Hold it," said Witt. "Stop moving a minute."

Sonny thrashed few a few seconds more and stopped.

"Barbed wire don't weigh much, but this net has got big weights on the ends," Witt said. "We keep thrashing, we're going to wrap ourselves up and die here like Mr. Bones."

"Who the fuck?" said Sonny.

"Turn your head."

Sonny did. The net dug into Witt's skin again as Sonny jerked back from the body.

"Fuck me," said Sonny.

"What are we going to do?"

"One of us has got to get out. Then he can hold the net up for the other to get out."

"So who does what?" said Witt.

"I hate to admit it, and if you repeat it I'll deny it, but I think you're stronger. I can't lift for shit flat on my back here. You get me out and I can help you."

"Okay," said Witt. "Can you help push a little?"

"I'll do what I can. Just keep those goddamn bones away from me."

"How am I supposed to do that?"

"I don't know. Forget it. Just push."

Witt got hold of one of the weights holding the net in place. The problem was that it was wrapped in barbed wire. Each time he grabbed it, the metal barbs tore into his fingers and palms. On his first try, he moved the weight up about six inches before the pain got to be too much. The good news was that it allowed Sonny to turn and wriggle up next to him. They both got ahold of the weight and lifted it just high enough for Sonny to crawl out. Witt dropped the net back where it was. Sonny lay on the stairs, panting.

"Sonny?"

"Yeah."

"Think you can start helping me out of here? I don't want to spend the night with this dead boy."

Sonny got to his knees and came up a step to where the weight lay. He put his hands on it and yanked them away.

"What's wrong?' said Witt.

"That dead fucker touched me."

"Use your jacket," said Witt. "It'll help with the barbs and you won't feel the bones."

Sonny looked at him like Witt was speaking Chinese. Then he took his jacket off and wrapped it around his hands. Taking hold of the weight, he pulled up, leaning back against the staircase railing for support.

There was a spark and a thump. The weight came down, almost smashing into Witt's hand. Sonny flopped on the stairs next to it.

"Sonny," said Witt. "You all right?"

Sonny opened his eyes and looked at the banister.

"The railing is electrified. Zapped me good," he said.

"Can you lift the weight without touching it?"

Sonny reached up and pulled off his ski mask. His face was slick with sweat. He wiped it out of his eyes with his jacket sleeve.

"No, I can't," he said. He looked over. Witt knew Sonny was staring at the bones more than looking at him. Sonny frowned.

"I think I'm about done here, Hoss," he said.

"What do you mean?"

Sonny put his jacket back on.

"I'm done. I'm over. The old fucker won."

Sonny stood and pulled his ski mask back on. He jerked back when he almost touched the railing and shook his head.

"I'm sorry, man. I can't help you."

He turned and started down the stairs.

"Sonny," yelled Witt. "Please."

Sonny kept walking. Witt yelled after him.

"You can keep my share of the forks and stuff. Just don't leave me."

Sonny stopped at the bottom of the stairs. Witt waited for him to come back up. Sonny said, "Sorry, man." He turned and headed for the door.

"Sonny!"

Down in the dark, Sonny cursed.

"What is it?" said Witt.

"The goddamned door. It's locked."

Witt listened to Sonny walk around downstairs, cursing and punching things.

He came back into the hall.

"The windows are barred from the inside. What the hell kind of house did you bring me to? This is your fault, you hayseed prick. I hope you fucking rot up there with your dead pal."

Witt watched as the circle of Sonny's flashlight disappeared down the hall.

"Sonny?"

Silence.

"Sonny?"

Nothing.

Witt lay on the stairs sweating. He pulled his ski mask off too. He tried wrapping it around his hand to keep the wire from tearing into his palms, but when he lifted the net, the barbs cut into him and he couldn't hold on. His hands were ragged and bleeding. He lay there, breathing hard and trying not to completely lose his mind. Sonny was a thinker, but he lost it. Be a better thinker. What would a better thinker do?

Witt's elbow brushed against the skeleton. He reached over and twisted one of the bone hands and with some sweating and swearing, snapped it off at the wrist. He'd torn up his shoulders doing it, but it was worth it. He found the dead man's other arm and snapped off the second hand. That's when he noticed a doll duct taped into the dead man's mouth. Witt elbowed him away and turned back to the weight.

Balancing the skeleton hands over his palms, he grabbed the weight. When he pulled, the barbs dug into the bones, but didn't touch his hands. It took three tries, but he finally got the weight high enough to set it on the step above him. Slowly, he crawled forward, using the skeleton's hands to hold up as much of the net as possible.

He cut his legs up wiggling, but finally, he was out. Witt lay on the stairs facing the dead man. Another thief? he wondered. It couldn't be the old man. Maybe his family were embezzlers and it was someone from the bank come to confront him. That meant Sonny was right all along. There was a treasure somewhere in the house, and now neither one of them was going to get it.

Witt stood and started down, careful not to touch the railing. A gunshot boomed through the house. He went down the stairs as fast as he could, and crouched by the wall, keeping low. The place was quiet now.

"Sonny?" whispered Witt. "Sonny?"

He looked down the hall and saw an open door. Warm light, like dawn over a river, lit up the walls and floor. Yeah, he thought, Sonny was a yellow dog piece of coward shit, but if he left now, that would make him just as bad. Witt started down the hall. He'd lost his flashlight on the stairs, so he went slowly, looking for any tripwires he might have missed earlier.

The basement door was open. A doll was perched on the top step, nailed in place through the stomach. Witt looked at it for a good long while, searching for monofilament, funny floorboards, or electric wires. He didn't find any, but he couldn't make himself step past the doll. Maybe Sonny wasn't close-enough family to go searching this crazyass dump after all.

A voice echoed up the stairwell. Witt stood and looked downstairs.

"Sonny?"

Something hit him in the back of the head and the building seemed to tilt, swing around, and hit him in the face. His vision collapsed to a tunnel and went out.

Witt awoke handcuffed to a rough stone wall. His hands tingled with pins and needles and his face hurt like fire. He tried to say something but it hurt so much he screamed, only there wasn't any sound. His lips were sewn shut.

The basement stank. The moist reek of decay down here was why the rest of the house smelled like Death shitting in a Dumpster. The blow on his head made it hard for Witt to see clearly. The glare from the bare bulbs strung along the ceiling hurt his eyes. He heard a splash, like someone was dragging wet laundry across the floor. Witt blinked, shook his head, and tried to focus.

Sonny hung on the wall like Jesus on the cross, held there with nails through his hands. A scrawny old man in overalls and a barbecue apron that read I LIKE MY PORK PULLED was gutting him with a long, curved butcher knife. The old man sawed his way up Sonny's stomach, stopping when he hit the breastbone. Then he made a cut across Sonny's belly, set down the knife, and reached inside, yanking out a long tangle of intestines. The old man let them flop into a plastic trash can pushed up against the body. Sonny's head moved from side to side as the old man worked. His eyes opened, showing the whites. Witt's breath caught for a minute. Sonny was still alive. He wanted to scream, but remembered the pain.

The old man glanced at him, then turned back to his work.

"I'm not ignoring you, son," the old man said. "It's just that I'm a little busy right this second." His voice startled Witt. He'd expected an old coot, but the voice was strong and cultured, like someone in one of those ancient aliens documentaries on cable.

The old man pulled Sonny's stomach wide, pinning the folds of skin to the wall with hooks and monofilament line. Sonny's abdomen was splayed open like a wet red flower. The old man took the knife and cut a couple of more things from Sonny's gut and dropped them into the trash. When he looked at Witt again, the old man's gaze lingered on him.

"I suppose you're wondering what's going on," he said, and smiled. "Since you're in no position to ask questions, I'll do my best to guess what you'd like to know."

The old man tossed the knife onto a worktable and pulled off bloody dish-washing gloves, dropping them next to Sonny's gun.

The man's face was creased and yellow, like a kid Witt remembered from grade school. The one with hepatitis, and they'd all had to get shots because of him. The man's knuckles were swollen and bent like he had rheumatism. His teeth were gray. Still, as beat up as he was, the closer the old man got, the more Witt saw something hard and ferocious in his eyes.

"First of all, nothing you see here tonight is about torture or cruelty, though lord knows you boys deserve a little of both. Showing up here with a gun," said the old man.

He turned and pointed to a couple of little dolls lying on his worktable.

"My eyes and ears," he said. "I saw you two coming a mile away." He looked at Witt. "Made all these dolls myself. A trick my *grand-mère* taught me long ago and far away. Made them out of ambitious boys like you and your friend."

The old man wiped sweat out of his eyes and pushed back wisps of thin white hair.

"On the other hand, I'm grateful you're here. If it wasn't for boys, and a few girls, like you two, I wouldn't be where I am today." He held out his arms like the filthy basement was Hollywood Boulevard. "That was a joke," he said. "Don't try to laugh. It'll hurt."

When he got close, the old man held open each of Witt's eyes and looked at them, like a doctor examining a patient. His breath smelled like a swamp and he wheezed a little. Witt tried to squirm from his hands.

The old man looked away for a moment, like he was lost in thought.

"Did you ever think about living forever?" he said. "I don't mean like fluttering off on angel wings and sipping tea with Jesus on a cloud, but living forever right here. Like a man. Well, I'm here to tell you, it can be done." He smiled wide, showing his rotten teeth. "Now, I know what you're thinking. If living forever looks like me, you're not interested. But you see me, this body, it's only a part of the story."

Sonny moaned and the old man walked back to him. He put on his gloves, picked up his knife, and got back to work, cutting into Sonny's stomach. He talked as he worked.

"Immortality isn't what you think it is. It's not like in movies where you stay young and pretty forever. It's harder than that and in a way it's more poetic. You live your life and grow old and when the time is right, you're reborn in new flesh. A bit like a phoenix." He turned to Witt. "You know what a phoenix is, don't you? Surely even a crude lad like you must know that."

Things from inside Sonny fell into the can.

"Your young friend here is my phoenix. When I shrug off this old meat, I'll be reborn in his. But first," he said, "I have to clear away the clutter."

He winked at Witt and pulled out more of Sonny's insides, until Witt could see his friend's spine.

"The heart and the brain. That's all I need. They're the only things I don't take out."

The old man stood, kicked off his work boots, and started to undress. He moved slowly, like each joint was stiff and painful.

When he struggled to get the apron up over his head, Witt pulled at the cuffs holding him to the wall. The ring that held the cuffs in place felt loose. He put slow, steady pressure on it, not wanting the old man to notice what he was doing.

Finally, the old man was naked. His skin sagged like it was melting off his bones. Patches of white, stiff tumbleweed hair bristled on his crotch and under his arms. He picked up the knife and looked over. Witt stopped moving.

"I know you think what I did to your friend hurt him, but consider this: at least he didn't have to do it to himself. Watch this."

The old man took the butcher knife and reached behind his head. He made a deep cut at the base of his skull, dragging the blade up and over his head to just above his eyebrows. This time, Witt screamed, and the pain brought tears to his eyes.

The old man's hands were shaking when he set down the knife. He reached behind his head with both hands and pulled. The skin slid away from his skull like he was skinning a dead deer. He kept pulling and the flesh came down over his face, his neck, his chest, and down his legs. He moaned the whole time, but the old man's pain didn't give Witt any satisfaction. He pulled on the ring that held his handcuffs to the wall. They turned a little. He kept twisting, wondering how long it would take the old man to snake all the way out of his skin, and if it was enough time to get free.

It wasn't. Witt was still pinned tight when the last of the old man's skin hit the floor. He stepped out of it like he was kicking off dirty socks and fell against his worktable panting. A glistening wet mass of sagging muscle and bone, the old man reached over and picked up Sonny's pistol. He pointed it at Witt.

"Stop that wiggling or I'll do double worse to you what I did to your friend," he said. "Besides, you'll like this next part. Slithering out of my old skin isn't fun, but I'm used to it. This next part, is what really hurts."

He pushed a stool under Sonny's ass, then used a hammer to pull out the nails that held his hands to the wall. Sonny's body dropped onto the stool like someone had cut the strings of a marionette. The old man eyed the opening in Sonny's stomach like a Peeping Tom looking through a window, thought Witt.

The flayed man bent over, stiff and arthritic. When he was down as low as he could go, he grabbed his head and yanked it forward. Witt heard his neck snap. The old man screamed and his head hung like it was held in place by spaghetti. Then he reached his arms around in front, like he was trying to hug himself. He jerked hard, dislocating both of his arms at the shoulder. Another scream. Witt closed his eyes, afraid he might throw up and drown inside his sealed lips.

The old man continued with whatever it was he was doing, the ritual coming to Witt as a series of horrible sounds. A wet tearing of muscles and snapping of bones. The old man's screams. When the noise stopped, Witt opened his eyes a fraction of an inch. He couldn't believe what he saw.

The old man lay on the filthy floor. He'd folded himself up like a god-damned origami bird. His legs were up around his shoulders and his head was buried beneath his ankles. The only thing that still sort of worked were his arms, and even they were kind of loose and dangling. Groping blindly, the old man's skinless hands went up Sonny's body, finally stopping when they found the opening in his stomach. They got a good grip on the edges and hauled the rest of his body up and into the hole.

Witt knew that what he was doing would never work. There was no way he could get his whole body into Sonny's stomach. And yet, as Witt watched, the old man did it. By whatever magic or skill or madness he'd learned over the years, the old man kept squeezing and squeezing his body tighter and tighter until he'd worked his way completely inside Sonny. Then he reached out and pulled the loose stomach flaps closed. The slits he'd cut into them healed as Witt watched.

Sonny twitched. His body went stiff. His eyes fluttered. He relaxed and his head fell forward. He pissed himself. Then he laughed.

"That always cracks me up," Sonny said. "I start off each new life by piss-ing myself like an infant. It's all right. It's how I know all the plumbing is working."

Sonny stood, holding himself with his hand against the wall. He took a stiff step. Then another, his balance coming back to him. He breathed deeply, as if relishing this new younger flesh.

"*Que penses-tu de ma nouvelle poupée?*" he said, then, "What do you think of my new doll?"

As Sonny came over to him, Witt braced himself against the wall like maybe if he pushed hard enough he could pass through solid stone.

When Sonny reached him, he held Witt's head in his hands.

"The worst part is over. Don't worry about me gutting you like your friend. All I need from you is your head. I just pull out the skull, scrape the fat from the inside of the skin, and shrink the rest of it down for one of my dolls."

He looked around the basement.

"These dolls are old. I'll be moving on soon and I'll need new ones. You'll be the first in my new life. Try to relax. It'll hurt less if you're calm. Be extra good and I'll kill you quick with the gun."

The thing that used to be Sonny went and picked up the old man's skin from the floor. He dumped it into the garbage can with Sonny's insides. It took him a while to drag the can over to an ancient gas furnace. He didn't quite have the hang of the new body yet.

While Sonny had his back to him, Witt pulled as hard as he could on the ring holding the handcuffs. He picked his feet off the floor, using his body weight to pull down. The cuffs felt like hot metal digging into his wrists. He gritted his teeth and swallowed so he wouldn't make any noise. He felt the ring move an inch. Then another. But the pain was too much. His vision started fogging again and he was afraid he might pass out. He put his feet on the floor and looked over. The old man had the body parts in the furnace and was fiddling around with the controls. He touched handles and gauges randomly, like he was having trouble remembering how they worked. Good, thought Witt. He still had some time. If he could get to the table, he could get the gun. *That's all I need.*

Witt took a breath and raised his head, getting ready for the pain when he pulled his feet off the floor. Hanging there, his hands turning dark with trapped blood and feeling like they were going to pop off, he raised his head.

He stopped what he was doing when he saw the doll nailed to a beam a few feet above. That's why the old man was taking his time. He knew everything Witt was doing. He wasn't going anywhere. And probably, Witt thought, he wasn't going to get that quick death after all.

"Shallaballah" by Mark Samuels. Copyright © 2005 by Mark Samuels. First published in *Don't Turn Out the Light*, edited by Stephen Jones, PS Publishing. Reprinted with permission of the author.

"Sob in the Silence" by Gene Wolfe. Copyright © 2006 by Gene Wolfe. First published in *Strange Birds*, a chapbook, from Dreamhaven Books. Reprinted with permission of the author.

"Our Turn Too Will One Day Come" by Brian Hodge. Copyright © 2006 by Brian Hodge. First published in *Alone on the Darkside*, edited by John Pelan, Roc/New American Library. Reprinted with permission of the author.

"Dead Sea Fruit" by Kaaron Warren. Copyright © 2006 by Kaaron Warren. First published in *Fantasy Magazine*, 2006, edited by Sean Wallace. Reprinted with permission of the author.

"Closet Dreams" by Lisa Tuttle. Copyright © 2007 by Lisa Tuttle. First published in *Postscripts*, spring 2007, edited by Nick Gevers, Peter Crowther. Reprinted with permission of the author.

"Spectral Evidence" by Gemma Files. Copyright © 2007 by Gemma Files. First published in *The Chiaroscuro e-zine* 31. Reprinted with permission of the author.

"Hushabye" by Simon Bestwick. Copyright © 2007 by Simon Bestwick. First published in *Inferno*, edited by Ellen Datlow, Tor Books. Reprinted with permission of the author.

"Very Low-Flying Aircraft" by Nicholas Royle. Copyright © 2008 by Nicholas Royle. First published in *Exotic Gothic 2: New Tales of Taboo*, edited by Danel Olson, Ash-Tree Press. Reprinted with permission of the author.

"The Goosle" by Margo Lanagan. Copyright © 2008 by Margo Lanagan.

First published in *The Del Rey Book of Science Fiction and Fantasy*, edited by Ellen Datlow, Del Rey Books. Reprinted with permission of the author.

"The Clay Party" by Steve Duffy. Copyright © 2008 by Steve Duffy. First published in *The Werewolf Pack*, edited by Mark Valentine, Wordsworth Editions. Reprinted with permission of the author.

"Strappado" by Laird Barron. Copyright © 2009 by Laird Barron. First published in *Poe*, edited by Ellen Datlow, Solaris Books. Reprinted with permission of the author.

"Lonegan's Luck" by Stephen Graham Jones. Copyright © 2009 by Stephen Graham Jones. First published in *New Genre 6*, summer 2009.

"Mr Pigsny" by Reggie Oliver. Copyright © 2010 by Reggie Oliver. First published in *The Sixth Black Book of Horror*, edited by Charles Black, Mortbury Press. Reprinted with permission of the author.

"At Night, When the Demons Come" by Ray Cluley. Copyright © 2010 by Ray Cluley. First published in *Black Static* #20, December/January. Reprinted with permission of the author.

"Was She Wicked? Was She Good?" by M. Rickert. Copyright © 2010 by M. Rickert. First published in *Holiday*, Golden Gryphon Press. Reprinted with permission of the author.

"The Shallows" by John Langan. Copyright © 2010 by John Langan. First published in *Cthulhu's Reign*, edited by Darrell Schweitzer, DAW Books. Reprinted with permission of the author.

"Little Pig" by Anna Taborska. Copyright © 2011 by Anna Taborska. First published in *The Eighth Black Book of Horror*, edited by Charles Black,

Mortbury Press. Reprinted with permission of the author.

"Omphalos" by Livia Llewellyn. © 2011 by Livia Llewellyn. First published in *Engines of Desire: Tales of Love & Other Horrors*, Lethe Press. Reprinted with permission of the author.

"How We Escaped Our Certain Fate" by Dan Chaon. Copyright © 2012 by Dan Chaon. First published in *21st Century Dead*, edited by Christopher Golden, St. Martin's Press. Reprinted with permission of the author.

"That Tiny Flutter of the Heart I Used to Call Love" by Robert Shearman. Copyright © 2013 by Robert Shearman. First published in *Psycho-Mania!*, edited by Stephen Jones, Robinson. Reprinted with permission of the author.

"Interstate Love Song (Murder Ballad No. 8)" by Caitlín R. Kiernan. Copyright © 2014 by Caitlín R. Kiernan. First published in *Sirenia Digest* 100. Reprinted with permission of the author.

"Shay Corsham Worsted" by Garth Nix. Copyright © 2014 by Garth Nix. First published in *Fearful Symmetries*, edited by Ellen Datlow, ChiZine Publications. Reprinted with permission of the author.

"The Atlas of Hell" by Nathan Ballingrud. Copyright © 2014 by Nathan Ballingrud. First published in *Fearful Symmetries*, edited by Ellen Datlow, ChiZine Publications. Reprinted with permission of the author.

"Ambitious Boys Like You" by Richard Kadrey. Copyright © 2015 by Richard Kadrey. First published in *The Doll Collection*, edited by Ellen Datlow, Tor Books. Reprinted with permission of the author.